NAPOLEON

A remarkable figure in French public life, MAX GALLO is the author of eighty books – biographies, novels, historical novels, memoirs – which have sold in their hundreds of thousands. Formerly Professor of History at Nice University, he has been or continues to be an MEP, newspaper editor and éminence grise in the last French elections. He lives in Paris.

MAX GALLO

NAPOLEON

The Emperor of Kings

Translated from the French by William Hobson

MACMILLAN

First published 2004 by Macmillan
an imprint of Pan Macmillan Ltd
Pan Macmillan, 20 New Wharf Road, London N1 9RR
Basingstoke and Oxford
Associated companies throughout the world
www.panmacmillan.com

ISBN 0 333 90796 5

First published in French 1997 as *Napoléon: L'empereur des rois*
by Editions Robert Laffont, Paris

1 3 5 7 9 8 6 4 2

A CIP catalogue record for this book is available from
the British Library.

Typeset by SetSystems Ltd, Saffron Walden, Essex
Printed and bound in Great Britain by
Mackays of Chatham plc, Chatham, Kent

For Marielle

My master has no feeling and that master is the nature of things.

Napoleon to Josephine, 3 December 1806

He had an intrinsic need to transform confusion into order,
like all men of history who are not stage heroes.

André Malraux, *Fallen Oaks*

PART ONE

Everything has gone as I planned it

JANUARY 1806 TO 25 NOVEMBER 1806

I

HE IS THE MASTER.

Since 2 December 1805, since the Austerlitz sun rose over the frozen ponds where so many Russian soldiers were to drown, useless allies of the already conquered Austrians, Napoleon has been thinking the same thought: he is the master.

Now it is Saturday, 28 December 1805 and he has just left Schönbrunn Palace in Vienna to go to Munich. In the berline taking him to Melk Abbey, where he will stay the night, he has wrapped his legs in a fur rug, but he is wide awake.

He is the master.

From time to time, he sees the silhouettes of the troopers of his escort through the carriage windows, and the words of the proclamation he issued on the day of victory come back to him, rhythmed by every turn of the wheel, 'Soldiers, I am satisfied with you. In the Battle of Austerlitz you have justified all that I expected of your intrepidity. You have decorated your eagles with immortal glory ... My people will see you again with joy and it will be sufficient to say, "I was at the Battle of Austerlitz," for them to reply, "There is a brave man."'

He is the master.

He can do anything, it seems. As he told his soldiers, he has cut to pieces or dispersed an army of one hundred thousand men jointly commanded by the Emperors of Russia and Austria; and the King of Prussia only escaped a thrashing because France's victory at Austerlitz convinced him that he had better submit without a fight.

Napoleon is the master.

AFTER THE BATTLE Talleyrand came to see him in Schönbrunn Palace. The minister of foreign affairs brought the terms of the Treaty of Pressburg which would drive Austria out of Germany and penalize it for its defeat.

'Sire,' Talleyrand began in his shrill voice, 'everything that conquest has given you belongs to you, but your nature is a generous one.'

Examining the clauses of the treaty, Napoleon saw that, acting on his own initiative, Talleyrand had reduced the financial contributions he had himself imposed on Vienna.

'Monsieur de Talleyrand, you have contrived a treaty at Pressburg which makes things very awkward for me!' Napoleon cried, throwing the copy of the treaty to the floor.

He is the master – Talleyrand should have realized this – but as so often, the minister instead took refuge in politeness and cunning, flattery and argument.

'I rejoice at the thought,' Talleyrand enthused, 'that this latest victory of Your Majesty should put him in a position to assure the peace of Europe and guarantee the civilized world against invasion by the barbarians.'

Napoleon listened, watching the fires in Schönbrunn's vast fireplaces that lit up the panelling and giant tapestries.

'Your Majesty can now either crush the Austrian monarchy,' Talleyrand continued, 'or set it back on its feet. Once broken, it will no longer be in Your Majesty's power to reassemble the scattered remnants and restore them to a single mass. However, the existence of this mass is necessary: it is indispensable to the future safety of all civilized nations. It is a sufficient bulwark against the barbarians, as it is a necessary one.'

Napoleon did not reply. He is the master.

NOW, IN HIS BERLINE, he thinks that it is years since he has had such a feeling of sovereignty, such a sense of control over his destiny, of dominion over the lives of men and the fate of empires. He tells himself that Austerlitz is his true imperial coronation, just as five years ago, on 14 June 1800, he was convinced that victory at Marengo had assured his position as first consul. Everything would have been compromised back then if he had been defeated in the Italian plains; and what would his Emperor's crown be worth now if the Austrians and Russians had defeated the Grand Army at Austerlitz?

His crown would be lying in the dirt.

But he has carried the day. He is the master and now, like

another Charlemagne, he can model a Europe to suit his specifications.

He dreams and imagines as the carriage takes him closer to Munich.

HE ARRIVES IN the Bavarian capital on 31 December 1805. It is cold and wet. The berline drives alongside the royal palace's austere facade, which only has a statue of the Virgin for decoration. Soldiers of the Guard open the bronze gates and, at one forty-five, the carriage enters the palace. It passes slowly through the four courtyards, skirts the fountains and draws to a measured halt at the foot of the great steps that lead to the apartments.

Officers rush forward; the Empress's ladies in waiting hover at the top of the stairs.

Napoleon gets out and looks around. He remembers the last letter he wrote to Josephine. He was still at Schönbrunn, on 20 December. Everything still hung in the balance. Austria was debating the clauses of the treaty. Napoleon had written a few lines in his jerky handwriting,

> I do not know what I shall do: I depend on events; I have no
> will; I await the outcome of everything. Remain in Munich,
> amuse yourself; this is not difficult when one has so many
> amiable companions and when one is in such a beautiful country.
> I am myself fairly busy. In a few days I shall have decided.
> Farewell, my friend. A thousand amiable and tender things.

Now events have decided. The treaty has been signed. He is the master. He climbs the stairs; everyone bows to him; in their eyes he glimpses a mixture of admiration and servility, and perhaps, for the first time, a sort of dread as well, as if such a devastating victory over the coalition between Vienna and St Petersburg has revealed him to be part of a sacred dynasty, whom nothing can resist.

He passes rapidly through the antechambers and reception rooms, walks along the gallery decorated with Italian and dark Flemish paintings, then enters the bedroom. There, leaning against the great gilt bed, stands Josephine.

It is weeks since he has seen her. She has not even written to him. He had reprimanded her in a letter: had the festivities at Baden, Stuttgart and Munich 'made her forget the poor soldiers who live covered in mud, blood and rain? Mighty Empress, not one letter from you . . . Deign from the height of your splendours to take a little notice of your slaves.'

Now here she is, alluring, older, smiling with her lips pressed together so as not to show her blackened and decayed teeth. She makes a shallow, slightly ironic bow, but a bow none the less.

He is the master.

EVERYONE MUST KNOW this and accept it. He makes the decisions; their duty is to obey. He feels powerful, capable of prodigious feats which will make him the founder of a new dynasty, the fourth after Charlemagne. For this he must rally the different nations around his person and his family, make kings of his brothers and relatives.

Now, if he had a son . . .

But he has no son.

At the Munich opera on 6 January, during a performance of *The Clemency of Titus*, he does not let himself be swept up by Mozart's music. Instead, he furtively watches Josephine. She has not been able to give him the descendant he hopes for, the son who is so essential to founding the imperial dynasty without which all his work will crumble the day he dies.

Why must it always be like this? Why must new challenges present themselves just when he has climbed a summit?

He leans over to Josephine.

He has decided, he says, to waste no time and organize the marriage of Eugène, Josephine's son, and Augusta, the King of Bavaria's daughter. It will be the first strand in the web he plans, like Charlemagne, to spin from one end of Europe to the other. He will adopt Eugène, although without right of succession to the French throne. Then he will choose which of his brothers are to occupy the various European thrones. In Naples, why not Joseph? He must be rid of those Bourbons, the King and Queen of Naples, who are in compact with the English. Isn't the Queen of Naples, Marie Caroline, Marie-Antoinette's sister? Hasn't she declared to the French ambassador her wish that the kingdom of

Naples be the match sparking the conflagration that will destroy the French Empire? Marie Caroline of Naples is going to find out that one's fingers can get burnt if one plays with fire.

Napoleon stands up. He does not wait for the end of the opera, but returns to the royal palace. He must act fast. Time is short.

He writes to Eugène de Beauharnais, ordering him to start post-haste for Munich. He extracts the King of Bavaria's consent. He gives his daughter a magnificent dowry. Augusta of Bavaria will receive fifty thousand florins the day after her marriage, one hundred thousand francs a year for her personal expenses and an estate worth half a million francs on the death of her husband.

And now here is Eugène, Viceroy of Italy, with his long, turned-up moustache of a colonel of the chasseurs of the guard. Napoleon pinches his ear and gives him a little pat on the neck — his usual marks of affection. He must trim that moustache, says the Emperor, it's far too long to be to Augusta's liking. That too is an order.

He is the master.

He tells Cambacérès that he is delaying his return to Paris for a few days in order to arrange Eugène and Augusta's marriage. 'These days shall seem long to my heart,' he says, 'but after having been constantly absorbed by the duties of a soldier, I feel a sense of tender release at occupying myself with the details and duties of the father of a family.'

ON 13 JANUARY 1806, at one in the afternoon, in the great gallery of the royal palace, Napoleon witnesses the official signing of the marriage contract. And on the 14th, at seven in the evening in the royal chapel, he presides over the religious ceremony followed by a Te Deum and a banquet. On the King of Bavaria's arm, Empress Josephine is radiant. Still beautiful. Napoleon escorts Augusta.

'I love you like a father,' he tells her. 'And I count on you having all the affection of a daughter for me.'

The newly-weds are to return to Italy.

'Take care of yourself on the journey, and in the new climate when you arrive, take plenty of rest,' murmurs Napoleon. 'Remember that I don't want to have you falling ill.'

After the banquet, Napoleon retires to his study.

The still of night envelops him after the noisy brilliance of the festivities, the shimmer of dresses and uniforms, the allure of the beautiful women, the grace of Augusta and the joy of Eugène de Beauharnais. He loves this stepson of his, who is now his adoptive son. By this marriage a first link has been established with the ruling families of Europe. Max-Joseph, the King of Bavaria and father of Augusta, is a Wittelsbach, whose ancestors appear in all the dynasties.

How can I assure the future of my dynasty that sprang from the Revolution, other than by forcibly, on the battlefield, introducing it into those royal houses whose legitimacy derives from the passage of centuries?

But some people do not understand this plan.

On his desk, Napoleon finds a letter from Murat, probably dictated by Caroline, his wife and Napoleon's sister.

'When France raised you to the throne, she thought she would find you a popular leader, adorned with a title which would lift him above all other European sovereigns. Today you pay homage to great titles which are not yours, which are in opposition to ours, and you are only going to show Europe how much you value what we all lack, illustriousness of birth.'

So, the valorous Murat and the ambitious and jealous Caroline challenge my strategy – out of attachment to revolutionary principles, anxiety or spite? What matter? I am the master.

'Prince Murat, sir,' Napoleon replies, 'I always see you with confidence at the head of my cavalry. But this is not a military operation we are dealing with here, it is a political action and I have thought it through at length. This marriage of Eugène and Augusta displeases you. It is agreeable to me and I consider it a great success, a success equal to the victory at Austerlitz.'

HE IS THE MASTER.

And this marriage is only the first pawn, the first move. He is thinking of combining Holland, Switzerland and Italy into a single entity. 'My Federal States,' he murmurs, 'or the true French Empire.'

He decrees that the Civil Code will apply in the kingdom of

Italy. Hasn't he been crowned King of Italy in Milan? And isn't Eugène Viceroy of Italy?

On 19 January 1806, he offers the kingdom of Naples' crown to Joseph, his elder brother, and orders its occupation by French troops. The Bourbons have fled to Sicily under the protection of the English fleet.

Now the only hostile sovereign left in Italy is the Pope, Pius VII. His Holiness protests, writing to Napoleon to express his indignation at the French occupation of Ancona, papal land.

'I have always considered myself,' Napoleon replies, 'the protector of the Holy See ... I have considered myself, like my predecessors of the third and fourth generations, as the eldest son of the Church, as the sole possessor of the sword with which to protect it and shelter it from defilement by Greeks and Moslems.'

Why doesn't the Pope understand that?

Napoleon's indignation mounts. He says to Cardinal Fesch, his great-uncle who represents him in Rome, 'I'm religious, but I am no bigot. The Pope has written me the most ridiculous, the most lunatic letter . . .' There is no question, Napoleon rages: Pius VII must submit to his authority.

'As far as the Pope is concerned, I am Charlemagne, because like Charlemagne I join the crown of France to the crown of Lombardy and my empire touches the East. I therefore expect the Pope to accommodate his conduct to my requirements. I shall make no outward changes if he behaves well. Otherwise, I will reduce the Pope to a mere Bishop of Rome ... Truly, there is nothing more unreasonable than the Court of Rome.'

I am the master.

BUT TO RULE, one must be implacable. One must show no pity, no hesitation.

When he appoints General Junot as Governor General of the States of Parma and Piacenza, he says, 'You don't maintain peace in Italy with words. Do as I did at Binasco [during the campaign of Italy]: order a large village to be burned; have a dozen insurgents shot and form mobile columns to seize the brigands wherever you find them and set an example to the people of these countries.'

But will Joseph, the scheming, hesitant Joseph, be able to display the necessary firmness? Napoleon summons Miot de Mélito, who is leaving with the new King of Naples.

In a curt voice, Napoleon says, 'You will tell my brother Joseph that I am making him the King of Naples, but that the slightest hesitation, the least uncertainty, will ruin him entirely ... No half measures, no weakness. I want my blood to reign in Naples as long as in France. The kingdom of Naples is necessary to me ...'

Napoleon remembers his brother's reservations at the time of the coronation, his refusal to accept the viceroyalty of Italy, his older brother's jealousy at a younger brother's glory.

Napoleon draws closer to Miot de Mélito.

'At present all feelings of affection yield to state reasons,' he says. 'I recognize as my relatives only those who serve me ... It is with my fingers and my pen that I create children ... I can have no relations in obscurity. Those who do not rise with me shall no longer form part of my family. I am creating a family of kings, or rather of viceroys ...'

A few days later, Napoleon receives a letter from Joseph, King of Naples.

'Once and for all,' Joseph writes, 'I can assure Your Majesty that I shall approve of everything you may choose to do ... Do everything for the best and dispose of me as you judge most fitting for you and for the state.'

Napoleon is indeed the master.

II

HE LEAVES MUNICH on Friday, 17 January 1806, as night is falling. In his carriage, he reads dispatches by the flickering light of the paraffin lamps. When the horses are changed at the relays, he does not get out. He picks at a cold leg of chicken, drinks Chambertin from a silver goblet, then drowses.

He reflects that he has spent a great deal of his life on the road like this, on horseback or in one of these berlines whose jolting doesn't affect him. The opposite, in fact: he likes this sensation of movement, these long stages, sometimes forty hours at a stretch, which allow him physically to experience the dominion he exercises over countries and men.

He must be seen wherever he reigns.

When he arrives in Stuttgart at four in the afternoon, on Saturday, 18 January, it is the King of Würtemberg who welcomes him and shows him the royal palace.

The reception rooms and galleries are lined with bowing men and women, glancing up at him with curiosity and deference. Enough of this, he decides. He issues his instructions: tomorrow, Sunday, he will watch a play; Monday, at eight in the morning, he will hunt in the forests near Stuttgart; the King will join him, he trusts.

Then he withdraws to the study which has been prepared for him. The couriers have arrived from Paris.

Paris is the centre. Everything is decided there. Part of the reason he wins these victories is to convince Parisians that he is invincible. For public feeling is fickle in Paris. It is never permanently won over.

Napoleon opens the dispatches from the minister of police first.

'Sire,' writes Fouché. 'Austerlitz has shaken the old aristocracy to the core. The faubourg St Germain conspires no more.' The ancien régime nobility are now impatiently awaiting his return, to be able to rush to the Tuileries with their petitions. They want titles, positions, honours, livings.

Napoleon folds up Fouché's letter.

There, that's a true portrait of mankind. Who can resist the allure of power triumphant?

On Monday morning, in the forests that border the Neckar, he rides far out in front of the King of Würtemberg, the chasseurs of the Guard and the other aristocrats he has invited to come hunting. Freezing fog and darkness swallow him up; his horse rears. Napoleon holds the reins firmly and grips his horse's flanks tightly. He masters his mount just as he tames history.

At midday, he sets off for Karlsruhe, then Ettlingen, Rastatt and Lichtenau, before finally reaching the Rhine.

Napoleon orders the berline to stop. On the other side of the river, he sees the lights of Strasbourg.

He looks at the river, a bright trail in the night. From its source to its mouth, the Rhine should be the frontier of his empire, and the states on its right bank should come together to form a grand confederation of allies protecting the empire. At their head he will put sovereigns and princes under his tutelage; they will provide subsidies and troops, and in this fashion a new map of Germany will emerge, a new face of Europe which will consolidate what the Revolution has started and revive the legacy of Charlemagne's empire.

Everyone in Vienna, in Berlin, in St Petersburg, in London and in Rome will have to come to terms with this.

'I am Charlemagne, the sword of the Church, their Emperor.'

These were his words to the Pope, and if Pius VII does not accept this, 'I shall reduce him to the state he was in before Charlemagne.'

The other sovereigns will have to submit as well.

Napoleon gets back into his carriage. At six in the evening on Wednesday, 2 January 1806, he enters the brightly lit streets of Strasbourg. The soldiers who present arms and the massed crowds shout, 'Long live the Emperor!'

He gets out of the carriage and enters the Rohan palace where he spent the last days of September in 1805. He stops for a moment in the large gallery where the mirrors reflect his image.

He remembers leaving Strasbourg on Tuesday, 1 October, after watching the Imperial Guard march past in a downpour, crossing the Rhine by the Kehl bridge on their way to Germany.

Barely three months have passed since then. He has smashed the Third Coalition, an alliance of the two most powerful states in Europe. Once more he has convinced himself that he is now not merely the Emperor of the French, but also the Emperor of Kings.

He climbs a few steps of the staircase, then turns around towards the aides-de-camp and generals thronging the gallery. On Friday, he says, he will review the troops. On Saturday, he will leave Strasbourg to be in Paris by Sunday, 26 January. He is impatient to return to his study in the Tuileries, to his papers arranged by ministries and stored in boxes, the keys to which he always carries on his person.

'I was born and made for work,' he tells Méneval when he comes to his apartments with several dispatches that have arrived from Paris.

With a gesture Napoleon bids his secretary read them, and settles down in front of the fireplace as Méneval slits open the envelopes.

First comes a report from the treasury minister, Barbé-Marbois, who speaks of financial difficulties. Napoleon flies into a rage and pulls out of his pocket a strip of paper on which he writes the figures of what he calls 'France's fortune', the public and private Treasury.

'What is all this?' he exclaims.

They have to be able to pay the Imperial Guard a fortnight's wages. The Grand Army in Germany also has to receive the money it needs. These are the most pressing expenses. What have these United Merchants – the Ouvrard, Desprez and Vanlerberghes – been doing? They should have been supplying the army, they've had the necessary funds, yet they have met none of their obligations.

'Who is this Barbé-Marbois? Knavery has its limits, but stupidity, it seems, has none.'

Napoleon is impatient; he presses Méneval. On Monday, in Paris, he says, he will chair a session of the Council of State and resolve this question of the finances.

'Messrs Ouvrard, Desprez and Vanlerberghe must cede everything they own to me,' he says, hammering out each word, 'otherwise I shall throw these gentlemen in Vincennes.'

He dismisses Méneval, who, before leaving, reads the letter that Le Coz, the Archbishop of Besançon, has sent to the Emperor, 'Thus far,' writes the prelate, 'you have been the most perfect of heroes, issued from the hands of God.'

Napoleon stops Méneval.

'Have my orders been carried out?' he asks.

At Schönbrunn he had given instructions that captured enemy flags be sent to Paris, shown to the people, and then hung from the roof of Notre Dame.

Méneval scans the dispatches. According to police informants, there were joyous scenes when the flags were unveiled. The Archbishop of Paris has pronounced that the flags bear witness to 'the protection heaven vouchsafes France, the prodigious successes of our invincible Emperor and the homage he does God by his victories'.

Roustam and Constant have come in while Méneval is reading. They announce that the Emperor's bath is ready and help him undress. Napoleon scolds them, pinches their ears.

He is happy. Paris is waiting for him.

AT TEN IN THE EVENING, on Sunday, 26 January 1806, the Emperor's berline draws to a halt in the courtyard of the Tuileries. The Guard presents arms, the grand marshal of the palace, Duroc, steps forward. Napoleon starts to issue orders while climbing the stairs. He wants to see Arch-chancellor Cambacérès, convene the State Council, meet the treasury minister and hold talks with State Councillor Mollien.

When he is alone in his study with Constant, he pronounces a name: Éléonore Denuelle de la Plaigne. He looks at the clock. 'At midnight,' he says. 'And now for my bath.'

He remembers the body of this nineteen-year-old woman: tall, black hair to her waist, spilling over her shoulders, tanned skin. She is slender, lively and submissive. He is well aware that when Caroline Murat introduced her to him, it was with the express intention that he single her out. He knows only too well how jealous his sister is of Josephine, how adept she is at hurting 'the old woman', as she calls her. He knows her too well, with her unbounded ambition and hope that her brother will divorce, to think that meeting Éléonore under Caroline's auspices could be just by chance.

But what do Caroline Murat's plans matter? Éléonore has the freshness of youth and he desires her, on his first evening back in Paris, as if he wishes to celebrate his victory and vigour by clasping her youthful form in his arms.

After all, he is not yet thirty-seven.

He hears Éléonore Denuelle's footsteps in the 'dark corridor'. She is punctual, as usual.

'Sire . . .' she murmurs. He grasps her arm, pinches it, pulls her into the room. In love, he is just as he is in war. He does not like long sieges; he prefers to take the object of his desire by storm.

Éléonore surrenders.

Napoleon gets to his feet, laughs, strokes her cheek, and then goes back to his study.

ON HIS DESK facing the window, there is only one dispatch, which must have been delivered when he was with Éléonore next door. It is a letter from Fouché. The minister of police reports that, according to a traveller just returned from London, William Pitt, their great adversary, the opponent of every peace initiative, has died on 23 January in his house in Putney, up to his ears in debt, overwhelmed by the victory of Austerlitz, and asking, as a final gesture, for the map of Europe on his bedroom wall to be taken down. 'Roll up that map, we shall have no use of it ten years from hence,' he murmured. 'My country! In what a state I leave my country!'

Fox will replace him as head of the Foreign Office.

Napoleon paces up and down his study. It is as if destiny is giving him a sign, clearing the obstacles from his path and at last offering him a chance to conclude peace.

Napoleon goes through to the little room which serves as his Topographical Office. On the table lies a large map of Europe. He rests both hands on it. He wants peace with England, but he must impose it on her by taking control of the Continent, closing all ports to its goods, and by demanding that all the European states ban English products.

He moves round the table. In the south, Italy forms the right wing of the Empire. Joseph is the King of Naples. He will make Elisa a grand duchess, sovereign of the territories of Massa e Carrara and later, perhaps, Tuscany. He will give Pauline Bonaparte, who is already Princess Borghese, the Duchy of Guastalla, a fortified town on the banks of the Po. Then he will set aside twenty or so duchies to award to his most prominent servants as their own personal fiefdoms: Talleyrand will become the Prince of Benevento, Fouché the Duke of Otranto, and Bernadotte, since he is Désirée Clary's husband, for which he can be forgiven his reticence that at times borders on treason, will become Prince of Pontecorvo.

Napoleon straightens up. With his finger, he moves north from Italy. Berthier will become the Prince of Neuchâtel, and Murat the Grand Duke of Cleves and Berg. The King of Bavaria is already an ally through the marriage of his daughter Augusta to Eugène. All that then will be needed is to create a Confederation of the Rhine by grouping together the other German princes. Further north, Holland, the left wing of the Empire, will go to Louis, his troublesome and jealous brother who might see this as an occasion for gratitude. In the process, his wife, Hortense de Beauharnais, will become Queen of Holland.

NAPOLEON LEAVES the Topographical Office. It may take weeks, months even, for what he has conceived to become reality, but he is sure it's the right thing; it will come about because it has to, because it represents the interests of the people. The arrangement is a model of reason; it will complete what the Convention has begun. The Revolution paved the way; now he is furthering it and making its aims possible: if he manages to combine the Civil Code with the monarchy, to maintain dynastic structures whilst overhauling society from top to bottom, then a new Europe will come into being.

That's what he's doing, what he wants, laying foundations. He is the first of a new dynasty. The fourth dynasty to rule France since Charlemagne.

IN THE DAYS THAT FOLLOW he returns, with a sort of light-heartedness, to the familiar rhythm of his days. Work from seven in the morning, then hunting in the Bois de Boulogne, Marly forest, around St Cloud and Malmaison. He chairs sessions of the State Council, and increases the number of receptions and diplomatic audiences, at which he makes the acquaintance of a new Austrian ambassador, a man of thirty-five, grandson by marriage of Chancellor Kaunitz, by the name of Metternich.

Metternich strikes him as intelligent, discriminating and open, possibly a supporter of an alliance with France – in the tradition of Chancellor Kaunitz, in fact.

At one audience, Napoleon takes him by the arm, questions him. Metternich, who completed part of his studies in Strasbourg, speaks perfect French. He witnessed the upheaval of the Revolution in the Alsatian capital, he explains, and it still terrifies him.

'I want to unite the present and the past,' says Napoleon, 'Meld Gothic precedents with the institutions of this century.'

Does Metternich understand? For this, continues Napoleon, there has to be peace. There's every possibility of it and it is what he wants. He has so many things to do.

HE PAYS A VISIT to the works he has commissioned on the Louvre. He confirms his decision to have a column built in the place Vendôme, modelled on Trajan's Column in Rome, and a triumphal arch in the place du Carrousel, both monuments to the glory of the Grand Army, and then a second triumphal arch at the top of the avenue des Champs-Élysées, the first stone of which he will lay on 15 August, the day on which, throughout the Empire, the Feast of St Napoleon is celebrated.

When he takes decisions like this – to commission buildings, erect fountains in the different districts of Paris, throw a bridge over the Seine, fit out the embankments along the river, order the publication of the Imperial Catechism or convince representatives of the Jewish nation to adapt the customs of their religion to the necessities of modern life (for example, to agree to give up polygamy) – he experiences a sort of intellectual and physical joy.

He feels alert, quicker-witted than anyone he commands. Even if he has put on a bit of weight over recent months: fuller cheeks, higher forehead, because his hair's already thinning, sharp profile and bony face subsumed by fleshy features, he feels full of energy, invigorated by his success, his plans, his decisions and the cheers of the crowd.

When he goes to the Théâtre-Français on Wednesday, 29 January 1806, barely two days after his return to Paris, to see *Manlius*, a play by an author in vogue, Lafosse, the entire auditorium rises to its feet even though Talma is already on stage. The actor bows as the spectators applaud and cry, 'Long live the Emperor!' The same ovations greet Napoleon whenever he appears at the opera or reviews the troops.

Moreover, police spies report that everyone is praising the Emperor, extolling his merits. Confidence has returned. The Bank of France has resumed cash payments over the counter, and the financial crisis of December 1805 has been forgotten.

Everyone knows that Napoleon has returned from his German campaign with fifty million in gold, silver and bills of exchange drawn on the principal financial centres of Europe.

It only takes a few days for Napoleon to restore order to the nation's finances.

HE RECEIVES BARBÉ-MARBOIS, the treasury minister. The man is crestfallen; he offers to put his head on the block. Napoleon shrugs. What can I do with a head like yours? he asks.

'I esteem your character,' Napoleon continues, 'but you have been the dupe of men against whom I had warned you to be on your guard. You have handed over all the effects in the portfolio to them, on the employment of which you should have kept a far more vigilant eye. I regret to find myself obliged to withdraw the administration of the Treasury from you . . .'

After a session of the State Council, Napoleon detains Councillor Mollien. He looks him over, sizes him up. 'You will be sworn in as treasury minister today,' he declares.

Mollien, who had been one of the officials of the Farm General, the fiscal administration under the ancien régime, seems to hesitate.

'Don't you want to be a minister?' the Emperor demands, a mixture of displeasure and surprise in his voice.

Mollien says he will take the oath today.

THIS IS WHAT RULING IS: analysing, deciding, choosing men and imposing one's will on them, brushing aside their reservations, guiding them so that they become efficient, and therefore docile, instruments of one's policies.

But this presupposes ceaseless work, constant vigilance and an iron will, asserting itself at every moment.

'I had a great deal of trouble setting matters in order,' Napoleon writes to his brother Joseph, 'and compelling a dozen swindlers, at the head of them Ouvrard, to disgorge their ill-gotten gains. They duped Barbé-Marbois, somewhat like the Cardinal de Rohan in the necklace affair, except that in this case for no less than ninety million. I was determined to have them shot without trial. Thank God I have been repaid. The effect has been to put me sorely out of humour.'

IT'S TRUE, HE'S OFTEN furious; he throws dispatches to the ground, and sometimes if a book displeases him, he hurls it into the fire.

He finds it less and less easy to accept any form of dissent, or lack of promptness in carrying out his orders exactly as he wishes.

He tells Berthier, who is anxious about the attitude of the Prussians and wishes to intervene, 'Adhere strictly to the orders I give you, carry out your instructions promptly, let everyone be on their guard and at their post; I alone know what I need to do.'

I alone.

He feels it in every bone of his body, that he is the only one who can see and judge matters correctly.

Hasn't he been right at every decisive moment of his life?

And it is this conviction that makes any opposition, any reservations even, of any sort, unbearable to him. People must bend to his will.

HE TAKES UP HIS QUILL to go through the wording of the Imperial Catechism.

'To honour and serve the Emperor is to honour and serve God Himself,' he'd dictated. And to disobey the Emperor is a mortal sin. He is owed 'love, obedience, loyalty, military service, the taxes levied for the preservation and defence of the Empire and his throne.'

Reading this document, certain state councillors are amazed. Fouché, that old Jacobin, has an ironic glint in his eyes.

Napoleon slams the Catechism shut. He is not a man to hide his thoughts. He gets to his feet and, before leaving the council chamber, he says in a voice of command, 'It is not the mystery of the Incarnation I see revealed in religion, but the mystery of the social order. It suggests an idea of equality in heaven which prevents the rich being massacred by the poor.'

He looks around to see if there is any opposition, but everyone is looking at the ground.

'To think of it another way, religion is a sort of inoculation, or vaccine, which, while satisfying our sense of the supernatural, protects us from the charlatans and the magicians: priests are better than the Cagliostros, the Kants and all the dreamers of Germany.'

He paces up and down, seemingly talking to himself, as if thinking out loud.

'Until now the world has only known two forms of government, the ecclesiastic and the military. But the civil order will be strengthened by the creation of a teaching order, and even more so by the creation of a great corporation of magistrates . . . The Civil Code has already done much good. Everyone now knows the principles to observe and governs his property and business accordingly.'

But I am the Supreme Judge.

IT IS SOCIETY, in all its forms, that he needs to organize. Sometimes he feels as if he is the world's reason, the only one capable of bringing order to the lives of the world's peoples and states.

He thinks of this constantly when, between sessions of the State Council, audiences and hours spent at dictation in his study, he goes out hunting in the bracing air of spring 1806.

One day, towards the end of March, after a long ride in the woods of Versailles, he hurries into his study, calls Méneval and, in one breath, elaborates the status of the imperial family, which will form the corner stone of the great Empire he is creating. Louis is the King of Holland, Joseph the King of Naples, his sisters Grand Duchesses in Italy, Murat the Grand Duke of Cleves and Berg, and the Berthiers, Bernadottes, Talleyrands and Fouchés become heads of their own fiefdoms.

He is at the top of the pyramid.

'The Emperor is the joint father of his family,' he dictates. Napoleon's will is the only law for all his relatives. No contract of marriage, no adoption may be instigated without his consent. He aligns the kings and hereditary princes below him and then the vassal princes and the titular heads of fiefs below them.

This is a hierarchy which satisfies his reason and assigns him all relevant powers. The Emperor may even order members of his family to cease contact with individuals he considers suspect.

He is indeed the absolute master.

ON 1 APRIL 1806, HE WRITES to Marshal Berthier, who has devoted himself with unswerving passion to the Marchioness de Visconti for years, erecting a veritable altar to her, lined with portraits, on campaign. Napoleon writes to inform him that he has been made the Prince of Neuchâtel.

> I enclose *The Monitor*, you will see what I have done for you. I make only one condition, which is that you get married, and this is a condition of my continuing friendship as well. Your passion has lasted too long; it has become ridiculous . . . I insist, therefore, that you marry, otherwise I shall not see you again. You are fifty years old, but you are of a race that lives to eighty, and these next thirty years are when you will need the comforts of marriage the most.

How can anyone resist the Emperor? Berthier bows to his will and breaks with the Marchioness de Visconti to marry Maria-Elizabeth of Bavaria-Birkenfeld, thirty years his junior.

Napoleon is satisfied. Isn't he the head of his 'family'?

To Eugène, Viceroy of Italy, he writes,

> My son, you work too much. Your life is too monotonous. You have a young wife who is expecting a child. I think you ought to arrange things so as to spend the evenings with her and have a small social circle. Why don't you go to the theatre once a week in the royal box? There must be more gaiety in your household . . . I lead the same life as you but I have an old wife who does not need to be amused, and even so I indulge in more pleasures and distraction than you. A young woman needs amusement, especially in the condition in which she finds herself.

Speaking to Augusta, Eugène's wife, he adds, 'Take care of yourself in your present state, and try not to give us a daughter. I will tell you the prescription for that, though you won't believe it: every day drink a little unmixed wine.'

He remembers Augusta of Bavaria with pleasure. She writes to him frequently. 'Your wife has been more amiable than you,' he chides Eugène. And sometimes, when he sees Stéphanie de Beauharnais, Josephine's niece, coming towards him in the Empress's drawing room, he feels the same pleasure he had in Augusta's company.

The older he gets, the more he likes young women, and Stéphanie is only seventeen in 1806. She is a high spirited, mischievous girl, with regular features topped by blonde locks. Napoleon loves looking at her, joking with her, and he senses the anxiety and jealousy in the looks that Josephine and Caroline Murat shoot at the pair of them.

One evening when he enters the Empress's drawing room, he finds Stéphanie in tears. He learns that Caroline has demanded that Stéphanie remain standing in her presence, according to that article of imperial etiquette which prohibits anyone sitting down in the presence of the 'Princess Sisters of His Majesty'.

Napoleon puts his arm around Stéphanie's waist, sits her on his knee and spends the evening whispering in her ear, as Caroline Murat furiously looks on.

The next day, because he is the man who can do anything, he decides to adopt the young girl. From now on, he dictates to

Count de Ségur, Grand Master of Ceremonies, 'she will enjoy all the prerogatives of her rank in all social gatherings, festivities and at table. She will sit at Our side, and should We not be present, she will be seated on the Empress's right.'

That is how one shows that one decides everything.

A few days later, Napoleon chooses a husband for Stéphanie: Charles, the Crown Prince of Baden, who was engaged to Augusta and then passed over in favour of Eugène de Beauharnais.

This is what I want.

Stéphanie must defer to him as well. Paris is lit up for her marriage. The ceremonies are sumptuous. Napoleon endows his adoptive daughter with an income of one million five hundred thousand francs and a trousseau of five hundred thousand francs, but when he learns that Stéphanie is closing her door to her husband, he gives her notice to leave Paris for Karlsruhe.

'Be agreeable to the Elector of Baden, he is your father,' he tells her. 'Love your husband for all the attachment he bears you.'

I am the one who dictates how the members of my family should behave, and I expect to be obeyed.

EVERYDAY — EVERY HOUR, almost — he must give orders, advice, lectures, reminding those he has made kings or princes that they are merely vassals, agents to carry out the imperial project, cogs in the great empire he is creating.

Murat, for instance, the munificent Prince Joachim, now Grand Duke of Berg, writes asking for guarantees for his children. Has he forgotten the man thanks to whom he is a prince? The man who alone holds in his hands the future of the Empire and the federal states allied with it?

'As to the guarantee for your children,' Napoleon replies, 'your arguments are pitiful and they made me shrug my shoulders. I blush for you. You are a Frenchman, I hope; so will your children be. Any other sentiment would be so dishonouring that I must ask you never to mention such a thing to me again.'

Napoleon breaks off. The blindness of these men, whom he has showered with titles, honours and money, astonishes and disgusts him. He feels a surge of contempt and pity. He has a presentiment that most of them will turn their backs on him if he's defeated or even simply weakened. That's also why he must rule them with a rod of iron, badger them, keep them under constant surveillance, compel them to do his will.

He concludes his reply to Murat:

'It would be a very extraordinary thing if, after all the benefits the French nation has showered on you, you thought of giving your children the means to injure France. Once more, never speak to me about this again, it's too ridiculous!'

BUT ALL THE PEOPLE around Napoleon are like Murat and his wife Caroline Bonaparte: greedy, thinking about their lot rather than the state of the Empire.

Even the Emperor's mother, showered with gold as she is, has requested an appanage from the Treasury. Letizia Bonaparte, in other words, is contemplating her son Napoleon's death and taking precautions to protect her income should he die.

Napoleon just shrugs when he is informed of this application, and gives his consent with a bitter grimace, to satisfy his mother.

She too, just like all the others, is incapable of seeing beyond her immediate, personal interests.

Louis, King of Holland, for instance, bombards the Emperor with requests for help. Isn't he a king? Doesn't he have a state of his own?

'I have no money,' Napoleon writes back. 'How convenient, this means suggested to you, of having recourse to France! But this is not the time for jeremiads, energy is what is called for . . .'

HAVE THEY any energy, these brothers whom I have made kings, these men whom I've made princes, these generals in whom I have placed my trust?

Napoleon has to guide them with daily dispatches.

The couriers leave Malmaison, St Cloud and the Tuileries several times a day, bound for Naples, Parma, Düsseldorf and Amsterdam.

He tells General Junot, 'You can only be clement by being severe, otherwise this unfortunate country and Piedmont will be lost and a sea of blood will have to flow to restore tranquillity to Italy.'

Junot carries out his orders, destroys the rebel villages.

'I see with pleasure,' Napoleon comments, 'that the village of Mezzano, which was the first to take up arms, has been burned . . . This act of rigour will prove one of great humanity and clemency, because it will prevent further revolts.'

BUT THE TEMPTATION for these men is always to make themselves loved rather than to rule with the necessary force.

Napoleon is indignant when he reads the reports Joseph sends him from Naples. He has little confidence in this older brother who has never seen combat. He repeats, 'When one rules a great State, the only way one controls it is by acts of severity.' There's Joseph, thinking that the Neapolitans have taken him to their hearts!

He believes he is king for all eternity. He has blotted out the fact that he is only King of Naples because of the Emperor's wishes and military might! Who does he takes himself for?

'You compare the attachment of the Neapolitans to you with that of the French to me,' Napoleon writes. 'It sounds like an epigram. What love do you expect from a people for whom you have done nothing, among whom you are by right of conquest with forty to fifty thousands foreigners?'

But does Joseph want to face this reality?

Napoleon laughs bitterly.

They don't understand anything!

'Bear this in mind,' he tells Joseph. 'Within a fortnight, sooner or later, you will have an insurrection on your hands . . . Whatever you do, you cannot maintain yourself in a city like Naples solely by opinion . . . Impose order, disarm, disarm!'

He has to tell him again, 'Sentence the mob's leaders to death . . . Every spy must be shot; every ringleader must be shot; every lazzarone who indulges in dagger play with a soldier must be shot.'

But will Joseph understand that governing is a demanding, rigorous discipline?

Napoleon enters into details; a sovereign's kitchen must be kept under close surveillance, otherwise beware of poisoning. 'No one should enter your room at night except your aide-de-camp; your aide-de-camp should sleep in the room preceding your bedroom; your door should be locked on the inside, and you should not let your aide-de-camp in before having recognized his voice, and he should not knock at your door before he has closed the door of his room . . .'

I have to teach Joseph everything: the prudence of kings and the art of war. And what are the results?

'Your government is not vigorous enough, you are afraid of antagonizing people,' Napoleon has to write on 5 July 1806. A few days later, when he learns that the English have landed and defeated General Régnier, his indignation erupts, more scathing than ever. 'It would cause you useless pain to tell you all I think,' he writes. 'If you become one of those idle kings instead of being of use to me, you will do me harm since you will take my resources from me . . .' When Joseph requests an audience at St Cloud, Napoleon's response rings out like a slap in the face: 'A king must defend himself and die in his State. An exiled and vagabond king is a silly personage.'

WHAT JOSEPH AND LOUIS – and all of them, all the princes and the marshals – want is peace, peace so that they can enjoy their power and wealth. Napoleon knows this. He wants it too, he says.

One day in February 1806, he grants Talleyrand an audience. The minister of foreign affairs is wreathed in smiles. He has just received a letter from London. Fox, William Pitt's successor, informs him that he has found out about an assassination attempt against the 'leader of the French' and had the ringleader arrested. A sign of Fox's peaceful intentions, wouldn't the Emperor say? Perhaps there is going to be a return to the climate of opinion in 1802 which led to the Peace of Amiens, that great moment of hope.

'Thank Fox in my name,' says Napoleon. 'The war between our two nations is a quarrel useless to humanity . . .'

That's his view, but to achieve peace, there will have to be concessions on both sides – but each mistrusts the other.

In May, when Napoleon learns that the English have decided to blockade every port from the Elbe to Brest, he grows indignant. How can one respond to such a measure other than by demonstrating that the continent is unified, and hence that it obeys and accepts the Emperor's leadership, that it approves of the reorganization of states which, from the Kingdom of Naples to that of Holland, makes Napoleon an Emperor of Kings? He is the sovereign dictating his law, demanding in turn that all ports be closed to the English.

But already the Pope, as far as his ports are concerned, is refusing to comply.

'He will see,' thunders Napoleon, 'whether I have the strength and courage to support my imperial crown. The Pope's relations with me should be the same as his predecessors' with the Emperors of the West.'

The cogs begin turning again. The English negotiators, Lord Yarmouth and Lord Lauderdale, are in Paris, but they refuse to give up Sicily and renounce their blockade. Then Fox dies on 13 September 1806. Is this the end of the peace party? Napoleon wonders.

Continental Europe is his weapon, but every step he takes to unite it under his authority, triggers anxiety, provokes counter-measures.

IN AUGUST AND SEPTEMBER, which he spends at St Cloud, then Rambouillet, Napoleon is more impatient than usual to receive dispatches from Berlin and St Petersburg.

He knows Prussia has been in a state of anxiety since he created the Confederation of the Rhine. Russia, meanwhile, has refused to sign the treaty of peace. A fourth coalition is taking vague shape, comprising Prussia, Russia and, of course, England, but Napoleon is determined to be cautious. 'You don't know what I am doing,' he tells Murat. 'So keep quiet. With a power such as Prussia one cannot proceed too gently.'

No war, only peace – that is what he wants. The soldiers of the Grand Army are still quartered in Germany, dreaming of returning to France.

'I want to be on good terms with Prussia,' Napoleon repeats to Talleyrand. 'Laforest, France's ambassador in Berlin, must be fully informed of this.' But Laforest keeps sending alarming letters.

Napoleon reads them in a subdued voice. Prussian troops are

moving on Hesse and Saxony to anticipate Napoleon and enrol these states' armies in their ranks.

Can Frederick William and his wife, the beautiful Queen Louise, really be risking war like this? Where the Russian and Austrian armies have failed, do the Prussians hope to be victorious?

On 10 September 1806, Napoleon says to Berthier, 'The movements of the Prussian troops continue to be very extraordinary. They wish to be given a lesson. I am sending my horses on tomorrow and in a few days my Guard.'

III

ON THURSDAY, 11 SEPTEMBER, in his room in the Château of St Cloud, Napoleon stands for a long time at the open window without moving. It is barely seven in the morning. He has got up earlier than usual and sent for the grand equerry Caulaincourt, who is waiting in the antechamber. He needs to tell him to prepare the field-glasses, the portmanteaux, the tent with his iron bed, rugs and plenty of thick carpets for bivouacs, and the little campaigning cabriolet, then send off sixty horses to Germany.

Napoleon has already decided that his headquarters will be in Würzburg first, then Bamberg, in the south of Germany, at the junction between Prussia and Saxony. The Grand Army will assemble there to prevent the Russian troops linking up with their Prussian counterparts. From there they will be able to head up north, outflank Frederick William's troops and enter Berlin.

NAPOLEON LEANS ON THE windowsill. He has been living at St Cloud since the start of August. He loves the forests that surround it; he can go hunting when he wishes, at a moment's notice, if he is suddenly seized by a need to act, to breathe.

Today the forest is swathed in fog; the air is damp and cool. He thinks of the forthcoming winter which he will spend in unfamiliar, hastily prepared rooms or under canvas.

Caulaincourt must remember the thick carpets, the fur rugs, the Chambertin wine, the waggons stationed at every post stage with his dinner services and provisions, so that a familiar decor can be recreated within hours.

The Emperor looks at the forest. He has commanded too many campaigns to be under any illusions. He will have to march in his men's midst, endure downpours, ride for hours at a time, sleep in his greatcoat, brave the wind. He is surprised he is even having such thoughts. He turns round, paces up and down his room, catches sight of himself in the mirror that takes up an entire dividing wall.

Has he changed so much? Is it his youth that he has lost along with his slimness? Now he is stout, will he always be tired? Perhaps he is like his marshals and brothers, wanting peace to be able to enjoy palaces, luxury, young women.

He turns away, calls Caulaincourt.

He respects this marquis of an old aristocratic family, having had him made major general and chosen him as his equerry. Caulaincourt can show initiative; he sometimes even ventures to stand up for his own viewpoint. Useful independence of mind, since it allows Napoleon to refine his own thoughts.

Napoleon gives him his orders. They must make it appear that the horses are being sent to Compiègne, as if it were a matter of a hunting party in the forest.

'Prussia has lost its head,' he murmurs.

He begins to pace about. The war is perhaps not yet wholly inevitable. He has already sent intelligence officers out onto the German roads, between Bamberg and Berlin. He wants to know all the routes, the state of fortifications, the movements of the Prussian troops, but, he reminds Caulaincourt, they must give no sign of preparing for war, nothing that would allow one to guess the Emperor is getting ready to leave Paris.

'We must show the greatest prudence,' he insists. 'I have no designs on Berlin.'

Is that true or false? That depends. He would like to have peace, but how is that possible when Prussia and Russia, urged on by England, don't want it? Of these three nations, the only one he can rapidly overthrow, and thereby break the triple coalition, is Prussia. Therefore, he has already given his orders. Every day he inspects his troops on the plateau overlooking the Bois de Meudon. He has seen fifteen thousand men there, for the most part young conscripts, but today, he adds, as he ushers Caulaincourt out of the room, he is reviewing the Imperial Guard and the troops of the garrisons of Paris and Versailles on the Sablons plain.

He rapidly descends the château's staircase; his aides-de-camp surround him. Soldiers of the Guard cry, 'Long live the Emperor!' Napoleon goes over to them and remains with them for a while, pinching the ear of some grenadiers and saying a few words.

More cheers ring out. When he has mounted his horse,

Napoleon leans down and says to Caulaincourt, 'Military fanaticism is the only sort that is any good to me. That's what you need to get yourself killed.'

Then he digs in his spurs and his horse bounds off.

HE PASSES ALONG the front rank of the troops. They form a vast square in the morning fog, striped with the glinting steel of bayonets and sabres, and dotted with coloured and white uniform facings.

He sets his horse prancing on its hind legs. He listens to the soldiers' cheers. Something in him holds back, as if the élan and enthusiasm of the past are having difficulty making themselves felt, constrained by weariness and a sense of repetition.

Everything is starting again. Armies on the march, battlefields with the screams of the wounded, and victory, too. Because he is going to win.

His plan is already drawn up in his head. He will go to Mainz, then Würzburg. They will pass the Frankenwald and debouch on the Bamberg plain. The troops will assemble there, then cross the Thuringerwald and make for Erfurt, Weimar, Leipzig and Jena. Battle will be joined between those towns. Then, when the Prussians have been swept aside, they will reach Berlin.

He's never been to that capital. He thinks of Frederick the Great, the statesman, general and creator of an army he admires. He imagines entering Sans-Souci, Frederick's palace in Potsdam, and visiting his tomb where last year, in October 1805, Tsar Alexander, the King of Prussia, and Frederick William III and Queen Louise, swore an oath of alliance.

Against me.

Queen Louise is the dominant personality of the coalition. The French ambassador tells him that she is constantly saying, 'Napoleon is nothing but a monster from the gutter.'

Napoleon stops his horse, looks at his troops.

'I have about one hundred and fifty thousand men,' he says in a loud voice. 'I can put down Vienna, Berlin and St Petersburg with that.'

War, then.

He returns to St Cloud.

'If I truly have to strike again, Europe will only learn of my departure from Paris by the entire ruin of my enemies ... It is good, therefore, if the newspapers portray me as occupied in Paris with pleasures, hunts and negotiations.'

If only that were true ...

He surprises himself, imagining such a tranquil life amidst the calm splendour of his palaces. He'd organize Europe; he'd build; he'd go from one of his capitals to the next; he'd have so much to do.

On 12 September, he dictates a letter to Frederick William III.

'I consider this war as a civil war ... If I am compelled to take up arms to defend myself, it will be with the greatest regret that I use them against Your Majesty's troops.'

BUT THE PRUSSIAN TROOPS are already on the march. On 18 September, they occupy Dresden.

The die is cast. It is no longer time to question oneself. He must dictate the army's plan of movements to General Clarke, which takes more than two hours. He must order the Imperial Guard to set off for Germany. He must watch over every detail.

Napoleon writes to Eugène, 'Matters should be mulled over at length; to succeed one should spend several months contemplating what might happen.' Napoleon has thought about this war against Prussia for a long time, without wishing it, even hoping to avoid it, but none the less envisaging its course.

Now the only thing left is to let his thoughts unfold.

He tells Berthier, 'I do not want more than four hundred transports, but by this I do not mean that half should be tool waggons or companies' artillery effects. I mean infantry cartridges and cannon ammunition, so as to repair losses and have twenty to thirty more guns in battery on the day of battle.'

He tells Marshal Soult, 'I am debouching in Saxony with my whole army in three columns. You are on my right; half a day's march behind you is the corps of Marshal Ney ... Marshal Bernadotte leads the centre ... Behind him the corps of Marshal Davout, with the greater part of the Reserve Cavalry and my Guard ... With this immense superiority of force in such a narrow space, you will realize that my purpose is not to take any risks but to attack the enemy, wherever they choose to make a stand, with double their number ... You realize that it would be a fine feat to move around this city of Dresden, in a battalion square of two hundred thousand men. Still, all this demands some skill and certain events.'

THESE ARE HIS FINAL PLANS before the army truly gets under way, and he knows that from now on everything may turn on an unexpected event, that the most detailed plan may be rendered unworkable, and that the only thing that matters in the field is keenness of sight and speed of decision.

That's why he must be in the midst of his troops, that's why he must march with his advance guard, come under enemy fire, and get first-hand knowledge of the enemy's disposition.

That's why he must leave Paris, St Cloud.

At the thought of this he is overwhelmed by another wave of weariness, which he fights by looking at the maps, by organizing a diversion to the north, since he plans to approach from the south.

'As my intention is not to attack from your side,' he writes to Louis, King of Holland, 'I desire you to open your campaign on the 1st by threatening the enemy. The ramparts of Wesel and the Rhine will serve you for a refuge in any event...' And because he knows that his brother lacks energy and is hesitant, he reassures him, 'I shall crush all my enemies. The result of all this will be to increase your state and establish a durable peace; I say durable because my enemies will be overthrown and unable to stir for the next ten years.'

Perhaps this will be the last war, he thinks.

HE WALKS THROUGH the galleries of the château. Josephine comes to find him. She insists on accompanying him if he joins the army, if war breaks out as she fears it will. She will take up residence at Mainz, and wait for him in that town. He gives his consent. He is finding it hard to leave; it's the first time.

He sends for Cambacérès. During the Emperor's absence he will be responsible for chairing the Wednesday meeting of ministers, but – Napoleon raises his hand – the ministers will correspond directly with the Emperor wherever he is. He wishes to continue governing France just as if he were in Paris.

HOW LONG WILL he be away? He rides through the forest of St Cloud alone. He needs this solitude to line up in his mind all the cogs of his military machine that will pulverize the enemy. He returns, immediately starts dictating ten or more letters defining in detail the marches of the different corps of the Grand Army.

Then he receives an aide-de-camp of General Augereau, who has returned from Berlin. Napoleon circles Lieutenant Marbot, scrutinizing and questioning him.

Marbot has been a guest in Berlin's salons. What does he think of this Queen Louise who insults the Emperor? Beautiful? People say she wants to witness war at first hand. Blonde, isn't she? asks Napoleon.

He smiles as he listens to the young lieutenant, who says that Queen Louise has paraded through Berlin at the head of the regiment of the Queen's Dragoons and that, according to General von Blücher, she intends to enter Paris with them herself.

'Is she a beautiful woman?' Napoleon asks again.

Marbot nods. But she has one defect. She always wears a flowing scarf to hide a pronounced goitre which, from excessive meddling by her doctors, has burst and now oozes a purulent matter, especially when the queen dances, her favourite pastime.

Napoleon lowers his head. Is this all she is, this Queen Louise who is said to have put Tsar Alexander under her spell?

'And the Prussians?' asks Napoleon. Marshal Brunswick, who commanded the army that tried to punish Paris in 1792 and was defeated at Valmy, what's he worth?

Marbot hesitates, then simply reports that the gendarmes of the Noble Guard have ridden through the streets of Berlin shouting that they don't need sabres for these French dogs, clubs will suffice. They have also gone and sharpened their sabres on the steps of the French Embassy ...

Napoleon brings his hand to the handle of his sword.

'Braggarts!' he shouts. 'Insolent dogs!'

If the Duke of Brunswick is in command of the Prussian army, as he was fourteen years ago, he'll soon find that the French armies are in good order. Napoleon wishes Lieutenant Marbot a glorious war.

He remembers when he was a young officer. He feels a soldier of the Revolution.

AT FOUR THIRTY on the afternoon of Thursday, 25 September 1806, he steps into his carriage and leaves St Cloud. Josephine is in one of the carriages following. Night falls; they dine at Châlons, then set off again in the dark and drive as far as Metz, which they reach the following day, at two in the afternoon. Pushing on, they pass through St Avold, Saarbrücken, Kaiserslautern and finally arrive in Mainz early on Sunday the 28th, just as day is breaking.

He feels drained. He consults the dispatches. The Grand Army is already concentrated around Bamberg. He checks the position of each corps, the number of men: he should have almost a hundred and sixty thousand men at his disposal. But is it war?

Everything is poised for its outbreak. The Prussians, commanded by Marshal the Duke of Brunswick and the Prince of Hohenlohe, have formed up around Jena, but fighting hasn't broken out so far.

'There is no declaration of war yet,' Napoleon tells Berthier on 29 September. 'We should not commit any act of war.'

Nor, under any circumstances, should they let themselves be taken by surprise.

He orders the purchase of thousands of horses, has the roads between Leipzig and Dresden reconnoitred. He mulls over the reports filed by officers sent on reconnaissance to Thuringia and Saxony. War is here, there's no doubt about that. Brunswick is advancing through the Main valley to the Rhine. Napoleon dictates orders for Berthier and writes to Fouché.

'The fatigue means nothing,' he says. 'I should regret the loss of my soldiers if the injustice of this war I am obliged to wage did not ensure that all the evil mankind is again facing catch up with these weak kings who let themselves be led by treacherous muddlers.'

He is tense. 'It is possible that present events are only the start of a great coalition against us, the particular circumstances of which will cause the whole to take shape,' he writes to Louis.

He must face up to the situation. During the first day of October, he gives his final instructions. He is going to set off for Würzburg himself that evening. The army should complete its movement, converging on that town and Bamberg.

He sees Josephine with Talleyrand, who has also travelled to Mainz. He walks slowly towards them. He is going to leave this town, he says, he'll drive through the night, travel to Würzburg via Frankfurt.

Josephine starts to cry and suddenly Napoleon feels his legs give way. It's as if his body's melting. He clings on to Talleyrand and Josephine. He cannot hold back his tears. The accumulated tension, the exhaustion of all the hours he has worked to prepare for this war, suddenly crush him.

He is carried to a bedroom, where he is seized with convulsions, his body going into spasms. He vomits; his face is ashen. He stays like that for several minutes, his body rigid, dripping with sweat, jerking and trembling, his jaw clenched.

Then gradually he grows still; he looks around and, without a word, gets to his feet, waving away those surrounding him. Then he strides briskly to his carriage, as if nothing has happened.

He sets off for Würzburg, as planned. It is ten in the evening.

WHAT HAPPENED inside him?

He ponders on this as his berline drives through the night towards Frankfurt where he is meant to arrive at one in the morning on Thursday, 2 October 1806. He has decided to dine quickly with the Prince Primate and then continue on to Würzburg.

He stretches out his legs. He hates his body's betrayal. What does it mean? Should he see Doctor Corvisart? But he feels fine now; the energy starting to radiate through his body reassures him, puts him in a good mood. He hums a tune.

He is cheerful throughout dinner in Frankfurt and when he reaches Würzburg at ten in the evening he feels in fine fettle. He jokes with his aides-de-camp, marches vigorously into the palace of the Grand Duke, the former residence of the bishops of the city.

He stops at the foot of the main staircase and looks at the crowd of German princes who press around him. He recognizes the King of Würtemberg, goes up to him, takes him familiarly by the arm.

He has learnt to feel as alone and free in a crowd as in a forest. Other people's looks makes no impression on him, and when he meets someone's eyes they lower theirs instantly. He dominates them all. He is above the common, swarming run of men, at the top of the world, breathing the rarefied atmosphere of those who command the fate of nations and inscribe their names in the annals of history.

He tells the King of Würtemberg that, as head of the imperial family, he has decided to marry his brother Jérôme to the king's daughter, Catherine of Würtemberg. To this effect Jérôme – who has renounced his American wife, thereby bowing to Napoleon's will – has been made a French prince by a *senatus consultum*, and is now in line to succeed him as Emperor. The King of Würtemberg bows, then reports the pressure Prussia has been applying, specifically a letter he has received from the Duke of Brunswick threatening to plant the Prussian eagles in Stuttgart if Würtemberg does not leave the Confederation of the Rhine.

'I am your protector,' says Napoleon calmly. 'All our armies are on the move. I enjoy the best of health and I have every hope of seeing all this through.'

The expectations of this king, of all these princes, oblige him to be successful.

HE IS SHOWN Tiepolo's ceilings and his paintings which line the galleries, along with still-lifes of the Italian school.

In one of the drawing rooms, he draws Archduke Ferdinand, the brother of Francis II, the Emperor of Austria, aside. He questions the Archduke. He feels at the heart of the network of European dynasties now, and when the Archduke lauds the advantages of an alliance with Austria, he agrees. After all, it is a tradition of the French monarchy, temporarily interrupted.

When he withdraws to his bedroom, he sends for his secretary. Ideas and visions of the future jostle for space in his mind, as if this war which has not yet officially been declared were already over and won. He has never been able to prevent himself looking beyond the present and the immediate future to sketch in the next chapter of his destiny.

He dictates a dispatch to France's ambassador in Vienna, La Rochefoucauld.

'My position and my forces are such that I need not fear anybody; but all these efforts are a burden on my people.'

Therefore he must have an ally. Prussia doesn't merit the slightest trust. That leaves Russia and Austria. 'In the past the navy flourished in France through the benefit we derived from our alliance with Austria. Besides, that power needs to remain quiet, a sentiment which I heartily share.'

He reads his marshals' reports, then, his mind at rest, goes to bed. His thoughts are in order.

HE GETS UP EARLY. The sky is bright.

Let us pay a visit to Würzburg Cathedral.

He rides at the head of the galloping cavalcade of aides-de-camp and German princes.

Suddenly he feels a shock. He turns round and sees a peasant woman, who his horse has knocked down, lying on the ground. He reins in his horse, dismounts, rushes towards the woman, gives orders that she be picked up and demands that someone translate what he is going to say to her. He offers her money, expresses his regret at the accident and then bids her farewell with a gesture full of affection and compassion.

The world should be a place without violence. It should be ... but he can't even dream, or think of, that. War is a part of nature.

When he returns to the Grand Duke's palace, he quickly writes a few lines to Josephine, from whom he has received a tearful letter.

I don't know why you weep, you are wrong to do yourself
harm. Courage and gaiety, that is the recipe.
    Farewell, my friend; the Grand Duke has spoken to me
about you.
    Napoleon

HE LEAVES WÜRZBURG on Monday, 6 October, at three in the morning. As the darkness fades and the fog thins, he sees the forests and hills which his troops have already crossed. These are the landscapes he has been trying to picture for so long, as he poured over maps. It is on this terrain, on this patchwork of plateaus, mountains and valleys beyond Bamberg, that he wishes to join battle.

He enters Bamberg, rides along the banks of the River Regnitz and turns into the Neue Residenz, which towers over the town and is where Caulaincourt has established his headquarters. The town is swarming with troops.

Napoleon studies the dispatches. The couriers aren't making good enough time.

'In a war such as this,' he exclaims, 'it is only by very frequent communications that we can achieve the best results! Make that one of your primary concerns!'

Where are Brunswick's troops? he asks.

'They're not expecting what we intend to do; woe betide them if they hesitate and lose a single day!'

NOW EVERY MINUTE counts. He receives General Berthier who has brought an ultimatum sent to Paris on 26 September, in which Frederick William demands that the Grand Army withdraw behind the Rhine before 8 October.

Napoleon crumples up the piece of paper, tosses it aside and paces about the room, his hands behind his back. From time to time he takes a pinch of snuff. When he speaks, his voice is irritable. Who is this King of Prussia? Does he think France is the same as it was in 1792?

'Does he think himself in Champagne?' he asks. 'Does he want to reproduce his Manifesto? Truly I feel pity for Prussia; I pity William.'

The king, he continues, his voice rising, is the victim of a queen dressed as an Amazon, who wears the uniform of her dragoon regiment, and writes twenty-five letters a day to feed the fire.

'This king does not know what rhapsodies he is being made to write. It is too ridiculous! He has no idea.'

Napoleon stops in front of Berthier.

'Berthier, we have been given an appointment of honour on the 8th. A Frenchman has never missed one of those. But as we are told there is a beautiful queen who wishes to witness the conflict, let us be polite and, without sleeping, march into Saxony.'

He walks around the room several times in silence. The words well up inside him, as if from a deep, gushing spring. He turns to his secretary, then dictates a proclamation to the Grand Army.

'Soldiers! The order for your return to France had been issued; you had already made several marches; triumphal festivities awaited you!'

He stops. He knows only too well how keenly the soldiers were dreaming of going home, of peace.

'But cries of war were raised in Berlin,' he continues.

He thinks of Brunswick's Manifesto of 1792. The men of the Grand Army must remember those threats against Paris, the arrogance of the Prussians and émigrés, and their defeat at Valmy. He must bring this past back to life.

'The same faction, the same vertigo that carried Prussia to the plains of Champagne fourteen years ago now dominate their councils. Their schemes were dashed to pieces before; in the plains of Champagne they found only death, defeat and shame. But the lessons of experience fade and there are men for whom hatred and jealousy never die . . .'

He speaks to the soldiers and to himself.

'So let us march then, since moderation has not been enough to jolt them out of their astonishing intoxication. Let the Prussian army experience the same fate it experienced fourteen years ago!'

This proclamation is to be read to the soldiers, he orders.

This is war beginning, the skirmishes at the outposts. It is where he wants it, where it must be. Everything in him is on the move.

He starts out from Bamberg. Only trusting his own eyes, he wants to reconnoitre the Saalburg defile himself, take a look at the Prussian troops of General Tauenzien who are bivouacking on the heights in front of Schleiz, where the first engagement has just taken place.

His men get to their feet as he passes, shouting 'Long live the

Emperor!' He stops, congratulates them, calls out, 'The Prussians' conduct is shameful. They have incorporated a Saxon battalion into two Prussian battalions to be sure of them, a violation of independence and a violation against a weaker power, the likes of which can only revolt all Europe.'

But it is no longer time for protests; it is time for arms.

He hears a cannonade in the distance. That must be the troops of Marshal Lannes, who are attacking the Prince of Hohenlohe's vanguard at Saalfeld, which is commanded by Prince Louis of Prussia, one of the most fervent supporters of the war against France.

Napoleon wants to continue, push forward. He gives orders to Caulaincourt for his headquarters to be transferred to Auma, and this is where he receives the reports of first Lannes, then Murat. He reads them standing up, impatient.

Lannes reports that Quartermaster Guindey has killed Prince Louis of Prussia with a sword thrust after the Prussian, refusing to surrender, had lunged at the Frenchman.

'It is a punishment from heaven,' exclaims Napoleon, 'since he is the real author of this war.'

Then he dictates his orders: 'Our skill now will be in attacking everything we meet, so as to beat the enemy in detail and while they are concentrating . . . Boldly attack everything that is on the march . . . Flood the whole Leipzig plain with your cavalry.'

It is four in the morning on Sunday, 12 October 1806. He goes outside, into the darkness, and feels a sense of joy and power. 'I haven't been mistaken about anything,' he murmurs. Everything he had anticipated two months ago in Paris is coming to pass, 'march for march, almost event by event'.

He decides to go on ahead to Gera, to be closer to what will be the scene of the decisive battle. When he arrives, he writes to Josephine. It is already two in the morning on Monday, the 13th.

I am today at Gera, my good friend, and my affairs are going very well, quite as I hoped they would. With God's help, in a few days, matters will have taken a terrible turn for the poor King of Prussia, I believe, who personally I pity because he is a good man. The Queen is at Erfurt with the King. If she wishes to see a battle, she will have that cruel pleasure. My health is excellent; I have already put on weight since my departure, and yet I travel from twenty to twenty-five leagues a day, on horseback, in my carriage and by every means of transport. I retire at eight o'clock and rise at midnight. I sometimes imagine you not yet abed.

     Ever yours,
     Napoleon

He sends for General Clarke, his private secretary, pinches his ear and begins pacing.

'I am blocking their road to Dresden and Berlin. The Prussians have hardly any chance now. Their generals are perfect idiots. It is inconceivable how the Duke of Brunswick, who is supposed to have talent, can direct the operations of his army in such a ridiculous fashion!'

He gives Clarke a friendly slap on the back.

'Clarke, in one month you will be governor of Berlin and people will talk of you as the man who in one year, and two different wars, was the governor of Vienna *and* Berlin!'

He walks towards the door, calling over his shoulder, 'I'm mounting up to go to Jena.'

HE REACHES THAT TOWN in the early afternoon. Parts of it are in flames; the streets are full of troops. The Foot Guard form up around him as he stops under the limes in front of the Grossherzogliche Schloss. He calls his aides-de-camp over and points to the mountain range that dominates the town and seems inaccessible. This is the Landgrafenberg; its vine-covered slopes are bisected by a few narrow paths. The only way to reach the top is on horseback, explain the officers. The artillery won't be able to get up. Napoleon listens. An officer of Marshal Augereau's, whose troops occupy Jena, reports that the Prussians have left Weimar overnight in two columns, one heading towards Naumburg to the north of Jena led by Brunswick, the other advancing on Jena under the command of Prince Hohenlohe.

So those troops are on the other side of the Landgrafenberg; protected, they imagine, by these impassable mountains.

Napoleon impatiently returns to the ducal palace, the tallest, most imposing building in the town. He walks through its rooms, his eyes permanently trained on the Landgrafenberg. Seen from the palace, the abrupt slopes seem almost vertical; the smoke from the fires in Jena and the evening fog are starting to envelop them.

Raised voices. Napoleon turns round. Some officers have entered with a priest who appears beside himself. He is cursing the Prussians: they're the ones responsible for the whole city being on fire and for them being at war in the first place. He knows a path through the vines, he says, which will take them to the top of the Landgrafenberg.

Napoleon congratulates the priest. He is certain this is destiny giving him a sign.

He sets off into the vines, Marshal Lannes and his staff hurriedly following.

The path is abrupt and narrow — as steeply sloping as a roof, a grenadier of the Guard calls back down to them — but when they reach the top, Napoleon finds a little rocky plateau that looks out over the Weimar plain where one can see the Prussian army's campfires.

Napoleon takes a few steps. He will concentrate his troops here, on this plateau. The whole army, cannon included, must climb the Landgrafenberg.

STRIDING BACK DOWN towards the city in the gathering darkness, Napoleon gives his orders. On rotation, every battalion will work for an hour at a time widening the path. Every soldier will be given pioneering tools. They will work their way up, then the next will follow, and so on until the corps of Lannes, Soult and Augereau and the foot soldiers of the Guard under Marshal Lefebvre have all taken up position on the plateau.

He stops several times on the way down. They should dig here and over there. The artillery with its caissons must be able to get through as well. He looks at the officers surrounding him; they lower their eyes — they agree.

He walks the final stretch of the path on his own, leaving his staff to see that his orders are carried out. Night has fallen. French sentries positioned on the edge of the town open fire on him. He carries on walking, indifferent, as if he were sure he couldn't be hit, and he feels invulnerable, protected, as if he were being carried to victory.

THERE'S NO WAY he's going to stay in the palace. He wants his bivouac to be set up on the Landgrafenberg so that he can sleep in the midst of his men.

He lingers over his maps, then makes his way up to his tent.

His marshals are waiting for him; he has invited them to dinner. A small fire is burning in a pit in the ground. The order has been given that only three fires be lit for every company of 220 men. Just like everyone else, Napoleon has obeyed orders; but dinner has been laid out in a hut which the grenadiers have roofed with matting. His iron bed has been brought up, along with his trunks and his paraffin lamps; a few books and his maps are on a second table.

Roustam serves a local Jena wine to accompany the boiled potatoes with melted butter and cold meats. Then, one by one, the marshals doze off, overwhelmed with exhaustion, in a circle around the Emperor, who seems to be drowsing.

HE WAKES UP. Everyone is asleep. He leaves the hut. Apart from a few twinkling lights, it is pitch black. The soldiers have concealed their fires. The enemy is close. The plateau is so small one cannot take a step without touching someone.

Napoleon slowly walks around the grenadiers' bivouacs, stopping occasionally and standing silently in the dark.

He likes mingling with his soldiers like this, without being recognized. He likes being an Emperor on his own, incognito. He listens to the jokes, the stories. He also likes it when he is suddenly recognized, and the soldiers are flustered and salute him deferentially, reverentially. Then he moves on.

Caulaincourt finds him, urges him to return to his bivouac; it's dangerous out here like this, exposed to enemy fire, on his own. But Napoleon doesn't go back. He wants to see everything, twice if necessary.

In war, he knows, you never delegate. 'Only the commander understands the importance of certain things; and he alone, by his will and superior knowledge, can conquer and overcome every difficulty.'

He continues walking in the dark. Where are the guns? he asks. The men are massed on the plateau, but he cannot see a single artillery caisson. He rushes forward; this is the sort of unexpected circumstance that often decides the fate of a battle.

At the foot of the Landgrafenberg, he sees Marshal Lannes's entire artillery trapped in a narrow ravine. The spindles of their axles are wedged between the rock walls. More than two hundred vehicles have been brought to a standstill.

Anger courses through him. Where is the general in charge of this corps? Nowhere to be found. Napoleon pushes his way forward, calls for a lantern, lights up the walls of the ravine and then, in a calm, clear voice, orders that tools be distributed amongst the men to widen the path. As the gunners set to, he holds up his torch, goes from one group to the next and doesn't leave the ravine until the first vehicle has started up it, followed by a piece of ordnance drawn by twelve horses.

He is calm again by the time he gets back to his bivouac. The grenadiers he's passed on the way are returning from Jena, where they'd been authorized to go and look for provisions. They've found plenty of wine. He hears them toasting 'the King of Prussia's health'. But they do so in hushed voices. The enemy is close and does not suspect the presence of a mass of men concentrated on a plateau which is reputed to be inaccessible.

Napoleon looks at the maps one last time, then gives his instructions. He will give the signal to attack himself, at daybreak.

At midnight he goes to his tent. He is serene; he closes his eyes; he falls asleep.

AT THREE IN THE MORNING, he is on his feet. The ground is white under a layer of hoarfrost. Thick fog covers the hills, the palace and the plateau. At six, it is still not light.

He is even more sure of himself than he was at Austerlitz. He rides along the lines, and calls out a few words to the soldiers, who shout 'Let's march, march!' and 'Forward!'

Napoleon pulls on the reins, stops his horse and cries, 'What's that you say? Only a beardless youth would try to judge what I should do beforehand. Let him wait until he has commanded in thirty pitched battles before presuming to give me advice!'

He gallops away. He is everywhere, under fire from the Prussian cannon that have gone into action at six in the morning. The Prince of Hohenlohe has no idea the French are so close to his lines, at the top of the Landgrafenberg, and his gunners' roundshot fall far behind them, but still, they whistle over Napoleon's head, and they're joined by bullets when, at about nine, the attack is launched all along the line.

He's not afraid for his life, which has been endangered so many times. He sees the men struck down around him. The Prussian soldiers advance in serried ranks like automata, then suddenly collapse, broken jointed. The wounded French yell, 'Long live the Emperor!' He barely gives them a glance. Ever since he first saw men die at his side, he has known that 'a man who cannot remain dry-eyed while he looks at a battlefield will send men purposelessly to their deaths.'

He is dry-eyed.

He observes these hundreds of thousands of men, these seven hundred pieces of ordnance spreading death. He delights in what, for him, is one of the 'rarest sights in history': behind the skirmishers come columns, bands at their head, advancing as if they were on parade.

By two in the afternoon, the battle's fate is decided. The Prussian army has been reduced to a river of fugitives streaming towards Weimar.

Napoleon remains on horseback on the plateau until three. As he listens to the reports of his aides-de-camp, roundshot begins to fall in the midst of his staff.

'It is pointless getting oneself killed after a victory,' Napoleon says to de Ségur, who has just arrived with a message from Marshal Lannes. 'Let us dismount.'

HE RETURNS TO JENA. The town is lit up by the fires started by the Russian cannon. He rides past the church and hears the screams of the wounded crowded together inside; there are so many of them that others lie, covered in blood, on the church square and in the streets leading off it.

He remains dry-eyed.

He snatches a few moments' sleep in a tavern where Caulaincourt has had his bed set up in the corner of a vast room, then his aides-de-camp wake him. De Ségur reports that the Queen of Prussia has almost been captured. Napoleon gets up.

'She's the cause of this war,' he says.

An aide-de-camp tells him that Davout has gained a complete victory at Auerstadt over the Prussians under King Frederick William and the Duke of Brunswick. The latter has been gravely wounded.

Napoleon asks about the circumstances of the battle. He grows solemn. He gathers that, far from helping Davout as he should have done, Bernadotte played no part in the fighting.

'That Gascon will never wage another battle!' Napoleon exclaims.

He should have Bernadotte shot, but he is the husband of Désirée Clary, and so is Joseph's brother-in-law.

He dictates a letter to Bernadotte: 'I am not in the habit of quarelling over the past since it is beyond remedy. Your Army Corps was not on the battlefield, and that could have been catastrophic . . . All this is certainly most unfortunate.'

The pettiness of men. Bernadotte didn't want to contribute to Davout's victory, Davout who deserves to be made Duke of Auerstadt. I shall remember these two men.

It is three in the morning on 15 October. Napoleon sits down and, resting a piece of paper on the edge of a chest, by the glimmer of a candle stub, he writes to Josephine,

> My friend, I have performed some fine manoeuvres against the Prussians. Yesterday I gained a great victory. They had 150,000 men; I took 20,000 prisoners, 100 guns and standards. I was in the vicinity and close to the King of Prussia; I nearly captured him and the Queen.
>
> I have been bivouacking for three days. My health is excellent.
>
> Adieu, my good friend; enjoy good health and love me.

If Hortense is at Mainz, give her a kiss from me, and
Napoleon as well and the little one.*
Napoleon

HE GOES OUT INTO the streets of Jena, climbs into an open
barouche.

Take me to Weimar, he orders.

The roads are choked with troops. The fields on either side are
littered with dead and wounded. He tells Berthier that 'they must
charge head down at any resistance'.

He leans out of the window, stops the carriage, gets out and
goes over to a group of wounded. They are covered in blood.
Some draw themselves up and call out in a choked voice, 'Long
live the Emperor!' He asks their names, their units. He will see to
it that they are awarded the Légion d'honneur. He walks away,
gets back into his barouche.

'To win is nothing,' he murmurs. 'One must take advantage of
one's victory.'

He stays in the ducal palace in Weimar for a few hours. To his
great satisfaction, the arrival of an envoy of the King of Prussia is
announced, an aide-de-camp requesting an armistice.

Napoleon listens to the request, then replies, 'Any suspension
of hostilities which would give the Russian armies time to arrive
would be too contrary to my interests — whatever my desire to
spare humanity further ills and victims — for me to be able to
subscribe to it. But I do not fear the Russian armies one jot; they
are no more than a cloud: I saw them in the previous campaign.
Your Majesty will have more to complain of than me . . .'

The Russians! He feels more invincible than ever, so sure of
himself, so confident in his intuition. Marshal Lannes writes to him
that his men, on hearing the proclamation celebrating the victories
of Jena and Auerstadt, burst into shouts of 'Long live the Emperor

---

* Napoleon Charles, the 'Napoleon' of this letter, son of Hortense and Louis
Bonaparte, was born in 1802. He will die in 1807. The 'little one' is his brother
Napoleon Louis, born in 1804. He will die in 1831. The last son of the family will
be Charles Louis, born in 1808, the future Napoleon III. He will die in 1873. A
half-brother from the liaison between Queen Hortense and Flahaut will be born in
1811. He will have the title of Duke of Morny and will die in 1865.

of the West!' 'It is impossible to tell Your Majesty how much these brave men adore you; truly no one has felt such love for their mistress as they do for Yourself.'

Napoleon listens carefully to Lannes's letter. He loves his soldiers for the love they bear him, and he tells them as much in his proclamation.

Now Davout steps forward and repeats that his blood belongs to the Emperor. 'I shall shed it with pleasure at any time and my reward will be to deserve your esteem and good-will.'

He accepts these words as trophies. Isn't it only right that people admire him, love him? At five in the evening on 16 October in Weimar, he writes to Josephine again, 'Monsieur Talleyrand will have shown you the bulletin, my good friend; you will have seen my success. Everything has gone as I planned it and no army has ever been so defeated and more wholly lost.'

He had anticipated all this. He is the only one to have this talent, this genius.

He continues:

All that remains is for me to tell you that I am in good health and that tiredness, the bivouacs and long vigils have made me put on weight.

Farewell, my good friend, a thousand loving things to Hortense and big Napoleon,

Yours ever,

Napoleon

'WE MUST PRESS HARD on them,' he declares when he rejoins his marshals.

Then he sets off through Halle and on to Wittenberg where he sees Lucchesini, the King of Prussia's envoy, who has come to negotiate.

'The King strikes me as inclined to come to terms,' Napoleon tells Berthier, 'but that will not prevent me from going to Berlin, where I think I will be in four or five days.'

They wanted war! Now let them pay. This is the conqueror's law; these are the facts they must face.

He imposes contributions of a hundred and fifty million francs on the German States. Halle University is to be closed. 'If any students are found in town tomorrow, they will be put in prison to countermand the truculence that has been inculcated into this generation.'

He calls to General Savary. Does he remember the Battle of Rossbach, in 1757, where Soubise's French were spectacularly defeated by Frederick II?

'Half a league from here you should find the column that the Prussians erected in memory of this event.'

At the foot of the monument that Savary has found in a wheat field, Napoleon spends a long time reading the inscriptions celebrating the glory of Frederick II.

I am here. Forty-nine years have passed, and now I have erased France's defeat and Frederick the Great's victory.

He gives Berthier his instructions.

'Plenty of ceremony, plenty of formalities, plenty of decorum, but in reality take everything, especially military resources . . .'

This is the conqueror's law.

HE LEAVES WITTENBERG, but on the road a hailstorm forces him to take refuge in a hunting lodge. The rooms are dark. The thunder roars; it is cold. The fire draws badly, filling the rooms with smoke. Suddenly, he hears a voice. A woman comes towards him and the circle of officers surrounding him. She is Egyptian, the widow of a French officer of the Army of Egypt. She bows. The Emperor listens to her story, and grants her a pension for herself and her child.

Then he goes and stands alone by a window.

So few years separate Egypt and Saxony – barely eight! And yet those times when he bivouacked at the foot of the Pyramids seem to belong to another life, so many things have happened since then. This woman who makes the past rise up again is so young.

He suddenly feels as if he is a stranger to his own life, as if he's watching it unfold in front of him, as if he is both actor and spectator.

He stays like that for a long time, waiting for the storm to end. Then he turns round. The Egyptian woman is looking at him.

Nothing is impossible. The most extraordinary things can

happen. He is here. Tomorrow he will be in Potsdam, in Sans-Souci, the royal palace of Frederick the Great, that ruler whose genius he admired as a young lieutenant, and whose glory fascinated him.

ON FRIDAY, 24 OCTOBER 1806, he enters the courtyard of the palace of Sans-Souci. He walks with measured steps, his hands behind his back, and has himself shown to the apartments of Frederick II.

So, this is it.

He opens the books, many of which are French. He lingers over the notes jotted in the margins. The Prussian King used to write in his books, like him.

Napoleon looks round the rooms, goes out onto the terrace, and gazes out onto the sandy plain where the creator of the Prussian army used to hold reviews of his troops. He goes back inside to the royal apartments and picks up the King's sword, his belt and great sash. Pointing to the standards of the Royal Guard from the Battle of Rossbach, he says, 'I shall give them to the governor of the Invalides, who will keep them as testimony to the victories of the Grand Army and the vengeance it has extracted for the disasters of Rossbach.'

Perhaps he has never had such a sense of fulfilment, or felt himself so completely the Emperor of Kings, the conqueror, as he does at this moment.

HE CHOOSES TO SLEEP in the same apartments Tsar Alexander used in November 1805. He looks out of the window at the soldiers of the Imperial Guard bivouacked under the trees of the park. The sky is very bright. He stares at it for a long time, remembering the starlit nights of Egypt, the Pyramids. He feels almost intoxicated.

He summons Caulaincourt. He will hold a review of the Imperial Guard tomorrow, he says. Then, before going to sleep, he thinks that 'the greatest danger lies at the moment of victory', when one lets oneself be carried away, when one forgets that once one enemy is brought low, others spring up. Russia, England – perhaps even Austria.

From tomorrow, he will set about reinforcing the army; he will prepare a decree to levy the conscription of 1807, to distribute pupils of the Polytechnic and St Cyr among various units, and to request that Eugène and Joseph send regiments from Italy and Naples.

Reviewing his Guard the following morning, he says, 'This war must be the last', but when he dictates a proclamation to the troops, he concludes with the words, 'Soldiers, the Russians boast that they are coming. We shall march to meet them and spare them half the road.'

He has to say this, because the Russians really are advancing, and they will have to fight again.

ON THE MORNING OF Sunday, 26 October, he slowly makes his way to the small church in Potsdam that contains Frederick II's tomb. He stands in front of the brass-hooped coffin, with Duroc, Berthier, de Ségur and a few other officers in a line a few paces behind him.

He forgets everyone else there.

He communes with all the men who, like Frederick II, make up the great chain of conquerors; those whom Plutarch, whom he has read so closely, calls *Illustrious Men*.

He is one of them. Their conquering successor in this century.

He stays motionless in front of the tomb for a long time.

AS DAVOUT'S TROOPS enter Berlin on 26 October 1806 and Murat's march on Stettin, Napoleon, after receiving the keys of Berlin from Prince Hatzfeld, makes his way to the Charlottenburg palace on the outskirts of the Prussian capital.

The skies open. The roads are waterlogged. He loses his way, gets separated from his escort and finds himself alone in the countryside in the driving rain. When he reaches the entrance to the palace, he sees de Ségur trying in vain to open the door.

'Why didn't you deploy any troops on my route?' he yells. 'Why haven't you posted a guard?'

The door gives way finally. The palace is empty. Napoleon discovers Queen Louise's apartments and, in a dressing table, her letters.

He leafs through them, and laughs.

He feels as if she is another conquest.

IV

HE SLEEPS LITTLE and then, early on Monday, 27 October 1806, he sees the chasseurs of the Guard starting to gather in the courtyard of the castle of Charlottenburg. They will be his escort for his entrance into Berlin today.

He wants a military parade that will make an indelible impression on all who see it. He has already demanded that the Prussian Noble Guard, who had sharpened their sabres on the steps of the French embassy, march through Berlin between two columns of French soldiers as punishment for their bragging.

Yesterday evening, he told Daru, Intendant General of the Grand Army, that all the money found in Berlin was to go to replenish the army paymaster's coffers.

'My intention is that Berlin will abundantly furnish me with everything my army needs, so that my soldiers are lavishly provided for in every respect.'

Then he led Daru to Queen Louise's apartments. He showed him the papers she had left behind: not, as he had thought for a moment, a lover's correspondence, but documents revealing the queen's determination to go to war.

'Against me, Daru, against us.'

She calls Napoleon *Noppel*, which her parrot pronounces *Moppel* – in Berlin slang, 'a bragging little cur'. These are her exact words.

He has even found among her papers a report from Dumouriez – yes, Brunswick's victor at Valmy – about tactics to use against the French.

'How unfortunate are princes who allow women to influence political affairs!' Napoleon exclaims.

IT WILL BE a beautiful day, this Monday.

He looks at his regiments forming up. All these men hope to be finished with marches and bivouacs and battles. They have eluded death, now they dream of peace; but they do not know that peace still has to be won. The Prussians are waiting for the approaching Russians, who, reports indicate, have crossed the Vistula and entered Warsaw. Should he help the Poles who want their independence? But what exactly does *wanting* mean? This is the point Napoleon makes to Dombrovski, a Polish patriot who wants France to help his country to be re-established, 'I will see if you deserve to be a nation. If Poland provides forty thousand good soldiers whom I can count on as if I had a corps of forty thousand regular troops,' then the Polish people truly want their independence. Otherwise . . .

Besides, helping the Poles would mean opening a Pandora's box: an endless war with the Russians and, no doubt, the Austrians. And at their backs, the English, the evil genius of every coalition, the banker of nations, the power that must be broken if one wants one day to obtain peace.

GENERAL ZASTROV is announced; he seeks an audience in the name of Frederick William. The King of Prussia solicits an armistice and the opening of negotiations.

'Are the Russians already on Prussian territory?' Napoleon asks.

'The heads of their columns may, at this moment, be crossing the border,' General Zastrov replies, bowing, 'but the King is only waiting for a word of reassurance to turn them back.'

Napoleon spins on his heel.

'Ah, if the Russians are coming, I'll march against them and fight them.'

He walks away, and then turns back to Zastrov.

'But the negotiations can continue,' he says. 'Duroc, the Grand Marshal of the Palace, will conduct them.'

FIRST THE ENTRANCE into Berlin, however. These Prussians must behold the might of the Grand Army.

At three in the afternoon, Napoleon caracoles his horse on Unter den Linden. He is in the middle of the procession, a small man in the green uniform of a colonel of the chasseurs of the Guard and a cocked hat with a 'one sou cockade', as the grenadiers call it. Of his decorations, all he wears is the ribbon of the Légion d'honneur. Behind him rides his Mameluke, Roustam, and a few lengths further back, his staff and the officers of the Imperial Household, Duroc,

Caulaincourt, Clarke, his aides-de-camp, Lemarois, Mouton, Savary, Rapp and Marshals Berthier, Davout and Augereau.

Lefebvre and the Footguard precede the Emperor, while the chasseurs of the Guard come after the officers.

Everything Napoleon sees is what he wanted: the fanfares, the Mamelukes, the twenty thousand men, the towering grenadiers with their bearskins – and the huge crowds on Unter den Linden. He gallops around the statue of Frederick II, his hat raised. He is the conquering Emperor.

HE REVIEWS III CORPS, which is commanded by Marshal Davout, the Duke of Auerstadt. He distributes over five hundred crosses and spends a long time talking to the men. He promotes countless officers.

'The brave men who have died,' he says, 'have died with glory. We all should wish to die in circumstances as glorious.'

The men cheer him and Davout cries, 'Sire, we are your 10th Legion! The III Corps will at all times and places be to you what the 10th Legion was to Caesar!'

As he listens, he feels himself a Caesar of this century.

HE PAYS A VISIT to the town hall and vehemently addresses the assembled Prussian nobility, assuring them that he has seen Tsar Alexander's portrait in Queen Louise's bedroom.

'It's not true, Sire,' calls a voice.

Officers rush forward. Napoleon stops them, forgives Pastor Erhmann for having dared interrupt him. He recognizes the man's sincerity, his candour, but when he returns to the royal palace where he is to stay, he grows indignant when General Savary gives him a letter written by Prince Hatzfeld, who presented him with the keys of Berlin. Savary's agents have intercepted this correspondence between Hatzfeld and Prince Hohenlohe. It contains an exact list of French troops in Berlin, corps by corps, and even gives the number of their caissons of munitions.

In a voice choked with rage, Napoleon immediately dictates an order that Prince Hatzfeld be brought before a military commission and tried as a traitor or spy. He is to be arrested and shot. He sees consternation in the eyes of Berthier and de Ségur, but haven't they understood that the only way to rule is severely? Wasn't a Nuremberg bookseller shot, on 26 August 1806, for selling an anti-French pamphlet?

A short while later, on his way back from a review, as the drums beat outside, he sees a pregnant woman waiting at the door of his study, on the verge of fainting. Princess Hatzfeld has come to ask for mercy for her husband.

Napoleon looks at the young woman, hands her the letter, asks her to read it. She stammers, cries.

Being the Emperor also means having the right to pardon, having the depth of fellow feeling that enables one to restore life to one whom one has condemned to death.

Napoleon looks at the tearful princess sitting by the fireplace.

'Well then,' he says, 'since you hold the proof of the crime in your hands, destroy it and thereby disarm the laws of war.'

She throws the letter in the fire.

Soon afterwards, Prince Hatzfeld is released.

HE WRITES TO Josephine at two in the morning on 1 November 1806.

> Talleyrand has arrived and tells me, my friend, that all you do is cry. What is it that you want? You have your daughter, your grandchildren, and good news: that is enough reason to be contented and happy.
>
> The weather here is superb, not a single drop of rain yet during the whole campaign. My health is good and everything is going well.
>
> Farewell, my friend, I have received a letter from Napoleon; I don't think it's from him, but from Hortense.
>
> A thousand things to everybody.
>
> Napoleon

IT'S TRUE, his health is good. Every day he attends a parade in front of the royal palace. He reviews the cavalry, manoeuvres the Guard on the Charlottenburg plain. The rest of the day he spends working in the study he has had prepared for him in the palace, to which his library and his maps have been transferred. He follows the pursuit of the Prussians. First Kustrin, then Magdeburg, Stettin and Lübeck – a free city yet none the less where Blücher has taken refuge – fall.

'Everyone has been captured or killed or is wandering between the Elbe and the Oder,' he declares.

Lübeck is sacked. 'It only has to blame those who have drawn war to its walls. Everything is going as well as it is possible to imagine.'

Frederick William, however, rejects the conditions of peace conveyed by Duroc, still putting his faith in the arrival of the Russians. More than one hundred thousand of them are on the march, under Generals Bennigsen and Buxhowden.

So war is here and winter on its way. He needs men. 'Send me conscripts,' he tells Berthier, 'even if they've only had a week's training, so long as they are armed, and have breeches, gaiters, regulation hat and a greatcoat. It doesn't matter if they don't have a uniform. The rest will suffice.'

He bends over the maps, says to Marshal Mortier, 'It is possible that in a few days I shall myself proceed into the heart of Poland.'

Then, marching up and down with his hands behind his back, he adds, 'The cold is going to set in and brandy may be the saving of my army. I'm told there's plenty of wine to be found at Stettin. We must take it all, even if there's enough for twenty million men. Wine is going to ensure me victory in winter; we must take it in an orderly manner and give receipts.'

HE KNOWS THAT he is going to have to fight again, teach the Russians a definitive lesson, like the one he has just meted out to the Prussians. He has received a triumphant letter from Murat after the capture of Magdeburg on 7 November. 'Sire,' the Grand Duke of Berg has written, 'combat has ceased due to a lack of combatants.' But there are always new ones. Will the Russians be the last? For that, the moving principle behind all coalitions, England, must be defeated.

During all November 1806 in Berlin's royal palace, Napoleon meditates on what to do. He reads the memorandum Talleyrand has drawn up, arguing that England has infringed human rights by establishing a blockade of European ports, that it is imperative they respond and that the moment is propitious because, since the defeat of Prussia, the Emperor controls the European coastline from Danzig to Spain, and from Spain to the Adriatic.

Napoleon sends for his secretary and dictates a decree which, on 21 November 1806, implements the Continental System. 'All commerce and correspondence with the British Isles are forbidden,' he says. The Isles are declared in a state of blockade, since London's conduct is akin to that of the 'earliest ages of barbarity'. Any Englishmen found in France or allied countries are henceforth prisoners of war and their property will be confiscated. All English goods are decreed a lawful prize.

England must be made to suffocate under a glut of unsold merchandise; it must beg for peace, to purge its excess production, or else face unemployment and chaos.

Napoleon re-reads the decree. He knows the blockade can only succeed if it is truly continental. Everyone in Europe must adhere to it. He has the means to impose it on them all, doesn't he? Anyway, it's in Europe's best interests, he is sure of that.

A challenge, it may be, but he's taken up so many already, and he's always succeeded, hasn't he?

HE RELAXES AND SEEKS distractions. He writes to Josephine who has been shocked by the terms in which he spoke of Queen Louise in the Grand Army's bulletins. 'You seem angry about the way I speak ill of women. It is true I hate scheming women more than anything . . . I love good, naïve, gentle women, but it is because they are the only ones like you.'

He puts down his quill. Does he really think that? In the past, Josephine . . . but he prefers not to remember her betrayals, her duplicity. She is most often sad, anxious and jealous these days.

He writes to her on 22 November at ten in the evening:

Be content, and happy with my friendship, and all the feelings you inspire in me. I shall decide in a few days whether to call you here or to send you to Paris.

Farewell, my friend; if you wish, you can now go to Darmstadt and Frankfurt, that will divert you.

A thousand things to Hortense.

Napoleon

He calls in Caulaincourt, the grand equerry. He is going to leave Berlin, he says, go closer to the troops. Post stages must be prepared for the horses.

He has the dispatches and Paris newspapers brought in. He flies into a fury, throws them to the ground. He calls his secretary, and dictates a letter to the minister of the interior.

Monsieur Champagny, I have read some extremely bad verses that are being sung at the Opéra. Is there a deliberate intention then in France to degrade literature? . . . Forbid anything being sung at the Opéra that is unworthy of that great spectacle. An obvious thing would be to commission a fine cantata to celebrate the 2nd of December. Since literature is your department, I think you had better look after it, for really what they are singing at the Opéra is only too shaming.

ON 25 NOVEMBER 1806, Napoleon leaves Berlin. It is three in the morning. He goes to join the Grand Army which is advancing on Warsaw to meet the armies of the Tsar of Russia.

PART TWO

When the heart speaks,
glory itself is an illusion

26 NOVEMBER 1806 TO 27 JULY 1807

V

IT RAINS, then snows, then freezes.

Storms have been raging since Napoleon has left Berlin, and the roads and fields are churned to mud. His berline moves slowly, its wheels constantly snared in a black magma. The soldiers his carriage passes, marching at the side of the road, do not even look up. He sees grenadiers, muskets slung, grabbing their calves with both hands to pull their feet out of the treacherous bogs. When his carriage comes to a standstill, he sees men marching barefoot, their legs covered with the same icy, clinging muck. Their shoes have been swallowed up by the quagmire.

Without waiting he writes to Daru, Intendant General of the Grand Army: 'Shoes! Shoes! Pay the closest attention to this matter. And if we cannot have shoes, then get leather which our soldiers will be ingenious enough to use to repair their old shoes.'

HE FEELS COLD.

He hasn't been able to shake of this unpleasant sensation of never being able to get warm, no matter what he does, since Berlin receded into the distance and his carriage entered these plains that seem to stretch on and on and merge with the sky. The Polish villages he glimpses past the Oder consist of nothing but tumble-down cottages, some of which have thatched roofs. He sees chasseurs of his Guard feeding their horses on straw from these roofs.

His aides-de-camp have been unable to tell him the where-abouts of General Bennigsen's army. It abandoned Warsaw and on 28 November Murat enters the Polish capital to a delirious welcome.

Napoleon reads his report. Murat already imagines himself King of Poland, implying that he is just the man for this heroic people.

Murat must be disillusioned and reminded that, although he should put Polish patriots in positions of power, 'he should under no circumstances mathematically plan the re-establishment of Poland.'

Napoleon has often told Poles in person, 'Your fate is in your hands . . . but what I have done is half for me and half for you.'

But the further he advances into this country, the more he sees of this muddy ground, these swamps where one gets bogged, these crude, barely laid out roads, the poverty of these wooden villages and fortresses, the deeper his reservations become. Can one trust these Poles?

'I am old in my knowledge of men,' he explains to Murat. 'My greatness does not rest on the aid of a few thousand Poles. It is for them to take enthusiastic advantage of present circumstances; it is not for me to take the first step.'

HE REACHES KÜSTRIN. He lodges in a room in the little fortress which stands at the junction of the Oder and the Warta. Despite the intense fire kept stoked by Constant, he still feels cold. He calls for a glass of Chambertin. He takes a pinch of snuff, then slips his right hand into his waistcoat to try to warm it. He settles down to sleep for a few hours. He sleeps badly. When he wakes, he immediately takes up his quill, as if to restore the circulation in his brain and his fingers.

'It is two in the morning,' he writes to Josephine. 'I have just got up, it is the way of war.'

He wishes to make his way as quickly as possible to Posen, a town on the Warta, where he will be nearer his troops and in a position to decide whether to head towards Danzig and Königsberg down the Vistula – and then further north, why not, to the Niemen, the river that serves as Russia's border – or alternatively to go back up the Vistula to Warsaw, where Murat is waiting and Marshal Davout has joined him.

It will depend on the position of the Russian armies.

He bombards his aides-de-camp and marshals with questions. Where are Bennigsen's troops? In this boundless country, the Russian armies seem uncatchable. Have they really chosen to fall back, or are they concentrating north of Warsaw, along that tributary of the Vistula called the River Narev?

The uncertainty irritates Napoleon.

When Murat once again speaks of the Poles' enthusiasm and their desire to see the rebirth of their dismembered country, partitioned out between Prussia, Austria and Russia, he tersely replies, 'Let the Poles show a firm resolution to be independent. Let them pledge themselves to support the king who will be given them, and then I shall see what is to be done . . .'

But Murat must not labour under any misunderstandings. The re-establishment of Poland is an undertaking too grave and too fraught with consequences for Napoleon to decide on it simply in response to the crowd. How is one to make peace with Russia, sustain peace with Austria and put peace on a permanent footing with Prussia if Poland is restored?

'Stress, Murat, that I have not come here to beg for a throne for my family, for I am not in want of thrones to give to my relations.'

HE DOES NOT WANT to be swayed by the wave of sympathy he feels when, on entering Posen on Thursday, 27 November, at ten in the evening, he beholds the triumphal arches which the Poles have erected in the streets of their town. The icy wind shakes the lanterns hanging from the facades of the buildings. Banners have been strung up, saluting the 'Victor of Marengo', the 'Victor of Austerlitz'.

Despite the rain, a crowd is waiting in front of the Jesuits' monastery and college, large buildings abutting the parish church in the middle of the city, where he is going to stay. The town's dignitaries and the nobility of the province have flocked to pay him their respects.

He listens to their speeches. Their enthusiasm and will may be a card he can play. He's moved by their conviction, their patriotism as well. He takes a pinch of stuff as he walks up and down the vaulted, poorly lit, cold hall.

'It is not so easy to destroy a nation,' he says eventually, crossing his arms. 'France has never recognized the partition of Poland. I wish to see the opinion of the whole nation. Unite yourselves . . .'

He walks away, the audience is over. He declares, however, before leaving the hall, 'This is the only moment for you to become a nation again.'

IT CARRIES ON RAINING for the next few days. He listens to aides-de-camp and generals telling him about the difficulties the troops are encountering in their advance.

The men are hungry. Some are committing suicide, they're so exhausted. They don't know where to find shelter in this muddy land. The peasants' houses barely protect them from the rain and cold. The horses get bogged down. No one knows what to feed them on. They're already defeated before they've even fought. Besides, no one knows where the Russian army is.

Suddenly Napoleon's anger erupts.

'You'd be happy going and pissing in the Seine!' he cries at Berthier.

The officers look at the ground. Napoleon walks up and down in front of them, his face creased with fury. Don't they understand that if they want peace they must crush the Russians, just as they have defeated the Prussians?

HE SHUTS HIMSELF AWAY.

It is 2 December 1806, the anniversary of Austerlitz. It is already so lost in the mists of time – that battle, that sun breaking through the fog! He must remind everyone of that glorious day, that monument to glory that is proof of what he is capable of achieving.

He leaves his study, gives orders. He wants a Te Deum sung in the cathedral to commemorate Austerlitz. He wants a proclamation read to the soldiers and then distributed amongst them. He dictates it, 'Soldiers! A year ago today, at this very hour you were on the memorable field of Austerlitz; the terrified Russian battalions were fleeing in disorder ... The Oder, the Warta, the deserts of Poland, the bad weather of this season have not been able to halt you for a moment ... You have braved everything, surmounted everything; everything has fled at our approach ... The French eagle soars over the Vistula.'

The words intoxicate him. He speaks of universal peace, which still has to be fought for, but first they must be victorious.

'What could possibly give the Russians the right to hope that destiny could be evened out? Are not we and they the soldiers of Austerlitz?'

HE FEELS BETTER and goes to the castle where the nobility of Posen and the locality are giving a ball in his honour. He is surrounded by women. Some come straight up to him, provocative and alluring. He looks hard at them, appraises them, then leads one aside. She laughs. She will come tonight. An easy conquest which leaves no trace.

A few hours later, he writes to Josephine, 'I love you and desire you. All these Polish women are French . . . I went to a ball yesterday of the nobility of the province; the women quite beautiful, quite rich, quite badly dressed, although in Paris fashions.'

And because Josephine, astute woman that she is, has declared in one of her letters that she is not jealous, he jokes, 'So, you are convinced in your jealousy; I am enchanted! Besides, you are wrong; there is nothing I think of less, and in the desert wastes of Poland, one thinks little of beauties . . .'

HE IS ASSAILED by so many thoughts! The Russians, the rain and mud, the wounded: they don't know how or where to treat them, so in the meantime they are rotting in the mud. Women, of course, preoccupy him as well, since he has to write to Josephine. But if he has to write to her, what difference does that make? What the eye doesn't see . . .

He is also perpetually obsessed with events in France. Every day he waits impatiently for dispatches from Paris. Young auditors of the State Council cover the four hundred leagues that separate Posen from the capital at full tilt. Eight days in the saddle, only stopping a few minutes at the relays.

Napoleon avidly reads the newspapers and ministers' reports. He signs decrees, most of which he dictates straight off, without pauses.

Hence at Posen, on 2 December, he decides to have a monument to the glory of the Grand Army erected on the site of the Madeleine. Inside, he wants marble and gold tables engraved with the names of those who fought at Ulm, Austerlitz and Jena.

This is what he wants.

And yet sometimes, in these large, sombre rooms in the Posen monastery, he is convinced that his will is subordinate to a destiny that defies him. It torments him. What is he really able to do?

HE IS GIVEN A LETTER from Josephine who again asks to join him – because she wants to keep an eye on him, he knows perfectly well. He would rather she didn't come. There are these passing liaisons that distract him. There's the war, the rain and cold and mud. And there's the uncertainty of what's coming next. A battle, but where and when?

'SO YOU MUST WAIT another few days,' he writes. Then he stops. It is six in the evening. Rain is falling on Posen. The darkness is impenetrable, as dense as black mud.

He takes up his quill again. 'The older one is, the less of a will one should have, since one depends on events and circumstances,' he remarks.

Will Josephine understand that one must simultaneously want things with a superhuman force and know that one is never the master of the game? One fits in with events, tries to exploit them, but the chessboard can tip up at any moment.

He continues:

> The warmth of your letter makes me see that you pretty women know no boundaries. What you want must be; but I, I declare myself the most enslaved of men; my master has no feelings and that master is the nature of things.
>
> Farewell, my friend.
>
> Napoleon

THIS THOUGHT HAUNTS him as he drives towards Warsaw. Icy rain lashes the road which repeatedly disappears under the mud. The bridges are down. They cross the river on rafts made of tree trunks.

The night seems as if it will never end.

He has to abandon his berline, and they travel in the light but uncomfortable Polish carriages. Duroc's tips over. The Grand Marshal of the Palace breaks his collarbone. They leave him in a peasant's house and carry on in pelting rain, trying to avoid the bogs.

Here it is, the nature of things.

The army 'is grumbling', Berthier ventures to tell him. The 'grumblers' will fight, what else can they do? Napoleon replies.

A few leagues from Warsaw, even his light carriage cannot make headway, or only so slowly, getting bogged down at every turn of the wheel, that Napoleon cannot contain his impatience. He gets out. The darkness is total, intensified by fog. It is not so cold, but that means the ground is only the more boggy. Nothing's solid any more; every vehicle sinks into bottomless mud.

Napoleon chooses a horse. The animal rears; it is a skittish beast from the post stage that might throw him at any moment – but what does that matter? He wants to reach Warsaw. The generals' reports suggest that the Russian army is gathered to the north of the capital, on the banks of the Narev. Napoleon wants to join battle quickly, to be done with it once and for all.

HE ARRIVES IN Warsaw on Friday the 19th, when fog covers the town and surrounding countryside. He sets off again at dawn on Tuesday, 22 December, to be with the advance guard. He comes under Russian fire and climbs onto the roof of a house to observe the enemy's movements. He sleeps in barns.

They are searching for the Russians as it grows dark at three in the afternoon, and the mud prevents cavalry charges. The horses cannot gallop, and the infantrymen cut one another's throats in the fog. But Ney, Lannes and Davout win victories at Soldau, against the last Prussian corps, and at Golymin and Pultusk against the Russians.

But how to pursue them?

Napoleon has installed himself in the episcopal palace of Pultusk.

He wandered in the fog with his Guard, and only reached the battlefield at the end of the fighting.

He sits by the fireplace in a small, dark room and dictates a brief letter for Cambacérès: 'I think the campaign is over. The enemy have put swamps and deserts between us. I am going into winter quarters.'

He stands up, takes a pinch of snuff. He is not satisfied. The Russian army has not been cut to pieces. The rain, mud and fog have helped them, but so has the inaction of Bernadotte's troops. A spectator again, as at Auerstadt.

He starts walking to calm himself down. He is going to write to Joseph. Perhaps this brother of his will understand?

'We are surrounded by snow and mud, without wine, without brandy, without bread . . . We fight with bayonets and grapeshot. The wounded are compelled to travel fifty leagues in open sleighs . . .'

Who will understand?

'Having destroyed the Prussian monarchy, we are fighting against the rest of Prussia, against the Russians, the Kalmuks, the Cossacks and the northern tribes that long ago invaded the Roman empire. We are waging war in all its energy and horror.'

Napoleon is living this, seeing it with his own eyes.

He repeats in a loud voice, 'Energy! Energy!' Then, more quietly, he adds, 'It is only by defying the opinions of the weak and ignorant that one can achieve the good of a nation.'

Then he feels calmer. It is Wednesday, 31 December 1806.

In the largest room of the episcopal palace of Pultusk, sitting by the fireplace, he listens to two female singers accompanied by the opera composer, Paer. He closes his eyes. The pleasure he feels is even keener because he has been marching for so many days under fire 'with water up to his belly'. At last he can forget the 'horror'.

He reassures Josephine the same day, 'You have formed an idea of the belles of Poland which they do not deserve . . . Farewell, my friend, I am in good health.'

The courier from France has just arrived.

Napoleon chooses from among the dispatches a letter from Fouché which suggests asking Raynouard, a playwright, to write a tragedy in praise of the Emperor. Napoleon remembers *The Templars*, a play by Raynouard he had seen in Paris.

'In modern history,' he writes to Fouché, 'the tragic motif to be used is not fate or the gods' vengeance but' – the expression comes back to him – 'the nature of things. It is politics that leads to the catastrophes not caused by any real crimes. Monsieur Raynouard missed that in *The Templars*. If he had followed this principle, Philippe le Bel would have played a fine part; one would have pitied him and understood that he could not have done otherwise.'

CAN HE, NAPOLEON, do anything other than continue the war? Does anyone understand that?

He reads through the dispatches. Suddenly, he starts.

Fouché reports a piece of news which, he says simply, has reached the minister of police and might interest the Emperor.

On 13 December 1806, in a town house at 29 rue de la Victoire, Louise Catherine Éléonore Denuelle de la Plaigne, born 13 September 1787, of independent means, divorced 29 April 1806 from Jean Honoré François Revel, reader to Princess Caroline, has given birth to a male child. This child has been called Charles, and is known as Comte Léon. The father has been declared absent.

Napoleon feels a warmth radiating through his whole body.

My son.

He tries to dispel what has instantly seemed a certainty.

My son.

Can he be sure of Éléonore, that artful, intriguing coquette who Caroline thrust in his arms?

But she wouldn't have risked deceiving him then, in spring 1806, when he was in Paris and saw her almost every night at the Tuileries, and when she was living in the house he had bought for her.

It cannot be anything but his son.

He knew he could have a son.

He guessed Josephine was lying. She could only be lying, the poor, old woman, when she kept telling him that he couldn't father a child.

A son – what, in his Imperial project, has been missing since the very start.

He imagines marriage to a king's daughter.

He imagines many things.

Then he thinks of Josephine, of divorce. He goes over to the window. Pultusk Castle is enveloped in fog.

Divorce, marriage, birth. The nature of things.

VI

FROM TIME TO TIME, Napoleon starts to say something to Duroc, but then, as if he were distracted by this dismal plain which they've been crossing since leaving Pultusk, on the morning of the first day of January 1807, he breaks off after only a few words.

He leans his head out of the window to look at the low sky which threatens more snow. Then he makes another effort, beginning, 'Bennigsen, the Russian troops . . .'

Duroc listens, his face strained, ready to etch every word in his memory.

Then Napoleon suddenly falls silent. What's the use of carrying on? He feels a sort of disgust. For this country.

That morning, before leaving the episcopal palace, he dictated his instructions to the envoy he's sending to the King of Prussia, who is still refusing to sign a treaty of peace. The aide-de-camp must assure Frederick William that 'since the Emperor has got to know Poland, he attaches no value to the country'.

But what does he value on this morning?

He will have to fight Bennigsen again; he will have to bombard Ney and Bernadotte, who are on his tail, with dispatches to prevent them venturing too far forward. When they have hooked Bennigsen, Napoleon will head up north, envelop him and destroy the Russians, finally. But he feels no enthusiasm at the prospect. Once the Russian armies have been cut to pieces, others will take their place. When will it all stop?

That's why he can't talk to Duroc.

IF HE COULD JUST confide in him this piece of news which has held him transfixed since the previous evening: a son.

If he could just tell him that, for years, Josephine and Doctor Corvisart have been trying to persuade him that he is the one who can't have children, and have managed to make him doubt himself. Josephine even managed to convince him for a while that if he wanted a son, all he needed to do was adopt one secretly, and then she could pretend to be its mother.

If she only knew that Éléonore Denuelle has given birth to a son – but how can she fail to have found out? She must have been fantasizing about this moment for a long time, imagining all the possible ways to escape divorce.

Henceforth he is determined to dispense with all subterfuge. He can have a son. He is certain of that now. He will draw all the appropriate conclusions.

In any case, has anyone ever been able to prevent him seeking to exploit his power to the full, and doing so?

HIS CARRIAGE SLOWS; they are approaching Bronie. At the gates of this small town, explains Duroc, a post stage has been organized by the grand equerry. The stop, Caulaincourt said, shouldn't last more than a few minutes. The Emperor won't even have to get out of his carriage, while the teams are changed. This is the last relay before Warsaw, which they will reach by early evening.

Napoleon leans out of the window, sees Bronie's fortifications in the distance, and then, as they gradually draw nearer, a waving, cheering crowd.

He feels no joy. He thinks of the son whom he will not be able to acknowledge publicly; of the one who must be born one day, who will be his heir in the eyes of all; and of the wound he will have to inflict on Josephine, whom he has loved so deeply and who is now just a jealous old woman whose every letter is full of sighs and tears.

HIS CARRIAGE comes to a halt. The crowds surround it, as the horses are unharnessed.

Duroc gets out and forces his way through to the post house. Napoleon sees him re-emerge after a few minutes, holding by the hand a young woman with curly blonde hair poking out from under her fur cap. She seems small. Duroc leads her towards the carriage.

The young woman disappears for a moment, as if swallowed up by the crowd, and then all of a sudden Napoleon sees her by the door. She has regular features, glowing, rosy cheeks and eyes that are at once alert and ingenuous.

She looks straight at Napoleon and he feels himself instantly suffused with merriment and energy. He hears, but does not see, Duroc saying, 'Look, Sire, this beautiful lady has braved the dangers of the crowd for your sake.'

Napoleon inclines his head, and leans half out of the window. He wants to touch that face, so fresh, so new to him. She can't be more than twenty years old.

She is different from all the others.

He wants to talk to her, but she has raised herself up on tip-toe. He sees her thin body, her slender waist clasped in her fitted coat. Her French is soft and lilting, as she gasps out, 'Be welcome, Sire, a thousand times welcome to our land. We have been waiting for you to rise up again.'

She carries on talking for several minutes, but he stops listening. He sees her eyes, her heaving breast. She exudes an aura of gentleness and innocence.

He is certain that she is different from all the women he has known, from that first woman in the arcades of the Palais-Royal to that schemer Éléonore Denuelle, who, even so, is the woman with whom he has had a son.

What would it be like to have a son with someone like this Polish woman?

He gives her one of the bouquets which were put in his carriage when he left Pultusk. He would like to see her again, he says.

The carriage begins to move. He turns round, leaning far out of the window. He sees her for a moment longer before she is hidden by the crowd.

'WHO IS SHE?' he questions Duroc. He castigates the grand marshal of the palace for not having asked. He wants to know everything about her. He wants her to be invited to the dinner he will give tomorrow evening in Warsaw. He wants her to be at all the dinners, all the balls.

He wants this woman.

He doesn't say anything else. He listens to what is growing in him which is not just desire, that wish to possess that he has felt so many times, but a combination of the need to dominate this woman, to hold her in his arms, and a kind of enthusiasm and joy. He hasn't felt this for so long, perhaps not since the very early days, when he was passionately in love with Josephine.

But he is another man now. He has had so much experience, and he is not yet thirty-eight. This young woman whose name he does not know, whom he is unsure if he will see again, but wants to – what attracts him about her is her charm, her youth, her naïve freshness.

She has not been Barras's mistress.

These are his thoughts, and he feels the desire to start something new, something different, which will divorce him from the past, from the old woman to whom he is attached but who embodies his beginnings, who reminds him of so many wounds.

As soon as he reaches the royal palace, Zamek, Napoleon strides through the galleries and the reception rooms decorated with frescoes by Lebrun and Pillement, giving instructions to Duroc. He wants to receive the entire Polish aristocracy during his stay in Warsaw. He wants a court organized: concerts twice a week, receptions, dinners, a military parade every day in front of the palace, on Saxony Square. He stops in front of a painting by Boucher. 'I want to know everything about her,' he says.

He waits impatiently, breaking off dictation or his work on maps if he so much as hears footsteps. Eventually Duroc appears.

Her name is Marie Walewska. Her husband, Anastase Colonna Walewski, is a rich aristocrat, related to the Colonna of Rome.

'He's old, very old,' says Duroc.

Marie's family, the Laczinscy, wanted her to marry this prosperous, widowed nobleman.

Napoleon feels a jolt of scorn and impatience. Send her an invitation, he says. Then he leans over his maps again, as if he were only concerned with anticipating his troops' movements north.

He sticks pins into towns near the Baltic, Eylau, Friedland, Königsberg and Tilsit. It is there, between these towns and rivers, the Vistula, the Passarge, the Niemen, that the final chapter of this campaign will play itself out.

SHE HAS FINALLY COME to the Balcha palace where the entire Polish nobility is gathered in honour of Napoleon. He sees her wearing a long white dress and guesses from the way everybody looks when he goes up to her that they all know already. But what's that matter to him!

When he stops in front of her, he mutters reproachfully, 'White on white does not go, Madame.'

He senses that she is panic stricken, withdrawn. She refuses to join in the dancing. He would have liked to see her dance. She doesn't say a word. He can't stand her evading him like this.

Before the party is even over, he writes to her; his writing is enraged, the letters black:

I saw only you, I admired only you, I desire only you. A quick answer to calm the ardour of
    N.

HE WAITS. What woman has ever resisted him? They often want to make themselves desired so that their stock rises. Perhaps she is one of these 'creatures'? Suspicion tugs at him, but he is almost ashamed to put it into words. So he sends for Duroc and presses him. Nothing is more urgent than this.

He tries not to think of this Marie Walewska, towards whom he feels sudden bursts of rage. He immerses himself in his daily work, alerts Marshal Ney to the fact that he has advanced too far north, thereby risking exposing his flank to the Russians. They are the ones who must be surrounded.

Often he stops working and starts pacing about, taking snuff, as he tends to do when preoccupied.

He can't stop himself thinking about this woman, as if she is the element of surprise and excitement he needs. Everything else seems utterly familiar to him. Even the war he is waging, even the sovereigns he is facing.

'Your aunt, the Queen of Prussia, has behaved so badly!' he writes to Augusta, the wife of Eugène de Beauharnais. 'But she is so unhappy today that one shouldn't speak of her any more. Send me news soon that we have a big boy, and if you should give us a daughter, let her be as good and lovable as you are.'

He cannot help it if thoughts of birth have haunted him since he's found out that he can have children.

But in that case, Josephine . . .

She is still in Mainz. She writes almost every day, bemoaning her lot; she wants to join him. Has she guessed what he is feeling? Had she known for a long time that Éléonore Denuelle was pregnant, and wanted to be with him when he heard the news?

He believes her capable of that.

He writes to her on 3 January 1807:

> I have received your letter, my friend. Your grief touches me, but you must submit to events. The distance between Warsaw and Mainz is too great; events therefore must allow me to return to Berlin before I can write to you to come there . . . But I have a great many affairs to settle here. I am inclined to think that you should return to Paris where your presence is necessary . . . My health is good; the weather is bad. I love you with all my heart.
>
> Napoleon

Is IT LYING, just to tell one side of things?

He feels himself attached to Josephine by the thousand ties of memory, but this complicity has become a habit. Josephine occupies a corner of his heart. She does not occupy him body and soul. In fact she hampers him, in a sense, because she represents an obstacle. He is overcome with desire for this woman, Marie, who seems inaccessible.

He writes to her on 4 January:

> Have I displeased you, Madame? Yet I was entitled to hope the opposite. Was I mistaken? Your zeal flags as mine grows. You shatter my repose! Oh, grant a little joy, a little happiness to a poor heart that is only waiting to admire you. Is it so hard to send a reply? You owe me two.
>
> N.

NAPOLEON'S IMPATIENCE turns to anger as he waits for replies that do not arrive. He berates Constant each morning, as his valet tries to go about his work and help him dress. He paces from one end of the room to the other, eventually sits down, only for the touch of Constant's hand to be unbearable so he gets up again.

He remembers that two of his aides-de-camp paid Marie Walewska marked attention during the reception at the Blacha palace. He summons Berthier, gives orders that these two officers be transferred far from Warsaw: Bertrand to Breslau, which Jérôme Bonaparte's men have just taken, and Louis de Périgord to the front, to one of the units pursuing the Russians on the River Passarge.

He cannot endure the thought that Marie Walewska could either prefer another man to him, or else refuse herself to him.

When finally he sees her coming towards him at a dinner he gives in the royal palace, he goes to her and says brusquely, 'With eyes as sweet as yours, one lets oneself be swayed, one does not take pleasure in inflicting torture, or else one is the most coquettish and cruellest of women.'

Why doesn't she say anything?

HE CANNOT ACCEPT this silence. He has to act, or at least write. His whole will is straining, taut, as if his life were at stake. Putting all his energy into every challenge he chooses to take up – that is what he calls living. He never playacts. He is completely present in everything he does, everything he writes.

'There are moments when too much exaltation weighs one down and that is what I feel,' he begins. 'How can I satisfy the needs of a smitten heart which would like to throw itself at your feet but finds itself held back by the weight of serious considerations, paralysing its keenest desires?'

Suddenly he feels helpless.

'Oh, if only you would!' he resumes. 'There is no one but you who can remove the obstacles that keep us apart. My friend Duroc will make it easy for you. Oh come! Come! All your wishes will be fulfilled.'

He hesitates. She is a patriot, so he has been told. She must remember who he is, what he can do. He writes, 'Your country will be dearer to me when you have had pity on my poor heart. N.'

HE KNOWS EVERYONE of importance in Warsaw is pushing her towards him. The means don't matter. She must come. It is what he wants.

When at last, in the middle of January, she comes to his room in the royal palace, he kisses her passionately and is indignant when she refuses him and tries to escape his embrace. As if she hadn't imagined what he was expecting from her! What game is she playing? What price does she want him to pay?

She bursts into tears and confides in him. He in turn speaks, tells her stories about his life, woos her with the sincerity of a young man. This innocence regained for a few hours, this freedom, these disinterested confidences they share move him deeply. The hours fly past. She leaves without him having tried to force himself upon her.

'Marie, my sweet Marie, my first thought is of you, my first wish is to see you again,' he writes at dawn.

These words that have been lost for so many years, since the Italian campaign when he used to write beseeching letters to Josephine, now spring to his mind, as clear and fresh as the first time he used them.

> You will come again, won't you? You promised. Otherwise the eagle will fly to you. I shall see you at dinner, my friend tells me. Deign therefore to accept this bouquet: I wish it to be a secret link which establishes a private rapport between us in the midst of the crowds that surround us. Observed by all, we will be able to understand each other. When my hand presses my heart, you will press your bouquet! Love me, my sweet Marie, and never let go of your bouquet!
> N.

SHE IS HIS, since she comes back, but he cannot content himself with this platonic sentiment. She's refused to accept the jewellery he sent her, has she? That does not mean she is free. Hasn't he showed her how much he esteems her? That she isn't just one of those women one picks up, then discards?

He flies into a fury, dashing his watch to the floor, trampling on it. He is also a man who can't be rejected.

At last she gives in.

But this is not enough. The young body he has taken, he wants it to give itself of its own accord to him. 'Love me, Marie, love me.'

He keeps her close. She is his. He is overjoyed by her gentleness and tenderness, her amenableness. He can look at her for hours on end. She is so bright, so young. He sees in her an image of himself that he thought he had lost.

When she leaves, he goes and finds her.

'I am inviting myself, my sweet Marie, for six. Have us served in your boudoir, do not prepare anything special.'

She will be there and that will be enough.

EVERYTHING IS NOW in order again. He has attained his goal. Calmly, and with heightened lucidity, he can now set about drawing up a plan of battle.

As Ney and Bernadotte engage in the initial fighting with the Russians in the north, this month, January 1807, will be a period of waiting.

That is another reason why he had to be swept up by a new passion.

Now he returns to the maps, his mind clear. He feels regenerated by this love, this renewal of youth, by Marie who is so completely disinterested.

He is going to leave Warsaw to snare Bennigsen's troops in a noose of which Eylau and Friedland, north of it, will be the centre. He will go to Willemberg, south of these two cities.

ALL MONTH, day after day, he has had to reply to letters from Josephine, intuitive, demanding and probably already in the know.

She has used every possible argument to make him agree to her coming to Warsaw, but he has not given in.

'Why these tears, this chagrin? Have you not more fortitude?' he asks her.

She must 'show character and strength of mind. I require greater strength of mind from you. I am told that you are always crying. Fie! How ugly that is! . . . Be worthy of me. An empress should have a brave heart.'

He is so distant with her now. 'Farewell, my friend,' he signs his letters.

She has finally returned to Paris, but she is still in tears. He doesn't like her making a show of her grief.

In the berline taking him from Warsaw to Willemberg, he starts another letter to make her understand what he expects from her.

> My friend, your letter of the 20th of January has pained me: it is too sad. There's the trouble of not having any religion! You tell me that your happiness is your glory. That is not generous: you should say the happiness of others is your glory; that is not conjugal: you should say the happiness of my husband is my glory; that is not maternal: you should say the happiness of my children is my glory; and since nations, your husband, your children cannot be happy without a little glory, you must not say fie to it.

He stops. He never likes rereading when he writes; his mind races ahead and the stream of his ideas is justified by their spirit of élan. One does not go over what has been thought or done or written.

He senses that she won't like this letter; but time has ploughed a furrow between them. It is the nature of things.

He resumes writing, 'Josephine, your heart is excellent, but your mind is weak; your instincts are wonderful, but your reasoning less so.'

She has to be aware of the distance there is between them now.

'Come, no more quarrelling. I want you gay, contented with your lot, and obeying not with scolding and tears but with a joyous heart and some degree of happiness. Farewell, my friend, I am off to my outposts tonight.'

VII

NAPOLEON LOOKS DOWN at the ravine from the top of the hill. Across a narrow bridge, in a little wood which partly conceals the town of Hoff, he sees Russian grenadiers' uniforms. He will have to deploy cannon to flush out the troops swarming under those snow-covered trees. There are several battalions there, without a doubt.

Is this the start of a real battle, finally? Bennigsen has been eluding them for a week, withdrawing towards Eylau and Königsberg.

'I think we're not far from an affair,' Napoleon remarks.

But he is not sure. He has already joined battle at Allenstein, and Davout bowled over the Russians at Bergfriede, but these have only been limited encounters.

'I am manoeuvring on the enemy,' Napoleon tells Murat. 'If he does not withdraw in time, he is very likely to be stormed.'

He leans forward on his horse's neck. He wants to snare these Russians, pin them down so he can surround them and crush them, but it is almost as if Bennigsen is aware of his manoeuvre. He withdraws at the very place Napoleon hopes to catch him. Perhaps he has seized one of the couriers sent to Ney and Bernadotte who are moving up the River Passarge on the left wing, while Davout holds the right wing.

'Charge immediately,' Napoleon tells Murat.

The light cavalry, hussars and chasseurs race off, followed by General Klein's dragoons.

HE MUST REMAIN impassive, watch the horses and men toppling off the bridge amid grapeshot, collapsing in the snow, slipping on the ice.

A curse on this country.

He has written to Joseph, who is swaggering about in his kingdom of Naples: 'Therefore it is a pretty poor joke to compare us with the army of Naples, making war in a lovely country of

Naples, where one can get wine, oil, bread, cloth, sheets, social life and even women.'

Here, nothing.

Since he left Warsaw eight days ago, Napoleon has lived amongst his soldiers. Their stomachs are empty, their eyelids burnt by the cold.

'Staff officers, colonels, officers have not undressed for two months and sometimes four,' Napoleon carries on explaining to his elder brother. 'I myself have gone a fortnight without taking off my boots . . . In the midst of these great fatigues we have all been more or less sick. As for myself, I have never been stronger and have become fatter.'

HE GETS OFF his horse. The remaining cavalry are regrouping. Corpses and fallen horses lie in heaps on the other side of the bridge. Hoff is a strategic point. It commands the road to Eylau and Königsberg: that is why Bennigsen is putting up such resistance, organizing a counterattack. If Hoff falls, he will have to stop withdrawing and accept battle. Finally.

Napoleon issues an order to an aide-de-camp. The cuirassiers of General d'Hautpoul are to charge.

He sees them pass, strapping figures with their buckled iron breastplates, helmets with gleaming crests and black horse-tails. Their heavy, broad-chested horses tear down the slope; the bridge shudders, the ground reverberates. The Russian grapeshot decimates them, but they keep going and break through the lines.

The Russian battalions scatter into the woods. Hoff falls, the road to Eylau is open. Eylau is where they will fight.

D'Hautpoul comes to report, a fine, tall cavalryman who towers over Napoleon.

Napoleon embraces him in front of the men.

'To show myself worthy of such an honour, I should get myself killed for Your Majesty,' d'Hautpoul calls out.

Napoleon stares at d'Hautpoul.

This man is mine. And I must be worthy of him. His sacrifice creates an obligation for me to achieve victory and greatness.

D'Hautpoul gives me his whole life.

As do all the troopers, who d'Hautpoul turns towards to cry,

'Soldiers, the Emperor is satisfied with you. He embraced me for you all. And I, soldiers, I, d'Hautpoul, am so satisfied with my terrible cuirassiers that I kiss all your arses.'

Cheers reverberate through the ravine filled with dead.

Such is the law of life. Until today.

IT IS DARK. The cold is intense. Napoleon paces around a glowing fire lit by soldiers of his Guard. His hands are behind his back. He has just been through the fallen city of Hoff. The streets were littered with dead, the houses full of wounded. He murmurs, 'War is an anachronism. One day victories will be won without cannon and without bayonets.'

He drops off to sleep for a few minutes, sitting beside the fire, then gives the order to advance on Eylau.

Day breaks, the sky is clear. The cold is brisk, but the sun is shining.

He walks around the plateau of Ziegelhof, looks it over, gives orders for his bivouac to be established. The Guard will camp around him.

'There's a suggestion that I take Eylau tonight,' he says to Marshal Augereau, 'but apart from the fact that I do not like night fighting, I do not wish to push my centre too far forward before Marshal Davout arrives with the right wing and Ney with the left.'

He looks at the members of his staff.

'Consequently I will await them until tomorrow morning on this ridge which can be protected with artillery and will offer our infantry an excellent position.'

He thinks of Jena, of the Landgrafenberg plateau.

'Then, when Ney and Davout are in line, we can march simultaneously on the enemy.'

Suddenly, below them, in the direction of Eylau, they hear the sound of intense musketfire.

Fires are breaking out all over the city. An officer arrives, and explains that the Emperor's quartermaster-sergeants had entered Eylau with the caissons and baggage and installed themselves in the postmaster's house, thinking the town was taken. They were starting to prepare the Emperor's cantonment and cook when they were attacked by the Russians. Marshal Soult's troops have intervened to defend them and the Russians have counterattacked. The battle is general.

'We must go into action,' Napoleon says.

A leader must encourage his troops with his presence. He mounts his horse, abandons his bivouac and goes to install himself in the postmaster's house in Eylau. The Guard surrounds him. The Russian cannonballs start to fall. It is the night of 7 February 1807.

THE WEATHER IS changing. The sky is overcast. On Sunday, 8 February, at eight in the morning, the Russians launch a fresh attack. The fighting centres on Eylau's cemetery. Dense flurries of snow suddenly start, which a northerly wind drives into the face of the French.

Napoleon does not move. He sees men being slain in their hundreds. Dead horses are piled atop the wounded and the slain. Artillery caissons and charging cavalry crush the living and the dead. The cannon go into action. The ground shakes.

He has to launch more men into this torment. He sees Augereau's troops ahead, disappearing into the snow, blinded.

Suddenly, the sky clears. Napoleon hoists himself onto a caisson, from where he can see the whole battlefield: dead stretching for as far as the eye can see, blood staining the snow red.

Wounded and desperate, Augereau is laid at Napoleon's feet. A few men are all that is left of his regiments, decimated by Russian grapeshot. The Emperor must keep his nerve, not let the gangrene of despair take over.

Napoleon calls Murat. 'Well, are you going to let those fellows eat us up?'

Murat spurs his horse. His men swing into a gallop. There are more than eighty squadrons of chasseurs, dragoons and cuirassiers in the charge. The Russian attack is halted.

But where are Ney's infantry?

Napoleon must hold firm, wait, refuse to send the Guard into action.

He stays standing in the cemetery, amongst the graves blown open by the cannonballs, dead soldiers jumbled in with skeletons.

He hears the shouts of thousands of Russian grenadiers as they charge.

Don't move. Reject with a disdainful look the horse Caulaincourt brings up for you to get away.

In a calm voice, he orders General Dorsenne to place a battalion of the Guard fifty paces in front of him.

Dorsenne shouts, 'Grenadiers, arms *au bras*. The Old Guard only fights with bayonets.'

NAPOLEON STANDS with his arms crossed, waiting for the Russian attack to be broken.

An aide-de-camp who has managed to get through the barrage of fire announces that a Prussian column under Lestocq has just reached the battlefield and is already attacking Marshal Davout.

Don't give any hint of the blow I have just received. Simply turn to Jomini, this Swiss strategist on Ney's staff whom I have become attached to. I must calmly analyse the situation and consider everything, even withdrawal.

'The day has been a harsh one,' Napoleon begins. 'I did not plan on engaging the enemy until midday, not having all my corps to hand, and this has led to some memorable losses. Ney hasn't come. Bernadotte is two marches behind. They alone have troops and munitions unscathed . . .'

Napoleon looks around. The dead form dark mounds which the snow is gradually covering. He lowers his voice. 'If the enemy does not withdraw at nightfall, we shall leave at ten. Grouchy, with two divisions of dragoons, will form the rearguard; you will be with him. You will go on patrol and promptly report to me what the enemy is up to . . . Absolute silence about this mission.'

Napoleon takes a few steps and then turns back towards Jomini.

'Come back this evening at eight to receive your definitive orders. Perhaps there will be some changes.'

HE IS STILL WAITING. Night falls. When there is a lull of several minutes in the firing, he hears the screams of the wounded and sees the shadows of the marauders who, risking their lives, are searching and stripping the corpses.

Exhaustion is beginning to grind him down. Suddenly, heavy fire breaks out on the left.

'Ney!' someone cries. 'Marshal Ney!'

He feels no joy, but his tiredness fades. Fifteen thousand men, he estimates, are going to take the Russians in the flank and in all likelihood compel them to fall back.

He knows this is the moment he mustn't let his concentration lapse, even if victory is taking shape. What victory is it, though? So many dead. Sadness grips his heart. He thinks of Marie Walewska, of Josephine. He wishes he could write, get away from all this cruelty just for a moment, but instead he straightens himself up and issues orders.

They must plan for tomorrow. Will Bennigsen withdraw or, on the contrary, will he hold his ground? He must think of the wounded, see that they are attended to and stretchered off the battlefield, all of them.

'All of them,' he repeats.

He must check the distribution of bread and brandy. He knows that none of it has been organized as it should have been.

At eight in the evening, he gives the order for the bivouac fires to be lit.

HE LEAVES the cemetery. The dead are everywhere. He stops two kilometres from Eylau, in a little farm. He lies down fully clothed on a mattress, beside the stove.

He has the impression, when he is woken at around nine in the morning on Monday, 9 February, that he hasn't slept at all. A colonel of chasseurs is standing in front of him. It is Saint-Chamans, Soult's aide-de-camp.

'What news?' asks Napoleon. His voice is hollow, he knows. He is weary.

Saint-Chamans answers that the Russians have begun their retreat.

Napoleon gets up. He draws a long breath. He walks outside. He has won.

The sky is low; it is dark. Wounded men are dragging themselves along the road, supporting one another, some using their muskets as crutches. Their heads are bowed as they trudge along.

He watches them for a long time. With the troops at his disposal, with these battered men, he cannot pursue the enemy. This victory is like this country's climate – doleful.

He goes back inside the farm. He needs to write, to allow a little tenderness to express itself in this universe of death. He knows that Marie Walewska has left Warsaw for Vienna. He would so love her to be there, like a wellspring of life.

My sweet friend,
    You will have learnt more than I can tell you today about events by the time you read this letter. The battle lasted two days and we have been left masters of the field.
    My heart is with you; if it could decide, you would be the citizen of a free country. Do you suffer as I do from our estrangement? I am entitled to believe so; it is very true that I want you to return to Warsaw or your castle, you are too far from me.
    Love me, my sweet Marie, and have faith in your
    N.

He folds and seals the letter, then takes another sheet of paper. He needs to write to Josephine as well,

My friend, there was a great battle yesterday; victory was mine but we have lost a great many men; the loss of the enemy, which is still more considerable, does not console me. I write these few lines to you myself, although I am very tired, to tell you that I am well and that I love you.
    Ever yours,
    Napoleon

Now he must talk to the grumblers, to these men who are trying to warm themselves at their bivouac fires, whose silhouettes he sees lying in heaps on the snow. He has never felt such a feeling, almost of despair, as he thinks of those thousands of mutilated, crushed, buried men.

He gives orders. He wants to revisit Eylau's cemetery where he stood all yesterday, in a hail of canister shot. He cannot leave this battlefield where twenty generals have been wounded or killed, some of them the best he had. He thinks of d'Hautpoul, dead as he had said he wanted to be. How many men have fallen with him? Perhaps twenty thousand dead and wounded, perhaps double or triple that on the Russian side?

HE RIDES SLOWLY through the thick snow, surrounded by his staff. The pine forests surrounding the battlefield block off the horizon; the clouds in the dark sky snag on their crowns.

Dead everywhere, naked bodies mingled with the carcasses of horses, wounded slowly dying on the dirty-yellow and blood-red snow. He does not avert his eyes. He tries to make sure his horse does not tread on human remains. He hears piercing screams that go on and on, as shrill as birds' cries. Wounded drag themselves towards him, stretching out their arms, imploring him to help them.

Men shout 'Long live the Emperor!', but he hears other voices yelling, 'Long live peace!', 'Bread and peace!', 'Long live peace and France!'

France seems so far away.

He climbs the small mound where the soldiers of the 14th of the Line, Augereau's men, were massacred, blinded by the snow. The bodies are in rows, crowded together.

'Lined up like sheep,' says Marshal Bessières.

Napoleon swings round, his eyes red.

'Lions, like lions,' he says through gritted teeth.

When he sees that the soldiers of the 43rd of the Line have draped black crêpe from their eagles, he stands up in his stirrups. 'I do not ever want to see my flags in mourning!' he cries. 'Our friends and brave companions have died on the field of honour; their fate is to be envied. Let us see that we avenge them, not mourn them, for tears only befit women.'

HE RETURNS to his quarters, sits in front of the stove, and leans his elbows on a chest he is using as a desk. He hears Caulaincourt asking when they will leave Eylau, where the Emperor's next residence is to be prepared. He doesn't know. He doesn't want to answer. He cannot leave this place that has drunk so much blood.

He dictates the bulletin of the Grand Army and issues a proclamation to the troops.

'Soldiers, we were beginning to enjoy a little rest in our winter quarters when the enemy attacked I Corps . . . The brave men who have stayed behind on the field of honour have died a glorious death, the death of true soldiers. Their families will have constant claims on our solicitude and our benefactions.'

He hesitates and then, with head bowed, continues, 'We are going to approach the Vistula and return to our cantonments.' But this will be a mere respite. The war is not over. 'We shall always be French soldiers, and French soldiers of the Grand Army,' he says.

Yet words only come with difficulty. He thinks of 'that space of a square league where one sees nine or ten thousand corpses, four or five thousand slain horses. This spectacle is fit to incite in princes a love of peace and a horror of war.'

Like an expression of remorse, he adds as a postscript to the 58th Bulletin of the Grand Army, 'A father who loses his children draws no pleasure from victory. When the heart speaks, glory itself is an illusion.'

HE WANTS TO STAY longer at Eylau. Assure himself that the Russians are indeed retreating, even if he cannot pursue them, even if he has decided to pull the Grand Army back to the Passarge.

The weather changes. Two days after the battle, the snow begins to melt and he smells the stench of death and rotting bodies. The wounded are dying of gangrene.

He wants to see the army surgeons and the official in charge of medical supplies. What is being done for the wounded? he asks. He listens to their answers and grows indignant. Time and time again he has tried to reinforce the medical service, but there is never any improvement. Only the Guard has its own ambulances and surgeons, like Larrey.

The other corps are short of men and equipment. 'What organization, what barbarity!' Napoleon bursts out. He gives orders, then withdraws and begins writing to Josephine,

My friend, I am still at Eylau. This country is covered with dead and wounded. This is not the finest part of war; one suffers and one's spirit is oppressed at the sight of so many victims.

He can admit this to his old companion, but it is only a sigh. He goes on:

> I am well. I have achieved what I wanted and I have repulsed the enemy and defeated his plans.
>
> You must be worried and that thought upsets me. However, put your mind at rest, my friend, and be merry.
>
> Ever yours,
> Napoleon

ON 17 FEBRUARY, finally, he orders the withdrawal to the Passarge.

He travels by short stages through this countryside that seems to hesitate between the numb sleep of winter and the awakening of spring.

'The season's strange,' he murmurs to Caulaincourt.

It freezes and thaws within the space of twenty-four hours, but damp and mud gradually predominate. The snow melts, the rivers overflow, flooding the roads along which the thirsty, starving wounded drag themselves.

He goes into his cantonments at Osteröde.

He writes to Josephine on 2 March:

> I am in a wretched village and will remain here for quite some considerable time.
>
> It's not up to the big city. Once more, I have never been in such good health: you will find that I have put on a great deal of weight.
>
> Be cheerful and happy, this is my wish.
>
> Farewell, my friend, all my love,
> Napoleon

He looks at himself in the mirror Constant is holding. His face has become round. He touches his stomach. Sometimes, during the past week at Eylau, he has suffered violent stomach pains, but they have gone now.

'I am very well, my health is excellent,' he repeats to Josephine when he writes to her in the little room with the fire that draws badly which he occupies in Ordenschloss's old castle at Osteröde.

The building is damp. The pine forests surrounding it create, despite the imminence of spring, an atmosphere of sadness in which each day is steeped.

He would like to see Marie Walewska. He has asked her to return to Vienna and she is en route. She must come and join him, not at Osteröde, but perhaps at Finkenstein Castle, which Caulaincourt has visited and which lies a few leagues to the west.

BUT FOR THE MOMENT, comfort is of no matter.

He wants to forget his surroundings, this morose landscape which the warmer weather has done nothing to cheer up. Often the fog lasts all day.

He wants to forget his body, whose heaviness is starting to trouble him.

But he cannot forget what people are saying all over Europe, even in Paris: that Eylau is a defeat, that General Bennigsen carried the day.

He indignantly draws up an account of the battle, by an 'eyewitness', which he has published in Berlin and Paris. He corrects the number of losses: '150,000 dead and 4,300 wounded,' he says. When General Bertrand, who is transcribing the account at his dictation, looks up, Napoleon stares back at him and, in a voice thick with scorn, says, 'This is how history will speak of it.'

He walks across the room, letting Bertrand read back to him this 'account of the Battle of Eylau'.

How is one to fight the lie of someone like Bennigsen, who claims to have won a victory, other than by fighting oneself to win over opinion? Men's minds are a battlefield.

BUT HE IS WELL aware of the reality: he hasn't destroyed the Russian army, even if he has beaten it at Eylau. In spring he will have to embark on war again until peace is imposed on the King of Prussia, the Tsar and England, all of whom reject it.

And this next campaign, which will be — will have to be — decisive, is readying itself.

First they need men. He tells Berthier that the thousands of stragglers, marauders and runaways roaming about the countryside have to be rounded up.

'They must be made to feel ashamed of their cowardice.'

Then they need provisions.

'Our position will be a fine one when our supplies are assured. Beating the Russians, if I have bread, is mere child's play.'

He sends for Daru, intendant general of the Grand Army, who talks of problems carrying out his orders.

Who are these men? He feels their uncertainty. He must shake them up, take them in hand again.

'I have been making war for a long time, Daru. Carry out my orders without discussion . . . In any case, even if what I say is disagreeable to everyone, it is my will.' Perhaps they thought him weakened, hesitant, ready to give in after the Battle of Eylau.

He goes for gallops in the surrounding countryside to take his body back in hand.

Perhaps this sombre, bloody victory has damaged him, but what would be the point of so much sacrifice if he were to back down now? The opposite is what he should do, keep a tight grip on the reins.

He returns to Ordenschloss Castle. The dispatches from Paris have just arrived. He begins with the police spies' reports: mutterings about peace; criticism in the salons, even in the Empress's salon. He writes furiously to Josephine:

> I learn, my friend, that the scurrilous remarks bandied about in your salon at Mainz are starting again; make them stop. I should be extremely annoyed with you if you did not remedy this. You let yourself be distressed by the language of people who should be consoling you. I recommend a little spirit and the ability to put people in their place . . .
>
> This, my friend, is the only way to earn my approval. Greatness has its inconveniences: an Empress cannot go where a private individual can.
>
> A thousand, thousand tokens of friendship. My health is good. My affairs are going well.
>
> Napoleon

'Friendship.'

He wounds her with this word, he knows, but how can he not use it when she refuses to understand, when she tells him again and again in her letters that she wants to die?

There is no occasion for you to die. You are in good health and you can have no reasonable cause for sorrow.

You must not think of travelling this summer; it is not possible. You cannot be allowed to run about inns and camps. I want to see you as much as you do me, and even to live in peace.

I know how to do things other than make war, but duty comes before anything else. All my life I have sacrificed everything – tranquillity, interest, happiness – to my destiny.

Farewell, my friend.

Napoleon

If I don't hold the reins, they will let themselves go.

He opens a letter, then immediately throws it on the floor.

'Junot is always writing to me on heavy mourning paper, which produces a sinister effect on me when I receive his letters,' he exclaims. 'Tell him that it is contrary to practice and respect, and that one never writes to a superior with the forms of mourning for a personal grief.'

Have they forgotten who I am?

They are growing slack. They are talking. That Madame de Staël has gone near Paris despite being ordered to keep away.

'This woman continues her trade of intriguer. She is a perfect pest . . . I shall be obliged to have her seized by the gendarmerie. Keep an eye on Benjamin Constant as well . . .'

What do they think? That I'm going to let things drift?

IN THE SINGLE ROOM he occupies in Ordenschloss Castle, one of the few to have a fireplace, he watches Colonel Kleist, envoy of the King of Prussia, make his entrance. He listens to what the officer has to say, observes him as he talks. All this man wants is to gain time for Prussia and Russia.

Napoleon is sitting facing Kleist. He wants peace, he says, even with England. 'I should look upon myself with horror were I to be the cause of the shedding of so much blood.'

Kleist cannot hide a look of joy.

He too must think that I am ready to give in.

Napoleon stands, turns his back to Colonel Kleist.

If the powers do not want peace, he says, 'I am resolved to make war for ten more years. I am only thirty-seven. I have grown old under arms and in the affairs of state.'

Such is my destiny.

VIII

NAPOLEON, his hands behind his back, walks through the rooms of this large castle set in a vast park, extended by forests of fir trees on all sides. Beyond the trees he can make out the little village of Finkenstein, which he has just ridden through, coming from Osteröde by the Marienwerder road.

He senses that this residence will suit him. It is not heavily furnished and the decoration, consisting of paintings of battle scenes and a handful of tapestries, is austere and typically Prussian.

He likes the fact that it was built by Count Finkenstein, a Governor of Frederick II's, and today belongs to Count Kohna, Grandmaster of the King of Prussia's household.

He will establish his headquarters here until hostilities resume, he tells Duroc.

The Grand Marshal of the Palace must impose a strict etiquette which the Emperor desires to be respected by everyone.

Napoleon goes over to one of the windows in the corner room he has chosen as his study.

He only wants a reduced staff in attendance here, but the entire infantry of the Guard. They will install themselves in the park. Huts must be built; there must be order. He wants to make the most of this period of calm to restore the Grand Army to full strength before the inevitable encounter – inevitable since Bennigsen's troops haven't been destroyed. Parade every day in front of the castle, in the park, he says. Manoeuvre in the neighbouring countryside. Supplies are to be sent for, horses bought in their thousands in Germany, the cavalry regiments reformed. He'll hold reviews. He wants to see everything.

He has already sent for his surgeon-in-chief Percy. He tells Duroc and his aides-de-camp that he will no longer tolerate the wounded dragging themselves about the roads. In the hours following Eylau, he gave up his carriage to help their transport. The medical service must be funded.

His head seethes with ideas. He is impatient to get down to

work. He feels at ease here. Marie Walewska must come and stay with him. After these sombre months, this winter of cold and blood, he will recover the peace of mind he needs to organize the future, to prepare for the battle which will finally oblige the Russians and Prussians to conclude peace. And once they are conquered, what will England be able to do except give in, strangled by the Continental Blockade?

He is in high spirits, for the first time since the Battle of Eylau. He goes out into the garden and spends a long time walking there accompanied by Murat, who has just arrived at Finkenstein and, as is his wont, swaggers about in an extravagant uniform, plumed fur cap and fur waistcoat. Napoleon listens benevolently to him. Murat has been heroic and will be again. Let him lead his regiments and ready himself.

THE WEATHER IS PLEASANT at the start of April 1807. Birdsong can be heard, despite the sound of sledgehammers as the sappers work on building a little wooden town at the edge of the forest for the regiments' cantonments – two grenadiers', two chasseurs' and one fusiliers'.

He will go hunting in the forest. He sighs deeply. He is going to make Finkenstein the centre, the head and heart of his Empire.

He goes back to the castle.

Grenadiers stand guard on either side of its huge, carved wooden door. He tells Duroc to find out as quickly as possible where Marie Walewska is so that . . . He does not need to finish. Duroc bows and leaves.

In his study, Napoleon writes his first letter. It is Thursday, 2 April 1807.

'I have just moved my headquarters to Finkenstein,' he tells Josephine. 'It is a country where forage is abundant and my cavalry can live. I am in a very fine castle which has fireplaces in all the rooms, which is very pleasant, as I get up often in the night. I like to see the fire. My health is perfect. The weather is fine but still cold.'

NEXT MORNING he is up at dawn. In the fog he sees the first fires the grenadiers are lighting in the park. He is in a hurry to get down to work. He browbeats Constant and Roustam for being too slow getting him dressed. Important matters await him: dispatches from Paris, decrees, regulations to dictate, orders to send back to Marshal Lefebvre who is conducting the siege of Danzig where the Prussian troops of Marshal Kalkreuth are refusing to surrender.

Danzig is his most urgent priority: once he makes this fortified town fall, he can have his flank free to move against Bennigsen if he makes the mistake of advancing.

For this is his plan. Napoleon studies the maps again. Marshal Ney is ahead of the French lines, as bait. He will pull back in order to draw Bennigsen forward, then they will surround Bennigsen by the flanks and destroy him as they destroyed the Russian troops once already, at Austerlitz. They need an equally resounding victory so that Tsar Alexander will finally realize that he must treat for peace, and perhaps then they will be able to conclude an alliance with him that will divide Europe into two zones of influence, and make England submit.

NAPOLEON raises his voice. He dictates a letter to Talleyrand. He has just learnt that the Duke of Portland has formed a new cabinet in London with Canning, Castlereagh and Hawkesbury as members: all Pitt's men, all supporters of war to the death with France. How could anyone think it's possible to treat with these men? He must defeat them – in other words, he has to beat the Russians, take control of the continent and then make the English listen to reason.

But who understands these stakes? In Paris, the whispering is starting, the dreams of peace, and these siren songs are to be heard even in the Empress's salon.

'Ridiculous clique!' Napoleon exclaims.

He writes to Fouché, minister of police. Shouldn't he be keeping this sort of thing under surveillance and curbing it?

'We must give opinion a firmer direction,' Napoleon says. 'It's not a matter of constantly talking about peace, that's how not to get it . . .'

Napoleon crumples up the newspapers and throws them into the fire. These men of letters say and write any old thing, revealing military information in articles which the enemy will find instructive. It is extremely stupid.

He grows calmer.

'Party spirit is dead,' he dictates, 'and so I cannot see it as anything less than a calamity that ten scoundrels without talent or genius constantly peddle baseless gossip attacking the most respectable of men.'

But who apart from him analyses the situation clearly? Talleyrand, the adroit, cunning Prince of Benevento, deludes himself about the different countries' attitudes, and about Austria's offers to mediate.

Napoleon turns to Caulaincourt, his equerry. He questions him, probing until Caulancourt says that he's sorry 'the hopes for peace are receding, Sire'. General Clarke nods in agreement.

They all hope for peace.

And who wouldn't? But do they think that's what London wants, or even Vienna? Do they think one resolves on a course of action on the basis of one's feelings?

'Loving: I'm not too sure what that means in politics,' Napoleon exclaims.

Can he make people understand that he wants peace too, a European congress?

He summons Talleyrand to Finkenstein, leads him out into the park, has him attend the parades that take place every day at midday. He is familiar, relaxed.

'We must be circumspect in the negotiations,' he tells him. 'Tread softly and see what happens.'

He observes Talleyrand at length. He guesses the thoughts hidden behind that powdered, smiling face that never lets any emotion show. Rather than be in Poland, in Warsaw or Finkenstein, Talleyrand would prefer to be enjoying his fortune in his town house in rue de l'Anjou!

These gentlemen — Talleyrand, Caulaincourt and all their set — don't like bivouacs or chance lodgings.

Do they think I do? Do they imagine that I'm a fanatic of war? Or else, as Caulaincourt has been whispering, that I'm succumbing to 'Polish fever'?

SINCE MARIE WALEWSKA arrived at Finkenstein one night at the start of April in the company of her brother, Theodore Laczinski, a captain in the Polish Lancers who is serving in the Grand Army. Napoleon has sensed reservations amongst his entourage, despite their bowing and scraping and silence. They speak of his 'Polish wife', who will urge him to prolong the war because she wants to see her country reborn.

Spiteful gossip! As if he were the sort of man to let his choices be dictated by a woman!

He lives with her in tender, peaceful harmony. She does not leave her room, she does not go to parades, often she keeps her blinds closed. But she is there every night, young, brimming with energy, sitting near him in silence as he writes and takes notes.

Sometimes he reads her a few sentences from the directives he's composing, but they seem distant matters to her: regulations concerning the intellectual and moral education of girls at the boarding school for members of the Légion d'honneur, or the creation of a history class at the Collège de France, or the text of a decree differentiating the four principal theatres of Paris: the Comédie-Française, Odéon, Opéra, Opéra-Comique.

He looks at her. He wants her to come to Paris, he says. She will get to know his city, and France. He is the Emperor. He has the power to decide everything.

She stares at him for a long time, then bows her head. She is humble, tender. A woman who soothes his soul.

ALL THE OTHER WOMEN he knows – his sisters, Josephine of course, and even his mother – he has to take to task, flatter and, from time to time, make fun of. They are always at his heels, following him around or pestering him, leaving him no choice but to give them a good talking to.

'Madame,' he has to write to his mother, 'as long as you are in Paris, it is befitting that you dine every Sunday with the Empress, where the family dine. My family is a political family. While I am absent, the Empress is always its head . . .'

He needs to stand up for Josephine in front of his mother, but he also needs to remind Josephine that she is the Empress and therefore has a duty to be discreet.

'I want you to dine only with people who have dined with me; the list of guests for your evenings must be the same, and you must never admit ambassadors and foreigners into Malmaison, into your private residence. Were you to do otherwise, you would displease me. Lastly, do not let yourself be talked round by people whom I do not know, and who would not visit you if I was there.'

He must always be on the lookout, keeping an eye on everything.

Marie is my only peace.

Is Josephine jealous of her? Making fun of her will be enough. 'Your little Creole blood is up and taking everything to heart, and you become a complete devil . . .'

What more can she do?

It is for me to decide her fate, just as I decide everything.

I MUST DECIDE for Marshal Lefebvre who is marking time in front of Danzig. Lefebvre is impetuous, courageous, but he must be allocated officers of the engineers, such as Lariboisière and Chasseloup-Laubat, who will be able to open breaches in the fortifications.

He must encourage him. 'It is when one stoutly wishes to conquer, that one imparts vigour to men's souls.' He must counsel him. 'Send all petty fault-finders packing with a good kick up the backside.' He must also keep him in check.

Napoleon remembers the siege of St Jean d'Acre, the fruitless attacks, the pointless carnage, and he can see Eylau cemetery so clearly in his mind's eye.

'Reserve your grenadiers' courage for the moment when science tells you it can be used productively,' Napoleon writes. 'And in the meanwhile, know how to have patience . . . Aren't a few wasted days worth several thousand men whose lives it will be possible to save?'

MEN'S LIVES?

He thinks about these constantly, while alone with Marie, while walking in the gardens, during his long rides through the forest, or when he receives the Persian ambassador Mirza Reza Khan and, with great pomp, holds a parade in his honour. The infantry and troopers, uniforms good as new, young mounts stamping their feet, march past the ambassador, marshals and Napoleon.

All these lives in motion, plus another eighteen thousand

cavalry, whose pounding hooves make the earth tremble as they gallop in front of him on the Elbing plain — how many of these lives will be left after a few days' fighting this spring, when the decisive battle will take place? The Russians and Prussians have confirmed their alliance at Bartenstein, on 26 April 1807. So now it is arms that will decide.

DANZIG, LUCKILY, has fallen and the fort of Weichselmunde with it, delivering up its warehouses, its supplies of wine, its thousands of English muskets.

At the news of the fall of this city, Napoleon immediately has the team of six horses harnessed to his berline. He wishes to go to Danzig to congratulate Marshal Lefebvre.

He meets him en route, at the Abbey of Oliva.

This is one of the most satisfying moments of one's life, when one can congratulate and reward another man.

'Good day, your Grace, sit here next to me,' the Emperor says. 'Do you like Danzig's chocolate?'

Napoleon laughs at the bewildered Lefebvre, who takes a while to realize that he has been created Duke of Danzig — Lefebvre the commoner, the former NCO in the French Guard, married to a laundress of rue Poisonnière — and that instead of chocolate, he will receive an income of hundreds of thousands of livres.

There's talk.

Let them chatter! A non-commissioned officer of the French Guard made a duke, and a laundress made a duchess, that is the new nobility! By merit. As for the rest, the nobility of the ancien régime, let them join the queue.

'I have émigrés in my court as well,' Napoleon says to his brother Louis, 'but I don't let them lord it over me.'

What does someone like Louis know of what to do and what not to do?

Louis wants to be loved, to be 'the good king', fawned upon by the Dutch!

'The affection inspired by kings must be a manly one, combining respectful fear and high esteem,' Napoleon writes to him. 'When a king is said to be a good man, his reign is a failure.'

Louis must beware.

'You may do some stupid things in your kingdom, that's all very well, but I do not intend to let you do any in mine.'

Louis is interfering, awarding decorations to French citizens! Can his brother really be that blind?

He lectures him from Finkenstein, as Bennigsen's Russian troops start to advance. So much the better! They are entering the trap.

'I will be very glad if the enemy wishes to spare me having to go to him. My plan is to be under way on the 10th of June. I have made all my arrangements of supplies and magazines to go and find him at that time,' he tells Marshal Soult.

From now on, hour after hour, from morning until night, and on into that too, he must settle all the questions the Empire poses, from the positioning of a bust of d'Alembert in the halls of the Institut de France to the conscription of 1808, which is to be levied early since the forthcoming battle is upon them.

THE STAKES ARE critical. The goal is a matter of peace in Europe through an alliance with the Russians, after their defeat. Napoleon often grows impatient at being plagued with ridiculous questions that none the less he must resolve.

Louis, again, is quarrelling constantly with his wife Hortense de Beauharnais.

Napoleon has to explain to him that one 'does not treat a young wife as if she were a regiment. Let her dance as much as she likes, she is just that age. I have a wife of forty: from the battlefield I write to her to go to balls, while you wish a young woman of twenty to live in a cloister, to be like a nurse, always washing the baby?'

He leans over to Marie Walewska, looks at her. She is like 'a pretty rose-bud'. 'Be calm and happy,' he murmurs.

Tenderness like this – that's what he has been looking for. But Louis! Napoleon picks up his quill again. 'You should have had a wife like some of those I have known in Paris. She would have played you false and you would have been at her feet. It is not my fault, I have often told your wife this.'

HE IS ATTACHED TO HORTENSE, and to her elder son Napoleon Charles, who bears his name, and who, if he doesn't have a son –

but he will have a son, he wants to have one and he knows he can – will be his heir.

He remembers the first steps the child took at Malmaison. He is glad when he hears, on 12 May, that Napoleon Charles has got better after being ill for a long time.

'I can conceive of all the pain his mother must have felt; but measles is an illness to which everyone is subject,' he writes to Josephine. 'I hope that he has been vaccinated and that he will be free of the smallpox at least.'

He goes for walks in the garden after the midday parade.

Life. He wants to have a son. His whole being craves it, as does his political will.

He goes back indoors. He looks at Marie Walewska for a long time. A woman like her could be the mother of his son, but she would have to be fit for imperial life. That's what he wants, what he must look for now. If the war turns out as he intends, then he will be able to marry a Russian princess. Why not?

He daydreams.

THEN, ALL OF A SUDDEN, on 14 May, an unexpected letter announces that Napoleon Charles has died of croup.

Napoleon shrinks back in his chair. So many dead around him, and now this child. Such an unfair death.

But what is a life? He writes to Hortense, 'Life is strewn with so many dangers and can be the source of so many ills that death is not the greatest of them all.'

But the sorrow is there, boring into him. He writes to Josephine:

I can conceive of all the grief which the death of poor little Napoleon must cause you; you can understand the pain I feel. I should like to be near you, so that you might be moderate and discreet in your sorrow. You have had the good fortune never to lose a child, but this is one of the conditions and penalties incumbent on our human misery. Let me hear that you are reasonable and in good health. Would you augment my pain?
    Farewell, my friend.
    Napoleon

HUMAN MISERY.

He gallops through the forest, repeating 'Poor little Napoleon.' But what can one do? He says, 'It was his fate.' He writes it. But he rebels, and writes to the minister of the interior: 'In the last twenty years an illness named croup has become prevalent, taking off many children in northern Europe. It is our desire that you establish a prize worth twelve thousand francs which will be awarded to the best medical report on this illness and the means to treat it.'

What else can one do? Lament the cruelty of destiny? What for? But neither Hortense nor Josephine nor Louis is reasonable.

'Don't impair your health, search for some distraction,' he tells them. Don't they know what life is? What fate is?

And the living? What are they doing with their lives when they endlessly mourn the dead?

'Hortense is not reasonable and doesn't deserve our love since she only loved her children,' he writes to Josephine. 'Try to calm her! For all ills beyond remedy one must find consolations.'

HE DOES NOT ALTER the rhythm of his days for a moment. Every day, at midday, he reviews the troops. He administers the empire. He dictates. He gives orders. He studies maps.

When he learns on 5 June that Bennigsen's troops have attacked those of Marshal Ney, his heart leaps. At last! He questions the aides-de-camp Ney sends him: 'Is it a serious attack or just a skirmish?'

He senses that the bait has played its role. Bennigsen is advancing. Napoleon gives Ney the order to withdraw. Bennigsen must fall into the trap; they will attack him on the flanks – and this time he won't escape.

ON SATURDAY, 6 June 1807, at eight in the evening, Napoleon gets into a barouche and leaves Finkenstein for Saalfeld.

His Guard parts, and he passes through their midst. Murat holds the reins like a coachman.

IX

At Saalfeld, in the little parlour of the low house where he is to spend the night, Napoleon has the maps laid out on the floor. Lamps are brought up. He kneels down. Around him, the aides-de-camp and marshals look on in silence. He gets back to his feet.

'I am still guessing at what it is the enemy really intended,' he says. 'Today I am assembling my reserves of infantry and cavalry at Möhrungen and I am going to try and find the enemy and force a major battle to finish him off.'

He retires to what serves as his bedchamber, a sort of garret. He hears the galloping horses of orderly officers who are bringing news of the army on the march. He closes his eyes. He is going to win. He must: for the dead in Eylau cemetery; because he always finishes what he has started; and because victory is the only way of obtaining peace. He is sure of himself, mind and body both straining towards a single goal: victory. He has only one concern, anguish even: that Bennigsen may elude him. Has he been well enough hooked so that he can't get out of the trap?

Nothing counts any more except these questions. Forgotten, everything that is not the coming battle.

He gets up at first light. The day dawns clear and bright. Even the weather presages victory. The road to Güttstadt, Helisberg and Eylau runs past fields of rye, oats and wheat. The peasants' houses are surrounded by gardens with scurrying flocks of fat geese. Where has the winter mud gone? What has become of the desolation of those cheerless fields?

The doleful days are over. It is hot, the air heavy with the smell of grass. The wheels of the artillery caissons bump along dry roads, throwing up just a thin, white dust that quickly subsides.

Napoleon gallops out in front of his escort. Often he rides so fast that it's hard for the grand equerry and the chasseurs of his Guard to catch him up. Now he rides onto a rise, which overlooks the countryside, and stands up in his stirrups. His staff surround him. He calls for his maps, which are spread out on the grass. He gets off his horse, almost lying down to study every sinuosity of the terrain.

With his finger, he follows the course of the Alle, this meandering river that flows past the small village of Friedland on its left bank.

Orderlies confirm the news that Bennigsen's troops have established three pontoon bridges on the Alle. They are crossing the river, from right to left bank, by means of those three bridges and a wooden bridge.

Napoleon, his hands behind his back, paces about the knoll.

Is this the moment? He mustn't attack too soon. He must let Bennigsen become more and more deeply embroiled, entice him to transfer his troops onto the left bank by making him think that there are only a few French troops in front of him, while the bulk of the Grand Army marches north, towards Königsberg. Bennigsen will think he is in position to make a flank attack and thereby sweep aside Ney and Lannes who have entered Friedland. Then, when Bennigsen's entire forces are on the left bank, Napoleon must destroy the bridges, pull the trap shut and leave him no choices other than surrender, drowning or retreat.

Napoleon points at the map with the tip of his riding whip. 'Friedland,' he says.

ON WEDNESDAY, 10 June, there's fighting at Heilsberg. Napoleon is furious, demanding to be informed of every detail of the battle. Murat has charged and his troopers have been mown down by grapeshot, his horse killed under him; he even lost a boot, and charged again.

Too soon, too soon.

Napoleon gallops to the battlefield. The Russians have fallen back with victory in their grasp. Napoleon walks among the wounded. Around the ambulances, he sees mounds of severed arms and legs stacked pell-mell amongst the corpses.

He gives orders for the wounded to be helped. Then he mounts up again. He cannot sleep for more than quarter of an hour here, a quarter there, but he doesn't feel tired. Does an arrow fall to the ground when it has been fired at its target with all the archer's strength and skill?

He is that arrow.

ON SUNDAY, 14 June, Napoleon realizes that the die is cast: Bennigsen's troops are crowded together on the left bank. Lannes's soldiers, like Ney's, have fallen back in good order, drawing the Russians after them, who are now occupying Friedland.

Napoleon is certain that nothing will prevent him now: Bennigsen is hooked. He mounts his horse, starts towards the first fighting and finds himself in the midst of Oudinot's men.

'Where is the Alle?' he asks Oudinot.

The general stretches out his arm and indicates the fifty-metre wide, steep-banked river.

'There,' he says, 'past the enemy.'

'I'm going to dump them in that water,' says Napoleon.

Cannon-balls begin to fall around Napoleon; more and more men are wounded. He stands perfectly still under fire, his arms crossed. Oudinot approaches, explains that the grenadiers are threatening to stop fighting if the Emperor continues to expose himself to danger like this.

Napoleon gets back on his horse. He has his bivouac installed at Posthenen, a little village facing the Russian troops under Bagration.

He engages the artillery and paces up and down the hill, lashing the tall grass with his crop.

It is 14 June. A sign.

He turns to Berthier.

'The day of Marengo, the day of victory,' he says. 'Friedland will equal Austerlitz, Jena and Marengo whose anniversary I am celebrating.'

He walks quickly. It is a sign from destiny. He feels invigorated, full of a joyous energy which nothing can staunch. When Captain Marbot brings him a communication from Marshal Lannes, he questions him.

'Have you a good memory, Marbot? Well then, what anniversary is today, the 14th of June?'

Marbot replies.

'Yes! Yes!' says Napoleon. 'The anniversary of Marengo, and I shall beat the Russians as I beat the Austrians!'

He mounts his horse and, as he passes the columns of soldiers shouting 'Long live the Emperor,' he calls out, 'Today is a happy day, the anniversary of Marengo.'

THE DAY DRAWS ON. It is hot. He still has not given the order for a full attack. Not all the troops have reached the battlefield.

He looks through his field-glass. The members of his staff, close to him, keep saying that the Russian troops are continuing to cross to the left bank and that there are so many of them that they should wait until the next day to attack, when the Grand Army will be up to full strength.

Napoleon lowers his field-glass. He knows that this is the moment.

'No,' he says, 'you don't catch the enemy making a mistake like this twice.'

Everything is simple now. Thoughts become orders and actions. He goes up to Ney and grasps him by the arm.

'That's the goal,' he says.

He points to the Russian troops and beyond them, the town of Friedland.

'March straight ahead without looking around you, penetrate into that dense mass whatever the cost. Enter Friedland, take the bridges and do not concern yourself about what might happen on your right, your left or your rear. The army and I are here to watch over that.'

Ney hurries away. Napoleon watches him go.

'That man is a lion,' he murmurs.

AT FIVE-THIRTY in the afternoon, when the sun is still high in the sky, Napoleon gives the order to attack. Twenty guns emplaced in Posthenen open fire at his signal and the entire artillery begin their barrage. Amid the explosions, Napoleon hears shouts of 'Long live the Emperor! Forward! To Friedland!'

His thoughts have become this battle.

He indicates to General Sénarmont the bridges that have to be destroyed. That way the trap will shut. Through his field-glass, he sees the Russians breaking into a rout, trying to cross the river and drowning.

And when the firing stops, at around ten-thirty, all he sees in the night are Friedland's houses on fire, lighting up the dead and wounded and the remains of the Russian artillery's caissons.

The screams of pain are often drowned out by the shouts of 'Long live the Emperor!' which the soldiers break into when they see Napoleon pass.

MONDAY, 15 JUNE, has already dawned. Napoleon passes through the ranks. The soldiers are sleeping; it makes them look dead. He gives orders for them not to be woken to present arms, and keeps walking, reaching the mounds of Russian corpses torn to pieces by the artillery, piled on top of one another, their bodies marking out the squares they had tried to hold, their disembowelled horses revealing the position of their cannons.

Surrounded by his escort, he slowly makes his way back up the road that winds along the left-hand side of the Alle valley towards Wehlau. Bodies float downriver.

It is raining. He stops in the village of Peterswalde, instals himself in a barn and begins a letter to Josephine.

> My friend, I write you only a few words, for I am very tired. I have been bivouacking for a number of days. My children have worthily celebrated the anniversary of the Battle of Marengo.
>
> The battle of Friedland will be as celebrated and as glorious for my people.

He could stop there, but he must also explain to Josephine what has happened so she can tell it to her entourage.

> The whole Russian army routed, eighty guns captured, thirty thousand taken prisoners or killed; thirty-five Russian generals killed, wounded or taken prisoner; the Russian guard crushed; it is the worthy sister of Marengo, Austerlitz and Jena. The *Bulletin** will tell you the rest. My losses are not serious. I successfully out-manoeuvred the enemy.

* The Bulletin of the Grand Army.

Put your mind at ease and be glad.
Farewell, my friend, I am just getting into the saddle.
  Napoleon

P.S. This news can be published as a notice if it gets to you before the *Bulletin*. The cannon can be fired too. Cambacérès will take care of the notice.

He stretches his legs and shuts his eyes for a few seconds.

He has carried off victory, but what can force achieve that will last? Force is powerless to organize anything.

'There are only two powers in the world: the sword and the mind. In the long run, the sword is always beaten by the mind.'

He has just brandished his sword and laid low the enemy. Now the mind must be allowed to organize. He must speak to Tsar Alexander. He must conclude peace with him.

He stays like that for another few minutes. He is serene. Then he starts to write again.

'For me,' he writes to Marie Walewska, 'you are a new sensation, a perpetual revelation. It is because I study you impartially. It is also because I know your life up to today. Thence comes your singular mixture of independence, submissiveness, good sense and lightness which makes you so different from all other women.'

He is happy.

ON TUESDAY, 16 JUNE he rides alongside the River Pregel towards Tilsit. He has a pontoon bridge built, and then personally conducts the search for a ford, wading his horse out into the river at the head of his squadrons, lifting his feet up above his saddle holsters.

Sometimes he breaks into a gallop. He loves this feeling of independence, this mark of a freedom which permits him to sweep aside all ceremony, all caution. He takes his escort by surprise and rides alone like this for half an hour or more until he reaches a hill, where he stops and looks at the grey countryside which is becoming blurry in the rain. His officers and the grand equerry, Caulaincourt, catch him up, out of breath, anxious. He laughs.

He is told of the fall of Königsberg, which Murat and Soult

have entered. Everything is unfolding as he planned. Later, he writes to Josephine:

> Königsberg, which is a city of eighty thousand souls, is in my power. I have found plenty of cannon, a good number of magazines, and lastly, more than sixty thousand muskets that came from England.
>
> Farewell, my friend; my health is impeccable, although I have caught a slight cold from the rain and cold of the bivouac.
>
> Be happy and merry.
>
> All yours,
>
> Napoleon

ON DAYS LIKE THIS after a battle, a victory, his mind relaxes and embraces the full range of his thoughts again, as if the horizon were no longer limited to a particular space to conquer, to armies to be swept aside, but instead grows into a stage full of memories and the people he loves.

He has already written to Josephine and Marie. He takes up his quill again to write to Hortense: perhaps another reason he was so determined to win this victory was that Napoleon Charles was dead and so he had to prove to himself that the vital energy had not abandoned him, that he was capable of carrying on, as he felt he was, of surpassing Marengo and Austerlitz, despite the death of this child he loved.

He writes to Hortense on 16 June 1807:

> Your pain touches me, but I wish you were braver. To live is to suffer, and a man of honour fights constantly to remain master of himself. I do not like seeing you being unjust to little Napoleon Louis* and to all your friends.
>
> Your mother and I hoped to occupy more of a place in your heart. I gained a great victory on 14 June. I am well and love you very much.

What is the good of talking of battle to a mother choked with grief who understands nothing save her pain? He understands her, but he cannot accept such submission to one's suffering, such self-

---

* Younger brother of Napoleon Charles. Born 1804, will die in 1831.

indulgence, such indifference to the world which carries on its way despite death.

ON FRIDAY, 19 JUNE, he enters Tilsit and rides through the city. The streets are straight and broad, and cobbled with uneven stones on which the horses stumble and slip. He goes to the banks of the Niemen. A bridge is still burning. On the right bank, Cossack riders are caracoling their horses. The river is broad.

He remembers the rivers in Italy, the bridges at Lodi and Arcola which he crossed under case-shot. He is here on the banks of these fast-flowing blue waters which mark the start of that other great Empire, Russia.

He learns, on his return to Tilsit, that Prince Lobanov has just arrived, conveying from Bennigsen a request for an armistice.

Napoleon wants more than that. He is in the stronger position.

'Russian boastfulness has been brought low,' he says. 'They confess themselves defeated; they have been furiously cut up. My eagles have been hoisted over the Niemen; the army has not suffered at all.'

What he wants to impose is not an armistice but peace.

In any case, everyone is calling for it – Talleyrand, Caulaincourt, even the marshals. The grumblers want it too. It's more than a year now since they've seen France.

What about him? Do they think he doesn't want it?

He sends Grand Marshal Duroc to Bennigsen. He invites Prince Lobanov to dine with him. He observes Bennigsen's envoy for a long time, then solemnly raises his glass. He drinks, he says, to the health of the Emperor Alexander. He takes Lobanov by the arm, leads him over to a map, points out the Vistula, following its course with his finger.

'This is the frontier between the two Empires,' he says. 'On one side your sovereign should rule, I on the other.'

On Sunday the 21st, an armistice is concluded.

'I am in marvellous health and wish to hear you happy,' he writes to Josephine.

He is light-hearted.

Perhaps this is peace at last, the agreement with the Tsar that will force England to accept France as it is now for the first time since 1792.

ON MONDAY, 22 JUNE, he orders the cannon to open fire to salute the introduction of the armistice. It rains unremittingly, but he sees the soldiers embracing in the downpour. In high spirits, he starts to dictate his proclamation to the Grand Army that will bring the campaign to a close.

> Soldiers! On the fifth of June the Russian army attacked us in our cantonments ... The enemy realized too late that our slumber was that of the lion. Now they regret having troubled it ... From the banks of the Vistula we have flown to those of the Niemen with the swiftness of an eagle. At Austerlitz you celebrated the anniversary of the coronation; this year you have worthily celebrated that of Marengo.

Now he must talk to them of peace.

> Frenchmen, you have been worthy of yourselves and me. You will return to France covered with all your laurels and having secured a glorious peace which will contain guarantees for its duration.

He wants this peace, as much as the soldiers whose silhouettes he sees marching in the rain, the butts of their muskets propped in the crooks of their arms, the barrels resting on their bearskins.

> It is time to be done with all this, for our country to be able to live quietly, freed from the malign influence of England. My beneficence will prove all my gratitude and the extent of my love for you.

He must win the battle of peace.

When he sees Prince Lobanov again, he raises his glass of champagne to Tsar Alexander once more. Then he asks after the health of Tsarina Elizabeth.

He notices that Lobanov is so moved his eyes are filled with tears.

'Look, Duroc,' he cries. 'Look how the Russians love their rulers.'

X

Napoleon gallops along the banks of the Niemen on 25 June 1807. The sun is at its zenith. It is nearly one in the afternoon.

Suddenly, behind a clump of trees, Napoleon catches sight of the raft in the middle of the river which the sappers were building last night and this morning, and have moored so that it is an equal distance from either bank of the Niemen. He sees it distinctly now, with its two tents of white canvas which he has instructed should be richly decorated and have two doors and a sort of salon. On the larger one, in which he will meet Tsar Alexander, he sees a giant 'N' painted on the canvas. An 'A' of the same size should be facing the right bank.

He looks at the Russian troops, who are amassed on that bank of the river, then turns his head towards the line of soldiers of the Grand Army who stretch along the left bank. They break into shouts of 'Long live the Emperor', yelling so loudly and merrily, that the words overlap one another and become indistinguishable. Their voices form a single, identical explosion of noise that rolls between the banks, joyous and airy and irresistible.

He feels light-hearted. He looks behind him. He has chosen five officers to accompany him out to the raft for this meeting: Marshals Murat, Berthier, Bessières and Duroc and his grand equerry, Caulaincourt, but he wants to be alone with the Tsar, this heir of a centuries-old Empire that straddles Europe and Asia. He has constructed his own empire with his own hands, he is its founder, only equalled by the conquerors of antiquity who started dynasties and gathered together whole peoples – he is going to be face to face with a Romanov!

This is the meeting of two eagles, the Romanovs' and mine, flying over the Niemen after ten victorious years.

When Prince Lobanov brought word from Alexander, Napoleon felt as if he had attained his goal. Who could seriously threaten the edifice he has constructed now?

This Romanov who welcomed French émigrés to his country – including Louis, brother of Louis XVI, who claimed to be eighteenth in line – this hereditary Emperor was saying to the Emperor Napoleon: 'The union between France and Russia has constantly been the object of my desires and I am firmly convinced that it alone can assure the happiness and tranquillity of the world. An entirely new system should replace the one that has existed up to now and I flatter myself that we shall easily come to an understanding with the Emperor Napoleon provided that we negotiate without intermediaries. A lasting peace can be concluded between us in very few days . . .'

NAPOLEON REINS in his horse, dismounts and walks to the large boat that is to take him out to the raft.

The breeze picks up. It chases white ripples of cloud across the sky that veil the full glare of the sun like gauze, tempering its heat. On the raft, the tent walls billow slightly, like sails swelling.

He will never forget this moment. Men will never forget this meeting of two Emperors, the Emperor of centuries past and the Emperor of the present century, Napoleon, Emperor of the French, who has had to cross so many rivers with his armies to arrive at this point.

He feels a sense of satisfaction that he has never felt before, even at his coronation.

This sky, this River Niemen, this raft, these armies facing one another, this Emperor who is on the right bank preparing to embark to come and join him – all this is *his* cathedral, *his* work. The fruit of thirty-eight years of his life. He feels proud, glad of his destiny.

He jumps into the large boat, followed by the marshals and grand equerry, and stands at the prow. The rowers, dressed in white smocks, plunge their oars into the waters of the Niemen.

HE REACHES THE RAFT first and strides forward quickly to welcome the Tsar whose boat is approaching.

Napoleon holds out his hand and, with a glance, appraises this man who is twelve years younger than he is and was responsible for the assassination of his father, Paul.

Alexander is tall and pink-complexioned. His powdered, curly chestnut hair and long side whiskers show beneath a tall hat with white and black feathers. He wears the green uniform with red facings of the Proebrajenski Regiment, a sort of Imperial Guard. On his right shoulder gold knots gleam. His sword hangs at his side and he wears short boots that stand out sharply against his white breeches. The pale blue ribbon of the Order of St Andrew runs across his chest.

I am wearing the red ribbon of my Légion d'honneur.

The Tsar has limpid eyes, a comely, youthful face.

Napoleon embraces him. Walking side by side, they make their way towards the large tent.

'I hate the English as much as you do,' Alexander begins. His voice is melodious, his French perfect.

'I shall second you in all your actions against them,' he adds when they are on the threshold of the tent.

Napoleon raises the flap. 'In that case, everything can be arranged,' he says, 'and peace is made.'

Napoleon continues talking, swept up by a feeling of exhilaration. His mind has never been so quick. He wants to persuade, charm and steer this Emperor whose elder he is, whose troops he has defeated, who he does not want to humiliate but rather rally to his side, in order to build a Europe of two faces.

That of the Tsar as far the Vistula, and mine from there west.

There is no alternative, in any case.

Prussia? He tells Alexander, 'An objectionable king, an objectionable nation, a power that has deceived everyone and does not deserve to exist. Everything it has it owes to you.'

Austria? Napoleon does not want to bring it up, but he read Andreossy's dispatches as he was leaving his residence in Tilsit to go to the Niemen to meet Alexander. France's ambassador in Vienna reports that the Austrians hoped that the Grand Army would be defeated and had made preparations to intervene and finish it off when it was beaten; victory at Friedland plunged the court at Vienna into despair.

That leaves Turkey, but a palace revolution has just overthrown Sultan Selim III, Napoleon's ally.

Napoleon murmurs to Alexander, 'It is a dispensation of

Providence that tells me that the Turkish Empire can no longer exist.'

Let us share its remains.

He speaks of the East, observing Alexander as he does so.

This man seems sincere. He is still young. I dominate him. I want his alliance, but I shall never let him have 'Constantinople, which is the Empire of the world'.

TIME HAS PASSED, more than an hour and a half. They agree to meet the next day, Friday, 26 June, on the raft.

King Frederick William of Prussia should be present, Alexander says.

Napoleon replies irritably, 'I have often been two in a bed, but never three.'

Then he recovers himself, proposes that the next talks take place in the town of Tilsit, half of which he will give to the Russians so that Alexander can reside there.

'We shall talk,' he says. Then he adds, 'I shall be your secretary and you shall be mine.'

Napoleon takes Alexander's arm and starts towards his boat. From both banks arise the cheers of the soldiers watching this scene.

THAT NIGHT, Napoleon's sleep is fitful; he lies awake for long periods in the large house he occupies in Tilsit.

The fires of the soldiers of the Guard light up his room. He hears a song rising up into the night sky in the distance. The tune is that of a popular marching song. The first voice is joined by other joyful voices who take up the song in unison,

> On a raft afloat midstream
> I saw two of Earth's lords
> And that was the noblest scene;
> Well I saw peace, I saw war
> And I saw all Europe's fate in store
> On a raft afloat midstream

His tiredness evaporates. Why bury himself in oblivion and silence when these days are the richest, fullest of his life?

He wakes Roustam, sends for his secretary. He dictates a letter to Fouché, 'See that no silly things are said, directly or indirectly, about Russia. Everything indicates that our system is going to link up with that power in a stable manner.'

He dismisses his secretary with a brusque gesture. He paces up and down the room, his hands behind his back, as is his habit.

Can he trust Alexander, this Romanov who only recently signed an agreement with the Prussians to wage war to the death on France? Is the Tsar one of those two-faced men dynastic heirs so often are?

Can I count on his loyalty? On his alliance against England? It is in my interest. Is it in his?

All I can do is back him.

Napoleon takes up his quill; he wants to pin down his impressions, write without inhibitions. He writes to Josephine.

My friend,
    I have just seen the Emperor Alexander in the middle of the Niemen, on a raft on which was erected an extremely handsome pavilion. I am very pleased with him; he is a very handsome, good and young Emperor; he has more intelligence than is generally supposed. He is coming to stay in the town of Tilsit tomorrow.
    Farewell, my friend. I very much wish to hear that you are well and happy. My health is very good.
    Napoleon

WHEN HE GREETS ALEXANDER at twelve-thirty the next day, 26 June, on the raft, the man already seems familiar. Napoleon feels drawn to this figure who comes from such a long line and he cannot help but be flattered by the warmth the Tsar seems to display towards him.

Yet he knows that all anyone talks about in St Petersburg is the 'Corsican ogre', 'the usurper'. He knows how the salons welcomed the émigrés, how people grieved for the Duke d'Enghien, wore mourning for that Bourbon, and what curses they rained down on the head of that 'Jacobin Bonaparte'.

And now I'm taking the Emperor of Russia by the arm and we're agreeing that tomorrow the password to go from one sector of Tilsit to another will be 'Alexander, Russia, Majesty', and Alexander is choosing the password for the day after tomorrow, 'Napoleon, France, Gallantry'.

Every day the sense of intimacy between us grows: troop reviews, long conversations, rides in the forest.

I surprise him, charm him, dazzle him.

Napoleon tells Duroc, 'He's like the hero of a novel, he has all the manners of one of the most charming men in Paris.'

But I am his superior. I am the founder of an empire, not its heir.

WHEN THEY RIDE through the countryside and forests that surround Tilsit, Napoleon spurs his horse, rides ahead of the Tsar and then waits for him. He is happy. Since their second meeting on the raft, Frederick William III, King of Prussia, often accompanies them. He is no sort of horseman and has the sad air of a defeated man. Napoleon pokes fun at his appearance, shows his contempt.

'How do you manage to do up so many buttons?' he asks.

He has to receive him, but only as an unwelcome addition whose presence one accepts solely because one's distinguished guest wishes to see him at table.

'The Emperor of Russia and the King of Prussia are lodging in town and dining with me every day,' Napoleon writes to Fouché. 'This makes me hope for a prompt end of the war, which I devoutly wish for in the interest of my people.'

However, he excludes Frederick William from all the meetings he considers private, and these he arranges with Alexander in the evenings after dinner.

'Europe, the Orient,' Napoleon says. He indicates on the maps how their two Empires could expand. Will Alexander allow himself to be convinced that, as allies, the two Empires can dominate the bulk of the world?

Napoleon does not tire of conjuring up this prospect. These conversations, these dinners, even with Frederick William present, enchant him. He feels himself an Emperor of Kings.

'I believe I have told you,' he writes to Josephine, 'that the Emperor of Russia takes a great interest in your health in a most amiable manner. He as well as the King of Prussia dines with me every day.'

NAPOLEON IS PROUD.

He shows off his grenadiers, organizes a march past of his Imperial Guard, his cuirassiers with their 'iron waistcoats'. From time to time he glances at Alexander and catches an admiring, anxious expression on his face. These divisions filing past seem like a moving rampart that never stops advancing, full of menace.

Alexander will have to agree to an alliance between them, recognize the Confederation of the Rhine and the kingdoms of Louis in Holland and Joseph in Naples, agree to Jérôme becoming King of Westphalia – he will, in short, have to admit that Napoleon is the Emperor of the West. Besides, Prussia's the one who's going to pay. Russia is only giving up the Ionian isles and Cattaro. Napoleon is giving it a free hand in Finland and Sweden. And Russia undertakes to declare war on England if it refuses mediation.

As for Prussia, Napoleon makes an offhand gesture, it must be punished, lose half its land and population. He listens to Alexander pleading Prussia's cause, affectingly evoking Queen Louise's despair. Napoleon waves towards the grenadiers of both Imperial Guards who have gathered in the country near Tilsit for a huge banquet. The men are carousing.

What does Prussia matter?

What about Queen Louise, Alexander asks. She has arrived in Tilsit, she wants to see Napoleon.

So she's come to beg me too, has she, to petition for her kingdom?

This woman who dreamt of war, who incited Prussian officers to sharpen their sabres on the steps of the French Embassy in Berlin, who is said to be so beautiful, who swore an oath of alliance against France on the tomb of Frederick II with her husband, that simpleton Frederick William III, and Alexander.

This Tsar who is abandoning them both.

NAPOLEON CALLS ON HER in the miller's house in Tilsit to which Frederick William III has been consigned.

Beautiful – yes: dressed in white crêpe embroidered with silver, her face as white as her dress, but regal none the less with its collar of pearls.

Napoleon observes her with an ironic glint in his eye. She speaks of Prussia's woes, calls for Magdeburg to be restored to Prussia when, in fact, it is to be part of Westphalia.

'Is that crêpe, Italian muslin?' Napoleon asks, complimenting her on her appearance.

'Are we to talk of dress at such a solemn moment?' she bursts out indignantly.

Napoleon admires her skill at negotiating, her determination. He invites her to dinner and tells Caulaincourt, 'She was like Mademoiselle Duchesnois in the tragedy.'

He does not want to give way on anything.

'The beautiful Queen of Prussia is to dine with me tonight,' he writes to Josephine.

He hesitates for a few seconds.

So here she is, submissively paying me a visit, this sovereign of whose beauty and will all Europe sings the praises.

'The Queen of Prussia is really charming,' he continues. 'She is full of coquetry towards me, but do not be jealous; I am an oilcloth off which all that runs. It would cost me too dear to play the gallant.'

But still, he can let Queen Louise think she will be able to seduce him, get round him.

SHE COMES TO DINNER dressed in red and gold, wearing a turban, and sits between Alexander and Napoleon.

Does she remember that she used to call him 'the monster', 'the son of the Revolution' and make fun of him in front of Berlin's entire nobility? Does she remember that she used to call him as ugly as a dwarf, and that she trained her parrot to insult him?

He remembers.

'Why does the Queen of Prussia wear a turban? It can't be to pay her court to the Emperor of Russia who is at war with Turkey?'

She looks him up and down. He doesn't like her look, her voice.

'It is rather, I think, to pay my court to Roustam,' she replies, looking at Napoleon's Mameluke.

She's wounded, he can tell. He has refused her Magdeburg, which he has left to the King of Westphalia, Jérôme. She has tried to charm him. He has listened to her saying, 'Is it possible that I am lucky enough to see the man of this century and of history at such close quarters, and yet he will not give me the liberty and satisfaction of assuring him that he has earned my undying attachment for life?'

What does she imagine? That he confuses coquetry, feelings and affairs of state? He is not another Frederick William.

'Madame,' he replies, 'I am to be pitied, I was born under an unlucky star.'

HE MAKES HIS WAY back to his quarters with Murat, whom he has seen paying his court to the Queen. She relaxes by reading 'the history of the past', Murat reports, and when Murat replied that 'the present age offers actions worthy of record as well', she murmured, 'It is already too much for me just to live in it.'

Napoleon falls silent. This woman has retained her dignity and her command of the conversation; she has even dominated it, constantly bringing it round to the subject that obsesses her, Magdeburg.

The beautiful Queen of Prussia to whom, despite everything, he will make no concessions.

He feels a desire to tell someone how when he offered her a rose, she drew her hand back, saying, 'On condition that Magdeburg is with it', or again, how he invited her to sit down 'because nothing undermines a tragic scene so well, for when one is seated, it becomes comic'.

He writes to Josephine.

My friend,
   The Queen of Prussia dined here with me yesterday. I had to defend myself against being obliged to make some more concessions to her husband; I was gallant, but I kept to my policy. She is very amiable. I will give you all the details that I cannot go into now without this becoming far too long a letter.

When you read this, peace will have been concluded with Russia and Prussia, and Jérôme will have been recognized as King of Westphalia with a population of three million. This news is just for you.

Farewell my friend, I love you and wish to know that you are happy and in good spirits.

Napoleon

THESE ARE THE LAST HOURS he spends in the company of the Tsar. The treaties have been signed, Prussia is dismembered, humiliated, Russia intact. The two nations have undertaken to act against England.

'The greatest intimacy has been established been the Emperor of Russia and myself,' Napoleon writes to Cambacérès, 'and I hope that our system will from now on work in concert. If you wish to fire a sixty-gun salute to announce peace, you have my full permission.'

He accompanies Alexander to the boat that will take him to the right bank of the Niemen. The time for farewells has come. He would like this moment not to end. He knows only too well that once men are away from him, the Tsar as much as anybody, they elude his influence, they slip away. There is also the sapping work of London's agents in St Petersburg to consider.

He wants to reassure himself and says to Alexander, 'Everything suggests that if England does not make peace before November, it will certainly do so when it knows Your Majesty's arrangements and when it sees the mounting crisis that will close the whole continent to it.'

Can he be sure of Alexander?

They review the regiments of the Tsar's personal Imperial Guard together.

'Will Your Majesty permit me to award the Légion d'honneur to your bravest man, the soldier who conducted himself best during the campaign?' he asks.

A grenadier is pointed out. Napoleon pins the Légion d'honneur to his chest.

'Private Lazarev, you will remember this as the day your master and I became friends.'

He embraces Alexander.
Who can I be sure of?

IN HIS IMMEDIATE circle, anxieties are already making themselves heard. Alexander can't be trusted, he is told repeatedly. He hesitates, then sends for General Savary. He stares at him hard. This man is one of his most faithful servants. He showed it at the time of the arrest and execution of the Duke d'Enghien.

'I have confidence in the Emperor of Russia,' he says to him. 'We have each shown each other marks of the greatest friendship after having spent twenty days here together, and there is nothing between the two nations that stands in the way of a thorough rapprochement.'

He goes up to Savary, pinches his ear.

'Go and work there.'

Savary will be Napoleon's ambassador to St Petersburg, and the salons will have no choice but to accept him, this general accused of being responsible for the death of the Duke d'Enghien.

'I have just made peace,' Napoleon continues. 'People tell me I'm wrong, that I'll be deceived; well, that's enough war. We must give the world a rest.'

He walks around the room.

'In your conversations in St Petersburg, never speak of war, don't criticize any customs, do not draw attention to anything ridiculous. Every people has its customs and it is only too like the French to compare everything to their own practices and set themselves up as a model. It is a bad habit . . .'

He accompanies Savary to the door.

'Global peace lies in Petersburg,' he says. 'The affairs of the world are there.'

NAPOLEON LEAVES TILSIT on 9 July at ten in the evening. He is in a hurry now to get back to Paris, the heart of the Empire. He has been away for six months.

He passes through Königsberg and Posen. He stops for a day here, a few hours there. He is impatient at the reservations of some people, the opposition of others.

'Make it known to the inhabitants of Berlin that if they do not pay their contribution of ten million, they will have a French garrison for all eternity!' he tells General Clarke when he stops at Königsberg.

Don't they know that he is the conqueror, the Emperor of Kings?

Have the Portuguese not heard of this either? They must close their ports to the English before 1 September, he writes to Talleyrand on the way to Dresden, 'otherwise I shall declare war on Portugal and the English merchandise will be confiscated'.

He no longer wants, nor can tolerate, any stupid resistance. Prussia and Greater Russia have either succumbed or sought to ally themselves with him. Do people think he is going to be dictated to by the Portuguese or the Spanish? Or by the Pope who, according to a letter from Eugène de Beauharnais, is considering denouncing him. 'Does he take me for Louis le Débonnaire? I shall always be Charlemagne in the Court of Rome.'

HE ARRIVES IN DRESDEN on Friday, 17 July.

The city is beautiful, decked out, lit up. The King of Saxony bows and respectfully invites him to attend the festivities he has arranged in his honour. Bejewelled, the women come forward to welcome him, curtseying low.

He stays for a few days. He receives Polish delegates and presents the King of Saxony to them. The King will be the ruler of the Grand Duchy of Warsaw which he has decided to create out of the Polish provinces wrested from Prussia. However, French troops will remain in the grand duchy so the Emperor will be its true master. It is not the Poland Polish patriots were hoping for, he admits, but perhaps it is the germ — and perhaps that is already too much for Alexander, even if the Tsar has accepted the grand duchy in principle.

He thinks of Marie Walewska. And he writes to Josephine.

My friend,

I arrived in Dresden yesterday, at five in the afternoon, quite well, although I spent a hundred hours in my carriage without getting out. I am staying here with the King of Saxony, with whom I am highly satisfied. I am now halfway back to you. One of these fine nights I shall turn up at St Cloud like a jealous husband, I warn you.

Farewell, my friend, it will give me great pleasure to see you again.

Always yours,
Napoleon

Now HE DOESN'T STOP any longer than is needed to change horses.

He passes through Leipzig, Weimar and Frankfurt.

At Bar-le-Duc, this silhouette, this man who steps forward and seems to be from another world, yes, this man who calls him Sire, who gives his name as 'de Longeaux', he was one of his fellow pupils at Brienne military school.

Napoleon remembers it — twenty-five years ago.

He listens to de Longeaux speak for a few minutes, then grants him a pension and sets off immediately for Épernay.

At seven o'clock on Monday, 27 July 1807, he reaches St Cloud.

PART THREE

Destinies must be fulfilled

28 JULY 1807 TO DECEMBER 1807

XI

'IT IS MY WILL,' says Napoleon.

He looks hard at Caroline, his sister, who is on her feet, defiant, straight-backed, making no attempt at denial. He has yelled at her and she has fallen silent. How can she refute what she has flaunted at the Opéra, in the Tuileries, and in the streets and salons of Paris – her liaison with General Junot, the military governor of the capital? While her husband, Murat, was leading the cavalry charge at Heilsberg and Friedland. Now Murat wants to fight a duel with Junot!

Ridiculous. No such duel will take place.

Napoleon paces up and down, gripping the handle of his sword. He feels the contours of the Regent with his fingertips, the enormous diamond he has had set into his imperial blade. He learnt of Caroline and Junot's affair the day he got back to Paris. She must break it off immediately.

'It is my will,' he repeats.

Since his first audience yesterday, Tuesday, 28 July at eight o'clock, here in the palace of St Cloud, he has uttered these four words almost constantly. He wants things and he will no longer brook any discussion of his orders.

He has already decided to do away with the Tribunate. What use is this assembly of chatterers who discuss drafts of bills?

He has decided to change ministers. He wants to be done with Talleyrand. He observed him, at Tilsit, behaving not like a minister of foreign affairs at his Emperor's beck and call, but like a prince with his court, keeping his distance, an ironic look in his eye. But it gets worse. This minister is for hire, at all times.

'He's a man of many talents,' Napoleon says to Cambacérès when he announces the change of departments, 'but one can't do anything with him unless he's paid. The Kings of Bavaria and Würtemberg have made so many complaints to me about his rapaciousness that I am withdrawing his portfolio.'

Talleyrand will become Vice Grand Elector with four hundred

and ninety-five thousand francs a year. And Champagny will replace him. Berthier is made Vice Constable and Clarke becomes head of the War Office.

It is my will.

The ministers must be kept in hand. They are only executants, but they must set an example of submissiveness that the whole world must follow. In these ten months of imperial absence, people have developed bad habits. Some had even been hoping to hear the Emperor had died! He is sure of it.

NAPOLEON LOOKS at Caroline. He can read this ambitious woman's mind. It is not enough for her to be the Grand Duchess of Berg. If she has won a place in brave Junot's heart, it is undoubtedly because she is hoping, in the event of Napoleon's death, to be able to count on her passionate lover to propel Murat to the head of the Empire.

THERE ARE OTHER little conspiracies being hatched in the salons of St Germain, in the houses of the old nobility.

'The titles of Duke, Marquis and Baron are reappearing, coats of arms and liveries are being taken up again,' Napoleon says to Cambacérès. 'It was easy to foresee that, if these old habits were not replaced by new institutions, they would spring up again in no time.'

He leads Cambacérès by the arm through the palace's galleries.

'I want to create a nobility of the Empire; such a scheme is the only way of uprooting the old nobility entirely.'

NOW HE IS ALONE in the great reception room at St Cloud where it is already oppressively hot on this Wednesday, 29 July 1807. Napoleon has been slowly pacing about this palace he loves, slipping back into his old routine, recognizing the smell of the forest. He looks at himself in the mirrors that line the galleries. He has put on weight in these ten months of campaigning far from France. His face is rounded; he has lost more hair; he looks like a Roman emperor.

He takes a pinch of snuff.

The Return of Hadrian is playing in Paris in his honour. Rank boot-licking, he knows. Crowds have cheered him; the streets are lit up.

He wanted to visit the different quarters of the capital. He got out of his carriage at Palais-Royal and walked through the arcades where once women's scent had intoxicated him.

He was recognized; the shouts went up, 'Long live the Emperor!' All of a sudden he is pensive.

DESPITE Josephine's whining, he has chosen not to return to the marital bed, which he abandoned several years ago now. On his second night, he went to Éléonore Denuelle's house. She was as desirable and coquettish as ever, but with an unpleasant undertone of insolence and authoritativeness. She drew back the gauze veil covering the crib and he saw the child, Count Léon, a baby just over six months old, asleep.

His feelings suddenly welled up. This son is his, there can be no doubt about it. He can see it, feel it. He touches the round head.

He remembers Napoleon Charles, the joy he felt playing with Hortense and Louis's son, on the terrace at St Cloud, the same feeling of resemblance that he feels today. He had often said, 'I see myself in that child . . . He deserves to succeed me, he could even outdo me.'

Death has taken Napoleon Charles. Fate has imposed its law. Count Léon will not be my heir. But if I don't have a son, what will be the use of all these stones I am piling up, one on top of the other, to construct an imperial palace that will be heirless?

Even my sister Caroline anticipates my death.

And these brightly lit streets, this cheering, this bowing and scraping, this flattery, even the price of public stock, which is soaring – higher than it's ever been during his reign at ninety-three francs – what will become of all this when the Emperor's death is announced?

He feels alone in this welter of tributes coming from all sides. Neither the paper lanterns that light up Paris on 15 August to celebrate St Napoleon's day, his thirty-eighth birthday, nor the courtiers' compliments exhilarate him.

HE GOES OUT into the summer night accompanied just by Duroc. He wishes to mingle with the crowds taking the air in the Tuileries' gardens on this 15th of August, a holiday. No one notices him, but they cheer his name; he sees these disinterested folk applauding his victories.

These people reassure him. He laughs when Duroc tells him Fouché's remark on hearing of Talleyrand's new title, Vice Grand Elector, 'That vice was the only one he was missing; it'll be lost in the crowd.'

These people and the Fouchés and Talleyrands are a world apart!

He thinks of what he will say to the Legislative Body tomorrow. 'In all I have done, I have had in mind solely the welfare of my people, which is dearer to me than my own glory ... People of France, your conduct lately has increased still further the esteem and good opinion in which I hold your character. It has made me proud to be first amongst you.'

He loves this country, this people. He is deeply moved. He needs to confide in someone. He returns to the Tuileries and, alone in his study, writes,

My dear, sweet Marie,
    You who love your country so, you will understand the joy I feel to be back in France after almost a year's absence. This joy would be complete if you were here, but I have you in my heart.
    The Assumption is your name day and my birthday; this is a double reason for our souls to be in accord on this day. You have written to me, I'm sure, as I write to you now sending you my good wishes; this is the first such exchange. Let us pray that many others will follow over many years.
    Farewell, my sweet friend; you will come and join me. It will be soon, when affairs give me the liberty to send for you.
    Believe in my unfailing affection,
        N.

BUT HE KNOWS THAT 'affairs' never cease and that if he wants to see Marie Walewska again, it will have to be at moments stolen from his Emperor's days. He even thinks sometimes that they will never again share intimate moments as peaceful as those at Finkenstein Castle.

Here, in Paris, one audience follows after the other, the dispatches pile up and he has to visit the works that have started on the Louvre or the Pont d'Austerlitz. He must review the troops, write to the King of Würtemberg to confirm that the marriage between his daughter Catherine and Jérôme Bonaparte, King of Westphalia, will take place on 22 August.

He must constantly be on his guard.

He learns that the Austrians are recruiting fresh troops. He summons Champagny, the new minister of foreign affairs. 'I would like you to write a confidential letter to Monsieur Metternich – mild, measured but explicit – saying something as follows: What spirit of vertigo has seized the people of Vienna? You are calling the whole population to arms, your princes roam the countryside like knight errants ... How is one to prevent this becoming a crisis?'

After Champagny leaves, he remains lost in thought.

He feels as if he is being compelled to rush from one end of Europe to the other to shut the gates of war. They bang and when one is shut, the other swings open and the bolts knock against one another.

Austria is already arming. England is assembling a fleet at Copenhagen to compel Danish ships to join the English. Prussia refuses to pay the contributions it owes, and Portugal is not closing its ports to English merchandise.

How is one to stifle England if the continental blockade is not total and without exception?

HE SENDS FOR General Junot.

He walks up and down in front of his faithful comrade, whom he has known since his first engagement at the siege of Toulon. Napoleon slowly describes the army of twenty thousand he has decided to form at Bayonne in order, if Portugal refuses to apply the principle of the blockade, to occupy Lisbon, after crossing Spain, and impose the ban on English merchandise on the Portuguese.

Junot, Napoleon concludes, will be appointed General in Chief of this army.

He stops in front of Junot, who stammers, 'You're exiling me! What more could you have done if I had committed a crime?'

Napoleon takes a step closer and gives Junot a friendly clap on the back; Junot his aide-de-camp, his friend, his support in the dark days.

'You have not committed a crime, simply a mistake,' he says.

Junot must leave Paris for a while to make people forget his liaison with Caroline Murat.

Junot hangs his head.

'You will have unlimited authority,' Napoleon says to him as he sees him out. 'The marshal's baton awaits you there.'

These troops will be obliged to go and impose imperial law on Lisbon. Napoleon is certain that monarchs only see reason when they are defeated.

HOW CAN ONE fail to react, so long as England does not give up? In the sweltering, late August heat, as the religious marriage ceremony of Catherine of Würtemberg and Jérôme, King of Westphalia, is drawing to a close, Napoleon learns that English troops have landed on the Danish coast, and have begun constructing gun batteries to bombard Copenhagen. 'I feel deep indignation at this horrible crime,' Napoleon says.

These are the winds of war that are still blowing, buffeting that corner of Europe. He must face up to it, rely on his alliance with 'the powerful Emperor of the North'. Flatter him, show him that one is now family.

'This union between Catherine and Jérôme,' Napoleon writes to Alexander, 'is all the more agreeable because it establishes between Your Majesty and my brother family ties to which we attach the greatest price. I take this opportunity with genuine pleasure to convey to Your Majesty my satisfaction at the relations of friendship and trust that have recently been instituted between us, and to assure him that I shall leave nothing undone to cement and consolidate them.'

But what are friendship and trust worth in politics? And how long do they last?

XII

NAPOLEON WALKS SLOWLY through the galleries of Fontainebleau Palace. He does not like these October evenings. He feels sleep stealing up on him before they've properly begun. After a day's intense work, then hunting – he gallops for several hours at a stretch through the forests surrounding the palace – time often weighs heavy. He is bored.

At the door of the main drawing room where the Empress assembles her circle, he sees the women watching him approach. Which of them would balk if he chose her for the night? Not a single 'cruel soul', he told Josephine yesterday to provoke her, irritate her, add a bit of spice to one of those drab, pointless conversations that wear him out so quickly.

'You have only ever applied to souls who aren't like that,' Hortense retorted, sitting next to her mother.

That amused him, but the heavy weight of boredom quickly redescended. Even at the court theatre, which he has had fitted out and where actors from the Comédie-Française give performances twice a week, he can't stay awake. He knows *The Cid*, for instance, or *Cinna*, off by heart. He yawns through a play of Marmontel's, with music by Grétry, *The Friend of the House*. One ought not to have seen what he has seen, cannonballs falling around one, Queen Louise biting her lips in humiliation, anger and resentment, to enjoy these sorts of shows, which no longer divert him.

He prefers his study: the excitement of the dispatches, the constant necessity of coming up with a response, devising a plan, anticipating a policy, imagining. Ah, imagining! That is what keeps one awake!

OUT HUNTING earlier this afternoon, riding far ahead of his guests on horseback or, in the case of the women, crowded into barouches, he suddenly finds himself alone in a clearing, with no idea where he is any more. A Polish forest, or a German one? Fontainebleau forest?

He stays like that for a few minutes, swept up by his memories and his imagination.

HOW SHOULD HE respond to the English who, after bombarding Copenhagen for five days, have forced Denmark to capitulate and made off with the Danish fleet like pirates?

Cursed England! I must wring its neck.

That morning he has dictated a decree reinforcing the blockade. It must be fully effective from Holland to Portugal, from the Baltic to the Adriatic. He has been obliged to write to Louis to ensure that he will at last have Holland's ports closed to English goods. 'One is no sort of a king when one cannot make oneself obeyed in one's own country!' he tells him.

As for Portugal, 'I regard myself as at war with it,' he has explained to Champagny, who hasn't the abilities of Monsieur de Talleyrand but is undoubtedly the less venal.

Is it to be war again?

HIS HORSE STAMPS its feet in the clearing. Napoleon feels a wave of despair, imagining fresh forests in Portugal and in Spain too, perhaps, where so many men may be scythed down, which he will have to cross in all weathers.

But can he let the English dictate their law? Holland and Portugal must close their ports. The Adriatic must become a French lake. Russia must be an ally in this battle between land and sea.

As the pack draws nearer, filling the forest with its barking, once again he thinks, 'I am determined not to tread carefully any more with regard to England; since that power is the sovereign of the seas, the moment has come for me to be the ruler of the continent. In accord with Russia, there is no one I need fear now. The die has finally been cast.'

The stag races past, chased by the dogs that soon reappear in the clearing, tongues lolling out of their mouths, with nothing to show for their efforts.

Anger courses through Napoleon's veins.

What sort of pack is this? What sort of beaters?

He sets off alone for the hunting lodge which he has had comfortably furnished.

Madame de Barral is waiting for him.

He needs a woman to divert him for a few minutes. She is there with her thickset silhouette. Can he tell her what he thinks when he sees her, that all she's missing is an iron vest to look like a cuirassier, but that she couldn't take a charge?

SHE IS ONE OF THE women who are milling around the door of the Empress's salon that evening. She stands near Pauline, whose lady's companion she is.

He ignores Pauline's conspiratorial look. His sisters Pauline and Caroline – and not only them, Talleyrand and Fouché too – have their muffs or pockets lined with women for him. Even Josephine turns a blind eye, so long as it is solely a matter of brief encounters.

She is only afraid of one outcome – repudiation, divorce. She has been haunted by it since Léon, my son, was born and Napoleon Charles, Hortense's son, died.

She knows that I'm thinking of the future of the Empire and of my dynasty.

So then she pushes some woman or other towards the imperial bed, who won't be able to take her place on the throne.

She approved of Carlotta Gazzani, a member of her entourage, moving into one of the palace's apartments. What has she to fear from this beautiful Genoan? Josephine has never worshipped fidelity!

She knows how quickly ennui springs from the encounter of two bodies only seeking pleasure, and she knows Napoleon cannot abide ennui or any feeling of emptiness.

HE PACES ABOUT the Empress's salon. He sees Talleyrand in his full Vice Grand Elector's uniform. The Prince of Benevento's face seems even paler than usual, by contrast with his red velvet coat with gold facings, its sleeves covered with gold-lace embroidery from shoulder to wrist, his neck hidden by a lace cravat.

Napoleon takes him by the arm, leads him to a corner of the

room. 'It is a strange thing,' he says. 'I have gathered quite a number of people in Fontainebleau . . .'

He turns round and indicates with a wave the family of kings he has founded. There's the King of Westphalia, Jérôme, a handful of German princes, the Queens of Holland and Naples and sundry marshals and ministers.

'It has been my wish that people enjoy themselves; I have organized every pleasure.'

In consultation with the grand marshal of the palace, Duroc, he has determined the etiquette, and even the standards of dress to be observed by women at hunts and dinners. 'You know my taste in clothes is pretty good.'

He has arranged how evenings are to be spent. He has personally allocated the thirty-five apartments in the palace for princes and high officials, and its forty-six state apartments; the rest of the six hundred apartments go to the secretaries and servants. He has established the frequency of theatre performances and hunts.

Napoleon leans towards Talleyrand.

'Every pleasure,' he repeats, 'and yet . . .'

He points out the people surrounding them.

'. . . all these long faces; everyone looks very tired and sad.'

Talleyrand bows his head contritely.

'Pleasure does not march to the beat of the drum, Sire . . .' he murmurs. He raises his head.

Smile at him so he finishes what he's saying.

'Here just as in the army, Sire, you always seem to be saying to each of us, "Come now, ladies and gentlemen, quick march!"'

Napoleon laughs, does a tour of the room and then leaves.

NEXT MORNING he sends for Talleyrand. He watches him enter his study, which is lit by dim sunshine on this October morning. The fog has not yet cleared from Fontainebleau forest or the lakes in the park.

As usual, Talleyrand is impassive, distant, almost ironic. He is no longer the minister of foreign affairs, but this sagacious man can still be worth consulting.

Napoleon walks about the room, taking several pinches of snuff.

'We will only be able to arrive at peace by cutting England off from the continent and closing all ports to its commerce,' he begins.

Talleyrand agrees with an almost imperceptible nod of the head.

'For sixteen years Portugal has offered the scandalous example of a power sold to England,' Napoleon continues, his voice steadily growing louder and more impassioned. 'The port of Lisbon has been a mine of inexhaustible treasures for the English; they have constantly found every sort of resource there . . . It is time to close both Porto and Lisbon to them.'

Talleyrand isn't moving a muscle.

Clever man.

Napoleon goes towards him.

'I have ordered Junot to pass the Pyrenees and cross Spain. I am impatient for my army to arrive in Lisbon. I have written all this to the King of Spain.'

'Charles IV is a Bourbon,' murmurs Talleyrand. 'His son Ferdinand, Prince of the Asturias, is the great-grandson of Louis XIV. Queen Maria Luisa has a favourite, Manuel de Godoy, the Prince of the Peace, as he is known. He is the one who governs, with the agreement and indulgence of the King.'

Talleyrand smiles.

'Charles IV is a Bourbon,' he repeats. 'He has, so one is assured, the character of Louis XVI.'

BOURBONS! He has already thought of this many times, but Talleyrand has stressed it, in that way he has of cleverly choosing and steering one in a particular direction without seeming to say anything.

Talleyrand leaves the study and several times Napoleon exclaims, 'Bourbons!'

He remembers Louis XVI, that craven king whom he saw not daring to fight on 20 June 1792.

The Bourbons: a spent dynasty!

Napoleon seizes the letters that Ferdinand, the Prince of Asturias, heir to the Spanish crown, has sent him, soliciting the hand of a Bonaparte princess in marriage (him, the great grandson of Louis XVI!), and snivelling like a woman, accusing Godoy, his mother the Queen's lover, of trying to supplant him.

A Bourbon!

And here is the father's letter. Napoleon rereads it, waving it as if it were soiling his fingers. Charles IV writes,

> My eldest son, heir presumptive to the throne, has formed the horrible plot to dethrone me. He has gone to such extremes as to make an attempt on his mother's life; such an appalling crime must be punished with the most exemplary rigours of the law ... I do not wish to lose a moment in instructing Your Imperial and Royal Majesty in this matter and ask for the assistance of Your knowledge and counsel.

Napoleon throws the letter aside.

Bourbons!

The son denounces the mother's lover, the father protects that lover and accuses the son of wanting to murder the mother, then has him arrested.

The Bourbons: a dying race.

I WAS BORN from the fall of the Bourbons. They tried to assassinate me and I had the Duke d'Enghien executed. I drove the Bourbons out of Naples.

I have had the Tsar expel from Russia the Bourbon who claims to be Louis XVIII and tried to buy me. Me!

By dethroning the Spanish Bourbons, I could create an Empire the equal of Charlemagne's.

HE HAS GIVEN HIS imagination free rein. Such an expansion is only a vision; the time hasn't yet come. For the moment, Portugal is the question.

He sits down to calm himself. Dreams are like wine: they warm one up, banish the ennui.

He dictates a letter to Junot, who is marching towards Lisbon.

'There is not a moment to lose if we are to forestall the English ... I hope that on 1 December my troops will be in Lisbon.'

That's all for today – but how can one forget one's dreams?

Napoleon walks back towards his secretary and dictates a final sentence. 'I do not need to tell you that we mustn't put the Spanish in charge of any fortresses.'

Yet the Spanish are already allies with whom Champagny has been ordered to sign a secret convention, organizing the partition of Portugal between Madrid and Paris.

No fortress, especially in a country that is to remain in my hands.

HE ENTERS THE LONG gallery at Fontainebleau where he entertains the ambassadors of the various powers. He stops in front of Monsieur de Metternich, says a few words to the Austrian diplomat in an indifferent voice.

In a salon, one must act strategically too.

He heads for the Portuguese ambassador and vehemently cries, as if launching a surprise attack, 'If Portugal does not do what I want, the House of Braganza will no longer reign in Europe within two months.'

Then, for all to hear, like an artillery salvo, he says, 'I will not suffer there to be a single English envoy in Europe ... I have three hundred thousand Russians at my disposal and, with such a powerful ally, I can do anything.'

He passes along the row of ambassadors, like a general inspecting the enemy officers he has captured.

'The English declare that they do not wish to recognize neutrals at sea any more. Well, I shall no longer recognize them on land.'

He walks away.

'I have more than eight hundred thousand men equipped and ready,' he says before leaving the gallery.

HE GOES OFF TO HUNT. He goes off to dream.

XIII

NAPOLEON GESTURES to Fouché to take a seat, but the minister of police remains standing. Napoleon observes him. Fouché is holding a portfolio in his hand.

His expression is even more inscrutable than usual. Deep lines furrow his cheeks and frame his mouth. His cheekbones are high, his lips so thin they're almost invisible. A stony face, Napoleon thinks.

What does Fouché want? He is not the sort of man to request an audience for trivial reasons or travel from Paris to Fontainebleau simply to pay court.

'Monsieur the Duke of Otranto,' begins Napoleon.

Fouché inclines his head. Perhaps he wishes to talk about the expedition to Portugal or Spain's affairs which are becoming complicated.

A new letter has arrived from Charles IV. Ferdinand, Prince of the Asturias, has now acknowledged his wrongs and eaten humble pie.

'Outrageous!' exclaims Napoleon.

He has decided to send a new army of twenty-five thousand men under the command of General Dupont into Spain to support Junot's troops. They are advancing by the Lisbon road, climbing the rugged massifs of the Iberian mountains in heavy rain and freezing winds.

What, he wonders, does the Duke of Otranto think of these Bourbons, regicide that he was?

Fouché remains silent, still standing, his eyelids so heavy one cannot see his eyes.

The silence is irritating. Napoleon turns away from Fouché.

'Talleyrand assures me that several thousand men will suffice to put an end to the Spanish Bourbons.'

'Do not misjudge the character of the peoples of the peninsula, Sire.'

Napoleon looks fixedly at Fouché. His face still has no expression; the eyes have stayed half-shut.

'Take care,' Fouché continues. 'The Spaniard is not phlegmatic like the German; he prizes his customs, his government, his habits. I say again, take care not to transform a tribute-paying kingdom into a second Vendée.'

'Monsieur the Duke of Otranto . . .'

Napoleon starts to pace up and down the salon.

'What are you saying?' he continues. 'Every reasonable individual in Spain despises the government. As for that motley rabble you are talking about, still in thrall to monks and priests, a volley of cannonfire will disperse them. You saw Prussia's army . . .'

He stops in front of Fouché.

'Frederick the Great's patrimony crumbled before our armies like an old club. Well then, if I wish it, you will see Spain fall into my hands without even realizing, and then applaud it afterwards.'

Fouché remains impassive.

Napoleon goes to the window. The wind is shaking the autumnal, russet leaves off the tall trees in the forest.

He walks slowly back towards Fouché. He has decided nothing so far. He has simply asked his chamberlain, Monsieur de Tournon, to go to Madrid to deliver a reply to Charles IV, gather information about the state of the country, its army, its posts, and also carefully examine the state of public opinion.

Is Monsieur the Duke of Otranto satisfied?

Fouché slowly raises his arm and displays the portfolio he is holding in his hand. He wants to read a memo to His Majesty, he says. This is why he is here.

'Read?'

Napoleon sits down and gestures to him.

Fouché begins to read in his metallic voice.

NAPOLEON LISTENS to Fouché who says, without meeting his eyes, that the welfare of the Empire demands that the Emperor dissolve his marriage, form a better matched, more harmonious bond immediately and provide an heir for the throne, onto which Providence has caused the Emperor to ascend.

Fouché eventually falls silent and closes the portfolio.

How to reply?

The words fail him. Fouché has always been an acute thinker. He guesses and senses a great deal.

In my mind the decision to divorce has been taken. It is, as Fouché has said, a political necessity. But how can I break with Josephine without destroying her or humiliating her?

How can I separate from her, when she has seen me climb all the steps of destiny? How can I not fear that breaking with her will not be the downfall of my lucky star?

Unless she consents to a divorce, unless she is protected in this upheaval to the extent that she resolves on it herself — or even better that she suggests it.

Her understanding of my situation must disarm fate and protect me from its vengeance.

Napoleon dismisses Fouché.

HE NEEDS to be alone.

He thinks about this divorce constantly. When he looks at Josephine, she is sad more often than not, as if crushed by the death of her grandson, Napoleon Charles.

Caroline and Pauline and his mother are birds of prey watching for the moment when the repudiation will finally come. Anyway, they have already turned their backs on her, preferring Caroline Murat's salon at the Élysée, where Fouché and Talleyrand plot. They all want this divorce.

But Napoleon hadn't imagined that Fouché could have such a nerve.

Fouché must be the one spreading the rumours round Paris that he's heard from police spies. The divorce is settled, people are saying in the salons. Napoleon hesitates, observes Josephine all through evenings when she presides over dinners or her circle. She is touching in this despair that she cannot conceal. Sometimes she looks at him like a drowning woman.

He turns his head, leaves the room, shuts himself in his study.

What can he do? Adopt Count Léon? He has seen Éléonore Denuelle's child again, wide awake this time and full of energy. He picked him up. He was touched but, at the same time,

Éléonore's pretentious chatter irritated him. He'd happily have this child, but he does not want the mother. He can't have her. He is the Emperor. He needs a mother and son that measure up to his dynasty. Has he arranged better marriages for his brothers than for himself?

He rebels.

He goes hunting so that the wind, as he gallops through the forest, will sweep away this consuming obsession.

WHEN HE RETURNS to the palace, Josephine is there, waiting for him, huddled up, her eyes full of tears. Fouché spoke to her in a window recess when she was coming back from Mass. He has asked her – after a thousand circumlocutions, of course – to perform 'the most sublime and at the same time most inevitable of sacrifices'. Those were his words. Was he speaking on the Emperor's orders? Does Napoleon want to repudiate her?

He looks at her for a long time. He remembers what she has been to him. He takes her in his arms.

'Fouché acted on his own initiative,' he murmurs.

'Well, then get rid of him,' she says, clasping him to her.

Napoleon pulls away. Fouché acted for political reasons, he explains without looking at her. Will she understand that by saying that, by refusing to dismiss Fouché, he is revealing his thoughts? But he can't, nor does he want to, separate from her yet.

He goes back to her, reassures her.

Only he will choose the moment. He will decide alone.

ON THURSDAY, 5 November 1807, when he returns to his study after this night spent with Josephine, he writes a letter so fast, that the paper is dotted all over with ink blots,

> Monsieur Fouché, for the last fortnight it has been reported to me that you commit nothing but follies; it is time you put an end to them and cease meddling directly or indirectly in a matter that could not concern you in any way. Such is my will,
> Napoleon

He has closed the drawer in his mind marked divorce. For the moment. He is even surprised he has devoted so much time to it.

He does not hold it against Fouché. Perhaps this has prepared the way for the future.

HE GETS UP ON Friday with a feeling of lightness. The great things he has to accomplish will not wait. He sends for the minister of the interior, Crétet. What stage have the main projects reached? What has been done to put an end to begging?

'I have made the glory of my reign change the face of my Empire,' he says.

He examines the projects. Let us open 'sixty or a hundred establishments for the eradication of begging', he says. To work, energy! 'Hurry this along and see that you don't fall asleep on your routine office work!'

Will this minister understand?

'One must not tread this earth without leaving some traces that will commend one's memory to posterity,' he exclaims, then calls in Constant. Today – all day – he wants to wear his St Andrew ribbon, which he was awarded by the Tsar. Men are sensitive to these sort of trivial details, and he is receiving the new Russian ambassador, Count Tolstoy.

HE WALKS TOWARDS Count Tolstoy in the great gallery at Fontainebleau. He must smile, charm him – this alliance with Russia is necessary – but this pale-complexioned man does not please him. Count Tolstoy responds in monosyllables. He does not thank him for the residence he has been given, a town house on rue Cerutti which has been bought from Murat. He is evasive when questioned.

What sort of ambassador has the Tsar sent me?

When he does say a word, it is to demand the evacuation of French troops from Prussia.

'The Prussians will play you more dirty tricks,' says Napoleon.

Evacuate Prussia? Why not? He takes Tolstoy by the arm and senses him stiffen.

'But one does not move an army the way one takes a pinch of snuff,' Napoleon adds.

The ambassador does not smile; he does not even seem to have noticed the ribbon of St Andrew.

This man seems worried by every mark of attention I show him. Does he know what happened at Tilsit between Alexander and me? Still, I need a Russian alliance. Reality always imposes its law.

And so he has to be solicitous all day, and show Tolstoy every consideration.

NEXT DAY HE SENDS for the grand equerry, Caulaincourt.

'I need a man of good birth at Petersburg,' he says. 'A man whose manners, dignity and attentiveness towards women and society will meet with the court's approval. Savary wants to stay in Petersburg, but he is not right there. Alexander is well-disposed towards you . . .'

He moves closer to Caulaincourt. He knows the grand equerry doesn't want to be his ambassador in Russia.

'You are headstrong, Caulaincourt.'

He pinches his ear.

'World peace is to be found in Petersburg, you have to go.'

What does it matter to me if Caulaincourt refuses this ambassador's post again?

'It is the beautiful Madame de Canisy who keeps you in Paris.'

He pinches Caulaincourt's ear once more.

'Your affairs, since you wish to be married, will be more easily arranged at a distance than in close proximity.'

This is how it is. One does not argue: one obeys; one listens.

Napoleon starts pacing back and forth, his hands behind his back.

'This Monsieur de Tolstoy thinks just like the faubourg St Germain, and he has all of the prejudices of the old Petersburg court before Tilsit,' he says. 'All he sees is French ambition and he fundamentally deplores Russia's change of policy, especially regarding England.'

Napoleon shrugs.

'He may be a very gallant man, but his stupidity makes me miss Markov.* One could talk to him, he understood matters. This one takes fright at everything.'

---

* Former Russian ambassador to Paris who was recalled at the end of 1803 after complaints from Napoleon.

BUT WHAT WEIGHT do the prejudices and reservations of Count Tolstoy actually carry?

'The people want liberal ideas,' Napoleon tells Jérôme, his brother whom he has put on the throne of Westphalia. 'They want equality. For many years now I have conducted the affairs of Europe and I have had reason to be convinced that the buzzing of the privileged classes is antithetical to public opinion.'

He stops, leaves his study.

The sentence he has just dictated troubles him. Is he certain of that? Since he came to power, hasn't he been trying to win over the privileged classes of the old nobility? Doesn't he want to form a dynasty that will be an ally of the old ruling families?

He returns to his study, pushes aside the letter he was writing to Jérôme. He feels hesitant, torn. He can't stand it.

HE'S GOING TO LEAVE Fontainebleau château, he announces suddenly, to go to Italy. It is two years since he last visited that kingdom, in spring 1807, whose iron crown he wears. It is time to go back.

He barely responds to Josephine's demands to come too.

He is also going there to get away from her, not to have to see that face whose sadness is a reproach.

'Can you believe that that woman cries whenever she has indigestion, because she thinks she has been poisoned by the people who want me to marry someone else? It's loathsome,' he says impatiently to Duroc.

Perhaps he'll be able to come to a decision in Italy.

Suddenly he remembers Augusta of Bavaria's sister, Charlotte. He organized Augusta's marriage to Eugène de Beauharnais. What if he marries Charlotte? He feverishly dictates a letter to the King and Queen of Bavaria inviting them to meet him at Verona with their daughter. We'll see there!

Then, on 15 November, the day before his departure for Milan, he is again assailed by doubts. He resumes his letter to Jérôme.

'Be a constitutional king,' he writes to him.

Not that Napoleon is one. He has chosen to combine the old and the new, to clothe liberal ideas in the tawdry finery of old prejudices, whose importance he has come to understand. That is why he has woven this plot with the ruling families. That's why he is going to meet the King and Queen of Bavaria in Verona. But Jérôme shouldn't misunderstand him: 'The majority of your Council must be made up of men not born into the nobility,' he writes. Smiling, he then adds, 'Without anyone failing to observe the habitual benevolence involved in maintaining the third estate's majority in all positions of employ.'

For, if he is certain that it is never the past that carries the day, he knows one must still use guile. Even when one is Emperor of Kings.

XIV

NAPOLEON BEGINS TO HUM. His carriage has barely left the courtyard of Fontainebleau, on Monday, 16 November 1807, and already he feels cheerful. He remembers the words of the song his soldiers often strike up when he rides along the ranks before a battle,

> Napoleon is the Emperor
> Valour's stout adventurer
> Enemies quail at his merest glance
> Shield and hope of our beloved France . . .

He laughs, pinches the ear of his secretary who is sitting next to him in the berline.

He feels rejuvenated, free of the burden of Josephine's tearful presence.

She hasn't been able to give him a son. She bore her children before meeting him. Is that his fault? Isn't it legitimate for him to want a son to succeed him? It's the demands of his dynasty, his politics.

He is going to resolve this question, since it is already settled in his mind. Will it be a German princess, Charlotte of Bavaria, or a Russian grand duchess? He laughs again, then continues the song,

> He comes to restore it to all its splendour
> Hail him, the true defender!

He feels as if he is heading towards a second youth.

He leans out of the window. He loves this road which leads through the Bourbonnais to Lyon, Chambéry and Milan. It's the road to Italy where his fate was decided, at Lodi, Arcola and Marengo. He proved there what he could become. At Campo Formio, he began to draw up a new map of Europe. He is revisiting the scene of his glorious youth, but he has become an

Emperor and King and he is going to gather around him all the sovereigns he has crowned who are his vassals.

He sings,

> Surely this is a second Charlemagne
> Who ensures the welfare of France, of all our kind.

He is happy to be alone, at last, a young Emperor of thirty-eight to whom everything is promised and everything permitted.

THERE'S CHEERING when he enters Milan Cathedral on Sunday, 22 November, to attend a Te Deum.

That evening, at La Scala, the standing ovations go on and on. He looks at the women; he makes the men drop their eyes. He gathers together the ministers, gives orders to Eugène de Beauharnais, the viceroy, and goes to Augusta of Bavaria's bedside, this wife he has given him.

He walks slowly through Milan's streets. He loves the cheering, the homage people pay him when he grants them an audience. He feels happier than in Paris. He is free of the ties that sometimes fetter him in France. Here he is Emperor and King. There, Talleyrand, Fouché, Josephine and his sisters remember that once he was just a Bonaparte and that they contributed to his glory. Josephine is that past; now he wants to experience the future.

He writes a few hurriedly scribbled lines to her.

> I have been here, my friend, for two days. I am very glad not to
> have brought you; you would have suffered horribly crossing
> Mt Cenis, where a blizzard held me up for 24 hours.
>   I have found Eugène in good health: I am very pleased with
> him. Princess Augusta is ill; I went to see her in Monza; she has
> had a miscarriage; she is better now.
>   Farewell my friend,
>   Napoleon

IT IS RAINING in the Po Valley, but what does it matter? He recognizes these hills, these poplars bordering the wash of rivers, these towns: Brescia, Peshiera and lastly Verona.

Crowds line the roads and throng the streets and wait in front of Verona's theatre which he attends with Elisa, Princess of Lucca, Joseph, King of Naples and the King and Queen of Bavaria.

He only needs to take one look at their daughter. Charlotte is ugly. Why didn't he marry Augusta?

In his bedroom in Strà Castle, near Padua, where he spends the night of Saturday, 28 November, he receives the dispatches from Paris. The newspapers are still going on in a roundabout way about the repudiation of Josephine.

He is enraged. He decides to write to Maret, his secretary of state; the letter must go immediately.

'It troubles me to see from your reports that people are continuing to talk about subjects that must pain the Empress and are in every way improper.'

This woman must not be persecuted: he has loved her and he will leave her at the time of his choosing.

Irritated, he sleeps badly. He issues his orders in a curt voice. The cheering in the small port of Fusina irritates him too, and he goes aboard the frigate, which is to him to Venice, with his head bowed and his hands behind his back.

IT IS A BEAUTIFUL day. A breeze swells the sails; the flotilla of the Adriatic arrays itself around him.

Suddenly he sees the Grand Canal, the Basilica San Giorgio, the maritime customs house and a mass of craft and flower-decked gondolas heading towards his frigate. Cheers and fanfares ring out when he steps onto the Piazzetta.

It is five o'clock on the afternoon of Sunday, 29 November 1807.

A great wave of joy snatches him up. He instals himself in the Palazzo Balbi on the Grand Canal. From his window, he looks out at the interplay of the elements. He is the ruler of one of the oldest republics in the world, the Doge's successor. He attends the Fenice Theatre, surrounded by generals who fought the Italian campaign with him. Kings and queens flock round him.

He wants to see everything, the canals, the lagoons, the palazzi, the library.

He gives instructions that from now on bodies are to be buried on an island, and not in churches where there is a danger they will contaminate the city. He strides across the Piazza San Marco. He likes its theatricality: it's like a stage set; he wants it to be lit.

Standing at the window of the Palazzo Balbi, he waits for a woman to join him, a Venetian countess with long hair who he noticed at the Fenice.

He possesses her; he possesses the world. He feels as if nothing can resist him.

The next morning, before leaving Venice, he signs the decrees he issued at Milan which reinforce the continental blockade. Since England is demanding that neutral vessels land at one of her ports before touching Europe, he has decided that any ship that submits to this law is to be regarded as English and their cargoes are fair game.

If one wants to rule, one must impose one's law.

He writes to Junot whose troops have just entered Lisbon, 'You act like a man who has no experience of conquest, you indulge in vain illusions: the people before you are your enemy ... The Portuguese nation is brave.'

I must bend men to my will.

HE REPEATS THIS phrase, sitting at a large round table in Mantua's fortress on Sunday, 13 December, the day he arrives.

He has a map of Spain spread out in front of him. He studies the relief, and carefully sticks in coloured pins to mark the route his troops will take if he decides to make Spain submit, impose his law on it, and replace those incapable, flabby Bourbons.

He hears the door shut. He forces himself not to look up, although he knows that his brother Lucien, the rebellious Lucien, has just entered the room, having come from Rome where he still lives with that Madame Alexandrine Jouberthon, whom he refuses to leave.

I must bend men to my will.

Lucien should divorce and return to the imperial family fold like Jérôme, because it is in the dynasty's interests that his daughter Charlotte be in a position to marry Ferdinand, the Prince of the Asturias.

Eventually Napoleon stands up.

He is overwhelmed by a rush of emotion. He has not seen Lucien for years, this brother who may have saved him from the delegates' stilettos on 18 Brumaire, but has since opposed him. He embraces him, presses him to his breast.

'Well then, it really is you . . . You look very well; you were too thin, but now I find you almost handsome.'

Napoleon takes a pinch of snuff.

'I am well too,' he adds, 'but I am putting on too much weight and I fear I will put on more.'

He barely listens as Lucien talks about his wife, his honour, his religion, his duties.

'And politics, sir?' Napoleon exclaims. 'Politics? Does it count for nothing for you? You always say your wife . . . I have never recognized her, I never will recognize her . . . a woman who entered my family against my wishes, a woman for whom you have deceived me . . . I know that you were useful to me on the 18th of Brumaire . . .'

He breaks off, and then states flatly, 'What I want is a divorce, pure and simple.'

He looks at Lucien for a long time, but his brother does not lower his eyes.

'To my mind, Sire,' Lucien murmurs, 'separation, divorce, nullity of marriage and anything else that would pertain to a separation from my wife appear dishonourable, both for myself and for my children, and I will do nothing of the sort, I can assure you . . .'

'Listen to me carefully, Lucien, and weigh up everything I say. Most of all, let us keep our tempers.'

He paces about the room, breathing heavily.

'I am too powerful to wish to put myself in a position where I risk becoming angry. However . . .'

He walks back towards Lucien.

'If you're not with me, I tell you, Europe is too small for the two of us.'

A log collapses in the fireplace with a loud crash.

Napoleon takes another pinch of snuff. He finds this brother who resists him irritating and fascinating.

'I don't want any tragedies, do you understand?'

He must compose himself, talk to his brother, speak of Josephine, 'that woman who cries every time she has indigestion'. He has already said this to Duroc, but Lucien has to know that the Emperor himself is determined to go through with the divorce.

'I am not helpless, as you all used to say,' Napoleon continues. 'I am in love, but always in a manner subordinate to my politics, and this dictates that I marry a princess although I would much prefer to crown my mistress. This is how I would like to see you with your wife.'

'Sire, I would think like Your Majesty if my wife were merely my mistress.'

'Come now, come now, I see you're absolutely incorrigible.'

He puts his hand on Lucien's shoulder.

'You should stay with me for three days: I'll have a bed set up next to my chamber.'

Lucien shakes his head. He talks about one of his children who is ill.

'Well then, go, since that's your wish, but abide by our agreement.'

THE NIGHT IS OVER. This discussion has exhausted him more than any night of battle.

Unshakeable Lucien! My brother who never bends. Will I always meet the fiercest resistance from my family?

He wants to explain himself. He writes to Joseph, the elder brother whom he has made King of Naples.

My brother, I saw Lucien at Mantua. I spoke with him for several hours. His thoughts and his way of expressing them are so far from mine that I had trouble understanding what he wanted. I think he promised to send his eldest daughter to Paris, to be with her grandmother . . . I have exhausted all the means in my power – and he is still quite a young man – to persuade Lucien to employ his talents for me and his country; I don't know what argument he can put forward against this arrangement. His children's interests are safe; I have provided for everything . . . Once the divorce with Madame Jouberthon has been pronounced, if he chooses to live with her in whatever form of intimacy he wishes, although not as if she were a princess and his wife, I will not oppose it in any way. For it is politics alone that interests me in this matter. Henceforth, I have no desire to interfere in Lucien's tastes or passions. These are my proposals. He must send me a declaration that his daughter is setting out for Paris and that he is placing her entirely at my disposition, for there is not a moment to lose. Events are marching rapidly and destinies must be fulfilled . . .

IT IS THURSDAY, 24 December 1807. He sets out from Milan at six in the morning to return to Paris.

PART FOUR

*When my great ship of state
is launched, it must pass.
Woe betide anyone
who finds himself in its path*

XV

HE IS IN PARIS, at last. The journey seemed interminable; rain, hail, wind, bumpy roads. After Turin, he decided not to travel by stages, but straight through, and ordered that his carriage only stop long enough for the horses to be changed at the double.

He knows that Marie is here, in Paris, having arrived from Warsaw with her brother. She is waiting for him. Duroc has installed her in a town house, 48 rue de la Victoire.

Napoleon leaps down from the carriage and stalks across the courtyard of the Tuileries. It is 1 January 1808. Despite the cold night air, the ministers and dignitaries hurry down the steps to greet him. The palace is lit up. He ignores them, makes for Talleyrand and leads him off to the drawing room by his study.

Marie is here, but there are decisions to be made. Politics is his only unconditional mistress. He cannot join Marie if he hasn't ordered his thoughts first.

DURING THE week's journey from Milan to Paris, he has written, dictated and thought a great deal.

He has given orders for fresh troops to enter Spain. He must be ready to seize the opportunity, if it presents itself, of subjugating this kingdom to the Emperor. 'A country of monks and priests which needs a revolution!' he mutters, turning to Talleyrand. And as all things are interconnected, he adds, he has demanded that General Miollis occupy Rome, since Pius VII doggedly refuses to ban relations between the Pontifical States and England.

Marie is here, but he needs to confer with Talleyrand. With a word, he silences the litary of conventional observations and compliments which the Prince of Benevento has embarked upon. What does Talleyrand think of the situation in Spain?

'If war flares up there,' Napoleon says, 'everything would be lost. Politics and negotiations are the appropriate realm for deciding Spain's destiny.'

Talleyrand agrees, bows his head. 'The Spanish crown has

belonged to France's ruling family since Louis XIV,' he murmurs. 'It is therefore one of the finest shares of the great king's legacy.'

He raises the tone of his voice.

'And the Emperor should recoup this legacy in its entirety; he should not, he cannot, give any part of it up.'

Napoleon looks at Talleyrand for a long time. The vice grand elector is rarely so forthright in his opinions.

'And Turkey, the Indies?' asks Napoleon. 'France and Russia together . . .'

He has cherished this dream of the Orient for such a long time! Perhaps this is the moment to make it a reality, with the help of Alexander.

Talleyrand seems pensive. He must press him, make him speak.

'If Russia obtains Constantinople and the Dardanelles,' Talleyrand says finally, 'we will be able, I believe, to make it envisage anything without anxiety.'

Talleyrand then speaks at length of the relative positions of the different powers. England is determined to wage war to the death. Austria may be an ally. Prussia is already stirring again. Russia wishes to conquer Finland and the Danube provinces and, with the support of France, get to the sea and Constantinople, its great, abiding ambition.

Napoleon listens. He has needed this long conversation with Talleyrand, to immerse himself in the implacable order of the world the minute he got back to Paris. Their conversation, he suddenly realizes, has lasted five hours. He dismisses Talleyrand with a nod. Now it is for him to decide.

THE NIGHT IS ALREADY far advanced. He tells Constant to go and fetch Marie Walewska and bring her to his apartment by the hidden staircase.

The Empress will not dare come in without being announced. In fact, she has taken to burying herself away. She is so afraid of divorce that she would rather make herself forgotten, as if discretion were enough to render her immune to repudiation, her abiding nightmare.

He waits for Marie in a fever of anticipation. It is months since he has seen this 'angel'. The other women, those of just a few nights, are nothing.

In taking them in my arms, I rid myself of them and of the desire to win them . . .

But Marie . . .

Constant opens the door, stands aside

She is just as he left her, so young, so unspoilt. She is his greatest luxury, his blessing, 'My Polish wife'.

She loves him for who he is and not for what he gives or promises.

NEXT MORNING he sends for the grand marshal of the palace. From now on Duroc is to watch over Marie Walewska. He is to receive his instructions from her every morning and ask Doctor Corvisart to inform himself regularly about her health.

A fleeting smile crosses his face, then he sits down at his desk.

This matter is settled. Let us take a look at the dispatches.

But when he is reading the first one, he looks at Duroc again and smiles at him for longer, as one does to an accomplice.

He feels well, as if he has just added a happy chapter to his life, and he thanks destiny for its generosity.

Marie's being in Paris seems proof that everything is possible when one is able to seize what destiny offers without hesitating and furnish oneself with the means to keep it. One must be organized, anticipate the obstacles and circumvent them.

Destiny proposes, but everything is also a question of will and strategy, in love as in war.

DURING THAT JANUARY of 1808, Napoleon feels gripped by a joyful determination, as if he is only a little way from the summit, having been able to cling to every purchase life has offered and haul himself up day after day.

But sometimes in the morning, when Constant and Roustam are dressing him, he has a moment of distress.

He sees how much weight he has put on, his protruding stomach that is becoming unmistakable, his fleshy face. In a fit of bad temper, he rejects a pair of breeches that are too tight. He rushes Constant who is busy suggesting another pair, another frockcoat. He puts them on impatiently, his face sombre. Might his body be getting out of his control?

Sometimes he has violent pains in his stomach and the image of his father haunts him. He remembers the autopsy report, the stomach cancer the doctors diagnosed Charles Bonaparte as suffering from.

He remains hunched over for a few seconds, then straightens up. He orders his horse saddled. He wants to go hunting, despite the cold, to bend this body to his will, to prove to himself that all the old vigour and energy are still there inside him.

He starts his horse off at full gallop. He loves the wind that lashes his face, brushing aside all anxiety. He races along the rides in the woods. He can hunt at whichever of his residences he pleases: the Tuileries, St Cloud, Malmaison, Fontainebleau, Bois de Vincennes and Rancy, in the Versailles or St Germain's forests.

He takes Count Tolstoy with him. It fills him with joy to outride the ambassador and then find him in a clearing, exhausted and chilled to the bone. He expresses naïve surprise. 'Tired, Count?'

This Monsieur de Tolstoy is a fine fellow, brimming with prejudices and mistrust of France. He must convince him.

When they return from the hunt, he invites him to follow him to the Tuileries.

He reassures this cold man, who, his police spies inform him, attends the salons of the faubourg St Germain as assiduously as ever, and has even fallen in love with Madame de Récamier, that unbearable woman and friend of Madame de Staël. But he must tolerate this fellow.

NAPOLEON SHOWS Tolstoy to a chair and begins to walk up and down in front of him.

'Imagine an army of five hundred thousand men,' he begins. 'Russian and French and perhaps Austrian as well, marching via Constantinople on Asia. It would only have to reach the Euphrates for it to make England tremble and go down on its knees before the Continent. Nothing would stop it reaching the Indies . . .'

He pauses in front of Count Tolstoy; he longs to seize him by the shoulders and shake him. He cannot stand that sceptical look.

'It's not a reason to fail in this enterprise, the fact that Alexander and Tamerlane were not successful,' he resumes.

He stamps his feet.

'It is simply a matter of doing better than them,' he booms.

Does this man understand what I'm saying to him?

Napoleon picks up his hat with both hands and hurls it to the ground, then, pacing back and forth, stopping frequently in front of the ambassador, he says in an irritated, urgent voice, 'Listen, Monsieur de Tolstoy, this is no longer the Emperor of the French speaking to you but one major-general speaking to another.'

He breaks off, and leans down towards Tolstoy.

'I shall be the vilest of men if I do not scrupulously fulfil what I contracted to do at Tilsit, and if I do not evacuate Prussia and the Duchy of Warsaw when you have withdrawn your troops from Moldavia and Wallachia!'

He straightens up.

'How could you doubt that? I am neither a madman nor a child not to know what I have contracted, and what I have contracted I always fulfil!'

A FEW MOMENTS later, Napoleon watches Tolstoy leaving, accompanied by the grand marshal of the palace.

With a kick, he sends his hat skidding across the room.

Even if he changes what I said, Tolstoy will talk about my anger and the hat I threw on the ground.

There is always a moment with men when one must back up words with gestures, a movement of one's body, feigned anger. One must surprise them, terrify them, so that they submit or simply remember. One must also know how to seduce them, as women do. He calls in Méneval.

He catches the look his secretary darts at his hat, and sees the way he hunches his shoulders, as if a storm is brewing.

For those who serve and surround him, for all the citizens of his Empire, whether peasantry or kings, he must be an invisible threat, an unforeseeable act of kindness, a mystery – the man above them all who they venerate and fear. The one who rewards them more richly than they could imagine and punishes with a rod of iron.

This is how one reigns; it applies to everybody. It requires a will that is active at every moment. It would be so easy to be 'good', to give in to those who one commands, to renounce one's goal, to delight in inactivity.

He signals to Méneval. He wants to write to Alexander to confirm what he has said to Tolstoy and evoke a joint march to the Euphrates and the Indies, for the purpose of threatening the English from the East.

> Your Majesty and I would have preferred the pleasures of peace and to pass our lives in the middle of our vast empires, regenerating them and making them happy . . . The enemies of the world do not wish it.
>
> We must become greater in spite of ourselves.
>
> It is both wise and politic to do what destiny ordains and to go where the irresistible march of events leads us.
>
> Then this swarm of pygmies who only want to see whether the events of today are such as to invite comparison with history, rather than newspaper accounts of last century, will yield . . . And the Russian people will be content with the glory, the wealth and the fortune that will be the result of these events . . . What was done at Tilsit will rule the destiny of the world.
>
> A little faint-heartedness led us to prefer a certain and immediate benefit to a better and more perfect result; but since England will not accept it, let us recognize that the time has come for great changes and great events.

HE WANTS THESE great events to happen. He anticipates them, instigates them, organizes them. He submits himself to their march.

A dispatch Méneval puts on his desk reports that General Miollis's troops have entered Rome. Pius VII is going to submit. An end, at last, to the Court of Rome's boundless impertinence.

He calls Méneval back. Actions must be seen through to their conclusions. He dictates a letter to Eugène, Viceroy of Italy.

'The slightest outbreak of insurrection must be repressed with grapeshot, and severe examples must be made.'

He takes a pinch of snuff, then goes into the Topographical Office. He leans over the desk where the map of Spain is spread out. That's where the game's afoot.

There needs to be a single hand controlling all the troops advancing in extended order through the peninsula.

Why not Murat?

He goes back to the study. 'Murat is a hero and a fool,' he murmurs.

The Grand Duke of Berg, urged on by Caroline, will imagine that he is destined to be the King of Spain. But his courage, his ambition and his illusions can be of use to me. I must simply hold him in check as one does a fiery horse. Let him enter Madrid and then we'll see!

'I do not think we should rush anything,' he writes to Murat. 'It would be advisable to take counsel from forthcoming events.'

But Murat should be on his guard; he had better warn this 'fool' of a Grand Duke.

You are dealing with a simple people. They will have all the courage and all of the enthusiasm one encounters in men who have not been worn down by political passions.

The aristocracy and the clergy are the masters of Spain. If they fear for their privileges and for their existence, they will organize levées en masse which could make the war drag on forever. I have supporters at the moment; I won't if I appear as a conqueror.

Napoleon stops dictating. He has just had a presentiment of what might happen, but he also senses that events are slipping through his hands, that he can't hold them back.

DISPATCHES ARRIVE in a constant stream, day after day.

Following a riot in Aranjuez, Godoy, the Queen's favourite, has been imprisoned, Charles IV has abdicated and his son Ferdinand, Prince of the Asturias, has been proclaimed King of Spain amid enthusiastic scenes of celebration.

That man who wrote me imploring letters! I can't see him having any of the qualities necessary to lead a nation.

'That will not prevent them making a hero of him, just to set him against us,' Napoleon writes to Murat. 'I do not want us to use any violence against members of the family; it never serves any purpose to make oneself odious and inflame hatreds.'

The Prince of the Asturias has become Ferdinand VII, King of Spain. He has entered Madrid and been greeted by delirious crowds. Murat's troops have followed. The actors are face to face.

I do not want hatred, but I can imagine what is going to happen next.

NOW HE MUST wait, let events unfold and spend every minute passionately.

Napoleon goes into his bed chamber. He sees, carefully laid out on the bed, the domino that Constant has prepared. The black masque has been put next to the hood. This evening there is a masked ball at Caroline's. He stands in front of a mirror, calls Constant and tries on the mask while his valet helps him put on the domino.

Is anyone going to recognize him?

He loves stealing into a crowd of people in fancy dress. All the young women that winter of 1808 – Pauline, Hortense, Caroline – are giving balls and vying with each other to see whose is the most imaginative and ambitious. But they're mistaken if they think they can get round him by thrusting women into his arms, like that Mademoiselle Guillebeau who appeared half-naked at one of Caroline's parties.

'The Grand Duchess of Berg dreams of the Spanish crown for Murat,' Napoleon murmurs to Duroc.

He enters the ball masked, leaning on the arm of the grand marshal of the palace, who is himself in fancy dress.

He hails the women in a different voice. He surprises and shocks them with salacious remarks. Behind his mask, in that domino, he loves seeing their anxiety. They know the Emperor is behind one of these masks. Might this be the one?

'Sire,' says one of the women.

He hates being recognized. He ushers Duroc out and returns to the Tuileries, cursing. He was enjoying himself at that ball. Constant suggests another disguise, which he immediately puts on and reappears among the crowd, but people back away from him.

They must have recognized him again, by his bearing, his silhouette, his hands crossed behind his back.

He stays a while none the less. The women are beautiful; twenty-four of them are dancing a quadrille representing the hours of the clock. The modulations of colour in their dresses illustrate the sun's course, its rise during the day and then descent into night. He watches the dance, applauds, and then suddenly feels tired. The bright lights dazzle him. He wishes he could have remained unknown for a little while longer; he senses everybody is looking at him. He is the Emperor. That is all he can be, even in a mask and the domino.

He leaves the ball, the crowd. There is only one person with whom he can let himself go.

He tells the coachman to drive to 48 rue de la Victoire, Marie Walewska's house.

HE TELLS HER what it was like. He would like her to come to these parties, but, at the same time, he is glad she doesn't want to, that she stays here hidden, discreet, peaceful. She never asks him questions, as if she were uninterested in what an Emperor does. She only becomes animated, she only badgers him, when it concerns her country, this Poland she wishes to see reborn.

He clams up. He cannot respond openly to her and this hurts him. Would she understand that he needs the Russian alliance and so cannot risk breaking it by giving the Poles satisfaction?

He limits himself to saying, 'This summer, important affairs may well be settled.'

He gets to his feet. The spell is broken. Politics, the world's passion, has seized him again. He returns to the Tuileries.

IT IS DAWN on 27 March 1808. The palace is deserted, icy. His footsteps echo through the galleries as the valets rush about and Méneval, just woken, reports for duty.

Napoleon immediately dictates a letter to Louis, King of Holland, to inform him that Murat has entered Madrid and that Charles IV has abdicated in favour of the Prince of the Asturias, now Ferdinand VII.

Then, still walking at a brisk pace, Napoleon raises his voice.

My brother, the climate of Holland does not suit you. Besides, Holland will not be able to rise from its ruins; in this whirlwind that sweeps the world, whether peace be concluded or not, it has no means of existing.

In this situation, I have thought of you for the throne of Spain. You will be the sovereign of a generous nation . . . Answer me categorically and say what your opinion is on this plan. You realize that this is still only a plan . . . Answer me categorically, if I name you King of Spain, will you accept? Can I count on you? Reply in just these two words, 'I have received your letter of such a date, and I answer "yes" ', and then I shall count on you doing what I wish, or 'no' which will mean you do not accept my proposal . . . Take no one into your confidence and do not speak to any one about the purpose of this letter, for a thing must be done before one admits to having thought about it.'

At last, he has decided.

He feels as if a great weight has been lifted off him. He has chosen to follow the rhythm of events; they will dictate his conduct from now on.

He is going to leave Paris and go to Bayonne, to be nearer Spain, because he never truly grasps the reality of events unless he sees them, touches them, clasps them in his arms.

The world is like a woman: one only knows her and understands her when one has possessed her.

He jokes with Méneval, 'We're in the fifth act of the tragedy; soon we will reach the climax.'

XVI

HE IS IMPATIENT and furious. In the courtyard of the bishop's palace at Orléans, on Sunday, 3 April 1808, he seethes with rage. It is four-thirty in the morning. He is waiting for the horses to be put to his berline. He paces from one wall to the other, ignoring Champagny who stands in the middle of the courtyard. Occasionally he stumbles on the cobbles that a fine rain has made slippery. Nothing is going as he wants it to.

Since leaving St Cloud yesterday at midday, it is as if destiny has been trying to hamper his journey to Bordeaux, Bayonne and Spain. His suite's carriages weren't ready. They were going to catch up the Emperor's berline at the first stop, Orléans, with his portable library, china, provisions, wine, portmanteaux and the quartermaster-sergeants and servants. But when he got to Orléans, at nine in the evening, no sign of any carriages – and where are they this morning as the last of the horses is being put to his berline?

He gets in, gives a signal that they can start, and Champagny has to run to take his seat on the bench facing Napoleon.

The latest dispatches and letters are put next to the Emperor. He seizes them, and waves them in front of Champagny's face.

The Minister of Foreign Affairs should know that my brother, the King of Holland, has refused the Spanish throne. And what reason does he give, this brother whom I put on the throne, who was nothing? Louis says that he is not 'a provincial governor. There is no other promotion for a king than that of heaven. They are all equal.'

Napoleon tosses the letter aside. That is what becomes of a man to whom one gives power. He grows blind.

Would he claim to be my equal?

NAPOLEON LEANS back into a corner of the berline. Where, apart from among the heroes of antiquity, could he find someone of his own stature? Or even somebody who can understand his plans and support them intelligently?

He looks out at the peaceful Tourraine countryside as day is breaking. Mist is clinging to the trees along the streams. The fields are still empty.

He feels alone in the world, with no one to talk to. Perhaps Tsar Alexander is the ruler and man whom he can communicate with best. But the others? The cunning operators, like Talleyrand and Fouché, do not deserve trust, and they are only subordinates playing their part.

Talleyrand is venal and Fouché has his own goals. He continues to spread rumours about the divorce.

'I have let him know my opinion of that countless times,' Napoleon says. 'All this talk about divorce does terrible harm; it is as indecent as it is pernicious. It is time people stopped concerning themselves with that matter, and I am scandalized to see his persistence.'

But Fouché digs his heels in.

Who can I count on? My brothers? Louis thinks he's my equal and refuses Spain. Jérôme is too attached to the throne of Westphalia to agree to go to Madrid. With a Lutheran wife, what would he do among the Papists? Lucien is an incorrigible rebel. When French troops entered Rome, he took the Pope's side! He thinks he has become a Roman prince.

That leaves Joseph, to whom I could propose to exchange the Kingdom of Naples for that of Spain and I will give Naples to Caroline and Murat, 'that hero and fool', who at least knows what he's worth. 'Never doubt my heart, it is more valuable than my head,' he wrote to me.

I am alone. Without an equal, and so without an ally. Without anyone to understand my politics!

NAPOLEON SITS UP straight. Day has broken. They are entering Poitiers; they stop at the relay. He gets out of the berline.

A carriage is already there with an escort. Three richly dressed men come forward and greet him. He ignores them. What manner of ambush is this?

Three Spanish grandees, Champagny explains: Duke Medinacelí, Duke de Frías and Count de Fernán Nuñez, have come to inform the Emperor of the accession of the Prince of the Asturias to the Spanish throne under the name of Ferdinand VII.

Napoleon walks away.

The Prince of the Asturias, King of Spain! It's too late. Napoleon has decided. The King of Spain will be a Bonaparte. Napoleon will not receive the three Spanish grandees.

He sets off again. 'Tell them Ferdinand is to come and meet me; I will wait for him in Bayonne.'

He gets into the carriage without looking at the three men, who bow low.

'The interests of my dynasty and my Empire demand that the Bourbons cease to rule in Spain,' he tells Champagny. 'Monks' countries are easy to conquer. If it were going to cost me eighty thousand men, I wouldn't do it, but it won't take more than twelve thousand; it is child's play.'

THE SUN IS SHINING brightly; they have driven through Angoulême. 'I don't want to harm anyone,' he continues, 'but when my great ship of state is launched, it must pass. Woe betide anyone who finds himself in its path.'

At Barbezieux, in the vaulted parlour of the La Boule-Rouge inn, he invites Champagny and his secretary to join him. He dines quickly on a roast capon and a glass of Touraine, then, stretching out his legs, a hand slipped into his waistcoat, he dictates dispatches and talks.

It is as if he were under canvas, on campaign. Isn't that what he loves?

He spent his last night in Paris with Marie Walewska, before returning to the Château of St Cloud. A peaceful night, like a ship in the roads. But now he must weigh anchor, take to the high seas if he wishes to discover new continents. He left Marie Walewska with a mixture of regret and enthusiasm. At last, after three months of palaces and imperial châteaux, he feels the wind of the open road; once again he is ready for surprise lodgings, for new landscapes and faces, for everything that has made up his life since his youth: movement, change, the unexpected. He will never be a sedentary ruler, but that does not mean, as they whisper in Madame de Récamier's, and even the Empress's, salon, or as Talleyrand implies, that he loves war.

He leans towards Champagny.

'I want peace by all the means that are reconcilable with the dignity and power of France. I want it at the cost of all the sacrifices that the national honour will permit.'

He gets to his feet.

'Every day I sense that peace is becoming more necessary. The princes of the continent want it as much as I do; I entertain neither passionate prejudices nor an invincible hatred for England.'

He starts to walk about the room and takes pinches of snuff with jerky, awkward gestures.

'The English have pursued a policy of repulsion against me; I have adopted the continental system to lead the British cabinet to have done with us. What does it matter if England prospers and is wealthy, so long as France and her allies are like her.'

He sits back down. That is why his dynasty must rule Spain and French troops must be in Portugal.

'Only peace with England will make me put up my sword and restore calm to Europe.'

He bangs his fist on the table, turns to Méneval. At his dictation, he is to write letters to Berthier, Prince of Neuchâtel, Chief of Staff of the Grand Army, and to Murat, Grand Duke of Berg, Lieutenant-General in Spain.

He begins to walk again and, with his hands behind his back, in a trenchant tone, he begins,

> You should remember the previous circumstances in which, under my command, you have waged war in large cities. You do not enter streets. You occupy houses at the start of streets and establish good batteries . . . Generals must be made responsible for unattached men . . . No small groups; soldiers will march only in columns of five hundred. In countryside or villages that could foster insurgencies or have seen acts of violence against soldiers or couriers, set a major example. If there is a movement in Madrid, you shall repress it with cannon and impose severe justice . . .

He sets off towards the door, and calls out the last sentence over his shoulder, 'When I judge the moment has come, I shall arrive in Madrid like a bomb.'

ON THE EVENING of Monday, 4 April, he enters Bordeaux.

The town is deserted. In front of the prefecture, the officer in charge of the guardhouse rushes forward and explains that they have been waiting for the Emperor since morning. The troops have returned to their quarters.

Napoleon barely looks at the officer or the prefect, but has himself shown to his room. Without turning round, he orders, 'Review of the Guard and cavalry tomorrow, Champ de Mars, visit to the port.'

He is certain that if he could do everything himself, as quickly as he thinks and wishes, then he would already have organized the entire world. But there are other rulers, prefects, soldiers, enemies, and to transform them into efficient subordinates or make them submit, he has to see them in person and urge them on or reduce them to obedience.

He is the heart of his empire, the principle that holds together everything that he has conquered and built.

That is why he wants a son to keep near him, so that, when the day comes, his succession will be natural and beyond argument.

A son means divorce, a son means rejecting Josephine.

HE SEES HER getting out of her carriage in the courtyard of the prefecture, when he is manoeuvring the soldiers of the 108 Regiment of the Line. It is his Emperor's duty to see he has seasoned, loyal troops. He has to be there, leading them, even for drill. He loves this movement of men in line, the mechanical perfection of their gestures and their steps. He loves issuing orders, his body straining forward, heels pressing hard on his stirrups. This is his life, this is what it always has been.

Josephine has come to a halt. She is dressed in white. Her silhouette, still youthful and elegant under her veils, moves him. It feels as if the past and all its feelings are flooding back again.

He goes towards her, greets her ceremoniously. She bows, smiling. They are like two old accomplices.

The sun is mild. A sea breeze blows on the Gironde. On Tuesday, 12 April, Napoleon travels down the river with Josephine from Quai du Chapeau Rouge to the grain depot. He takes her hand. Spring brings out the tenderness in him. Everything would be simple if it wasn't for the demands of politics and the force of destiny.

He looks at Josephine. When the moment of separation comes, for it will come, he will have to protect her. But for the moment, since the time hasn't yet come, he must look after her, and, with an air of insouciant lightness, make sure she enjoys every day.

She joins in this game. She whispers confidences in his ear; she reminds him of intimate moments.

He has to leave her to go to Bayonne, but as soon as he arrives, he writes to her

My friend,

I'm giving the order for a supplement of twenty thousand francs a month to be added to your privy purse, while you are travelling, starting as from 1 April.

I have terrible lodgings half a league away in a country house. The Infant Don Carlos and five or six Spanish grandees are here. The Prince of the Asturias is twenty leagues away. King Charles and his queen are on their way. I don't know where I shall put everybody up. They are all still in the tavern. My troops are in the best of health in Spain.

It took me a moment to understand your sweet words; I laughed at your stories. You women have wonderful memories.

My health is good, and I love you with all sweet friendship. Please remember me kindly to everyone in Bordeaux; my affairs did not allow me to do so in person.

Napoleon

THE BELLS ARE RINGING in Bayonne when he leaves the town to go to Marracq Castle. He explores the vast park on horseback and makes out a turret, which serves as a dovecot at the corner of a high wall bounding the park. A few hundred metres below flows the Nive. This is where he will stay, he decides; the place is vast. Other châteaux situated close by can accommodate members of the court. He wants them to join him in a few days. He loves having his people around him. And the park is large enough to manoeuvre troops.

He will receive the Bourbons of Spain here.

WEDNESDAY, 20 APRIL. Here is Ferdinand, Prince of the Asturias, who believes himself the King of Spain!

Napoleon observes him in silence. He accompanies him to the top of the staircase, invites him to dinner, tries to draw him out. The Prince of the Asturias has round eyes and a round face. His body exudes a sense of flabbiness.

'The King of Prussia is a hero compared to the Prince of the Asturias!' exclaims Napoleon. 'He has not yet said a word to me; he is indifferent to everything; very material. He eats four times a day and has no idea of anything . . .'

Soon afterwards, Charles IV, Queen Maria Luisa and her favourite Manuel Godoy arrive.

Is this a Bourbon dynasty?

'King Charles is a good fellow, he has the air of an honest, kind patriarch. The Queen's heart and history are written on her face, which says it all,' Napoleon confides in Talleyrand. 'It surpasses everything one could imagine . . . The Prince of the Peace, Godoy, looks rather like a bull . . . He has been treated with unexampled barbarity: one month suspended between life and death, constantly under threat of perishing. Can you imagine, all that time he didn't change his shirt and he had a beard seven inches long . . .'

He feels pity mingled with scorn and disgust for these Bourbons.

These people don't deserve to rule any longer. It is only fair to drive them off the throne. And it is in the interests of my dynasty, of Europe and of Spain. Ferdinand VII, who claims to be king, is the real enemy.

'The Prince of the Asturias is very stupid, very bad-hearted and a great enemy of France,' Napoleon explains to Talleyrand. 'I have had his couriers arrested, on whom were found letters full of bile and hatred for the French whom he several times calls: those cursed Frenchmen. You can imagine that with my knowledge of how to handle men, his twenty-four years' experience makes no impression; it is so self-evident to me that it would take a long war to induce me to recognize him as King of Spain.'

HE WATCHES THEM quarrel. The father accusing the son of having stolen his crown, the son answering insolently, the mother beside herself with anger, insulting her son, defending her lover, who remains silent, exhausted.

They're ugly, cowardly. Charles IV weeps like a child; Ferdinand eats like a glutton.

They are waiting for me to choose between them.

I have made a choice which they can't imagine. My plan is decided upon. I will have to carry it out, make them accept it. There will be some shouting, some tears. But these people are nothing any more.

On 2 May he dictates a letter to Murat. The Grand Duke of Berg should be informed too. He writes:

> I am pleased with King Charles and the Queen. I intend to give them Compiègne.
>
> I intend the King of Naples to reign at Madrid. I wish to give you the kingdom of Naples or that of Portugal. Reply at once what you think of this, for it must be done in a day.

JOSEPHINE ARRIVES at the castle light-hearted and content. Hortense has just given birth to a son, on 20 April, whom she has called Charles Louis Napoleon.*

Napoleon leads her off. He finds her more beautiful than when he saw her last. They go down to the Nive. It is hot; he pushes her into the river. They splash one another, get in a boat and go to Lauga Castle where Caroline Murat has recently arrived.

Caroline will have to accept that Spain can no longer figure in her dreams, but instead Naples, a beautiful kingdom. He laughs, then writes to Joseph that 'Spain is not like the kingdom of Naples ... In Madrid you're in France. Naples is the end of the world. Therefore I wish that, as soon as you receive this letter, you entrust the regency to whoever you choose ... and set off for Bayonne via Turin, Mont-Cenis and Lyons.'

Joseph is the eldest of the family. He is entitled to this Spanish throne which the other brothers have refused. He will accept it. He will have no choice.

If the Bourbons but knew!

He sees them walking across the park towards Josephine. She

---

* The future Napoleon III, possibly the son not of Louis but of the Dutch Admiral Verhuell.

is grace personified. He takes her hand and leads her into the dining room. She will preside over dinner.

A SMALL COURT has formed itself at Marracq Castle, under the guidance of Grand Marshal Duroc. Among the young women who comprise Josephine's suite and bow in his presence, Napoleon notices a young woman whose name he remembers immediately, Mademoiselle Guillebeau; he had noticed her at one of the masked balls given in Paris by Caroline or Hortense. He stares at her; she does not look down. Everything about her attitude says that she accepts. His spirits soar. He glances at Josephine. She has seen; she smiles, giving her assent. She's not afraid of it. His politics and his heart are elsewhere. In divorce and with Marie Walewska. But Marie is in Paris, and one must always take what destiny offers.

That evening he will pay a visit to Mademoiselle Guillebeau at the very top of the castle.

He sits opposite Josephine and Charles IV, with Queen Maria Luisa on his right. He finds them a pitiful couple. Ferdinand sits at the end of the table; his heavy features bespeak greed. 'Whatever one says to him,' Napoleon later relates, 'he doesn't reply; whether one hauls him over the coals or pays him compliments, his face never changes. To anyone who has seen him, his character can be summed up in one word: sly.'

When shall I constrain them to renounce what they think they still possess, the Spanish crown?

He hesitates. He thinks of Mademoiselle Guillebeau, of the night to come. There will need to be some event, a sign that will enable him to sweep aside the illusions of this family he despises in a handful of words.

By 5 May 1808, he still hasn't said anything.

HE GOES WALKING that Thursday, in Marracq park.

It is the middle of the afternoon, very mild.

He has not been able to refuse his arm to that fat, ugly, vulgar little woman, Queen Maria Luisa, who is puffing and panting at his side, and complaining in a shrill voice about her son Ferdinand, the 'traitor'. She bewails the suffering inflicted upon 'her' Prince of the Peace, Godoy, by the rioters. She is putting herself completely in the Emperor's hands, she says, squeezing his arm. Charles IV agrees with his wife. He is on the other side of Napoleon. They're like two subjects petitioning a king.

Napoleon turns round and sees Josephine between Duroc and Ferdinand. All of a sudden he feels a rush of gratitude towards her. She has always supported him intelligently and here she's no different, listening to the rulers of Spain because it's necessary; she has a sovereign's natural grace.

HE SEES AN OFFICER coming towards them from the castle, preceded by an aide-de-camp. The officer, whose uniform is covered with dust, is carrying a large leather portfolio. It should be from Murat. Napoleon goes to meet him with Maria Luisa and Charles IV.

'What news from Madrid?' he asks, recognizing Captain Marbot, an aide-de-camp of Murat's. He is surprised by the officer's silence as he hands him the dispatches, a fixed look on his face.

'What is happening?' Napoleon asks again.

The officer still says nothing.

Napoleon takes the dispatches, leads the officer away from the Bourbons, and when there's some distance between them, Captain Marbot starts to talk. Under the trees, as he walks beside the wall, Napoleon listens and reads Murat's dispatches.

On the first day of May, a crowd gathered in the Puerta del Sol in Madrid; it was only dispersed with great difficulty. On Monday the 2nd, in the morning, the announcement that Charles IV's youngest son, Don Francisco, had left the capital triggered a riot. Unattached French soldiers in Madrid had their throats slit. Several thousand rioters attacked squadrons of Dragoons and the Guard, which entered the capital from the suburbs. In the Puerta del Sol, the Spanish soldiers threw in their lot with the rioters and fired case-shot at the French. The fighting lasted until Tuesday, 3 May.

Napoleon interrupts Captain Marbot. It is not the details of a battle that matter, but the conclusion, he says.

He reads Murat's last letter. The Mamelukes charged with the Guard.

'Several thousand Spaniards have been killed,' Marbot says.

The people, he continues, are desperate. They cannot accept that the royal family has been taken to France. The rioters displayed ferocious courage; even the women and children attacked the French.

'They hate us, even after our victory . . .'

Napoleon interrupts him.

'Nonsense!' he says, turning back towards the centre of the park where the Spanish sovereigns are waiting for him. 'They'll calm down and bless me when they see their country shake off the opprobrium and disorder into which it has been plunged by the weakest and most corrupt administration that ever existed . . .'

He claps Marbot on the shoulder, pinches his ear.

This is the event he was waiting for to sweep aside the Bourbons of Spain.

He calls Ferdinand over in a loud voice, tells him about the riots in Madrid, the blood shed, the French murdered, the unavoidable severity of the repressive measures taken by Murat, and the rebellion finally crushed after the days of 2 and 3 May.

He watches Charles IV rush at his son, yelling 'Wretch!' and accusing him of being responsible for the riot. It is his criminal rebellion, his usurpation of his father's crown, that has triggered this massacre. Then Queen Maria Luisa throws herself on Ferdinand and hits him, screaming, 'On your head be this blood!'

Napoleon walks away. Josephine, Duroc, the ladies in waiting and the officers of his suite leave the King and Queen insulting their son who is pale and silent.

Now it will be enough to pick up the Spanish crown which they have sent spinning into the dust.

HE SENDS FOR Ferdinand and talks to him without even looking at him, as one does to a man one despises.

'If you have not recognized your father as your legitimate King and communicated this to Madrid by midnight, you will be treated as a rebel.'

It will be enough then to obtain Charles IV's abdication. Duroc has already prepared the treaty. They'll pay off the Bourbons like a valet who has been fired.

Napoleon doesn't even read the text of the treaty. He walks

around the reception room of Marracq Castle, which has smoke-blackened beams.

'The Château of Compiègne and the forest of the same name are given to Charles IV for life and the Château of Chambord is bequeathed to him in perpetuity,' reads Duroc. 'The French Treasury will pay Charles IV annually a civil list of 7,500,000 francs.'

Until then the King and Queen will stay in Fontainebleau and Ferdinand will be put up by Talleyrand at his Château of Valençay.

NAPOLEON IS ALONE in the park, in the walk that leads down to the banks of the Nive. It is growing dark. He is waiting for the castle to be asleep before joining Mademoiselle Guillebeau in her little room in the eaves, where it's so hot they have to leave the window open.

He loves the smell of the countryside, the murmur of the wind. At the Tuileries, he feels hemmed in, suffocated. He needs the horizon, wind.

He slowly walks back up to the castle.

So, he has driven the Bourbons out of Spain, just as he drove them out of Naples. That dynasty is dead. It hasn't been able to protect its rights. When a man or a dynasty or a people lack energy, it is only fair that they succumb.

Will the Spanish accept it or will they rise up in defence of their sovereigns?

He must convince them.

He walks quicker. Entering the castle, he summons Méneval. Mademoiselle Guillebeau will wait.

IN HIS STUDY, amidst the sounds of the countryside and the distant song of the river, he dictates,

> People of Spain, long in its death throes, your nation was perishing. I have seen your troubles. I am going to remedy them ... Your princes have transferred to me all their rights to the Spanish crown ... Your monarchy is old; my mission is to rejuvenate it.
>
> I will improve your institutions and delight you, if you

support me, with the benefits of a reform which will cause neither offence, disorder nor convulsion . . .

I shall place your glorious crown on the head of someone other than myself, whilst guaranteeing you a constitution that will reconcile the holy and salutary authority of the sovereign with the liberties and privileges of the people . . .

I want your descendants to preserve my memory and say: he restored our country.

He thinks of Joseph, who must be on his way by now. Will he have a firm enough hand to hold the reins of this country? To make himself accepted by his people?

'The hardest part of the job is done,' he murmurs.

He signals to Méneval. He wants to dictate a letter to Talleyrand.

'I consider that the hardest part of the job is done,' he begins. 'Some agitation may still occur, but the proper lesson the cities of Madrid and, latterly, Burgos have been taught ought necessarily to bring matters to a prompt resolution . . .'

As long as no one incites the Spanish to revolt.

'I have the greatest interest in the Prince of the Asturias not making any undesirable moves. I wish him therefore to be amused and kept occupied . . .'

Ferdinand will stay at Valençay, with Talleyrand, a peerless connoisseur of entertainments.

'I have decided to send him to the countryside, to stay with you, and to surround him with pleasures and surveillance.'

Napoleon goes up to the window. The park seems lit up in the milky white glow of the moonlight.

He walks back towards Méneval and says in a merry voice, 'If the Prince of the Asturias becomes attached to a pretty woman, there will be no harm, especially if we could depend on her.'

Then he quickly crosses the room and takes the staircase that leads up to Mademoiselle Guillebeau.

EARLY IN THE MORNING he goes walking in the park of Marracq Castle. A light haze blurs the blue of the sky, but, beneath this veil, the day looks as if it is going to be fine, dazzling.

He travels down the Ardour by boat with Josephine. He goes aboard a frigate that has just entered Bayonne harbour. He travels as far as St Jean de Luz. The long lines of the tiller form white parallels against the dark sea.

He persuades Josephine to walk on the sandy beach.

These last days of May 1808 and the start of June presage a peaceful summer, sometimes disturbed by stormy midday heat.

He learns on the last day of May that Murat is ill, and amongst the bundle of dispatches announcing the Lieutenant-General's jaundice are others reporting that here and there French troops are being attacked.

'It's brigands. They kill us when we march in small numbers.'

Napoleon is furious. He had given orders. They must, he repeats, advance in columns, disarm the inhabitants, use artillery against towns and set examples.

He demands that dispatches be got to him as quickly as possible.

'It is of first importance to achieve good communications,' he insists in his letters to Murat. 'I am sorry to hear of your illness, but the doctors' consultation is reassuring; I hope soon to learn that the emetic and a little sweat have done you good.'

But when he returns to Marracq Castle in a storm, which broke just after he left Bayonne, the first dispatch he opens reports the massacre of three hundred and thirty-eight soldiers in Valencia. The rioters who slit the French garrison's throats were led by a canon, Calvo.

He stops reading.

Perhaps this is an insurrection of fanatics, led by monks and priests. Who knows if the Pope and his Roman cardinals are not behind this escalating uprising? Every dispatch reports the insurrection of another town – Saragossa, Barcelona, Malaga, Cadiz, Badajoz, Grenada. In Oviedo the inhabitants have been incited to rebel by a canon who, his informants are sure of this, called Napoleon the Antichrist. The French soldiers are 'hell-hounds' or 'Voltaire's troops'.

The fire must not spread.

Napoleon writes to the minister of war, Clarke. Reserves must be sent to Spain, but without panicking public opinion with rumours of war.

'So as not to make too much of a stir in Paris, these regiments can perform the first march on foot, as usual, and only get into carriages a day from Paris.'

Joseph must be ready to get down to work in Madrid as soon as possible.

HE GOES TO MEET his brother on the outskirts of Bayonne. Joseph is worried; he assures him that the Pope has instructed the Spanish bishops to refuse to recognize 'this Lutheran, heretic, Freemason King, like all the Bonapartes and the French nation'. Pusillanimous as ever, worried by the slightest of rumours, Joseph is terrified.

Napoleon takes him by the arm, leads him into the dining room in Marracq Castle where a dinner has been prepared in his honour. He reassures him. The Spanish delegates have formed a junta and recognized him as King.

'Don't worry, you shall lack for nothing. Be of good cheer and above all be well!'

Joseph hesitates. He has his own sources of information about Spain.

'No one has told Your Majesty the whole truth,' he murmurs.

He bows his head as if he dare not confess what he thinks, the presentiments he has.

'The fact is there isn't a single Spaniard who is for me, except for the small number involved with the junta.'

Are these the words of a sovereign? Does Joseph think one becomes a king effortlessly? Does he think one does not have to fight?

'You should not think it so extraordinary to have to conquer your kingdom,' Napoleon says.

He stares at Joseph, whose eyes look away.

Is this the King I need in Spain? Why do I have to keep everyone I entrust with a position, or with some sort of task, at arm's length? Am I so alone?

'Philip V and Henri IV,' he continues, 'were forced to conquer their kingdoms.'

He must reassure Joseph.

'Be gay, let nothing trouble you, and do not for a moment doubt that everything will finish better and more promptly than you think.'

But Murat is still confined in Madrid on a stretcher. Saragossa is holding out against assault, cannonballs, grapeshot. The English are landing in Portugal, interfering in Spain. The Spanish armies are reforming, marching towards Madrid. The days pass and the insurrection continues to spread.

IN THE PARK of the Castle of Marracq, Napoleon organizes his troops. He hesitates. There is a great temptation to put himself at the head of the cavalry squadron, to march with the Guard and enter Madrid which Joseph, who has only just arrived, is already thinking of leaving, terrified by the thought of being captured. He is appealing for help already; he is afraid of being killed, he says.

This fear his letters exude does not befit a king; it is not worthy of a man who is my brother.

'I don't like the style of your letter,' Napoleon writes back. 'It's not a question of dying but of living and of being victorious, which you are and shall be. I shall discover the Pillars of Hercules, not the limits of my power, in Spain. Don't be uneasy about the outcome of all this.'

Hasn't Marshal Bessières just won a victory at Medina de Rio Seco? And haven't General Dupont's troops just engaged with the Spanish at Baylen? They are in a position to defeat the rebels.

Napoleon watches the troops march past in the park of the Castle of Marracq.

If he rushed to Spain, he could settle all this, he's sure, but he must consider all the pieces on the chessboard. Police reports indicate plots in Paris. Nothing very significant, a few Republicans bad-mouthing the Empire, but how much can he trust Fouché, minister of police?

Napoleon feels he should be everywhere. He should be in Madrid, but also in Paris. And in Germany, because Austria is reforming its armies. Why?

Is Vienna preparing to open war, thinking I am bogged down in Spain? It is in the nature of things!

'Since Austria is arming,' he writes to Berthier, 'we must arm. Therefore I have ordered the Grand Army to be reinforced ... If there is a means to avoid war, it is by showing Austria that we are taking up the gauntlet and that we are ready.'

WAR AGAIN, ALREADY!

Napoleon leaves the Castle of Marracq on 20 July. The heat is torrid. It's swelteringly hot on the road to Auch, Toulouse, Montauban and Agen. They drive at night to avoid the sun that, from daybreak, sets the countryside ablaze.

Napoleon has decided to return to Paris. He has chosen to stop the gaps that are opening in the north and then to settle the question of Spain later, if the insurrection has not been put down before then. He thinks it will have been. He hopes it will have been.

Every time they stop, he waits for the couriers.

At Bordeaux on 2 August, he sees the emotion on the face of the aide-de-camp who hands him the dispatch. He reads it at a glance. General Dupont has surrendered at Baylen to General Castaños's force of soldiers and insurgents. Twenty thousand men have surrendered their arms and their flags in exchange for the promise of being repatriated!

Napoleon hurls the dispatch to the ground and yells, 'Fool! Imbecile! Coward! Dupont has lost Spain to save his baggage.'

He kicks the dispatch.

'It's a stain on our uniform!' he cries.

He asks for the maps and Dupont's dispatches in the order they have been sent. He writes to General Clarke, minister of war.

'I send you the reports for yourself alone; read them, map in hand and you will see if, since the world existed, there has been anything so stupid, so inept and so cowardly ... Everything that has happened is the result of the most inconceivable ineptitude.'

It makes him wild, just thinking of it. He is alone. The cowardice, blindness and stupidity of the people serving him are his worst enemies.

But he must confront the situation.

At Rochefort, on Friday, 5 August, he sequesters himself with his generals and a handful of ministers who have come from Paris. Half the troops stationed in Germany must be sent to Spain. Marshal Ney is to take command.

Then he goes off alone.

It is the first time since he has been in command, since he has ruled the country and waged war throughout Europe, that a unit of his army has surrendered.

The first time.

He grits his teeth. He tries to master the pain gnawing at his stomach. He knows that all around him his enemies are watching and waiting for this very event. The loss of twenty thousand men will resound from one end of Europe to the other.

He issues an order. A courier is to set off and ride without stopping to St Petersburg before the news of the surrender at Baylen reaches Alexander.

Never give the other a reason to suspect that one is weakened; always anticipate the other's reaction, imply that one is ready to evacuate Prussia, as he wishes, suggest a meeting. Show one is afraid of nothing; that one is more determined and more powerful than ever.

HE RETURNS to Paris by the western cities: La Rochelle, Niort, Fontenay.

On Monday, 8 August, he enters Napoléon-Vendée and the memories come back. He had decided to build this town on 25 May 1804, when that month was still known as Prairial and the year was Year XII. He wanted to eradicate the name of La Roche-sur-Yon and show that he had pacified the Vendée.

He rides through the streets of the straggling settlement. Is this his town? Adobe cottages? Big cob houses?

Rage overwhelms him. He draws his sword, drives it into the mud walls up to the hilt.

Is this building for the future?

He becomes gloomy. Perhaps everything is like this, friable. His glory, his dynasty, his Empire.

Is this a reason to give up? He summons the engineer, dismisses him, gives orders.

Only action can help.

He has learned since childhood that one never gains anything by hanging one's head.

If everybody had had the same experience as him, he wouldn't feel so alone, constantly forced to urge others to resist, to fight.

In the berline driving towards St Cloud, he writes to Joseph:

My friend, you have been called upon to deal with events for which neither your habits nor your natural character suit you. Dupont has besmirched our flags. Events of this nature require my presence in Paris. My grief is really great to think that I cannot be with you at this moment in the midst of my soldiers.

Tell me that you are in good spirits and health and performing the duties of a soldier; this is an excellent opportunity for studying them.

He hasn't any other card to play in Spain for the moment.

He must back Joseph.

But to win the hand, he will have to commit himself to the game, enter Madrid at the head of the Grand Army. It is imperative; it is his duty.

When he reaches St Cloud on Sunday, 14 August, at three-thirty in the afternoon, he knows he will only have a brief stay here.

He strides across the courtyard.

That evening, he tells Duroc that there is a party at the Tuileries in his honour. Tomorrow is St Napoleon's day.

He will be thirty-nine tomorrow.

'Let's go and dance,' he says.

XVII

WHEN HE ENTERS the ballroom in the Tuileries, on Sunday, 14 August, a little after eight, and joins the throng of dignitaries, who clear a path for him, bowing, Napoleon senses the beady eyes trained on him.

Here is Talleyrand the Pallid, as Metternich, the Austrian ambassador, calls him, according to police reports. The Prince of Benevento approaches. He is so powdered that his scent is overpowering. He wears his usual, cunning half-smile. He knows, they all know, that General Dupont has surrendered, that General Junot looks as if he'll do the same at Cintra to Wellesley's Englishmen, that the Spanish have entered Madrid, that Joseph, the King of Spain, has fled and that there isn't a single French soldier left south of the Ebro.

They're trying to see the scars of these defeats on my face. They are wondering: has the Emperor begun to doubt, is his power weakened, is he vacillating? They are lying in wait, ready to abandon me, betray me, if I waver. They try to guess what I'm going to decide. I walk past. They whisper.

Word has gone round that in Marracq Castle's park, on the banks of the Adour and Nive and on the beaches of Bayonne and St Jean de Luz, Josephine seemed light-hearted, reassured, happy. Has he given up the idea of a divorce?

Fouché observes him, without dropping his eyes. He needs to know if the plan to divorce he favoured has been abandoned, in which case he will have to re-establish himself in Josephine's good graces and make her forget what he dared suggest to her.

His spies already have 48 rue de la Victoire under surveillance, and they will tell him when the Emperor pays a visit to Marie Walewska later this evening and doesn't leave her house to return to St Cloud before dawn.

They spy on me.

I must show them that I'm just as sure, just as determined, as on the day after a victory.

NAPOLEON STOPS in the middle of the room. People surround him; he smiles and jokes. Then he declares in a loud voice, 'Peace is what the whole world wants, but England opposes it and England is the enemy of the world! The English have landed a fairly substantial force in Spain. I have recalled the I and II Corps and three divisions of the Grand Army to conclude the subjection of this country.'

He takes Marshal Davout by the arm, walks with him a little, speaking loud enough for the dignitaries following them to hear.

'Dupont,' he says, 'has dishonoured our arms. He has shown as much ineptitude as cowardice. When you learn the details one day, the hair will stand up on your head.'

He looks around him: the eyes lower.

'I will deal with them as they deserve, and if they have stained our uniform, they will have to wash it clean.'

Never reveal that one is hesitating, never confess one's anxiety or weakness. Shrug them off oneself.

He has himself driven to Marie Walewska's house. She opens her arms. The disinterested love of a woman, her youth and tenderness, are like victories: the resilience and energy of life.

On the afternoon of Monday, 15 August, he receives the diplomatic corps at St Cloud. The ambassadors are watching for the slightest sign of weakness. Here, appearing strong and assured is essential.

Napoleon goes up to Metternich and leads him off for a long discussion, away from the other diplomats. With a shake of his head, he dismisses Talleyrand as he approaches them.

'The Pallid,' Napoleon murmurs, smiling at Metternich. 'When I want to do something, I do not use the Prince of Benevento. I turn to him when I do not want to do something whilst giving the impression that I do.'

He laughs and then suddenly his face freezes and he says in a hollow voice, 'Does Austria wish then to make war or does it wish to frighten us?'

Metternich seems surprised, denies Vienna has any bellicose intentions.

'If that is so, why your immense preparations? Your militia will give you a force of four hundred thousand, trained and formed into regiments. Your fortresses are provisioned. Finally, a clear sign for me of war being prepared is that you have been buying horses; you now have fourteen thousand artillery horses.'

He controls himself so as not raise the tone of his voice; one must show that one is so strong one cannot be worried by the measures Austria has been taking.

'Do you want to frighten me?' he continues. 'You will not succeed. Do you believe that circumstances favour you? You are mistaken.'

He continues calmly walking up and down with Metternich while the other ambassadors watch.

'My politics is open because it is based on loyalty. I am going to withdraw one hundred thousand of my men from Germany to send them to Spain and I shall still be your equal. You are arming; I shall arm. If necessary, I shall levy two hundred thousand men; you shall have no power on the continent on your side.'

He slowly accompanies Metternich back to the other ambassadors.

'You see how calm I am,' he says. 'The Bourbons are my personal enemies; we cannot occupy European thrones at the same time.'

That is the fundamental reason for the Spanish affair.

'It is not a matter of ambition.'

He acknowledges the other ambassadors, then retires.

THESE ARE DAYS of waiting, like those that precede an attack. He is not impatient. He weighs every gesture and every word in order to analyse and plan for all outcomes. First he must ensure peace in the north, in Germany. Metternich has been persuaded. Vienna will not take up arms. He must therefore at all costs maintain the alliance with Alexander, and so arrange a meeting with him.

If I talk to him, I will convince him.

The meeting is arranged for Erfurt at the end of September 1808. He must gain a few months of peace, time to be victorious in Spain and then, if necessary, he will return to Germany and crush Austria once and for all, flattening it like Prussia.

It is a game of chess.

He walks up and down his study. He hunts in the forest of St Germain or at Grosbois, Marshal Berthier's estate. He holds reviews at Versailles and on the Plaine des Sablons.

And at every moment, he holds the chessboard in his mind. He anticipates. He prepares Jérôme for what might happen in the future in Germany. As King of Westphalia, Jérôme must be ready.

'It is incalculable what may happen here in April.' He sends him a letter from Stein, the Prussian minister of Frederick William III, that was intercepted by the police. It is addressed to General Wittgenstein, a Prussian serving in the Russian army. Stein declares that he is organizing a national insurrection across Germany. The French will be attacked, the country devastated if necessary, the whole nation called to arms and the princes and nobility deposed if they do not join the uprising.

Does Stein think I'm going to wait?

Once Spain is subdued, I will have to go back to Germany. I will move the Grand Army, the Queen on my chessboard.

HE ENTERS THE Topographical Office. On the map of Spain, pins mark the route of three Spanish columns that are marching towards the Ebro. They must be allowed to carry on.

He closes his eyes. The plan of counterattack is beginning to take shape, but he needs men. The class of 1810 will be levied in advance; those exempted from 1806 to 1809 will also be called up.

Is there grumbling? Is it open season for wife-hunting because married men are exempted from military service?

I need men. Let the imperial police hunt down absentees. Every soldier is to get 3 francs when units being transferred from Germany to Spain come through France.

'Have some songs composed in Paris and sent to the cities the soldiers are going to pass through,' he tells Maret. 'These songs will celebrate the glory the army has won and the glory it shall win . . .'

He must keep the army in close order, compact. 'Everything is opinion in war.' He must inspire confidence, exalt his men's heroism, speak to them.

Soldiers, after having triumphed on the banks of the Danube and the Vistula . . . I now order you to cross France without giving you a moment's rest.

Soldiers, I need you. The Leopard's hideous presence has sullied the continent of Spain and Portugal . . . Let us carry our triumphant Eagles to the Pillars of Hercules.

Soldiers, you have surpassed the renown of modern armies, but have you equalled the glory of the armies of Rome, which in the same campaign triumphed on the Rhine and the Euphrates, in Illyria and on the Tagus?

WILL THEY LISTEN?

He tells the minister of war, General Clarke, 'Everything that's happening in Spain is deplorable. We have done nothing to inspire confidence in the French. The army is commanded not by generals who have made war, but by postal inspectors.'

He sweeps aside the pile of dispatches on his desk with the back of his hand, keeping only one.

Does Clarke know the teachings of one Spanish catechism? He brandishes the piece of paper, then reads it in a voice rigid with anger:

Whence does Napoleon proceed?
From hell and sin.
What are his principal offices?
To deceive, steal, murder and oppress.
Is it a sin to kill Frenchman?
On the contrary, one would deserve well of one's country if,
    by this means, one relieves it of insult, theft and
    imposture.

He throws the piece of paper on the ground. This is the work of the Pope and his bishops!

It is for France to be free of such fanaticism that he wants the imperial university to have a monopoly of all education, and the Church not to be a weapon against the government.

He checks himself, dismisses Clarke.

It is always the same struggle, against the Bourbons, against superstition.

They do not accept what he is, what he represents. He must face up to that. There is no other choice.

On Wednesday, 21 September, he goes to Paris.

He gets out of his carriage on boulevard des Capucines to inspect the building works. Then he reviews a division of Dutch troops on the Sablons plain. He does not tire of watching his regiments.

Soon it's already dark. He goes to find Marie.

Tomorrow, he says, he will set off for Erfurt. Then he will go to Spain. Marie Walewska remains silent, but he senses her anxiety. She doesn't understand why he has to be at the head of his armies like this. Must he fight constantly?

He murmurs, almost as if to himself, 'One has to wage war for a long time to conceive of it.'

Then he stands up and adds in a louder voice, 'In war men are nothing; it is one man that is all.'

He is that man.

XVIII

IT IS STILL DARK, at five in the morning on Thursday, 22 September 1808, when Napoleon gets into his berline. He turns his head. He thinks he glimpses Josephine's silhouette hurrying through the galleries, followed by her lady's companions.

He instantly gives a signal to the colonel in command of the escort of chasseurs of the Guard. The berline swings into motion and sets off on the Châlons road.

At last he feels free. Josephine has been insisting for days that she come with him to Erfurt. He refused; she kept pestering him. She wanted to see the performances by the Comédie Française and go to the parties and dinners. Isn't she entitled to mingle with the kings and sit opposite the Emperor of Russia? Isn't she the Empress?

He didn't say anything. He is glad now not to have given in. He is alone, like an eligible bachelor. He lets himself be lulled by the jolting of the berline. He must suggest to the assembled sovereigns, Alexander especially, that he is looking for a new wife to assure the future of his dynasty. This marriage he is contemplating could be a great asset to his politics, a way to bind tighter the ties of alliance. Why not a Russian grand duchess? Doesn't Alexander have two unmarried younger sisters?

He daydreams as the sun rises over the grey expanses of the Lorraine plateau. The carriage is often forced to slow down. He leans out of the window impatiently. The road is clogged with waggons and berlines, saddle horses and carts and riders wearing the imperial livery.

In one of the carriages, he thinks he recognizes Mademoiselle Bourgoing, with her pointed chin, her curly hair, her mischievous expression. He remembers the slyness of this pretty actress who gave herself to him while she was still Chaptal's mistress. He smiles. Poor Chaptal: that love affair cost him his ministry.

He asks Méneval, who is sitting in the opposite corner of the berline, to list which actors have been invited to perform at Erfurt.

'Thirty-two,' he murmurs after listening to Méneval.

He cannot help calculating the expense, with travel expenses at one thousand écus a head, and several-thousand-franc bonuses for the leads on top of that.

'I am going to amaze Germany with this magnificence,' he says.

He hums a tune, then recites a few verses of *Cinna*,

> All crimes of State committed for a Crown
> Heaven absolves if the throne is handed down
> The recipient forthwith is rendered immune
> Justified his past, his future, his fortune
> No matter what he hath done or may seek to do

He says the lines again.

'Excellent, especially for the Germans, who are always stuck on the same notions and still talk about the death of the Duke of Enghien. We must expand their morals.'

The road is clear again, the weather beautiful, crisp and cold. The villages stand out against a blue horizon.

'Let's have a performance of *Cinna* then, on the first day. It's good for men with melancholy thoughts who you find everywhere in Germany.'

HE CLOSES HIS EYES.

It is going to be a close thing, this game he's playing; he will have to be both Master of Ceremonies and winner. He has invited the Kings of Saxony, Würtemberg and Bavaria, the princes, grand dukes and duchesses of Germany and Poland, their diplomats, and Marshals Oudinot, Davout, Lannes, Berthier, Mortier, Suchet, Lauriston, Savary and Soult. And Champagny, naturally. Talleyrand will be there in his capacity as Grand Chamberlain.

I shall have to use everyone as a trump to be played. Even the actors of the Comédie-Française. I must envelop Alexander, charm him, persuade him to put pressure on Austria to stop her starting a war before I have finished with Spain.

That's what's at stake.

'We are going to Erfurt,' he murmurs. 'I want to come back free to do what I want in Spain. I want to be certain that Austria remains anxious and contained.'

I need Alexander for that.

HE IS IN A HURRY to get to Erfurt where Talleyrand is no doubt already ensconced. He mulls over a doubt he has. Was he right to put the Prince of Benevento in charge of drafting a treaty with Alexander to renew the alliance of Tilsit and provide for a Russian intervention if Austria threatens France?

They reach Châlons. It is eight in the evening. He shuts himself away with Méneval and examines the text prepared by Talleyrand. The Prince of Benevento seems to have forgotten the article concerning Austria. That was the crucial part of the treaty!

He has a presentiment.

Perhaps the mercenary, the 'pallid' Talleyrand is going to play his own card, treat Vienna with particular consideration to ensure his own future. Because he too must be thinking about my fall, my death without an heir. I need a son.

He dictates a dispatch for Marshal Oudinot, who is to assemble the most prestigious squadrons in Erfurt for the parades, which will take place in Alexander's presence.

'Before starting negotiations, I want the Emperor Alexander to be dazzled by the spectacle of my power. There isn't a negotiation that won't be facilitated by this.'

HE PASSES THROUGH Metz, Kaiserslautern, Kassel and Frankfurt. He only sleeps for a few hours, starting off again at four o'clock in the morning, when it's still dark. He stops to witness a review. He must be seen. But, after Frankfurt, he does not get out of his berline for all of Monday, 26 September, and he carries on through the night.

The next morning, at nine o'clock, accompanied by General Berthier, he at last he enters Erfurt, the French enclave in the Confederation of the Rhine.

The carriage drives alongside the River Gera, surrounded by the squadrons of the Guard. Crowds are already pressing round the palace of the Lieutenant of the Elector of Mayence, now the seat of government. This will be the imperial residence. He sees the troops lined up on the neighbouring square, the Hirschgarden.

He greets the marshals perfunctorily, issues orders, dictates a letter to Cambacérès, but he doesn't want to waste any time. He must influence each of the participants in this meeting. He pays a visit to the King of Saxony, but it is Alexander who he has to bring round to his point of view.

AT TWO IN THE AFTERNOON he is on horseback. The marshals' horses surrounding him stamp the ground. The squadron of the Guard brings up the rear, as the procession sets off on the road to Weimar to meet the Tsar.

The first moments will be as decisive as the first engagement in a battle.

At Münchenholzen, he stops and watches Alexander's carriage approach. Alexander gets out; Napoleon dismounts. He embraces the Tsar. Then they ride to Erfurt. He keeps level with Alexander; their staffs ride together. In the crisp air, the horses' hooves kick up a fine white dust.

The bells of all the churches ring out. The cannon thunder. The troops in their brightly coloured uniforms present arms.

'THE EMPEROR seems disposed to do all I wish,' Napoleon says to Talleyrand when he is alone with him in the palace.

He is walking about, as usual.

'If he talks to you,' Napoleon continues, 'tell them that my confidence in him is such that I believe it better if everything happens between us. The ministers can sign afterwards.'

He reflects.

'Remember in everything you say that whatever slows things down is useful to me. The language of all these kings will be good. They fear me.'

The game must last as long as possible. The Emperor of Austria and the King of Prussia, who won't be coming to Erfurt, will imagine the worst if the conversations stretch on with all due pomp and festivity.

Alexander is announced. Napoleon opens his arms, introduces Talleyrand.

'He is an old acquaintance,' says the Tsar. 'I am charmed to see him. I was hoping he would have made the journey.'

Napoleon looks at Talleyrand, then at Caulaincourt, the ambassador in St Petersburg, who came to Erfurt with the Tsar. These two men seem close. Are they accomplices? They are excessively deferential to the Tsar. He feels irritated; he wants to dispel these suspicions gnawing away at him; he knows he will be able to convince Alexander.

THE NEXT DAY, Wednesday, 28 September 1808, in Government House, he waits for Baron de Vincent, who is the bearer of a letter from Francis, Emperor of Austria. The atmosphere in the salon is stifling. The marshals crowd round the table. The Tsar is surrounded by his officers. Napoleon hears him speaking German to the Archduke Charles.

Talleyrand, impassive, stands a few paces away, on the other side of the table. In the gloom, Napoleon makes out Caulaincourt. This pair are definitely not his favourites.

This morning, in conversation with Alexander, he had the impression that the Tsar was being evasive, refusing to bring up the question of an alliance against Austria, should the latter attack France. He noted an unexpected determination, a reticence and coolness behind Alexander's affected politeness and declarations of friendship.

It was only a first meeting, but the Tsar's resistance is surprising.

He seems not to want to let himself be enveloped. As if he already knows my manoeuvres and my aim.

Napoleon slips his left hand into his waistcoat. He extends the right to Baron de Vincent who hands him the letter from the Emperor of Austria. He will read the letter, he says, and see the baron in a private audience on Thursday. He retires. The dispatches from Vienna confirm that Austria is continuing to arm and is refusing to recognize Murat as King of Naples and Joseph as King of Spain.

What does he want? If Alexander refuses to bear down on Vienna, it's war. It must break out as late as possible, when Spain's affairs are settled.

He receives Baron de Vincent. He wishes to communicate his anger and determination to the Emperor of Austria's envoy.

'Must I always find Austria in my path, thwarting my plans?' he asks. 'I wanted to live on good terms with you.'

He paces about the drawing room of Government House, without looking at Baron de Vincent.

'What do you expect? The Treaty of Presburg settled your fate. Are you looking for war?'

He goes up to the Austrian, stares at him.

'I must prepare myself for that and it will be terrible for you if I wage it. I neither wish it nor fear it; my resources are immense; the Emperor Alexander is, and will remain, my ally.'

IS THIS DEFINITE?

They see each other every day. In the morning, they negotiate, then they hunt together. They visit the battlefield of Jena where another hunt has been organized. The game is surrounded and killed; the boars, does and stags are tossed in a bloody heap in front of the sovereigns.

Napoleon turns away and returns to his tent, where he is to receive the sovereigns.

He doesn't like this massacre in a place where armies have clashed. Cruel, pointless butchery.

But gradually, as he tells the story of the battle, his ill humour fades. Alexander is attentive, admiring.

Perhaps I have won him over?

During the theatrical performances, the Tsar is enthusiastic and when Talma, in a scene from Voltaire's *Oedipus*, declaims, 'The friendship of a great man is a blessing of the gods,' Alexander leans over, seizes Napoleon's hand and shakes it vigorously, for all to see.

Should I believe this man?

I should act as if I have confidence in this alliance and as if Alexander were finally going to sign the Convention which puts him on my side against Austria.

Napoleon returns to the palace. He sets to work, receives Caulaincourt.

The ambassador is dignified and grave, as usual.

'What do people think I am planning?' Napoleon asks.

Caulaincourt hesitates.

'To rule alone, Majesty,' he says finally.

Napoleon shrugs his shoulders. 'But France is big enough! What more can I desire? Haven't I enough with my affairs in Spain and war against England?'

He walks round Caulaincourt, observing him.

'Spain,' he continues. 'There has been an unfortunate, even disagreeable, combination of circumstances in that country, but what does that matter to the Russians?'

He shrugs his shoulders again.

'They weren't so particular about the means of Poland's partition and submission. Spain keeps me occupied far from them; that's what they need, so they are enchanted.'

He keeps on walking.

'In politics, everything happens because of, and is founded on, world peace, the necessary balance of power between states . . . I have done what I had to, given the situation the intrigues of Madrid's court had put this unfortunate country into.'

He spreads his arms, then gives Caulaincourt a friendly slap on the back.

'I wasn't able to take into account all the consequences of the weakness, stupidity, cowardice and bad faith of the princes of Spain, but what does it matter, when one has resolve and knows what one wants!'

Can Alexander understand that?

He must. Napoleon wants to try again to persuade him of it, the next time they meet, every time they meet, starting from tomorrow.

NAPOLEON HOLDS forth animatedly as Alexander listens. From time to time he stops and looks at the Tsar who smiles at him charmingly and seems to be in agreement. Then, suddenly, Alexander starts talking about Mademoiselle Bourgoing – such a remarkable actress, such an attractive woman. Would she be amenable? he asks.

Napoleon smiles. He feels like an older brother, knowing and experienced.

'I hope you may able to resist that temptation,' he says.

He implies he's speaking in full knowledge of the case, as he would do to a fellow garrison officer. Men, whether they are lieutenants or kings, are cut from the same cloth. He adds that Mademoiselle Bourgoing is a gossip.

'In five days Paris would know what sort of a man, from his head to his toes, Your Majesty is,' he says.

Alexander laughs, makes his bow and, after a complicit glance, leaves the room.

Napoleon feels reassured. He must continue weaving and mending the intimacy with Alexander which he established at Tilsit; that way he will undoubtedly manage to convince him, and make him understand that the alliance between the two of them must be extended to include a guarantee against Austria.

THAT EVENING at the theatre, during a performance of *Phèdre* by the Comédie-Française, he makes sure he is attentive to the Tsar and invites the Duchess of Saxe-Hildburghausen, who is the sister of Queen Louise of Prussia, into the imperial box. Better flatter these Prussians, since Alexander is still so infatuated with them. The Tsar seems alive to these marks of consideration.

During the concerts and dinners, the daily reviews and balls, Napoleon shows Alexander every sort of attention.

He must seduce this man, to whom, in any case, he feels drawn. Out of all the sovereigns of Europe, Alexander is the only one for whom he does not feel scorn. He would like to establish a relationship of trust and friendship with him, without illusions but also without hypocrisy.

When he returns from the theatre that evening, he cannot sleep.

In the middle of the night, he feels an intense pain in his chest, as if he is suffocating. He wakes in a sweat. He sees shadows around him. He thinks of Tsar Paul, murdered by Alexander's close relatives, who were obeying the orders of that parricide son.

He curls into a ball. He recognizes Constant and Roustam. They dry him. He gets out of bed and starts a letter to Josephine,

My friend, I don't write enough: I am very busy. Conversations all day long; it is no good for my cold, but all goes well.

He hesitates, then writes:

I am satisfied with Alexander; he should be with me; if he were a woman, I believe I would make him my mistress.

I shall be with you in a short while; look after your health, and let me find you plump and fresh.

Farewell, my friend.

Napoleon

AT THE BALL GIVEN at Weimar, Napoleon watches Alexander dance elegantly.

He does a tour of the room, his hands behind his back. The sovereigns bow. He recognizes Goethe, that little man who came one morning to Erfurt to attend his levée. He goes up to him.

'Monsieur Goethe, I am charmed to see you.'

He looks around. In that room, with the exception of Alexander perhaps, there are so many puppets, automata, so much stupidity hidden beneath uniforms and decorations.

'Monsieur Goethe, you are a great man. I know you are Germany's finest tragic poet.'

Next to Goethe stands the dramatist Wieland.

'Monsieur Wieland,' says Napoleon, 'we call you the Voltaire of Germany.'

Napoleon turns around. Alexander is still dancing.

'But why,' Napoleon continues, 'do you write in that ambiguous genre which imports the novel into history and history into the novel? For a man of your talent, genres should be clear-cut and exclusive. Everything that is a mixture leads all too easily to confusion . . .'

'The thoughts of humans are sometimes better than their actions,' says Wieland, 'and good novels are better than human behaviour.'

Napoleon shakes his head.

'Do you know what happens to those who always show virtue in their novels? They make it seem that virtue is nothing but a chimera. History has been slandered often enough by historians themselves . . .'

He stops for a moment, and then says, 'Do you know a greater and often more unjust detractor of the human race than Tacitus? Tacitus never taught me anything. He finds criminal motives for the simplest actions. Am I not right, Monsieur Wieland?'

He points to the ballroom.

'But I am disturbing you. We are not here to discuss Tacitus. Look how well Emperor Alexander dances.'

He listens to Wieland tell him that he is an Emperor who speaks as a man of letters.

'I know Your Majesty does not disdain this title.'

Napoleon remembers dreaming of being a writer, like Jean-Jacques. It was so long ago, in his room back in Valence. Wieland and Goethe are now talking about men's passions which one day will be mastered by reason. Napoleon starts to walk away, remarking, 'That's what all our philosophers say! I'm looking for this force of reason, and I can't see it anywhere.'

SUDDENLY HE FEELS weary, alone in the midst of this bejewelled crowd. With a flash of clarity, he realizes that he is deluding himself about Alexander, that he's wrong in thinking he's going to be able to bring him round to his point of view.

Who knows if the Emperor's policy of resistance isn't supported by Talleyrand and Caulaincourt, men who play their own hands, the former so mercenary and adept, the latter so avid for peace, and both ready to reveal my strategy so that I will fail?

He remains awake all night, even though tiredness has overwhelmed him and made his body heavy as lead. He finds it hard to breathe. His stomach hurts, and it seems swollen, enormous. He tries to calm down. He writes a few lines to Josephine:

> My friend, I have received your letter. I see with pleasure that you are in good health. I went to the ball at Weimar. The Emperor Alexander danced, but I didn't. Forty years are forty years.
> My health is basically good, in spite of a few little ailments. Farewell my friend.
> Ever yours. I hope to see you soon.
> Napoleon

IN THE MORNING, he has decided to find out what he should think of the Tsar's intentions.

He does not say anything when Alexander enters the room where they met yesterday, and begins speaking enthusiastically about the Weimar ball and the grace and distinction of Princess Stéphanie de Beauharnais, the wife of Charles, hereditary prince of Baden and brother of the Empress of Russia.

'Stéphanie de Beauharnais, my sister-in-law,' says Alexander.

Napoleon listens and then curtly speaks of Austria, and the threat of war it is putting France under. A diplomatic intervention by Alexander is the only way to maintain peace. Is the Tsar resolved to commit himself?

Alexander seems not to have heard.

He must know.

Napoleon takes his hat, throws it on the ground, tramples on it, shouting that he wants a definite answer. Alexander stands up and makes for the door.

'You are violent, I am wilful,' he says. 'Anger achieves nothing with me. Let us talk, let us reason, otherwise I shall leave.'

Napoleon grasps his arm, laughing, and leads him to the middle of the room, where he sits down next to him and starts to chat.

'Stéphanie de Beauharnais has a nice wit,' he says.

Now he knows.

Alexander will never sign an alliance committing him to France's side against Austria.

Here, at last, everyone's position is clear.

He has wasted a few days in pointless manoeuvres, but he has not let himself be fooled. Has Talleyrand sold himself to Vienna, as he senses, and has he urged Alexander to resist him? Will he ever have proof of his betrayal?

But that is how men and things are. One has to look them in the face, change one's ends and make sure that the war Vienna will inevitably declare starts as late as possible.

So, HE WILL have to wage war again, here, in Germany.

He looks at the countryside with a mixture of bitterness and melancholy. He has not been able to impose peace. He feels detached from everything that is going on around him. He is already elsewhere, in Spain, where he will have to hasten when he leaves Erfurt, and then he must face the Austrian armies.

He takes his seat at one of the dinners that no longer amuse him. On his right, he has the Tsar and the Kings of Westphalia and Würtemberg. On his left, the Duchess of Weimar, the Kings of Bavaria and Saxony. He speaks of the origins of the German Constitution. People are amazed at his erudition. He looks at all these assembled sovereigns.

He speaks about garrison life, the time he has devoted, the years of his life, to reading, studying and filling reams of exercise books with notes.

'When I was a lieutenant of artillery . . .' he begins, looking at each of the sovereigns in turn.

Then he starts again, 'When I had the honour to be a lieutenant of artillery . . .'

HE DOESN'T REGRET this surge of pride and vanity. That's what he was; now he is Emperor. He must change tactics with Alexander. It is so often like this on a battlefield. Unable to break through the enemy? Then one attacks on the wings. But don't let anyone imagine he considers falling back. He is not going to give up any of his fortresses in Germany, on the Oder, which will be so useful in this war that Alexander has not wanted to make impossible and Vienna is bent on.

Talleyrand requests an audience. Napoleon listens to him. The Prince of Benevento urges moderation, compromise.

Napoleon stares at him, then, as if distracted, says, 'You are rich, Talleyrand. When I need money, you are who I will turn to. Come now, upon your conscience, how much have you made with me?'

He knows he won't ruffle Talleyrand, or get him to confess anything.

'I have achieved nothing with Emperor Alexander,' says Napoleon, seeming to forget the question he'd asked. 'I turned the matter over and over, but he is of limited intelligence. I did not advance a single step.'

Caulaincourt has entered the drawing room. Napoleon turns towards him. 'Your Emperor Alexander is as stubborn as a mule. He turns a deaf ear to anything he does not want to hear. This confounded Spanish business is costing me dear!'

'The Emperor Alexander is completely under your spell,' says Talleyrand.

Napoleon laughs derisively.

'That's the face he shows you, and you are taken in. If he loves me so much, why doesn't he give me a sign?'

He interrupts Talleyrand who has again started speaking about the Oder fortresses, and the likelihood they will have to evacuate them.

'You are proposing a position of weakness there!' Napoleon bellows. 'If I acquiesce, Europe will soon treat me like a little boy.'

He takes a swift pinch of snuff and walks about the middle of the room, ignoring Talleyrand and Caulaincourt. He has learnt that one must always make use of every situation. He has not stayed at Erfurt this long just to abandon the field.

'Do you know why no one acts straight with me?' he says, going up to Talleyrand. 'It is because, there being no heir, they think all France depends on me alone. This is the secret of everything you've seen here: people fear me, and yet everyone is looking to their own future as best they can; it's a poor state of affairs for everybody. And . . .'

He articulates each word:

'One day it will have to be remedied. Continue to see the Emperor Alexander: perhaps I was slightly uncivil to him, but I want us to part on good terms . . .'

He detains Caulaincourt as he seeks to leave with Talleyrand.

The Tsar must be sounded out about a new marriage, Napoleon tells him, and the necessity of his having children to found a new dynasty.

Caulaincourt seems surprised, embarrassed.

'It's to see if Alexander is really one of my friends, if he takes a genuine interest in the welfare of France. I love Josephine. I'll never be happy again. But this way we will find out the opinion of the other sovereigns about his divorce which, for me, would be a sacrifice. My family, Talleyrand, Fouché and every statesman demand I go through with it, in France's name. And it's true, a boy would give France much more stability than my brothers, who are not loved and not very capable . . . Perhaps you favour Eugène? Adoptions, however, do not lay good foundations for a new dynasty. I have other plans for him.'

PERHAPS ALL that will remain of Erfurt is this idea of divorce, which he has broached so that Europe's sovereigns will not be surprised when the repudiation comes. Consulting the Tsar will make him feel that Napoleon still has every confidence in him.

Even though, on Wednesday, 12 October, he only signs a convention that is, at best, a simple renewal of the treaty of alliance concluded at Tilsit.

'I signed it with my eyes shut, so as not to see the future,' Napoleon murmurs to Berthier.

But he knows the future.

He has suggested to Alexander that they write a letter to George III, King of England. He chooses the wording: 'Peace is therefore in the interests both of the people of the Continent and those of Great Britain.' They must put an end to this 'long, bloody war' for 'the welfare of Europe'.

Words England will reject.

IT IS FRIDAY, 14 October 1808.

He is riding at Alexander's side on the Weimar road. He looks at their staffs rearing their horses on their hind-legs. The soldiers present arms. He hears the bells of Erfurt's churches ringing in the distance. The cannon boom.

He stops his horse at the exact spot where, eighteen days ago, he welcomed Alexander. His illusions and hopes have all fallen by the wayside since then.

The Tsar's carriage is waiting with his escort.

He embraces Alexander. He holds him for a few seconds by the shoulders, then watches him get into his carriage.

He feels heavy; slowly he heaves himself onto his horse and turns back onto the Erfurt road.

It's silent; no bells nor cannon; only the hollow drumming of hooves on ground that's wet from a thin but persistent drizzle.

Napoleon rides his horse at a walk, alone, out in front of his staff.

His head is bowed. He lets his horse pick its course. He closes his eyes to avoid looking at this future he can imagine.

PART FIVE

Impossible?
I don't know that word

14 OCTOBER 1808 TO 23 JANUARY 1809

XIX

HE LEAVES ERFURT in the early evening of Friday, 14 October 1808. It is raining and cold. The paraffin lamps blaze in his berline. He instals himself under one of them to read the dispatches that are starting to arrive from Paris and Spain. It only takes a few words from General Clarke or appeals for help from Joseph, who calls for reinforcements and advocates insane operations, to imagine what it must be like for his soldiers in the midst of a people in revolt. Their throats are being slit. They're looting and massacring. They're afraid. Tens of thousands of British have crossed over from Portugal and are now fighting in Spain under John Moore.

He pushes the dispatches aside. He begins to dictate a letter for General Junot who did surrender to the English at Cintra, and has since been repatriated to France, according to the terms of that surrender.

'The minister of war has shown me all your reports . . . You have done nothing dishonourable. You brought back my troops, my eagles and my cannon. I had, however, hoped that you would do better . . . Publicly I am going to approve your conduct; what I write confidentially is for you alone.'

Napoleon remains silent for a few minutes, then he resumes dictating, 'Before the end of the year I intend to re-establish you myself in Lisbon.'

HE FEELS TENSE. He doesn't want any stops, except to change the horses. They drive through Frankfurt and continue on to Mainz.

One game has just ended and now another is beginning. As he had anticipated, he must personally take command of his troops and enter Madrid and Lisbon. He must crush this revolt and drive the English from the pensinsula.

All his good troops are on the northern bank of the Ebro. He demanded they wait for the Spaniards, in order to envelop them, at the right moment, by breaking through the centre and then rolling up their flank. However, Joseph, who can't command an army, has given his own orders and Ney and Lefebvre, carried away by their ardour, have attacked on the wings, earning some success. But haven't they understood that the only thing that counts is the total victory that destroys the enemy?

He dictates a letter to Joseph. 'In war, one must have sound, precise ideas,' he says. 'What you propose is unfeasible.' Joseph must wait for him to get there.

He tells the coachman to pick up the pace.

He has to win this Spanish game fast, to be able to come back and fight here, against Austria.

If he'd been able at Erfurt to . . .

HE HAS NO REGRETS. He did what he could, but Alexander was elusive. He picks up one of the police reports which he has only just set eyes on.

Every evening in Erfurt, the Tsar went to Princess Thurn und Taxis's, where he met up with Talleyrand. Every evening they spent several hours in each other's company, often in private, away from the princess's other guests. Baron de Vincent, the Emperor of Austria's envoy, frequently participated in these discussions.

Talleyrand has betrayed me. His politics has always been to protect Vienna, but has he gone further? Not content with dissuading Alexander from joining me to threaten Austria, has he actually turned him against me? How much has this 'pallid' prince been paid by Vienna?

What does he want? To insure his future in case I die or am defeated? Or else to unite Europe in a coalition against me to bring me into subjection? Should I break him, or still put him to use, without any illusions?

He hesitates, then dictates an order for the Prince of Benevento. One must know how to exploit the enemy.

'You will give a dinner at your house at least four times a week for thirty-six people, mainly legislators, state councillors and ministers, to enable them to see each other, and to enable you to get to know the principal ones and cultivate their dispositions.'

Let the pallid prince be my valet.

He feels a sense of disgust. Deep down, he has regard only for men who expose their breasts to gunfire. The rest are slimy and make one feel soiled the minute one comes into contact with them.

HE ARRIVES AT the Château of St Cloud on Tuesday, 18 October, just before midnight.

He only sees Josephine the next morning. She has that anxious expression he can't stand. She doesn't ask him anything, but her eyes hound him. She knows he's waiting for an opportunity to separate from her, to conclude one of the princely marriages he's forced on all the other members of his family. Why won't he follow suit?

But she doesn't dare ask him openly. She's just anguished when he says he's only going to stay a few days in Paris. He wants to attend the opening of the Legislative Body, show himself in public with her, the Empress, in the streets, inspecting the building work at the Louvre and on the banks of the Seine and then he'll rejoin the army in Spain.

She clings to him. Does he have to leave to make war? Will it never end?

He is sharp with her, shrugging her off. Does she think he wouldn't prefer a good bed to splashing and floundering about in the mud of a bivouac?

He slams doors, shuts himself away in his study. He sees Cambacérès, Fouché, his ministers. They don't dare speak as frankly as Josephine. They obey, but he senses their reservations.

Yes, war, again! What can he do? England has responded to his offer of peace with unacceptable demands. Why should it stop fighting when its troops are having success and Austria is arming?

He doesn't order events; he obeys them. It is his duty to France. His destiny.

IN THE NIGHT OF Friday, 28 October, he has his coach stop in rue de la Victoire. He surprises Marie Walewska asleep. Making love to her, then leaving, moves him intensely.

Such is his life.

He sets off for Rambouillet and from there, via Tours and Angoulême, for Bayonne.

QUICK. This is the only word he says. At St André de Cubzac he orders the carriage to stop. The Landes's sandy roads keep forcing them to slow down and he can't stand it. He is going to finish the journey on horseback. He mounts up and sets off at a gallop. He is shattered when he arrives in Bayonne with Duroc on Thursday, 3 November. It is two in the morning. Staggering with tiredness, he shouts orders. He wants to see the army's stores. There are no uniforms, even though it is bracingly cold and Spain is rainswept.

'I have nothing left, I am naked,' he yells. 'My army is indigent. The army contractors are thieves. Never have we been so unworthily served and betrayed.'

He is too tired to continue his journey. He puts up at Marracq Castle once again, but he cannot sleep. He dictates a letter to General Dejean, the minister in charge of army administration.

Then, as if to think out loud, he writes to Josephine.

I arrived in Bayonne tonight, after quite a slog, having galloped across the Landes. I am a little tired.

I shall set off for Spain tomorrow. My troops are arriving in numbers.

Farewell, my friend. Yours ever.
Napoleon

HE WAKES WITH a start after less than an hour's sleep. He wants to see the officials responsible for the depots. He bawls them out, demanding they organize supply convoys to follow the army. He reviews a squadron of Polish Light Horse, then carries on to Tolosa, a little town a few kilometres south of St Sebastian.

He's in Spain. The game has started.

The parlour of the monastery where he's lodged is icy cold. It's pouring with rain. General Bigarre approaches, bows ceremoniously and pays his compliments in the name of Joseph, King of Spain.

Joseph takes himself for Charles V!

'He's taken leave of his senses,' he grumbles. 'He has become a king through and through.'

He hears murmuring. A delegation of monks steps forward. He stares at the round faces, listens to the honeyed voices protesting their goodwill and respect.

'Gentlemen, if you take it into your heads to meddle with military affairs, I promise you I will have your ears cut off!'

He enters the cell that has been prepared for him for the night. He throws himself fully clothed on the narrow bed. It's cold.

Such is war.

XX

He reaches Vitoria on 5 November 1808.

In the streets of the little town he passes units of Footguards and Horseguards who are heading for Burgos, the city he has ordered must be captured. If it falls, the Spanish front will be broken and the way to Madrid will be open.

The soldiers recognize him and cheer. He stops and acknowledges them, raising his hat and causing more shouts of 'Long live the Emperor!' These privates who he asks to give their lives are still enthusiastic. He watches them march past for a long time. He needs the trust these grenadiers are showing him.

At length he carries on to the bishop's palace where Joseph is waiting for him, surrounded by his court. He does not embrace him, but leads him aside immediately.

'War is a profession,' he says, 'and you don't know anything of it.' The orders Joseph has given are impossible to carry out.

In a louder voice, so that Marshal Ney, who has refused to obey Joseph, can hear, he declares, 'Any general who undertook such an operation would be a criminal.'

Joseph looks at him, scarlet in the face, but he says nothing.

Joseph has never been very brave. He is attached to his crown. He should — no, he will — give in.

He is my elder brother, but I am the Emperor. I have made him what he is.

Napoleon thunders his orders.

Joseph will follow my staff at a distance. There will be no further meddling in military matters from him.

I will give him Spain when it's been brought to heel.

He turns round, calls the marshals, generals, aides-de-camp. He doesn't concern himself about Joseph any more.

In war, one cannot waste one's time and one's energy tending people's pride, even a king's, even if he is one's elder brother!

When it grows dark, he goes for a walk round Vitoria. Soldiers have established their bivouacs on the square. The sky is so bright one can count the stars. This magnificent weather is auspicious. It is as beautiful and mild as the finest May night in France. He goes back and, without sitting down, writes a few lines to Josephine:

> My friend, I am two days in Vitoria; my health is good. Troops are coming in daily; the Guard arrived today.
>   The King is in excellent health. I am very busy.
>   I know you are in Paris. Do not doubt my feelings.
>   Napoleon

HE ASKS CONSTANT to wake him as soon as the aides-de-camp bringing dispatches from the marshals arrive.

He needs to be where the fighting is. He decides to join Marshal Soult, who has just bowled over the Spanish and taken Burgos. He rides so fast that he reaches Cubo, on the Burgos road, accompanied only by an aide-de-camp, Roustam and a few chasseurs. The rest of his escort and staff haven't managed to keep up. He reins in his horse and dictates a letter to an officer for Joseph:

> My brother,
>   I shall start at one in the morning so as to reach Burgos before dawn, where I shall make my arrangements for the day, for a victory is nothing, it must be turned to account.
>   While I think there need be little ceremony made over me, I do think there should be for you. As for me, it doesn't go with my profession of arms; in any case I don't want any. It seems to me that deputations from Burgos should come to meet you and give you a good reception.

He leaps back into the saddle. No time to wait for the escort.

On the outskirts of Burgos, he sees by the glimmer of their torches that the grenadiers accompanying him are fanning out to find their way through a jumbled mass of dead — soldiers, peasants and monks all atop one another.

It is still dark when he enters the town. Drunken soldiers are staggering about the rubble-strewn streets. On the square in front of the archbishop's palace, Church furniture is burning in huge bonfires. The smell is pestilential. Corpses lie everywhere amongst the rubbish and disembowelled horses. Women's screams can be heard above the soldiers' singing.

He passes through the middle of the soldiers who don't see him, so carried away are they by the frenzied revels, rape and pillage.

The room in which he is to sleep in the archbishop's palace is filthy, its furniture smashed. Three armed Spaniards have just been discovered hiding in it.

He sits down on the archbishop's stained bed. He is overwhelmed with tiredness. He is hungry. He has become a campaigning officer again. It is as if he had never known the luxury of palaces. Roustam brings him a bit of roast meat, bread and wine which he got from some of the grenadiers bivouacking on the square. He eats, his legs splayed, in that dirty, stinking, barely lit room. Then he lies down on the bed, still in his boots and clothes covered with dust and mud.

THE NEXT MORNING, he watches the smoke rising from Burgos for a moment. Some ruined buildings are still burning. He summons his aides-de-camp. He wants to know the positions of the different armies, under Soult, Ney, Victor and Lannes. The officers must take the men back in hand so that the pillaging stops. He goes on a tour of inspection of the town and the warehouses they've discovered which are overflowing with provisions.

On the square, he hears the first shouts of 'Long live the Emperor!'

'There's more Bacchus than anything else in this,' he says.

One cannot command an army of drunks and looters. Every day he will hold a review of the troops, he announces.

He returns to the archbishop's palace which the grenadiers of the Guard have started cleaning. The first couriers are arriving and reporting, as the hours pass, victories for Soult at Reynosa, Victor at Espinosa, Lannes at Tudela. Castaños's Spaniards are in flight, as are John Moore's English troops. He leans over the maps. Now they can march on Madrid.

Before leaving Burgos, he visits the wounded who are crowded into the Convent of the Conception. He sees his mutilated men, eaten away by gangrene, lying in rotten straw. They raise themselves, salute the Emperor, tell him what they've seen and what others have told them.

Captain Marbot, Lannes's aide-de-camp, was wounded bringing dispatches to the Emperor. On the road, they say, Marbot saw 'a young officer of the 10th Chasseurs à Cheval, still dressed in his uniform, nailed by his hands and feet to a barn door! The poor wretch was upside down and a little fire had been lit under his head. Luckily for him, his torments had ceased; he was dead! But blood still ran from his wounds.'

Napoleon is silent. He remembers some blood-stained dispatches he'd been given: they were the ones Marbot was carrying when he was wounded.

They must bring this war to a close and get out of this bloody quagmire.

He passes between the rows of wounded, has eight napoleons given to each officer and three to each soldier. Then, leaving the Convent of the Conception, he takes the road to Aranda.

He pushes his horse hard over the stony ground. His aides-de-camp and escort have difficulty following him. He seems not to feel any tiredness. He wants to enter Madrid.

AT ARANDA, he sees the Sierra de la Guadarrama on the horizon. This is the rocky barrier which Bacler d'Albe, staff officer and chief geographer, underlined on the map with a thick black line while still in Burgos. Behind this sierra lies Madrid and there is only one way to cross the mountain range: the Somosierra pass.

Napoleon leans over the map with Bacler d'Albe. They are so close their foreheads touch. Napoleon straightens up.

He trusts this man whom he has known for ages and always wants to have near him, in his tent, on campaign. He questions him. Bacler d'Albe has stuck coloured pins into the map marking out the route of the Somosierra. The pass is above fourteen hundred metres at its highest point; the road, hemmed in by mountains, is narrow and, according to voltigeurs, mountaineering troops, who have gone ahead to reconnoitre, it is barred by Spanish gun emplacements at every one of its hairpin bends. At the summit, there is a final obstacle, a battery of sixteen guns and thousands of Spaniards commanded by Benito San Juan.

'The only way,' Napoleon murmurs.

They have to cross by the Somosierra pass to be able to bear down on Madrid. He wants to appraise the situation himself.

ON WEDNESDAY, 30 November, he advances through the streets of the village of Ceroso de Arriba, which is at the foot of the sierra. Soldiers cheer him. He gives the order to the colonel of the chasseurs of the Guard, Piré, to go and reconnoitre. He waits, observing a squadron of 250 Polish Light Horse who are having trouble keeping their restless mounts still.

He sees Piré coming back, lying flat on the neck of his horse. Out of breath, he gasps that it is impossible to get through. Cannon are raking the road.

' "Impossible". I don't know that word.'

Napoleon signals to Captain Korjietulski who is commanding the Polish Light Horse.

The troopers race off up the pass road, their ardent throng ashimmer with the royal blue and scarlet of their uniforms, their black chapki undulating like waves.

Napoleon hears the crack of Spanish muskets, then shouting, drowned out by cannonades.

They must pass. Madrid is over these mountains.

But they sweep back in complete disorder. They charged without leaving any gaps between their lines, and courage alone is never enough.

Napoleon sees General Montbrun riding forward from the ranks of his staff; he's offering to take command of the Poles for a new charge. The man is tall, with a scarred face and a bushy black beard. An orderly officer, Ségur, steps up. He wants to be part of the attack as well.

Napoleon nods.

They must get over this pass.

He observes Montbrun give his orders, directing the riders to keep a certain distance from each other.

He watches them gallop up the steep slope. They disappear between the rocks.

A volley of musketry rings out, then artillery fire, and shouts of 'Long live the Emperor!' echo between the walls of the pass.

They are going to get through. They are dying for me.
More firing, more shouting amplified by the echo rolls down this road half a league long.
How many are going to die? Will they get through?
Explosions come from the summit of the Somosierra pass which is covered in smoke. They have reached it. They have got through.

Napoleon tears off, taking his staff with him. Behind, at the double, follows General Ruffin's infantry division.

Reaching the pass, he sees Ségur and the Polish Lieutenant Niegolowski lying amongst the Spanish corpses, both of them wounded, as is Montbrun.

Napoleon leaps off his horse. He looks at the forty or so survivors, most of whom are covered in blood. He bends down, takes off his cross, and pins it to the Polish lieutenant's chest.

Then he gets back on his horse and crosses the pass. In front of him lies a vast expanse. He imagines Madrid up ahead, on the horizon.

He gallops to the village of Buitrago. He will sleep there.

It only takes a handful of men to change the course of a war.

Next day he holds a review of the survivors. He raises his hat. He stands up in his stirrups. He cries in a loud voice, 'You are worthy of my Old Guard! I acknowledge you my bravest cavalry!'

In the deep voices that answer 'Long live the Emperor!' he hears the Polish accent, Marie Walewska's accent.

He starts his horse off at full gallop. He wants to sleep in the suburbs of Madrid tonight.

It is Thursday, 1 December 1808.

Four years ago, it was the eve of his coronation as Emperor. In a few hours he is going to conquer a new city, Madrid, the city of Charles V and Philip II.

When he is about to enter his tent, which has been pitched at San Agostino, he raises his eyes.

The sky is luminous.

He looks at the stars for a long time. He is worthy of his crown, he is loyal to his destiny.

HE GETS UP WHEN dawn has barely started to reveal the horizon and rides his horse along the front line. Madrid is there, in a rough of darkness that slowly fills with light. He sees the roofs of the city and its palaces take shape. He gives the order to mount the first attack at three in the afternoon, then he withdraws to Chamartín Castle, a league and a half from the capital.

But he cannot stay that far away from the fighting. He would rather bivouac on the start line.

The troops launch the second wave of their attack in milky moonlight. The Spaniards defending the Retiro Palace, the Observatory, the porcelain factory, the main barracks and the Medina Celí are routed.

Napoleon observes the fighting from a hill which is swept by the Spanish artillery. He wants to see the city fall. The gates are taken. He gives the order to stop the attack. He issues a third warning to the Spanish.

'A general attack is going to be launched, but I would rather Madrid surrendered to reason and humanity than force.'

He waits for a Spanish delegation led by General Thomas de Morla, who tells Napoleon's aides-de-camp that he needs a whole day, 4 December, to convince the people of the necessity to stop fighting.

He wants to see the Spaniards himself. He stands in the antechamber of his tent, arms crossed, and looks the three delegates up and down. He listens to them talk about their people's determination for a few minutes, then stops them with a wave of his hand.

'You are using the name of your people in vain,' he says. 'If you cannot manage to calm them down, it is because you have excited them, led them astray with your lies.'

He takes a step forward.

'Assemble the parish priests, the heads of monasteries, the magistrates, the main landowners and tell them that either the city surrenders between now and six in the morning or it ceases to exist.'

He goes still closer to General Morla.

'You massacred the unfortunate French prisoners who fell into your hands. A few days ago, you let two of the Russian ambassador's servants be dragged through the streets, then put to death simply because they were born French.'

He has learnt recently of the conditions in which prisoners

from General Dupont's army have been kept on the island of Cabrera.

'The incompetence and cowardice of one general,' he bursts out, 'delivered into your hands troops who had capitulated on the field of battle, and their capitulation has been violated. How dare you demand a capitulation, Monsieur Morla, when you violated that of Baylen?'

He turns his back on the delegates.

'Return to Madrid,' he says, pushing back the curtain that divides the tent in two. 'I am giving you until six o'clock tomorrow morning. Return then if all you have to tell me of your people is that it is submissive. Otherwise you and your men will be put to the sword.'

ON SUNDAY, 4 December 1808 he is woken a little before six.

His bedroom in Chamartín Castle is icy; a brazier has been set up in the middle of the room which has no fireplace.

Marshal Berthier is announced.

He calls him in. He guesses that Madrid has capitulated. Who can resist strength and determination?

Now he must change Spain. He dictates the text of a decree while the darkness outside is still unrelieved by any glimmer of dawn.

Madrid has surrendered and we occupied it at noon.
From the date of the publication of the present decree, feudal dues are abolished in Spain. The tribunal of the Inquisition is abolished as infringing on the sovereign power and civil authority. From the 1st of January next, the existing toll-gates between provinces shall be suppressed and the customs houses moved and set up on the frontiers.

He detains Berthier. They must extend the Civil Code to all Spain.

'The Civil Code is the code of the century; it not only preaches tolerance but organizes it.'

The Inquisition, he thinks, these monks, this fanaticism . . .

He seems to become aware of Berthier's presence. He wants the troops to parade through Madrid in gala order.

'At last I have it, this Spain of my desires.'

HE VISITS MADRID, but feels no attraction for this city which strikes him as cold and hostile, despite the restoration of order.

He prefers to stay in the Castle of Chamartín, where he receives the marshals and Spaniards who have rallied to him. He speaks to them of liberty, of the decrees he has just issued. He senses they have reservations, as if they do not understand that he wants to open Spain to new ideas.

'You have been led astray by perfidious men,' he tells them, 'who have involved you in an insane conflict.'

He reminds them of the measures he has taken.

'I have broken the shackles that have weighed on the people; a liberal constitution gives you, instead of an absolute monarchy, a moderate, constitutional monarchy.'

When they remain silent, his temper flares up. 'It depends on you whether this constitution becomes your law. If all my efforts are fruitless, all that will be left for me will be to treat you as a conquered province and place my brother on another throne.'

He spreads his hands over the brazier.

'Then I'll put the Spanish crown on my own head and I shall make it respected by the wicked.'

He goes towards them.

'God has given me the strength and will to overcome every obstacle,' he says.

He walks away, suddenly thoughtful.

What if one day God, or destiny, were to abandon me?

He turns back towards the Spaniards.

He will still have the strength and will; he is sure of it.

XXI

HE TOSSES JOSEPH'S LETTER onto the table covered with maps
in the room in Chamartín Castle which he uses as a study. The
brazier near the table glows red. Napoleon picks up the letter
again. Everything about it irritates him, from the very first line.
Joseph has written:

> Sire, I blush with shame at not having been consulted before the
> promulgation of the decrees of 4 December, after the capture of
> Madrid.
> I implore Your Majesty to receive my renunciation of all the
> rights which you have given me to the throne of Spain. I shall
> always prefer honour and probity to power bought at such a price.

Napoleon crushes the letter into a ball.

*What has Joseph ever bought? He has never shed his blood! He
hasn't even be able to give an effective order! And what general would
obey him, what grumbler respect him? He will stay on the Spanish
throne as long as is necessary. In any case, he won't abdicate. He's too
attached to his title!*

Napoleon paces up and down, then goes back to the table. He
lays his hand flat on the open map of Spain.

The one who decides, the one who's respected, is the one who fights.

He bends down. First he must drive out the English, take them
in a pincer movement. Moore will try to evacuate his army from a
port in Galicia or from Lisbon. He must destroy it first. And for
that he must take his troops in hand again.

He sends for Berthier.

'Looters must be shot!' he exclaims, the minute he enters the
room.

He shows Berthier a petition requesting that he pardon two
voltigeurs who have been caught with objects stolen from a church
in Madrid. They're good soldiers, their colonel testifies, who
deserve to be pardoned.

'No. Looting ruins everything,' Napoleon says as he walks

about the room, 'even the army that practises it. Peasants leave the land, which presents a double disadvantage: they become irreconcilable enemies who avenge themselves on the unattached soldier and swell the enemy ranks as we deplete them; and we are deprived of all local information, which is so necessary to wage war, and of all means of subsistence. Looters must be shot,' he repeats through gritted teeth.

That's the price of discipline.

He leads Berthier over to the map. Lannes, he shows him, is besieging Saragossa, Gouvion Saint Cyr has just defeated General Reding's army at Molinas del Rey.

'We are the masters of Catalonia, the Asturias and Old and New Castile.'

But now Moore and his English must be crushed; they must fling themselves into the pursuit and not give them a minute's respite.

'It will be hard for them to escape and they will pay dearly for this enterprise they've dared undertake on the continent.'

He goes up to the window. The sky is the purest blue. He wants to hold a review of the whole army, between Chamartín Castle and Madrid, and then set off with Ney, Soult, Duroc and Bessières.

He looks north, to the black line of the Sierra de la Guadarrama. He will have to cross it again, not by the Somosierra pass, but further south, by a pass that's not so high.

On 22 December he writes to Josephine.

'I am leaving at once to operate against the English who seem to have received reinforcements and wish to cut a swagger. The weather is beautiful; my health is perfect; do not worry.'

ON THE MORNING of Thursday the 22nd, he consults the latest dispatches brought by Soult's aides-de-camp. He is amazed.

'The English manoeuvre is extraordinary,' he says. 'It is probable that they have sent their transports to Ferrol, thinking they won't be safe retreating on Lisbon.'

He goes to the window.

'The whole of the Guard has set off. We shall probably reach Valladolid on the 24th or the 25th at the latest.'

But, to do so, they must march at backbreaking speed.

He goes out onto the steps of the castle.

It is two in the afternoon.

HE SPURS HIS HORSE but, after riding headlong for twenty minutes or so, he straightens up in the saddle. The weather is changing. An icy wind is blowing in squalls. The peaks of the Sierra de la Guadarrama are disappearing behind grey-black clouds.

At the foot of the sierra, he sees disorderly troops tramping along amid the horses and artillery caissons. They are foundering in a blizzard, blinded by the gusting snow. He is forced to dismount in a crowd of men that, despite the efforts of the Guard to keep them back, envelops him.

'One doesn't stop for a snowstorm,' he murmurs. 'One pushes on through.'

Ducking his head, he listens to the explanations the officers give him. The pass is being raked by a violent wind that has already driven several men over the precipices. The horses have slipped on the sheet ice. The cannon have hurtled down the slope. The snow and ice are making it impossible to make any headway. They cannot get across.

We have to pass.

He issues his orders in a loud voice. The men of each platoon are to link arms to brace themselves against the wind. Troopers are to dismount and proceed in the same fashion.

One must always pay with oneself.

He links arms with Duroc and Lannes. The staff is to divide up into groups.

'Forward march!' he shouts.

A league and half to cover to the summit. He pulls, bent double; he's pushed; he pushes. He is a man like any other, but he knows what he wants, why he's marching.

Halfway up the slope, he has to stop in the snow. His riding boots are impossible to walk in. He sits astride a cannon. He will get through. The generals and marshals copy him.

'Damned profession!' he yells, his face frozen, his sight blurred by the snow.

He hears furious voices speaking up from the crowd of infantry. 'Shoot him down, that damned swine, put a bullet in his head!'

He has never heard such cries of hatred before tonight. He doesn't even turn his head. Let them threaten him, what does it matter. Let them kill him, why not? If that is what destiny wants. He's not afraid of these men who are driven mad by exhaustion and cold.

He is with them. They won't dare shoot at their Emperor. But he feels anxiety taking root in him.

Is it here, in Spain, during this 'unfortunate war' that the threads of my destiny will loop themselves into their 'fatal knot'?

He bows his head against the blizzard. He thinks of the illustrious men whose rise and fall he has passionately followed in Plutarch.

All of them had a moment when their destiny turned. Is this that moment for me?

'Forward,' he yells.

The wind blows harder. In the swirling snow, he makes out the buildings of a monastery that stands on the top of the pass. The men need wine and wood; he organizes the distribution, on his feet in the driving wind for the men, issuing orders that the army should rest. Then, after half an hour or so, he starts down the other side. They must catch the English at all costs.

In Espinar, at the bottom of the sierra, he stops. He goes into the post house.

He collapses for a moment, prostrate with tiredness, then sits up and looks around. His staff officers are sitting on the floor.

Everything about them suggests despondency and exhaustion.

He calls Méneval over. He wants Bacler d'Albe found, the maps laid out. In the meantime, he dictates a few lines for Joseph:

'I have crossed the Guadarrama with part of the Guard in rather disagreeable weather. My Guard will sleep in Villacastin tonight. Marshal Ney is in Medina. The English seem to be at Valladolid, probably an advance guard, and in position at Zamora and Benavente with the rest of their army . . . The weather is rather cold.'

Damned profession that Joseph will never understand, even if he were the Emperor!

THE RAIN FALLING now is freezing, and then, when the weather turns milder, the torrential downpour turns the roads into quagmires.

At last, he can see the banks of the Douro. He rides along the columns of infantry. He observes these men who march hunched over, battered by the driving rain. He feels the rain coming through his overcoat and running off his hat, its soaking brim flopping down in his eyes. None of the soldiers looks up, none of them cheers.

He could let himself go, order a halt until there's a break in the rain.

He demands that they march faster. He sees infantrymen forced to strip to cross the icy-cold torrents.

They pass Tordesillas, Medina. Where are the English?

He goes on ahead. He ignores his aides-de-camp telling him that the troops can't keep up. He gallops across fields in the rain.

Sometimes he turns round and sees, through the cloudbursts, the squadron of chasseurs of the Guard following him, a few hundred metres back. He must be the best, because he is the Emperor.

At Valderas, he waits in the rain, with his arms crossed, for Marshal Ney to arrive. After an hour, he sees Ney coming towards him. 'The Emperor has been our advance guard,' says the marshal.

Napoleon stares at him.

'What I need to know is whether the enemy is retreating by the Benavente or Astorga road.'

He gives his orders in the rain. The chasseurs of the Guard commanded by Lefebvre-Desnouëttes are to push forward to reconnoitre the position of the English troops.

He waits for them to return. This weather is almost as bad as in Poland. He thinks of the cemetery of Eylau. He feels the anxiety mount in him again like a presentiment.

He decides to march on Benavente because he can't stand this inaction. A mud-splattered aide-de-camp hurries up. Lefebvre-Desnouëttes has been taken prisoner, he cries. The chasseurs of the Guard have had to withdraw after being taken by surprise by English cavalry.

Napoleon spurs his horse. He is the first to enter Benavente.

HE THROWS HIMSELF on the bed in a smoky room. He is cold, dirty, covered in mud. Suddenly he remembers that today is Saturday, 31 December 1808.

Already! In the year about to begin, he will be forty years old. And the English still elude him. And the army is tottering with exhaustion. And he has no idea what is happening in Austria, because he hasn't received any dispatches from Paris for days.

He gets up and dictates a few lines to Joseph.

Damned profession.

The English have been lucky, he explains. 'They should be grateful to the obstacles presented by the Guadarrama mountains and the foul mud we have encountered.'

He has barely finished when dispatches are brought in. Marshal Bessières confirms that the English have got away; they are marching towards Galicia, probably with the intention of embarking at Corunna. So, they must give chase on the Astorga road.

Before leaving, he writes to Josephine:

My friend, I have been pursuing the English for several days but they flee in terror. Like cowards, they have abandoned the remnants of La Romana's Spanish army so as not to delay their retreat by half a day. Over a hundred baggage waggons have been taken. The weather is very bad.

Lefebvre has been captured; he and three hundred chasseurs were involved in a skirmish; these jaunty lads swam their horses across a river and threw themselves into the midst of the English cavalry; they killed a good number, but on the way back, Lefebvre's horse was wounded and he almost drowned; the current took him back to the English bank and he was captured. Console his wife.

Farewell, my friend. Bessières with ten thousand horse is near Astorga.

Napoleon

Happy New Year to everybody.

THE RAIN HAS NEVER been so glacial. He hunches over in the saddle, but keeps his horse at a hard gallop. Soldiers are lying down in the mud, they're so done in. He hears isolated gunfire.

He remembers the men who, in the stifling heat of the Egyptian desert, committed suicide.

Don't see anything. Don't hear anything.

He just wants to get to Astorga. Be done with the English. Quickly. Lannes gallops at his side.

Now all he sees behind him, in the darkness, are his staff and Marshal Lannes's staff, and then, further back, a few hundred chasseurs of the Guard.

Probably they're celebrating the last day of the year in Paris. He thinks of Marie Walewska, who has had to return to Poland, as she told him she might.

It is hard to be true to his destiny, to want to grip it tight, not let it slip. It would be so good to fall asleep next to her, in a warm room with a fireplace.

He thinks of the palaces he has lived in. He imagines the dignitaries, Talleyrand and Fouché, giving balls, welcoming their guests in drawing rooms lit by hundreds of chandeliers.

He is the one who makes all that possible. And he is here, in the mud and rain!

An officer rides level with him. He shouts above the wind that a courier has just come from Paris and is looking for His Majesty.

Napoleon draws on the reins and jumps off his horse.

He will wait for him. They are at least two leagues from Astorga.

The chasseurs of the escort light a big fire at the side of the road. He walks around it to warm himself up, his hands behind his back.

The rain has stopped, but the cold is even more bitter. He shivers. He doesn't hear the courier arrive and give Berthier a portfolio bulging with dispatches.

A lantern is brought. Napoleon signals to Berthier to open the letters and pass them to him.

A LETTER FROM MARIE. He resumes walking. The grenadier follows him, holding the lantern up at arm's length.

Marie complains that he has forgotten his promises to the Poles. She echoes all those people who think he can change things with a word or that they're the only people in the Empire, when he is responsible for every particular and every person.

He crumples the letter and jams it into his overcoat pocket.

He seizes a handful of dispatches and stops by the fire. He recognizes the writing of Eugène de Beauharnais and one of his informers, Lavalette, a man in whom he has full confidence, one of his aides-de-camp in Italy who he has since put in charge of the Postal Service. Lavalette is the husband of one of Josephine's nieces. He is a loyal servant, like Eugène de Beauharnais. He reads the two men's letters, then he re-reads them. In Paris, Lavalette explains, Talleyrand and Fouché are now in league. They are often to be found at each other's houses, immersed in long discussions. They openly display their understanding. People are even saying that a ministry has been formed and is ready to take effect, should the Emperor die. Eugène has intercepted a letter addressed to Murat. They were asking the King of Naples to arrange relays of horses across Italy, so that he could get back to Paris without delay, to succeed the Emperor if he perished. Naturally Murat, on Caroline's urging, has accepted this proposition. The plot is also supported by everyone who wants to see the war end. Talleyrand is in constant communication with Metternich, the Austrian ambassador. He is inciting Vienna to form closer relations with St Petersburg, to make Napoleon submit. Caulaincourt, the ambassador to Alexander, is one of Talleyrand's men.

In addition, Eugène reports that Austria is continuing to rearm. It is buying horses and supplies throughout Europe. Its army is now several hundred thousand strong. Spies are emphatic that Vienna is convinced Napoleon is bogged down in Spain, mired in a national war. The Spanish Junta, which has taken refuge in Seville, has ordered its people to rise up against the French and has urged every Spaniard to kill their French foe. The moment is ripe, Vienna therefore considers, to start a war in Germany. Fouché and Talleyrand know this and the Prince of Benevento probably hopes as much. Murat is the man who, having a military reputation, could succeed the Emperor.

Napoleon crushes the dispatches in his fist then stuffs them in his pockets.

He had an intuition of all this.

He walks slowly round the fire. The soldiers move aside.

He didn't think the plot would be this far advanced though. Fouché! Talleyrand! Murat!

He remembers Erfurt, the intelligence he was given about the long evenings Talleyrand and the Tsar spent together.

He gets back into the saddle. He lets the horse set off at a walk. It is as if the momentum driving him towards Astorga has been shattered. The main front is no longer here, in Spain. He must change direction, as in a battle when an enemy springs out where one did not expect them.

He must return to Paris, stifle this conspiracy and crush Vienna if, as everything suggests, it dares to start a war.

All that remains is to choose the moment to leave Spain.

He looks up. The city of Astorga lies before him, dark and deserted.

He must stop here. He is no longer the one who will lead the fight against Moore's English. The principal battle he must give is in Paris, against Austria.

But he oughtn't to leave Spain until the English have been driven out and the army taken in hand, so that Joseph can be left a kingdom at peace and the wherewithal to stand on his own. Spain must not be a wound that can open again, when he is fighting the Austrians.

It is so cold in the house he enters that, despite the large fire lit by the quartermaster-sergeants, he carries on shivering.

ICY RAIN FALLS on Astorga throughout the first days of January 1809. He goes from house to house. The grenadiers are billeted there. He sits in front of the fireplace and questions them. He knows that three soldiers of his Guard killed themselves on the road, driven to despair by tiredness and the impossibility of stopping for fear of being tortured by the Spanish. Many others lay down to die in the mud. He has seen them.

He comforts these exhausted men with a few words and gestures. The soldiers form a procession behind him. They don't shout 'Long live the Emperor!', but shared suffering means he is one of theirs. For ever.

He holds a review of Soult and Ney's men who have arrived in

Astorga. He orders Soult to continue to Corunna, where John Moore has withdrawn to wait for the English ships on which he plans to embark.

Suddenly, shrill cries come from a barn a few paces from the ground where the review is taking place. Soldiers rush over, open the doors. Napoleon follows. In the gloom, he sees a thousand women and children covered in mud, huddled together, famished. They are English who were following the army, soldiers' families abandoned in the retreat. The women surround him, fall to their knees, beseech him.

He orders that they be lodged in Astorga, fed and sent back to the English as soon as the weather allows.

To RETAIN THE ADVANTAGE of surprise, he'd prefer not to express his mistrust of Fouché or Talleyrand or Murat, but his anger boils over.

'Do you think I've died out?' he writes to Fouché. 'I don't know, but it seems to me you haven't much knowledge of my character or my principles.'

He scans the dispatches in which Joseph and Cambacérès send him their New Year's wishes and talk of peace. They haven't seen those women and children who'd been eating raw barley for days. If they had, they would have understood English hatred.

'My brother,' he writes to Joseph, 'I thank you for your wishes for a good new year. I have no hope that Europe will be pacified this year. I have so little hope of this, that I yesterday signed a decree to raise one hundred thousand men. The hour of repose and tranquillity has not yet come!'

He signs, then collects himself and adds, 'Happiness? Ah yes! Happiness is the question these days!'

HE DECIDES to leave Astorga for Valladolid. The couriers from Paris can reach that town in five days, and it is what is happening in Paris that counts now, since Marshal Soult has caught up with Moore at Corunna. An English defeat is only a matter of days now.

He shuts himself in his study on the first floor of Charles V's palace which gives onto the Plaza de Armas in Valladolid. He walks from the fireplace to the window. His muscles are so tense they are starting to hurt. He grits his teeth. His stomach is sore. He berates Constant, Roustam and his aides-de-camp. Is there any news of Soult? Has he thrown Moore into the sea at last?

He writes with a sort of uncontrollable rage.

My sweet Marie,
You are an argumentative woman and it is a very ugly trait; you also listen to people who would do better to dance the Polonaise rather than meddle in their country's affairs.
Thank you for your congratulations on Somosierra; you may be proud of your compatriots, they have written a glorious page in history. I have rewarded them collectively and individually.
I shall be in Paris soon; if I remain there long enough, perhaps you can come back.
My thoughts are with you,
N.

But these thoughts fade quickly. He must also write to Josephine, who, as usual, is listening to all the gossips.

I see, dear friend, that you are worried and in a state of black anxiety . . . People are mad in Paris; everything is going perfectly well. I will be in Paris as soon as I think useful. I warn you to beware of ghosts; one fine day, at two o'clock in the morning . . .
But farewell, my friend; I am well and ever yours.
Napoleon

HE SLAMS THE DOOR and strides down the stairs. On the Plaza de Armas, as every morning, there's a troop review. He goes out, walks among the ranks, grabs a grenadier by the collar and pulls him roughly, forcing him to break rank. He shakes him so hard that the man drops his musket.

Without letting go of the soldier, Napoleon yells, 'Ah yes, I know, you want to go back to Paris, to your bad habits and your mistresses! Well, I will keep you under arms until you're eighty.'

He releases the soldier who goes back to his place, trembling.

Then he walks along the ranks. The soldiers must lower their eyes. These men must be tamed.

Suddenly he stops dead. Can this be possible? Standing in front of a row, he sees General Legendre, Dupont's chief of staff, the man who surrendered at Baylen.

'You are very bold, daring to appear before me,' he exclaims, walking towards the General.

He can't stop himself gesticulating. It is as if all the pent-up bitterness and anger of the last few days, all the resentment of those who 'betray' him and all the tiredness are suddenly overflowing.

'How can you show yourself when your shame is blatant, when your dishonour is written on the face of every brave soldier? Yes, men have blushed for you in the depths of Russia and France . . .'

He marches back and forth and glances at his troops who are standing, frozen. He must show these men a lesson, use Legendre to complete this job of taking them in hand.

'Where has one ever seen men surrender on a battlefield? One surrenders in a fortified place when all one's supplies are exhausted, when one has respected one's misfortune in sustaining and repelling three attacks . . . But on a battlefield one fights, sir, and when, instead of fighting, one surrenders, one deserves to be shot.'

He turns back towards Legendre again. He no longer even sees the man's twitching face.

'In the open country, there are only two ways to succumb: die or be taken prisoner, but only while using the butt of your musket! War has its odds, one can be defeated . . . One can be taken prisoner. I may be tomorrow . . . Francis the First was; he was captured with honour, but I never will be, only if I'm knocked unconscious by a rifle butt!'

Legendre stammers a few words.

I hear him, but I don't want to understand his reasons.

'We were only trying to preserve men for France,' says Legendre.

'France needs honour,' says Napoleon. 'It does not need men.'

He takes a step backwards.

'Your capitulation is a crime; as a general it is a mark of ineptitude, as a soldier, a mark of cowardice and as a Frenchman it is the first sacrilegious assault that has been made on the most noble of glories. If you had fought instead of capitulating, Madrid would not have been evacuated, Spain's insurrection would not be exulting in unparalleled success, England would not have an army in the peninsula. What a difference there would be in everything that has happened, and perhaps in the destiny of the world.'

He turns his back on Legendre.

Perhaps he has said too much, revealed that he is starting to think that Spain is the fatal knot of his destiny.

With a nod, he gives the signal for the review.

The drums roll. He watches the first platoon pass at charging pace. Then he returns to Charles V's palace.

There, another yell escapes him. The body of an officer with his throat slit has been found in the well of a monastery in Valladolid.

'This rabble only loves and esteems those who it fears!' he cries. 'We must hang twenty of the worst characters. We must do the same in Madrid. If a hundred brigands and firebrands are not got rid of, nothing will have been achieved.'

He writes to Joseph.

'Whatever the Spaniards' numbers, one must march straight at them, with a firm resolution. They cannot hold their ground. One must not use evasions or manoeuvres, but sweep down on them.'

He is going to leave Spain. Soult has crushed the English. John Moore has been killed; Wellesley,* the general who respected the terms of Junot's surrender, has replaced him. No matter. There are no redcoats left in Spain.

'Spread the word that I will be back in twenty to twenty-five days,' he tells Joseph.

He has relay stations established along the route home. He will ride from Valladolid to Burgos. With a wave, he silences his aides-de-camp who are stressing the danger of an attack by guerrillas, the poor state of the roads, the distance – almost thirty leagues† – between the two towns. All he wants, he says, are teams ready for a berline between Burgos and Bayonne, then on the road from Bordeaux to Poitiers and to Vendôme. He will drive at that back-breaking pace all the way to Paris.

---

* In July 1809, Wellesley is made Viscount Wellington.
† 120 kilometres.

On Tuesday, 17 January 1809, he leaps into the saddle at seven o'clock in the morning. He starts off with Savary in front and Duroc, Roustam and five guides of the Guard behind.

Faster.

He passes a barouche. He recognizes General Tiébault's carriage. He lashes the crupper of Savary's horse to make him get a move on. He digs his spurs in hard, repeatedly.

Faster.

He lays himself flat on his horse's neck and gallops into what lies before him. He doesn't feel the rain. He loves the driving wind, as sharp-edged as destiny.

PART SIX

Enough blood has been shed!

23 JANUARY 1809 TO 13 JULY 1809

XXII

WHAT, EVERYONE here's asleep!

He pushes past the officers who rush to meet him. He thrusts aside the lackeys who are too slow opening doors for him. He shouts that he wants to see Cambacérès immediately. He walks through the reception rooms, along the galleries and marches into Josephine's bedroom as her servants and ladies-in-waiting try to tell him that the Empress is still resting.

He is back, he booms, leaning over her as she squints up at him. He's well. She is too, isn't she? In her last letter she was complaining about toothache. She doesn't move, stupefied, hiding her face in her hands.

Old women don't like being surprised early in the morning.

He likes the truth. He wants the truth.

He leaves the room.

He only got out of his carriage in the Tuileries courtyard a few minutes ago, on this Monday, 23 January 1809, and yet already he's suffocating. These rooms smell musty, of lingering scent and old people asleep. For six days and six nights he has been racing back from Valladolid, keeping his energy and anger in check like springs wound tight, and now this sleepy palace is a stagnant pond.

These people are rotting away! Do they know where he's come from? Can they imagine what's happening in Spain? What he has experienced? What his finest soldiers, who he's left there, are going through?

Roustam has already prepared his bath. Damned bath!

He feels as if he has already let too much time pass without acting. He wants to question Cambacérès and the police spies to find out what is afoot, what has been hatched by Fouché, Talleyrand and all those who thought he was going to die in Spain or come back so weakened that they could replace him with Murat.

Murat! And my own sister Caroline!

But he is here, alive. They are going to have some explaining to do. What have they been saying? What have they done during his three-month absence? He wants to know everything. He wants the truth.

AFTER A FEW HOURS, he knows. It was at Madame de Rémusat's house that Talleyrand said, 'The unfortunate man is going to throw his whole position into doubt.'

The unfortunate man is me.

He listens to his informants who speak in trembling voices; they're afraid of Fouché's spies. The minister of police has been seen in the Prince of Benevento's house in rue de Varenne. The two men walked from room to room, arm in arm, in the middle of the guests. Talleyrand spoke in a loud voice about events in Spain.

'It's a low intrigue,' he said, 'and an enterprise totally contrary to the nation's wishes; by engaging in it, he turns his position on its head and declares himself an enemy of the people. It is a mistake that will never be put right.'

Napoleon remembers Talleyrand's advice, when he was urging him to drive the Bourbons out of Spain!

All he can think of is this betrayal, this covert war Talleyrand is waging against him. He wants to catch him by surprise, leave him dumbfounded.

He shows himself in the streets of Paris. He visits the building works at the Louvre and in the rue de Rivoli. He goes to the Opéra with Josephine, but he seethes with indignation; he cannot stay sitting down so long any more. He gets up, returns to the Tuileries on his own and calls for the regimental returns to be brought to him. He tallies up strengths, calculates his needs, redistributes troops. He is going to have to leave the men of what was called the Grand Army, and now is called the Imperial Army, in Spain. Which means he needs, in a matter of weeks, to reconstitute an Army of Germany, with conscripts, foreigners, soldiers from Baden, Westphalia, Würtemberg, Poles, Italians and even several thousand Spaniards. He will have 350,000 men, 250,000 of them French, of which 100,000 will be veterans whom he will put under Davout's command. Eugène in Italy has one hundred thousand at his disposal. Archdukes Charles and John can count on having three hundred thousand Austrians.

Closing the returns, he says, 'I double my troops' strength when I command them. When I give orders, people obey, because that is my nature. Perhaps it's a bad thing that I command in person, but it is my essence. Kings and princes should perhaps not command their armies; it's debatable, at least. If I command, it is because that is my fate, my lot.'

It soothes him to be working on this, at night.

Marie is not in Paris.

He dismisses Méneval, calls Constant.

ONE OF THE POLICE reports notes the birth on 11 November 1808 of a girl called Émilie Pellapra, daughter of Françoise Marie Leroy, wife of Pellapra, the Receiver General of Caen.

He remembers the young woman he first met in Lyon, probably in 1805, and whom he's seen on a number of occasions here, in his private apartments in the Tuileries. The last time was in March 1808, before he left for Bayonne. Less than a year ago. Time in which to have a child.

He wants to see this woman. Tonight.

HE WAITS FOR HER, surprising her as Constant shuts the door behind her. She smiles at him, letting down her hair. She's just started to be up and about, she says, and he knows, by the way she speaks, that he is Émilie's father.

It is the first time since his return to Paris that he feels intense joy.

He feels strong, invincible. Talleyrand had thought him weakened; he had planned his succession.

What surprises await these gentlemen who have united against me!

Tomorrow, he is seeing Fouché. The day after, Talleyrand.

HE WATCHES FOUCHÉ walk towards him and greet him.

This man is perfectly composed, but he must suspect that I know, that I've been making enquiries since I got back to the Tuileries.

'Monsieur the Duke of Otranto, you are one of those who sent Louis XVI to the scaffold.'

Fouché inclines his head slightly.

'Yes, Sire, and it was the first service that I had the good fortune to render Your Majesty.'

Fouché is a fox. He'll have all sorts of justifications. He'll say he warned of the problems my succession would create. Didn't he read me a report on my divorce?

Am I angry with him, actually? In his own way, he is both devious and straightforward. He is not slimy like Talleyrand, venal and sly like the former Bishop of Autun.

'There are vices and virtues of circumstance,' Napoleon continues. 'I know men. They are so difficult to grasp when one wants to be fair. Do they know themselves? Do they understand themselves? They will only abandon me when my luck runs out.'

He goes over to the window.

Spain is conquered, he says. If Austria wants war it will be destroyed.

And I can be a father whenever I want. I know that now.

He turns and walks back towards Fouché. 'You completely fail to police Paris,' he says suddenly in a brutal tone of voice. 'And you allow people of ill will free rein to spread every sort of rumour ... Take care of the police in your department and not foreign affairs!'

He has been gentle with Fouché, because it's good tactics to divide the parties in a coalition. The pallid Talleyrand is the one he has to hurt.

ON SATURDAY, 28 January, he ushers into his study Archchancellor Cambacérès, Arch-treasurer Lebrun, Minister for the Navy Decrès and Minister of Police Fouché. Talleyrand comes in last, limping, and leans on a small table.

Napoleon wanted these witnesses to be present. He must crucify Talleyrand publicly, so that Paris knows what sort of a thrashing traitors can expect from him.

He begins speaking in an intentionally scathing voice. He lets his anger mount. 'Men whom I have made high dignitaries or ministers must cease to be free in their thoughts and their expressions. They can only be organs of mine.'

He walks slowly about the room, stopping in front of each of the men.

'For them, betrayal begins when they allow themselves to doubt. It is complete if from doubt they pass to dissent.'

He takes a few steps back. Now's the time for the cut and thrust. He feels calm, as when he gives the order to open fire. Gunner and the gun; the dragoon and his mount Talleyrand. 'You are a thief!' he cries. 'A coward, a man without honour. You don't believe in God. All your life you have neglected your duties, you have deceived and betrayed everyone. Nothing is sacred to you. You would sell your father!'

He paces round Talleyrand. So, will this face never become distorted?

'I have showered you with favours and there is nothing you would not do to harm me. Hence, for the last ten months, you have had the impudence, supposing, without rhyme or reason, that my affairs in Spain are going badly, to tell whoever wishes to listen that you have always criticized my policies towards this kingdom, when *you* were the one who first gave me the idea and kept urging me to take it up.'

He thrusts his face into Talleyrand's.

'And who informed me of the unfortunate Duke of Enghien's place of residence? Who urged me to deal severely with him? What are your plans? What do you want? What do you hope? Have the courage to tell me!'

He walks away again, then turns back and shakes his fist in front of Talleyrand's eyes.

'You deserve to be smashed like a glass; I have the power to, but I despise you too much to take the trouble. Why haven't I hung you from the railings on the Carrousel? There's still plenty of time. You are shit at the bottom of a stocking.'

Talleyrand does not move. What must he say to make this man drop his mask?

'You didn't tell me that the Duke of San Carlos was your wife's lover,' he cries.

He has wounded him. He sees his cheeks quiver. Talleyrand murmurs, 'Indeed, Sire. I hadn't thought this news would be in the interest of Your Majesty's glory or mine.'

But even so, Napoleon is convinced that insults and scorn slide off this man. He forgets every affront one does him.

HERE HE IS again, on this Sunday, 29 January, in the Throne Room, as if I hadn't laid into him yesterday.

Napoleon walks past, snuff-box in hand, and takes several pinches. He wants to show his scorn again. He speaks to people on Talleyrand's left and right, without seeming to see him.

Talleyrand remains motionless.

Returning to his study, Napoleon dictates a note to appear in the *Monitor* of 30 January 1809. Talleyrand is no longer Grand Chamberlain. He is replaced by Monsieur de Montesquiou.

A mild penalty. But what else can I do? Talleyrand is the one in my entourage who represents the people of the ancien régime, who has the confidence of Alexander, and is Caulaincourt's friend. The alliance with the Tsar ties my hands.

So he must accept the situation, appear to laugh about it. When Hortense tells him a tearful Talleyrand came to see her, claiming to be a victim of slander, Napoleon exclaims, 'You don't know people, my dear. I know where I stand. Does he think I don't know what he's been saying? He was trying to do himself honour at my expense. Well I won't stop him any more. Let him chat away as much as he wants. Anyway, I haven't done him any harm. I just don't want him to meddle in my affairs.'

Now I know he's my enemy. A humiliated man is as dangerous as an animal one's wounded but not killed. But what could I have hoped of someone of Talleyrand's ilk?

HE THINKS ALOUD in front of Roederer. He needs to talk. War with Austria is approaching. He senses anxiety around him. Talleyrand's criticism and his plot with Fouché and Murat are only the visible tip of a seething mass of ambition and cowardice.

Those loyal to me are not those of the old court.

'I took some into my household. They've gone two years without talking to me and ten without seeing me. Besides, I don't receive any of them. I don't like them at all. They are fit for nothing. Their conversation displeases me. Their tone does not go with my gravity at all. Every day I regret a mistake I made in my government. It's the most serious I've made, restoring all their property to émigrés.'

Talleyrand is one of these men, obsequious and hostile and cowardly.

'I am a soldier, it's a gift I received at birth. It is my existence, my habit. Wherever I've been, I have been in command. I was in command aged twenty-three at the siege of Toulon. I was in command in Paris for Vendémiaire. I roused the soldiers in Italy the moment I arrived. I was born for it.'

He loves this 'damned profession' of soldiering, he murmurs. He turns to Roederer.

'Austria wants a slap. I'm going to give it one on both cheeks. If the Emperor Francis makes the slightest hostile movement, he will soon cease to reign. That is clear. Within ten years mine will be the oldest dynasty in Europe.'

He stretches out an arm.

'I swear that everything I do, I do for France. I conquered Spain; I did so for it to be French. All I think of are the glory and strength of France; all my family must be French.'

He goes over to his desk, shows Roederer the registers containing the regimental returns.

'I always know the position of my troops,' he says. 'I am fond of plays and tragedies, but if all the tragedies in the world were there, on one side, and the regimental returns on the other, I wouldn't even glance at the tragedies and there wouldn't be a single line of my regimental returns that I hadn't read intently. This evening, they will be waiting for me in my room and I will not go to bed without reading them.'

He goes up to Roederer.

'My duty is to preserve the army. It is my duty to France which entrusts me with its children. In two months, I will have forced Austria to disarm . . .'

He remembers years ago saying to Roederer, 'My sole passion, my sole mistress, is France.'

Now he says it again.

HE GOES HUNTING at Versailles and in the Bois de Boulogne. It's raining and cold at the end of that February, 1809.

When he returns to the Tuileries, he sometimes sits at the same pedestal table as Charles Louis Napoleon, the son of Hortense and Louis. He pats the child's head, very moved. His desire to have a child is so strong that he has to turn away, overwhelmed.

On Monday, 27 February, when Napoleon leaves the child in this frame of mind, Marshal Lannes's aide-de-camp presents himself with a dispatch.

Baron Lejeune has ridden at full gallop to announce the fall of Saragossa on 21 February. It had to be taken house by house, he explains. The women and children fought like soldiers.

Napoleon opens the letter. A round piece of lead, indented like a watch cog, falls out. A cross is engraved on both sides. It is a Spanish bullet. It grievously wounded Captain Marbot.

Napoleon weighs it in his hand. It must be sent to Marbot's mother, he says.

Then he reads Lannes's letter.

'What a war!' the marshal writes. 'To be constrained to kill so many brave men, or even fanatics. Victory is painful.'

Napoleon bows his head.

He loves Lannes, one of the best of the best, one of his oldest comrades in arms in Italy and Egypt.

But what is to be done? One must win.

None the less there is a bitter taste in his mouth, as if this will driving him on is becoming harsher, as if there were no longer any sweetness or joy in victory, only bitter necessity.

'Victory is painful.'

He has felt what Lannes felt at Saragossa before. But if victory is bitter, what would defeat be?

HE WALKS SLOWLY towards his study.

War is coming. He feels it draw nearer.

On his desk, he finds a message from Champagny. The minister of foreign affairs reports that Metternich has protested against the movements of the Imperial Army's troops. Vienna considers them a provocation.

Napoleon summons Metternich immediately.

'What is the meaning of this?' he asks the ambassador in a hollow voice. 'Has a spider stung you? Do you want to set the world ablaze again?'

Metternich dissembles. Napoleon observes him, then murmurs to Champagny, 'Metternich is close to being a true statesman. He lies very well.'

He barely acknowledges him.

War is here.

Whether I want it or not. I must win.

XXIII

IT'S ONLY A QUESTION of days now. He sends for Berthier constantly. He wants returns for each of the corps under Davout, Masséna and Lannes. He has put Lefebvre in charge of the Bavarians. He is furious when the King of Bavaria calls for the crown prince to command them instead. He dictates a reply like a door slamming: 'I have selected an old soldier, the Duke of Danzig, to command them ... When the Prince Royal has won his promotions through six or seven campaigns, he will be fit to command.'

He feels nervous, irritable. He has the feeling that people round him are trying to edge away, as if the reins are slipping from his hands, as if his horse were restless, exhausted. He constantly wants to push his entourage out of the way. He doesn't like their anxious expressions. He flees Josephine's sighs. Every time they dine together or sit side by side in a box at the theatre, she begs him to let her come with him, when he leaves on campaign.

He doesn't answer. He so wants this war, which he feels rumbling at his gates, to recede, like a storm blowing over. But he has known for months, since Erfurt, that it will break out, since Alexander has refused either to say, or put his signature to, the words that would check Austria on its path of confrontation with France.

Betrayal.

He goes hunting in Rambouillet forest, rage in his heart. Betrayal by the Tsar, but that's only natural, isn't it? Alexander is playing his card because the Spanish wound is still open and France is weakened. Betrayal by Talleyrand and the royalists of the faubourg St Germain.

He digs his spurs in fiercely twice. His horse bounds forward. The stag zigzags, panic-stricken, through the damp undergrowth. The pack is at its heels. It is a powerful animal, but its stride steadily grows heavier. It plunges straight into St Hubert pond. Napoleon rides round the bank and dismounts. A musket is handed to him. The animal emerges from the water, its breast pale and broad.

I must deal death.

He closes his eyes. The stag is lying on the bank, the pond is turning red. The pack howls.

HE TURNS AWAY and walks his horse back through the already dark avenues. In one of the château's drawing rooms he sees Andréossy, France's ambassador in Austria, who has hurried back from Vienna. He looks travel-weary, his face and clothes rumpled.

Napoleon tosses his riding-whip and hat aside and has the drawing-room doors shut.

He gestures to Andréossy to start.

He only listens to the start of each sentence. He only needs to hear a word to understand.

The Archduke Charles is assembling his troops. A citizens' militia is replacing the regular army in Vienna. The Archduke is preparing to issue a manifesto to the people of Germany, calling on them to rise up against the Emperor. English negotiators are in Vienna to agree on a treaty of alliance between England and Austria. London will provide the necessary credit for war.

Napoleon doesn't pass comment.

War is rolling towards me faster and faster, like a huge boulder.

In the Tyrol, the Austrians are urging people to rise up against Bavaria. The peasants have been radicalized by the Capuchin priest Haspinger. The name of a popular leader, Andreas Hofer, is bandied about a great deal. Vienna is supplying arms.

He dismisses Andréossy.

How many days before he leaves France and finds himself back amongst the bivouacs, in the rain and mud, seeing dead soldiers and hearing the screams of the wounded?

HE RETURNS TO the Tuileries. He has no choice.

The atmosphere in the palace oppresses him. The galleries, the salons, the court circles are silent, as if everyone was sitting up with a dying man.

Me, whom they're already bearing to my grave.

He reads a secret report sent him by Joseph Fiévée, one of the paid observers he has in every circle. This one was a royalist, but for years he has been spying, analysing, listening for the Emperor. He has a piercing intellect; his eyes and ears seem to be everywhere.

'France is sick with anxiety,' he writes. The words of a dignitary – it's not said who, perhaps Decrès, Minister for the Navy, unless it's Talleyrand – are doing the rounds of all the salons in the faubourg St Germain: in an unguarded moment, he declared, 'The Emperor is mad, absolutely mad. He will ruin himself and he will ruin us too, with him.'

Napoleon throws Fiévée's report into the fire.

Mad? They dare say such things because they think I won't be able to take up the challenge. I'm being strangled before their eyes. Austria is under arms, Spain is insurgent, the English are in Portugal, Germany is quaking, Russia is watching me like a hawk. And here in France, they plot, they betray me.

He returns to his desk. He recognizes the writing on a petition. Once again Monsieur René de Chateaubriand is pleading on behalf of his cousin, Armand de Chateaubriand, who was caught on a Cotentin beach, his pockets stuffed with letters from émigrés in London or Jersey to Brittany's royalists.

Armand de Chateaubriand is nothing but a royalist courier in the service of England and the Bourbons. Death for him.

To make me relent, Monsieur René de Chateaubriand sends me his latest book, The Martyrs. *What has that got to do with me? Does he know what war is?*

'The death of his cousin will give Monsieur de Chateaubriand the occasion to write a few pathetic pages which he will read out in the faubourg St Germain. All the fine ladies will weep and this will console him,' he exclaims.

Justice must be done and this spy, this émigré, this traitor must be executed on the Plaine de Grenelle.

He feels hard times have returned. No ovation when he took his seat in the imperial box at the Théâtre-Français; only looks, almost of panic, as if he were the bearer of a curse.

Fontanes, the servile Fontanes who I have made Grand-master of the University, comes up to me and murmurs, bent double like a lackey, 'When you leave, some fear, inspired by love and tempered by hope, upsets everyone's peace of mind.'

Their peace of mind or their bank balances?

He laughs derisively.

They have never exposed their breasts to bullets, roundshot, sabres. They only sense that the game now joined is the most formidable there could be. A coalition, and my armies in action in Spain.

He brandishes the regimental returns in front of Roederer's face.

'Yes, I'm leaving Joseph my best troops and I'm going to Vienna with my little conscripts and my great boots.'

Then he calls out in a loud voice as Roederer is leaving. 'Everything I do is prompted by duty and devotion to France.'

But can they conceive of that, all these men who have latched onto my power like parasites to suck out all the juice they crave? Do they think I go to war with joy in my heart?

It's a crushing burden, but all I can do is take up the challenge.

ON THURSDAY, 23 March, he reads a dispatch that has been sent by telegraph. 'A French officer has been arrested at Braunau and his dispatches, though sealed with the arms of France, have been forcibly taken by the Austrians.'

Must I accept this?

At four in the afternoon, he summons the Count of Montesquiou, the Grand Chamberlain.

He says in a hollow voice, 'Inform Monsieur the Count of Metternich that the Emperor and King will not be receiving this evening.'

A FEW WORDS and the war has come closer.

He orders Berthier to start for Germany and take command of the whole army until he arrives.

Every day the dispatches he opens announce that war has taken a step closer. On 6 April, Archduke Charles proclaims that 'the country's defence creates new obligations'. On the 11th, the English fleet attacks French ships in the roads of Aix island.

On Wednesday, 12 April, at seven in the evening, Napoleon

confers with his aides-de-camp Lauriston and Cambacérès. A courier from Marshal Berthier is announced. With a gesture, Napoleon has him sent in. He reads the dispatch. His chest suddenly feels gripped in a vice, his throat is choked. His eyes burn as if he were crying. Then, without turning his head so his eyes can't be seen, he slowly says, 'They have crossed the Inn. It's war.'

He will leave tonight then.

Now he is calm. At dinner the Empress again insists on coming with him. He looks at her distractedly, then says, 'Very well.'

In his study he dictates letters to Joseph and Eugène. Archduke John will have entered Italy through Caporetto. They must contain him, drive him back, march on Vienna.

He drinks coffee in little sips. He sees Fouché at eleven. He has to trust him to keep the country under control and flood Germany with spies. There can be no war without police and information.

HE GOES TO BED at midnight.

The time of interrupted sleep has returned.

At two o'clock, he wakes up. Leaving, fighting – this is his destiny. Winning is his duty.

At four-twenty he gets into his berline. The paraffin lamps are lit, the portfolios, so he can work, are stacked on one of the seats. Josephine is sitting in a corner, a fur wrapped round her legs. He doesn't look at her. He gives the signal to leave. He hears the gallop of the squadron of chasseurs of the Guard who are his escort.

It is the music of his life.

XXIV

FROM TIME TO TIME, when the berline is too violently jolted for Napoleon to be able to read or study his maps, he observes Josephine. She sleeps. The bumpy road gradually causes the veil to slip from her face which she wanted it to hide. He sees this 'old woman' whose features sag in sleep. Her breathing is noisy and when she parts her lips, he sees her tiny, chipped, black teeth which she has always tried to hide.

He will not look away. He dares to look at the corpses on the battlefield, or, harder still, watch the young soldiers charge when death is going to take them in their thousands. He has always confronted the truth.

He looks at Josephine for a long time. What would be the point of being victorious and sending men to die if he remained heirless, the husband of this old woman?

To assure the future of his dynasty, to give the battles he is going to join some sense, he should divorce her and, by a princely marriage and son, defuse the hatred of the courts – Vienna or St Petersburg, the ones with the most power who have not yet accepted him.

He is going to conquer Vienna again. He has to. He is going to compel the Tsar, once Austria is defeated, to abide by the alliance of Tilsit. One or other of these dynasties must give him the hand of one of their young daughters in marriage. There, those are the goals.

Can Josephine sense this when she wakes, shoots him a look full of anxiety and hastily, fearfully rearranges her veil?

She is to wait for him in Strasbourg, he says. He will go to Vienna alone.

THE BERLINE slows down. He recognizes Bar-le-Duc. He remembers that General Oudinot was born in this village; only a sergeant on the eve of the Revolution, he has since fought in every war. In his mind's eye, he sees him at Friedland amidst a hail of grapeshot or at Erfurt, welcoming kings, this grandson of brewers.

This is the man he's made a general and a Duke. This is the nobility of the Empire, a nobility of talent and courage.

He makes the berline stop and jumps down in the dark. He laughs at the surprise of the Duke of Reggio's parents, the terror of his two little daughters who are pulled out of bed. He kisses them.

He loves appearing in people's lives by surprise, like a magician who leaves indelible memories, whose coming is told of in stories. He leaves so quickly, people will wonder if they didn't dream his visit.

He wants to be men's dreams. He gets back into the berline. He murmurs, bending back down over his maps, 'I make my plans out of the dreams of my sleeping soldiers.'

HE DROWSES. He knows what his men are thinking. The conscripts are afraid and only want to shout, 'Long live the Emperor.' He will say to them, 'I am coming to you with the speed of lightning. Let us march. Our past successes are a sure guarantee of the victory that awaits us. Let us march then, and at sight of us, the enemy will recognize its conquerors.'

He will be among them. In front of their lines even. He will sweep them along. Didn't he transform the barefoot Army of Italy into an invincible force? But now there are the generals and marshals, who would like to enjoy their titles and properties and repeat with a sigh, 'I would gladly hang up my boots.'

And him? What do they think, these gentlemen? That he loves having his legs roasting in his leather riding boots?

He begins scribbling a few lines, 'I do not intend it to become customary for officers to request to be placed on the retired list in a moment of ill temper and then ask to be reinstated when the mood has passed. These caprices ill befit an honourable man, and army discipline does not allow of them.'

ON SATURDAY, 15 April, he reaches Strasbourg. He brusquely shrugs off Josephine who clings to him, weeping, as he is setting off with Duroc. Is this worthy of an Empress?

In the carriage, he reads Berthier's dispatches. The Austrians have superiority in numbers, They are close to half a million and he has only three hundred thousand soldiers in Germany and Italy. His lines stretch from Ratisbon to Augsburg. The foreign contingents cannot be depended upon. Berthier reports that prayer sheets printed in Vienna have been found in churches, calling on the Germans of Bavaria and Würtemberg to pray for 'Archduke Charles. It is God who has sent him to bring succour to us.'

He tosses Berthier's dispatches aside. He must wait before taking any action, understand what the enemy wants. He calls an aide-de-camp who, leaning in the carriage window, listens to the message he is to take to the marshal.

'Above all,' yells the Emperor, 'don't take any risks!'

He repeats the phrase, as he watches the officer ride away from the escort.

On Sunday, 16 April, he stops for a few moments at Ludwigshafen. He glimpses the King of Würtemberg who is waiting in the cold dawn air. He carries himself like a frightened man. He says in an anxious voice, before even greeting Napoleon, 'What is Your Majesty's plan?'

'We shall go to Vienna.'

He takes the King by the arm, reassures him. As they part, the sovereign speaks of the confidence he has in the 'Jupiter of the modern age'.

Napoleon gets into his berline.

Jupiter? I depend on men.

At that moment he receives Berthier's reply. 'I impatiently await Your Majesty,' writes the marshal.

What are these men without me? They'd hang up their boots!

ON SUNDAY, in the early afternoon, a storm breaks. There is a torrential downpour.

He enters a hotel in Gmünd like an ordinary traveller; he eats in a corner of the poorly lit dining room.

He loves these moments of anonymity, when his presence does not alter the daily rhythm of life a jot. It is at these moments he feels his power most clearly, when he knows that it would just take a word to electrify the atmosphere like lightning, and he says nothing, remaining in the shadows and paying like an ordinary customer.

But, once over the threshold, he is the Emperor again.

At Dillingen, he listens to the panic-stricken King of Bavaria who has been driven out of Munich by the approaching Austrian troops.

'Sire, all is lost for us if Your Majesty doesn't act quickly,' the King murmurs in an imploring voice. 'All is lost,' he repeats.

'Do not be concerned. You will be back in Munich in a few days.'

Why do these men need a protector? Why do they rely on someone else to reassure them, defend them, guide them?

YET, AS HE DRIVES towards Donauwörth, where he campaigned in 1805, he remembers those years, the most unbearable of his life, when he had to solicit a position from Pascal Paoli, or Barras. He had no rest until he only depended on himself. And destiny.

In a tavern in Donauwörth, which he reaches on Monday, 17 April, at six in the morning, he has the maps spread out on a large table. The dispatches arrive. Bacler d'Albe begins to stick in the pins that mark the progress of Archduke Charles's troops.

This is the decisive moment. He has a horse saddled and goes to inspect the fortifications of the little town. He stops at the top of a rise. Through the fog he makes out the banks of the Danube, the broad black stripe of its waters. And at the end, over there, Vienna.

He returns to the inn at a gallop and rushes to the map. A message from Davout confirms that Archduke Charles is heading towards Ratisbon.

Can it be possible?

The aides-de-camp confirm it. He bends over the map, paces around the room. He sees the whole game beginning. It plays itself out in his head.

'Ah, Prince Charles,' he exclaims. 'I'll get you the easy way.'

He gives orders, dictates messages. He is going to attack Archduke Charles on his southern flank. Now it's the 'damned profession' that must take over.

HE GETS UP at four in the morning on Tuesday the 18th. First the study of maps by the glow of lanterns, then the dictation of messages. To Davout, Masséna.

'In a word you will understand the situation. Prince Charles marched out yesterday from Landshut on Ratisbon with his whole army. He had three corps, estimated at eighty thousand men. So you see that circumstances never required that a response be more energetic and swift than ours. Activity, activity, speed! I put myself in your hands.'

Then, to horse.

On the highway from Neustadt to Oberhausen, he makes out a monument between the trees, the one to La Tour d'Auvergne. He raises his hat. He loves coming across traces of Frenchmen like this who came before him and whose memories he reveres.

Will someone come after him?

He speeds along the roads, over the fields. He stops in Ingolstadt, the royal palace, but sets off again immediately to see the heights that dominate the Danube.

When he reaches Ziegelstadel in the middle of the afternoon of Wednesday the 19th, he is exhausted and aching all over. The men of Davout's corps march past. A baker comes out of his house, bringing him a wooden armchair. He falls into it. He senses the looks of the soldiers marching past a few metres from him. He is as tired as they all are. They love this sharing, this equality of war. It is his work to be here, by the side of the road, on the battlefield, to study the maps at night and lead these men to victory.

He straightens up.

'Work is my element,' he says to Savary as he remounts. 'I was born and made for work. I know the limits of my legs. I know the limits of my eyes. I do not know those of my work.'

HE REACHES THE Castle of Vohburg after darkness has fallen. He opens a window. It seems as if he can hear the murmur of the river.

If the game goes as planned, if the men carry out the plans he has conceived, then Vienna will fall and once again, as at Marengo, Austerlitz and Friedland, he will have taken up the challenge. In

Paris the chatterers and pallid intriguers will return to their holes. But how long will this vortex of wars continue? The generals are complaining, he knows.

It is after eleven at night on Wednesday, 19 April. They will join battle tomorrow. He sees entering the courtyard the silhouette of Lannes, Duke of Montebello. Perhaps his best soldier.

Lannes slowly crosses the large room lit by candles from the next-door church.

I know that fatigue. I feel it too. But I am the Emperor.

'How many old wounds have you?' Napoleon murmurs.

Lannes shakes his head, 'I forget everything when our profession calls.'

Wounded at Arcola, St Jean d'Acre, Aboukir and Pultusk. Twice before Arcola.

Lannes paces up and down, his head bowed.

'I am afraid of war,' he says. 'The first sound of war makes me shudder. We daze the men the better to be able to lead them to their deaths.'

Is it my doing?

It's England who's organizing and provoking all these wars, even if Austria has instigated this particular one.

He speaks, explains. Lannes has the courage of a Murat or a Ney. If even the best are beset by doubts . . .

'Command, Sire,' Lannes says finally, 'and I shall carry out your orders. All the officers must step onto the battlefield as if they are going to a party.'

A messenger from Davout enters.

With just his one corps, Davout has defeated the whole Austrian army at Tengen. It is falling back on Thann.

Napoleon pinches Lannes's ear, leads him out.

We are going to win. I shall command.

IT IS ALREADY Thursday, 20 April 1809. He must sleep a few hours.

He gets up at dawn. The countryside is shrouded in fog which hasn't cleared by the time Napoleon sets out on the Ratisbon road; he rides as far as the hills that dominate Abensberg.

He looks around at the Bavarian and Würtemberger Light Horse escorting him.

Are these men going to be loyal, or will the Bavarians break ranks at the first onslaught and go over to the enemy?

He pushes his horse into a gallop and goes and takes up a position in front of these regiments. Then he gives the signal to attack.

If I am to die, what does it matter whether it is from an Austrian bullet in the chest or a Bavarian one in my back?

But I won't die. It's not my time.

After a few hours, the Austrian troops are broken up, cut in two.

HE SINKS INTO A CHAIR in Rohr's post house, in the market square. He drowses from two until four in the morning, then jumps to his feet.

'We mustn't lose a minute!' he cries.

He rides to the Danube. The Austrians are massed on the other bank, in the town of Landshut. Another bridge the infantry have to cross under a hail of bullets.

He watches them. They break into a run, get across, are confronted with the town gates and fall back, stumbling on the bodies that choke the roadway of the bridge. They launch another charge, and are again repulsed.

Landshut must fall.

He sees General Mouton coming towards him; an aide-de-camp, he is bringing a message from Davout.

An attack always needs a leader. Mouton is brave. He told me, 'I'm not made for palace life and it's not made for me.' He can take Landshut.

Napoleon turns to him.

'You've come at the right moment. Put yourself at the head of that column and take the town of Landshut.'

Mouton dismounts, draws his sabre and runs towards the bridge.

I will not forget that man! It is soldiers like him who make up my strength. I owe them everything. And I owe it to them to fight at their side.

HE HAS INSTALLED himself in the royal residence in Landshut. Through the window, as he dictates, he sees troops crossing the town. They are marching towards Eckmühl.

'I am determined,' he writes to Davout, 'to exterminate the army of Prince Charles today, or, at the latest, tomorrow.'

The signal to attack will be given by Davout, who will have his cannon fire a ten-gun salvo.

Suddenly he feels exhausted. He sits down, deaf to everything. When he wakes, barely an hour later, the first thing he sees is that it's growing light, the sky is clear and bright. His throat hurts. Roustam pours him a glass of milk and honey. Then he sets off on horseback. It is chilly. He doesn't like this boggy road his men are tramping along that runs through the Isar valley.

Eckmühl is to the north. He wants to see the battlefield. The ground is broken, dotted with hillocks and clumps of trees, but towards the Danube, past Eckmühl, he can see a vast plain at the end of which, by the river, stands Ratisbon. The Austrians have just driven out its small French garrison.

At one-fifty he hears Davout's cannon fire ten times. The battle has begun.

He is far forward, surrounded by his marshals.

When dusk sets in and the darkness spreads, he looks at the showers of sparks that fly when the heavy sabres strike the thousands of helmets and body armour. He doesn't hear the shouts of the men fighting; they're drowned out by the heavy impact of weapons clashing with redoubled vigour.

He is surprised by the resistance the Austrian cavalry puts up. The battle is lost, but they keep on fighting, protecting the infantry's retreat to Ratisbon.

Lannes approaches. They must pursue the enemy, he says, launch the whole army at them to finish off the Archduke Charles and the town of Ratisbon in one charge. Napoleon is poised to give the order to continue the attack. He has so often said that pursuit is everything, that one has to destroy the enemy, that, listening to Lannes, he seems to be hearing himself talking. And yet he hesitates. It would mean engaging in a night action, says Davout. The men are exhausted. Ratisbon is another three leagues.

He is like the soldiers, he feels tiredness grinding him into the dirt. It's days now since he last slept properly. He hesitates further, then gives the order to bivouac.

He sees Lannes's astonishment, the other officers' relief.

'We have carried the day,' he says.

He walks off a few paces. Now he can hear the screams of the wounded and dying rising up from the whole battlefield.

For the first time he hasn't ordered his men to take advantage of a rout to pursue the enemy.

He can't.

AT DAWN ON SUNDAY the 23rd, he watches the artillery pass in thick fog on its way to Ratisbon. The town must fall. He positions the cannon himself to demolish the old houses built against the walls that will, if he's lucky, fill the moats with their rubble. He walks over to a cannon and suddenly feels a violent pain in his right leg. He is thrown off balance, flings out an arm to Lannes for support. A bullet has hit him in the right toe.

'That can only be a Tyrolese: those people are very skilful,' he says.

He sits on a drum while the wound is dressed.

IS THIS WOUND a sign? He looks at it: it's not serious, even if the pain is intense.

He turns his head. Soldiers are running up. There are shouts of 'The Emperor is wounded', 'The Emperor is dead.' He stands up. He orders that he be hoisted onto his horse, the drummers beat to arms. He will ride along the ranks. He must be seen. He cannot die.

He rides up and down the lines and the cry rings out, the cry he hasn't heard for months: 'Long live the Emperor!'

He stops in front of each regiment.

I must reward these men. I am alive, victorious, generous, just.

This is my aristocracy. I am going to ennoble them on the field of battle.

The commanding officers single out the bravest men.

'I appoint you Knight of the Empire with a pension of twelve hundred francs,' he calls out in a commanding voice.

'But Sire, I prefer the cross.'

He looks at the soldier with his stubborn, scarred face and firm voice.

'You have both, because I have made you a knight.'

'But I'd prefer the cross.'

I should pin a cross on his chest, pinch his ear.

These men get themselves killed for me, because they know I risk my life like them and because I lead them to victory.

RATISBON IS CAPTURED, Ratisbon is burning. The road to Vienna is open.

He should be satisfied, but he doesn't feel the usual joy at winning. He hasn't destroyed Archduke Charles's army. It is falling back on Vienna along the left bank of the Danube. He throws his troops onto the right bank, then dictates a proclamation for them:

'Soldiers! You have justified my expectations. You have made up for numbers by your bravery. You have gloriously shown the difference which exists between the soldiers of Caesar and the armed mob of Xerxes.'

From the palace he is in, he sees soldiers with buckets running through the streets to help put out the fires ravaging the town. He is going to pay for the damage caused by the fighting out of his own purse. He is tired of war. He sees wounded leaning on one another as they drag themselves towards the infirmaries.

He resumes in a low voice.

'In a few days we have triumphed in three pitched battles, at Thann, Abensberg and Eckmühl, and in the actions of Landshut and Ratisbon. Within a month we shall be in Vienna.'

Will that be the end of the war?

Destiny is still benign. In four days of fighting, he has rolled over the Austrians – but at the cost of how many dead?

His leg and foot are still painful, he has difficulty walking, but it's nothing compared to the suffering of others.

A FEW DAYS LATER, when he sees the thousands of dead filling the streets of Ebersberg because Masséna, 'the Favourite Child of Victory', wanted to take this town by storm – for nothing; the Danube had already been crossed – he feels nauseous. He ignores Masséna's justifications. A thousand, two thousand wounded in vain.

He refuses to lodge in a house in the upper town, the only part of Ebersberg not destroyed. He has his tent pitched in a garden, in front of a house in the nearby village of Angtetten.

He walks about the part of the tent that serves as his bed chamber.

He should have stopped Masséna, but how can he control everything? Nowadays he'd like to be able to rely, in part, on men who are not just brave but also perceptive.

He'd like . . .

Passing through to the part of the tent he uses as his study, he murmurs, before starting to dictate his orders, 'All those who agitate for war ought to see such a monstrosity. They'd know the sufferings their plans cost mankind.'

But he must take Vienna!

HE GALLOPS TOWARDS the capital, stops at Ems where he watches the divisions pass who are pursuing the Austrians. At Mölk he finds a Benedictine abbey on a promontory, rising high above the Danube, which gives a good view of the left bank of the river. The Austrian campfires pierce the night.

He enters the building and takes a seat in a long gallery that overlooks the countryside.

If only this could be a long halt! But his work is not finished.

He hears the voices of the grenadiers who have overrun the abbey and are being given something to drink by the monks.

Men need these moments of revelry from which he abstains, reading the mail that has come from Paris.

He gestures scornfully as he reads through Talleyrand's servile letter. 'Thirteen days ago Your Majesty left and already He has added six victories to the marvellous history of previous campaigns.'

I am the victor. I am not dead. The courtiers fall to their knees.

'Your glory, Sire, is the cause of our pride, but your life is the cause of our whole existence,' Talleyrand goes on.

He exclaims, talking to himself out loud and not worrying whether the marshals can hear him, 'I have showered him with honours, wealth, diamonds and he has used them all against me. He has betrayed me as much as he could, at the first opportunity . . .'

He tosses aside Talleyrand's letter.

Josephine writes to him as well, worried about his wound. On a corner of a table, he replies,

> The bullet that caught me did not wound me; it just grazed my Achilles tendon. My health is excellent and you are wrong to worry. My affairs are going very well.
>> Ever yours,
>> Napoleon
>
> Give all my best to Hortense and the Duke of Berg.

BUT HE HAS TO TEAR himself away from these expressions of tenderness, these images of peace. He must exercise his profession.

He goes to the balcony that runs along the gallery. He wants to know which Austrian troops are camped on the other side of the river: General Hiller's or Archduke Charles's? An officer must take advantage of darkness to capture an Austrian they can interrogate. Lannes has suggested Captain Marbot, his aide-de-camp.

'Be aware that this is not an order I'm giving you,' Napoleon says to Marbot. 'It's a wish I am voicing; I recognize the undertaking is most perilous, but you may refuse it without fear of displeasing me. Go and think in the next room for a few minutes, and then come back and frankly tell me what you have decided.'

Marbot will accept, he knows. These men are not courtiers but soldiers, like him.

It is my genius to be able to command such men.

He tugs Marbot's ear, then the captain sets off unhesitatingly towards the river.

THEY ARE INDEED General Hiller's troops. So now the way to Vienna is open.

He arrives in St Polten. It is a beautiful day, the soldiers cheer him. At last he's able to sleep for a few hours.

He lets Josephine know:

My friend, I write to you from St Polten. Tomorrow I will be within sight of Vienna, only a month to the day since the Austrians crossed the Inn and violated the peace.

My health is good; the weather is superb and the men in extremely good spirits; there is plenty of wine in the area.

Take care of your health.

Ever yours,

Napoleon

ON WEDNESDAY, 10 May 1809, once again he walks in the gardens of the royal Palace of Schönbrunn.

His whole body relaxes. He casts an eye over the reception rooms, the elaborate gilding. He daydreams for a few moments, remembering the first time he stayed there, on 13 November 1809, before Austerlitz.

Must he be like Sisyphus, always rolling the stone of war to the top of the hill, only for it to roll down and him return to all the same places – Donauwörth, Schönbrunn? What will it be tomorrow? Warsaw? Eylau?

He feels tired, edgy.

He is told that the Austrians have wounded the officials demanding Vienna's surrender. He orders that it be bombarded until it capitulates.

Every time he undertakes it, the climb to the top is harder.

Vienna is mounting resistance. In Prussia, an officer of hussars, Major Schill, with a force of a hundred men, has set about massacring French soldiers. In Tyrol the insurrection is persisting. The French are not carrying the day in Spain and Portugal – the opposite, in fact.

He mounts his horse, pushes it into a gallop and suddenly feels his mount collapse beneath him and fall on its side.

IT IS ALL so black . . .

HE OPENS HIS EYES. Men are carrying him. He frees himself, looks around him. He sees the terrified faces of Lannes, his aides-de-camp, the chasseurs of the Guard. So, he has passed out. He berates Lannes who advises him not to get back on his horse. The incident must be forgotten. People believe in omens too much.

He gathers all the witnesses in the courtyard of Schönbrunn Palace: marshals, officers, privates. He tells them to form a circle around him. He walks round it.

He wants this to be a secret, he says. Nothing happened.

The men will keep quiet.

He returns to the palace.

ON SATURDAY, 13 May at two in the morning, Vienna capitulates.

He is standing in the palace's reception room. He looks at the immense pictures that decorate it.

'I will live here,' he murmurs, 'among souvenirs of Maria Theresa.'

Then, without stopping to rest, surrounded by his escort, he goes to Vienna which he slowly crosses. The streets are deserted. Where is the amiable curiosity of the last time?

When he returns to the Schönbrunn Palace, he dictates a proclamation for the army:

'Soldiers, the people of Vienna, forsaken, abandoned, bereft, will be the object of your respect. I place its inhabitants under my special protection.'

He wishes it were peace; he ought not to claim victory. Anyway, the war isn't over. Archduke Charles's troops have not been destroyed.

'Be good to the unfortunate peasants and the citizens who have so great a claim to our goodwill,' he says. 'We should not be proud of our success, but see in it only a token of that divine justice which punishes the ungrateful and the perjured.'

He orders that looters and stragglers be hunted down. He doesn't want Austria and Germany to become other Spains.

Discipline must be restored.

As it's growing misty, he decides to do the rounds of the sentries posted about Schönbrunn.

He identifies himself and is allowed to pass.

One of the soldiers repeats his challenge and shouts through the fog, 'If you come any closer, I'll bury this bayonet in your guts.'

Napoleon stops. He is just a man who can be killed. He moves closer. The grenadier identifies him and presents arms.

Destiny has decided not to pluck the thread of my life.

He asks the grenadier his name. It is Coluche, the man says. Napoleon congratulates him, gives his ear a tug, then slowly walks away.

In his room, he writes a note to Josephine, 'I am the master of Vienna, everything is perfect here. My health is excellent.'

XXV

THE AIR IS MILD in the gardens of Schönbrunn in the middle of May 1809. Napoleon sets off for a walk along its avenues after reviewing some regiments of the Guard, but then stops immediately. He cannot enjoy the spring, the tranquillity of this royal palace. He must bring this campaign to a close, have done with this war. He goes back, consults the aides-de-camp and sees the reports from patrols he has sent along the Danube, downstream from Vienna.

He calls Bacler d'Albe. They both stick pins in the map.

The Danube is at least a kilometre wide. He counts numerous islands which can serve as points of support for bridges thrown from the right to the left bank, because they have to cross the river; Archduke Charles's troops are concentrated on the left bank. They're there, Bacler d'Albe indicates, between the villages of Aspern and Essling, and the other side, further north on the Wagram plateau.

Napoleon is worried. Since the start of this war he did not want, he has fought against the feeling that bad omens are everywhere. Often, like a reminder of the threats hanging over him, he feels a sharp stab of pain in his right foot. He has been wounded. His horse has fallen and he has passed out. Then yesterday, as he was walking with Marshal Lannes along the banks of the Danube, Lannes lost his footing and fell into the icy river, its waters swirling like an Alpine torrent in spring. He had to go into the water up to his waist to reach out his hand to the Duke of Montebello. Neither of them laughed; instead they looked at one another for a long time with the same anxiety.

None the less the troops have to cross from one bank to the other, and so they have to build bridges below Vienna. The island of Lobau, which is four kilometres long and six wide, according to Bacler d'Albe, will be the pivot for a large bridge from the right bank and then one half the size, two hundred metres, from the island to the left bank.

Unhesitatingly, he orders the sappers to start work. They will take possession of Lobau, assemble ropes, timber, chains and chests of cannonballs to use as anchors; General Bertrand's pontooneers will stow the material. He sends for Bertrand. His men have one night to carry out this work.

IT IS WEDNESDAY, 17 May. Tomorrow he will leave Schönbrunn for Ebersdorf, the village on the right bank facing the island of Lobau.

He examines the latest dispatches. Spain is gangrenous, the same round of defeats and petty victories that resolve nothing. In Italy, Eugène's troops are proceeding towards Vienna, but the Pope is trying from Rome to cause all Catholics to rise up against the 'Antichrist'.

Me! He's succeeding in Spain and the Tyrol. Can I accept this?
He begins to dictate without even drawing breath,

Decree:
I, Napoleon, Emperor of the French, King of Italy, protector of the Confederation of the Rhine . . .
Whereas Charlemagne, Emperor of the French, our august predecessor, when donating various counties to the bishops of Rome, did so merely by way of fiefs and for the good of his States; whereas, by these donations, Rome did not cease to be a part of his Empire; whereas nothing we have proposed to reconcile the safety of our armies, the tranquillity and well-being of our people and the dignity of our Empire with the temporal claims of the Popes has come to anything, we hereby decree:
The States of the Pope are united to the French Empire.

This is how it is. They fight me, excommunicate me: I snap. Should I turn the other cheek? I am the Emperor, not a holy man, I am responsible for my people and my soldiers who get themselves killed at my command.
And whom I will kill if I must.
In the same voice, he resumes,
'Every straggler who, on the pretext of fatigue, leaves his corps to maraud will be arrested, tried by court martial and executed on the spot.'

One doesn't wage war with pity and compassion. I didn't want it but it's here and I will wage it.

HE CANNOT WAIT any longer. The bridge over to the island of Lobau isn't finished but Napoleon crosses the Danube by boat and instals himself with Marshal Lannes in the only house on the island.

He hears through the open window the laughter of his aides-de-camp lying on the grass around the house. He goes outside. The full moon lights up the island, the river and the left bank on which he can see the Austrian campfires. He listens. These young men, many of whom could die tomorrow, sing in merry, insouciant voices,

> You leave me to go where glory awaits
> My tender heart will accompany your every step . . .
> The stars, in all their quiet brilliance,
> Rain fire on the tents of France

He knows the army thinks these words were written by Hortense, Queen of Holland. A peaceful image comes to him, that of Hortense's child, Napoleon Charles, playing on the terrace of the Tuileries. A dead child. He wants a son. And for that too he must win.

On Sunday, 21 May, he joins the troops of Masséna and Lannes who, having crossed over the long bridge, the island of Lobau and the small bridge, have reached the left bank. They are fighting in the villages of Aspern and Essling.

HE SITS MOTIONLESS on his horse in the ruins of a tile works situated on a small hill. He has to grip the reins firmly, because the bullets and cannonballs are raining down. He sees the Austrian lines, like white waves, storming Aspern and Essling, then falling back, and then other waves, dark ones, break and the ground is bestrewn with white and blue, the uniforms of the dead and wounded.

Slaughter.

The cannonballs from the hundreds of Austrian guns smash into the French lines, knocking over several men each time. He only looks round when an aide-de-camp brings him a message. Aspern and Essling have been retaken for the sixth time. Suddenly his balance goes. His left leg feels hot. He's still astride his horse, but a bullet has torn away his boot and seared the flesh.

Another omen.

He represses his anxiety. An aide-de-camp announces that the main bridge has been swept away by floodwaters, collapsing under the battering it has received from whole tree trunks carried down by the torrential river. He steels himself to give the order to fall back and abandon Aspern and Essling which have cost so much blood.

Then a voice cries that the bridge has been repaired: munitions convoys and men can cross onto the island of Lobau and from there to the left bank again.

He hears the whistle of a cannonball; his horse rears, falls to the ground, its thigh shattered.

He takes another mount, but the grenadiers surround him, threatening to stop fighting if the Emperor insists on remaining in danger. 'Down arms if the Emperor stays here! Down arms!' they shout.

If that cannonball had struck a metre higher, he would be one of the bodies he can see lying on the grass between the shattered walls.

Someone seizes his horse by the bit and yells, 'Withdraw or I shall have you removed by my grenadiers.'

It's General Walter, that old Lutheran, that pastor's son whom I've known since Italy, who was wounded at Austerlitz, who I put in command of the grenadiers of the Horseguards, who charged so many times at Eylau that the word kept on going round that he was dead – General Walter's pulling my horse.

They don't want me to die.

He half-turns and walks his horse across the small bridge. He rides along the columns of young conscripts who raise their muskets and cry, 'Long live the Emperor!'

Gradually mist covers the river and it grows dark and silent.

He sits outside the little house on the island of Lobau and dictates a dispatch to Davout: 'The enemy attacked at full strength when we had only twenty thousand men over the river. The affair was a hot one. The field remains ours. You must send us as many troops as you can, apart from those you need to guard Vienna, and as much ammunition as possible. Send us supplies as well.'

He shuts his eyes. He must sleep a few minutes. He must.

A THICK FOG shrouds everything when Napoleon wakes up on Monday, 22 May 1809. He hears the tramp of men and the creaking of munitions waggons that are crossing the island and heading towards the left bank. If these convoys and reinforcements get over, the battle may be won, but if the bridges are broken again, tens of thousands of men will be caught in a trap.

He points to a fir tree. Carpenters are to build a lookout post from which he can see the battlefield. He waits impatiently as the fog lifts and the cannon start thundering again. At last, he climbs to the top of the tree. Aspern and Essling are holding. Now he can order Lannes's cavalry to charge in the centre and break through the heart of the Austrian army.

He jumps to the ground. He wants to be on the left bank before the attack begins.

HE MAKES HIS WAY along the bank as far as the gun positions held by a battalion of the Guard who are firing with redoubled intensity at the attacking Austrians. Suddenly he hears a voice, General Bertrand's.

The general of Engineers is furious. The main bridge has just been carried away. They won't be able to repair it in less than two days. The munitions, reinforcements, provisions – nothing can get over.

He turns away from Bertrand and immediately calls his aides-de-camp. They are to inform Marshals Lannes and Masséna, the commanding officers, that they have to fall back, still fighting, and cross the small bridge in good order; the island of Lobau must be fortified and held.

As he returns to the island, he looks at the prone bodies. Perhaps 20,000 men killed around Essling and Aspern. Many more Austrians, no doubt.

At the abutment of the small bridge, he sees some grenadiers carrying a stretcher made of branches. Among them he recognizes

Marbot, Lannes's aide-de-camp, who is holding the hand of the man lying down, wounded. Lannes. He wants to scream. He rushes forward. Lannes, Lannes. He pushes Marbot aside. Lannes's legs are just a bloody mush. They're going to operate.

He tears himself away from him, gets back on his horse. He can't take any more. He slumps forward on his horse's neck, gives it its head, jolting up and down in the saddle. This bitter taste on his lips, this burning in his eyes – these are tears.

He straightens up finally and issues orders. Essling must be held at any cost, so that the retreat of the troops on the left bank can be protected. He can't stay still; he gallops back to the small bridge. He wants to know what's happening. He sees Lannes with his left leg amputated. He is overwhelmed again. He doesn't want . . . He kneels down and embraces him. He breathes in the smell of blood. He holds Lannes tight in his arms. Blood stains his white waistcoat.

Lannes stops him leaving, clings to him.

He beseeches me as if I had the power to save him, as if I was his Providence. I want him to live. And I feel he is going to die.

Napoleon walks away.

Exhausted but marching in line, the troops cross the small bridge and establish their bivouacs on the island of Lobau; Austrian roundshot begins to fall.

They must hold the island and destroy the small bridge after the last units are across. When the main bridge is repaired, they'll only leave enough batteries of cannon and men on the island to defend it.

He returns by boat to the village of Ebersdorf on the right bank. He hasn't won this battle of Essling, nor has he lost it, but twenty thousand men are dead.

And everywhere people will say I retreated. So I must win again, despite the dead, despite Lannes's suffering.

The Marshal is dying in the suffocating heat at the end of that May.

His body is eaten away by infection, gangrene. He is fighting it. He needs my presence. I kneel down, talk to him. I would like to stay with him, but people are pulling me away.

The Army of Italy has finally joined up with the Army of the Rhine. He must salute this success.

'Soldiers of the Army of Italy, you have gloriously carried out the mission I gave you. Welcome! I am satisfied with you.'

I've said those words so many times, and so many times I have had to start fighting again.

It's the law of my life.

'Soldiers,' he continues, 'this Austrian army claimed it would break my iron crown. Defeated, scattered and decimated, thanks to you, it will be an example of the device, *Dio la mi diede, guai a chi la tocca!*'*

He sits down in the house in Ebersdorf which has become his headquarters. The shutters have been closed, the heat is so intense.

The gangrene must have eaten its way through Lannes's entire body.

He shouldn't think about it.

HE WRITES to Josephine:

> My friend, I send you a page to say that Eugène has joined me with all his army, that he has perfectly fulfilled the mission I asked of him . . . I send you my proclamation to the Army of Italy, which will explain it all.
>
> I am very well.
> Ever yours,
> Napoleon
>
> P.S. You can have the proclamation printed at Strasbourg and translated into French and German so we can promulgate it in Germany. Add a copy of the proclamation to the letter going to Paris.

HE REMAINS in the half-light of the house in Ebersdorf. It's a moment of calm between storms. He sees Berthier every minute of the day: they must prepare for the next battle, rebuild the bridges, fill the warehouses and move the wounded to Vienna's hospitals.

Every morning and evening he goes to Lannes's bedside in a nearby house.

Lannes is going to die.

---

* God gave it to me, woe betide any who touch it.

On Wednesday, 31 May, Marbot, Lannes's aide-de-camp, spreads his arms on the doorstep to stop him entering the house.

Lannes is dead. The stink of the corpse has spread through the house. It's dangerous to go in. Foetid miasmas, Marbot keeps saying.

Napoleon pushes him aside. He falls to his knees and clasps Lannes to him.

'What a loss for France and for me,' he murmurs.

He cannot take any more. He weeps.

He wants to keep the body next to him. Warm it.

Someone pulls him away, forces him to stand up. It is Berthier. General Bertrand and the officers of engineers are awaiting his orders.

Napoleon commands that Lannes's body should be embalmed and sent back to France.

He goes up to Bertrand. 'Now, the bridges . . .' he begins.

IN THE DARK ROOM of the house in Ebersdorf, he writes to Madame Lannes, the Duchess of Montebello,

> My cousin,
>
> The Marshal died this morning of wounds received on the field of honour. My grief is as keen as yours. I lose the most distinguished general in my armies, my comrade in arms for sixteen years, he whom I considered my best friend.
>
> His family and his children will always have a special claim to my protection. It is to assure you of this that I wanted to write you this letter, for I feel that nothing could alleviate the orrow you must feel.

He stays for a long moment with his head bowed, his chin on his chest. He must ask Josephine to try and console Madame Lannes.

He writes to her, 'The loss of the Duke of Montebello, who died this morning, has caused me great grief. Thus all things come to their end!'

XXVI

NAPOLEON IS SITTING in his study, looking out at the gardens surrounding Schönbrunn Palace. The windows are open. These first June mornings are mild; it could almost be peacetime. For a few moments he imagines his life here with Marie Walewska. The letters she has written him from Poland are there, on the table. He remembers those long days in Finckenstein Castle, after the Battle of Eylau, before the victory at Friedland. Back then he thought he had established a system of alliance with the Tsar that would prevent war. But nothing turned out as he hoped, everything as he feared.

Now the Archduke Charles's army is still on the left bank of the Danube, on the Wagram plateau.

It is erecting palisades, building redoubts, deploying artillery to ensure the river is impassable.

He must destroy it. He must cross the Danube.

I can only count on myself. The Tsar is manoeuvring his troops, but that is much more to neutralize Poniatowski's Poles and prevent a Polish kingdom being re-formed than it is to threaten the Austrians. A fine ally, this Alexander!

Napoleon gets to his feet and sends for General Savary. He wants to know which regiments will be on parade this morning, which marshals and generals will be present. He ought to award crosses of the Légion d'honneur, elevate some grenadiers to the rank of Knight of the Empire.

He wants to reinvigorate these troops who have been so roughly handled at Essling. He wants to erase the memory of their dead or wounded comrades – almost twenty thousand of them! He wants them to forget that they had to pull back. They must be ready to resume combat as soon as the bridges are rebuilt and reinforcements arrive. From Paris he is awaiting 20,000 infantry, 10,000 cavalry, 6,000 grenadiers of the Guard, as well as artillery. He will then have 187,000 men and 488 cannon to set against the Archduke Charles's 125,000 men.

He goes up to the window.

But there is still this river to cross, and there is still Archduke John, Charles's brother, who was beaten in Italy but has now regrouped in Hungary, and his army is more than thirty thousand strong.

Napoleon turns to Savary. He wants to go the island of Lobau every morning. Once again it is the pivot of his disposition. From there he will be able to observe the Austrians, gauge progress on the bridges and choose the moment when the troops will cross from the right bank onto the island and then over to the left bank of the Danube.

He will have to bring this off. There isn't a monarch in Europe who isn't waiting to launch themselves at him after his defeat.

The King of Prussia and my fine ally, Alexander, are just waiting for a sign of weakness.

'They've all arranged to meet at my grave,' he tells Savary, 'but they don't dare join together.'

HE SENDS SAVARY away; he's alone. He hears the tramp of regiments taking up their positions in the main courtyard. The parade will start at ten o'clock, the same as every morning.

He needs this precise organization of time.

After the tumult of battle, the shocks and deaths that negate every certainty, he wants order to reign here at Schönbrunn, the most rigorous Court ceremonial to be observed. He can only work effectively within a familiar routine. Then he's clear-headed, then he can imagine the imminent battle, the bridges, the movement of troops that will sweep over the Wagram plateau after crossing to the left bank where Archduke Charles does not expect them, downstream of Aspern and Essling.

For a brief moment, he feels a sense of joy. He sees the troop movements: he'll engage the artillery en masse, in a way that has never been tried before, deceive the Archduke Charles into thinking he is directing his attack at Essling and thereby turn his flank.

He goes back to the map table. He points his finger at Gross-Enzersdorf. That's where the battle will be decided.

He paces about the study a little. He cannot think of anything except this approaching conflict, the course of which he must try to predict.

Afterwards, when victory is won, perhaps peace will follow. He wants it to; he needs to live another way, to halt this frenzied progress he has not yet been able to check.

He picks up Marie Walewska's letters from the little table next to the one the maps are spread out on.

He writes a few words. He would like her to join him here, as she did at Finckenstein Castle.

Your letters give me pleasure, as always. I don't really approve of you following the army to Cracow, but I cannot reproach you for it. Poland's fortunes have been restored and I understand your anxiety. I took action; it was better than lavishing you with words of comfort. You have nothing to thank me for. I love your country and I see for their true worth the merits of a great number of your compatriots.

It will take more than the capture of Vienna to bring an end to the campaign.

When I've finished it, I will arrange to be nearer to you, my sweet friend, because I am impatient to see you again. If it is at Schönbrunn, we will enjoy the charm of its beautiful gardens and we will forget all these bad days.

Be patient and keep your faith in me.

N.

I HAVE NEVER had anyone I can turn to for reassurance.

I have to draw all the energy and all the faith I need from within myself, only myself.

God? He is silent. And the Pope, who claims to be his representative, is excommunicating me!

'No more circumspection in dealings with this Pope. He is a lunatic who should be locked up.'

What purpose would it serve, being cautious towards enemies who wish me in hell?

I must hold firm on all fronts, conquer here, rule everywhere; in Rome just as in Paris.

He writes to Fouché. The Duke of Otranto is to assume the

powers formerly held by the home secretary, Crétet, who has fallen ill from overwork.

Do I have time to be ill?

He turns to his secretary.

'Any man I make a minister shouldn't be able to piss after four years,' he snaps.

That is what power is, an exercise of utter dedication or nothing. Fouché is a resolute fellow who'll be able to keep the country under control.

In time victory will silence critics and dispel anxieties, but for the moment, as long as there is no military resolution, Fouché must control the police and Home Office with an iron rod.

'I feel very calm, knowing you will have everything in hand,' he dictates. 'Things here will all change in a month.'

When I've defeated Archduke Charles.

So, PARADES, reviews, inspections.

Every day he is on the island of Lobau; he walks around it, hands behind his back, for seven to eight hours. He stops in front of each of the hundred cannon with which he has fortified the island. He questions Colonel Charles d'Escorches de Sainte-Croix. He has taken to this young officer, barely thirty, who is the son of one of Louis XVI's ambassadors. Napoleon wants him to be at Schönbrunn every morning when he gets up, to report what has happened the previous night on Lobau.

Does Sainte-Croix realize my anxiety? Does he know that every night I'm afraid the Archduke Charles will attack?

But the Austrians are only thinking of strengthening their defences!

Napoleon climbs a huge double ladder which Sainte-Croix has set up on a hill on Lobau in such a way that one can see the entire left bank of the Danube from its top rungs.

Napoleon stays up there a long time up. He sees the enemy redoubts along the left bank, but over towards Essling and Aspern. They'll cross the Danube then, as he anticipated, by Enzersdorf.

Beyond it lie fields of ripe wheat which sway in the breeze, unharvested by any peasant. The cavalry and infantry will have to advance through this crop.

Napoleon gets down from the ladder. He sends for Marshal Masséna. He wants to see the enemy at closer quarters.

Napoleon and Masséna put on sergeant's greatcoats; Colonel de Sainte-Croix dresses as a private. Napoleon leads the way, making his way down to the island's shore. The Austrians are on the other side of the river, but during this lull the two sides are simply observing one another. The colonel strips. He's just a soldier wanting to have a swim. Napoleon and Masséna sit by the water like two sergeants who have taken a walk. The Austrian sentries watch them and make jokes. A sort of truce exists at this bathing spot.

Napoleon has seen enough. He goes back to the middle of the island. He will not alter his plan. They just need to wait for the bridges to be finished and ready to be put in place: four bridges between the island of Lobau and the left bank, and three bridges from the right bank to the island of Lobau.

HE GOES OVER to the island again. There are so many troops on it now that grenadiers of the Guard have to organize the flow of waggons and caissons that are piling up as they wait to cross to the left bank.

Suddenly Masséna's mount stumbles and falls into a hole concealed by the long grass. Napoleon jumps off his horse. Is it another of these bad omens, like those before the Battle of Essling?

He needs Masséna, this penniless orphan who travelled the world as a ship's boy, before rising up through the ranks under the ancien régime from corporal to staff officer, becoming brigadier-general in 1793 thanks to his talent and courage.

There's a gaping wound in Masséna's thigh. He can't ride or walk any more. Yet his troops are pivotal to the battle. The plan is to have them on the left wing; they will take the full impact of the Austrian attack which will start the minute the first troops land on the left bank; they will have to hold firm until Archduke Charles has been outflanked.

Napoleon looks at Marshal Masséna bending over his wound. Will he lose this officer too? – a fighter obsessed with money, a miser, but also a 'Favourite Child of Victory' and the Duke of Rivoli?

Masséna gets up, grimacing with pain, but he says he'll command his troops from a barouche, with a doctor at his side.

ON FRIDAY, 30 June, Napoleon invites Eugène de Beauharnais and Marshals Davout and Bernadotte to dinner at Schönbrunn Palace. He loves Eugène, brave, loyal soul, almost a son to him. He admires Davout, the Duke of Auerstädt, a former gentleman cadet at Paris Military School like him. A man who ordered his men to fire on Dumouriez in 1793 when he betrayed the Republic. A general who has never been defeated.

Napoleon talks without looking at Bernadotte. He mistrusts his old rival, Désirée Clary's husband. How far off all that is now, and how stubborn jealousy can be!

Bernadotte held back his troops at Austerlitz and Jena. He even conspired against me. He would not commit himself on 18 Brumaire. He is in command of the Saxon divisions. Can I count on him?

At ten in the evening, an aide-de-camp of Masséna's reports that the troops have started crossing onto the left bank, creating a bridgehead near Essling to hold the enemy.

The opening gambit.

Napoleon finishes what he was saying about the theatre in the same, level voice.

'If Corneille were alive, I would make him a prince.'

Then he stands up and turns to Montesquiou, the grand chamberlain.

'What time is sunrise?'

'Four o'clock, Sire.'

'Well then, we shall set off for the island of Lobau tomorrow morning at four.'

HE IS UP AT THREE. How could one sleep longer?

At five o'clock on Saturday, 1 July 1809, he steps onto the island of Lobau. He watches the troops crossing the bridges from the right bank to the island and with difficulty finding some space amidst the artillery caissons, horses and tens of thousands of men. He must make them wait until, on the day of the main attack, they are an unstoppable wave breaking on the left bank.

Napoleon doesn't sleep for more than one or two hours, when he can, in the middle of the day or night. He goes to his tent, pitched by the main bridge, and studies his maps. He goes out to conduct a fresh inspection. He interrogates a spy who for several days has been infiltrating the island and then crossing the Danube every night to report to the Austrians. The man cries, begs him. He offers to cross the river again and give the Archduke false information. He was born in Paris, he explains, he lost everything gambling, then fled his creditors. He needed money.

Napoleon turns away. Shoot this man, he orders.

ON TUESDAY, 4 July, the heat is stifling. It becomes overcast. Tonight is when the troops are meant to cross the Danube and head for where the Archduke least expects them, Enzersdorf. At nine in the evening the storm breaks.

Napoleon leaves his tent. The skies have opened on the island and river; the wind bends the trees; the Danube is churned into waves which batter the bridges. He stays standing in the rain, arms crossed. He sees Berthier hurrying towards him. The attack must be adjourned, the marshal says.

'No,' he replies unhesitatingly. 'Twenty-four hours' delay and we'll have Archduke John on our hands.'

He gives the order to open fire on Aspern and Essling, so that the Archduke is convinced that the attack will strike there, on the left.

He raises his face to the sky and rain. The warm water runs down it, washing away his tiredness.

He joins Masséna, who is sitting in a barouche. The four white horses, which lash out at every clap of thunder or cannonfire, strike him as a good omen.

'I am delighted with this storm,' he tells Masséna.

He speaks in a loud voice, so that the aides-de-camp caracoling their horses round the barouche can hear.

'What a fine night for us! The Austrians cannot see our preparations to cross opposite Enzersdorf and they won't know until we've taken that crucial position, until our bridges are laid and part of my army is formed up on the bank they claim to be defending.'

It's Wednesday, 5 July 1809. It is still dark.

He has crossed over to the left bank with the first troops attacking Enzersdorf. When the village is captured, he mounts up and begins to ride along the lines that are swinging inwards on the Austrians.

The day dawns; the sun is dazzling, the sky as if scrubbed clean by the storm. The heat is intense. He orders all the guns to fire, and here and there the tall wheat, already dried by the sun, goes up in flames. Through his field-glass, he sees men fleeing the blaze, others falling into the flames.

He goes from one bridge to the next. On the north of the plain, at the start of the Wagram plateau, Davout's men have crossed the Russbach stream which he can see glinting in the sun. Now they are swinging inwards to envelop the village of Wagram. Suddenly an aide-de-camp comes to report that Bernadotte's Saxons have broken ranks after exchanging fire with Macdonald's men who no doubt confused their uniforms with the Austrians'.

He mustn't let his anger with Bernadotte explode – once again he hasn't played his part – but nor must he forget.

Napoleon walks up and down in front of his tent as night falls and the fighting comes to a halt. He hears the screams of the wounded. The wheat is still catching fire in different places. A smell of burnt flesh hangs in the air.

He sits down, stretches his legs and lets his head sink onto his chest. It is one o'clock in the morning. He is going to grab three hours' sleep, he's decided. He wakes up as planned. A body, a mind are both machinery one must know how to control.

He goes out onto the battlefield.

Today, Thursday, 6 July 1809, will be the decisive day. It is already stiflingly hot. The cannonballs start raining down around him. One of them explodes in front of his grey, which he has chosen specially so that everyone will know that it's him, the Emperor, in the firing line.

'Sire,' calls out an aide-de-camp, 'your staff are under fire.'

Who is this simpleton?

Spurring his horse, Napoleon shouts, 'All sorts of accidents are possible in war!'

Archduke Charles has launched an attack on Masséna's troops, the pivot of his manoeuvre.

Masséna must hold fast. Napoleon gallops in his direction and catches sight of the barouche drawn by four white horses in the front line. There's a man! He jumps off his horse. Roundshot falls all around the carriage, killing the aides-de-camp flanking it. Napoleon gets in. They must hold the line, at any cost, he cries.

Getting to his feet, he scans the horizon with his field-glass. The Archduke Charles's troops are advancing. To the west, against a cloudless sky, he sees the houses of Vienna and the thousands of handkerchiefs the inhabitants of the capital are waving from roofs or windows to hail the Archduke Charles's advance.

They will see!

He mounts his horse again and orders the artillery batteries concentrated on Lobau to open fire.

This is part of his plan. The Austrian lines have been breached.

He catches sight of Marbot, the aide-de-camp.

'Run and tell Masséna that if he falls on everything that lies before him, the battle is won,' he bellows.

Now he must deliver the knockout blow.

'Take a hundred guns,' he yells at General Lauriston, 'sixty of them from my Guard, and go and crush the enemy masses.'

He joins Lauriston just as he is moving forward. He does not want the guns to open fire until they are three hundred metres from the Austrians.

He sees the gunners run forward amidst the bullets and roundshot, position their cannon wheel to wheel and only open fire when the Austrians are a few metres away.

The enemy lines are torn to pieces. The corpses pile up, the wheat bursts into flames, the powder caissons explode. He sees men hurled into the air, their cartridge pouches ablaze.

'The battle is won!' he cries.

But Archduke Charles is withdrawing with eighty thousand men and making for Znaym.

He sleeps for a couple of hours. At three in the morning on 7 July he is up.

He rides through the trampled, burnt wheat fields. Some of the wounded are screaming as it grows light. He orders detachments of cavalry followed by carriages to scour the plain to find any wounded hidden in the wheat who are going to rot in the heat.

Is it the screams, or the smell of corpses or the intense heat? Suddenly he feels exhausted and nauseous.

AT WOLKERSDORF CASTLE where he sets himself up, he begins to calculate his losses. How many dead and wounded? Fifty thousand? No doubt as many on the Austrian side. He has seen Marshal Bessières lying on the ground. He didn't want to go closer. No time to weep during a battle. Five marshals have been killed, thirty-seven wounded.

He listens as Savary talks to him about Bernadotte. On the evening of 5 July, Bernadotte criticized the Emperor and declared that if he had been in command, he would have forced Prince Charles, by means of a skillful manoeuvre, to lay down his arms almost without a fight. Bernadotte has also published an order of the day glorifying his Saxons.

'Get him away from me immediately! He is to quit the Grand Army within twenty-four hours!' cries Napoleon.

He is dripping with sweat, his mouth full of bitter-tasting saliva. Some die, like Lannes, or like General Lasalle, killed by a bullet in the middle of his forehead at the age of thirty, others are wounded and in pain, like Bessières – and this fellow swaggers about!

His whole body aches.

He goes out into the cool night air. The moon lights up the castle gardens. He vomits. His face is sunburnt. He slowly goes back inside, a searing pain in his stomach.

He calls Roustam; he wants some milk.

He is made to lie down. He raises himself up on his elbows. The campaign isn't over.

Archduke Charles still has troops in good order. They must make for Znaym, do battle.

But he is sick again.

This body is failing him.

He closes his eyes.

SICK? WHAT IS THIS WORD? This inadmissible state? He works, drowses off, wakes with a start and resumes dictating. On Sunday, 9 July, he feels better. At two in the morning, he writes to Josephine.

> Everything here is going according to my wishes, my friend. My enemies have been undone, defeated and wholly put to rout. They were a sizeable force, and I have crushed them. My losses have been fairly heavy. Bessières had his thigh grazed by a roundshot; the wound is very slight. Lasalle was killed.
>
> My health is good today; yesterday I was slightly ill from a defluxion of bile, caused by excessive fatigue, but I feel much the better for it.
>
> Farewell, my friend, I am well.
>
> Napoleon

ON MONDAY, 10 July, he leaves Wolkersdorf Castle and gallops towards Znaym. He knows this country. He makes out the slopes of the Pratzen plateau in the distance. Austerlitz was 2 December 1805. On the eve of the battle, the men celebrated the anniversary of his coronation with thousands of torches.

He hasn't stopped leading an army, but now he has to fight those they defeated then all over again.

He issues orders to attack the Archduke Charles's troops, which have just engaged to protect the retreat of the bulk of the Austrian army.

Victory.

He goes into his tent which has been erected in a field full of tall grass. A violent storm suddenly breaks, but through the thunder one can still hear the explosion of roundshot.

It is five in the afternoon on Tuesday, 11 July 1809. An Austrian cavalryman approaches, preceded by a French escort. It is the Prince of Liechtenstein, come to request a suspension of combat.

Napoleon is standing in his tent. The marshals surround him. Davout insists again that they must put an end to these Hapsburgs, these Austrians in the pay of the English. Oudinot, Masséna and Macdonald agree.

He goes out of the tent. The rain has stopped. The cannon roar. Below a strip of blue sky on the horizon, he can see Pratzen plateau again.

'Enough blood has been shed,' he says.

He signals to Marshal Berthier to grant a suspension of hostilities.

HE WILL RETURN to Schönbrunn. Perhaps Marie Walewska is already waiting for him. Perhaps this will be peace.

He scribbles a few words to Josephine.

I am sending you the suspension of arms which was concluded yesterday with the Austrian general. Eugène is over towards Hungary and he is well. Send a copy of the suspension of arms to Cambacérès in case he hasn't got one.

With much love and in good health, I am your
Napoleon

You can have this suspension of arms printed at Nancy.

Josephine is in Plombières. She is taking the waters: an old woman still full of vigour who wants to keep on pulling the wool over people's eyes, to keep on fighting time.

Everything is war.

PART SEVEN

We must make peace

14 July 1809 to 26 october 1809

XXVII

HE IS FORTY YEARS OLD today, 15 August 1809. He strolls along Schönbrunn's walks with Duroc. It is barely seven-thirty in the morning; on the horizon, the rising sun glints on Vienna's roofs. Napoleon turns and, through the bank of trees that screen the grounds, glimpses the white facade of Marie Walewska's house. She has been living there since the middle of July.

He stops. To the left of the path he recognizes the Roman ruin, obelisk and fountain, which he had seen in 1805, when he first stayed at Schönbrunn. Four years ago already. He is forty.

He runs his fingers over the nape of his neck. The skin is cracked and puffy, the itching infuriating. Sometimes he even thinks he can feel a dull throb of pain spreading from the red, inflamed area to his shoulders and up into his head.

But why does he have to pay any mind to his body's protests? He's alive; he sees Marie Walewksa every night; he makes love to her passionately. Last night was no exception, before he returned to the palace to receive the dignitaries who started arriving at seven o'clock this morning to present their compliments on this 15 August, his fortieth birthday.

Last night, lying next to Marie, he felt at peace. The shooting pains in his back and stomach disappeared; he even forgot about his smarting neck.

Marie never asks for anything; she's discreet; she doesn't even go to the plays performed in Schönbrunn's theatre. She simply waits in her house in Meidling next to the palace, as unruffled, serene and bright as the water in Schönbrunn's fountains. She displays none of the hypocrisy, cunning or trickery of every other woman he's known. She has a young woman's body, firm and curvaceous. She only ever complains about Poland, but she understands and accepts what he tells her.

HE TURNS TO Duroc and they resume walking towards the Gloriette, the porticoed belvedere on a little hill that affords views not just of Schönbrunn's gardens but of the entire surrounding countryside. Vienna is over there, in the distance, lit by the fiery blaze of dawn.

Poland – that's still the obstacle on which all the negotiations with Russia are foundering

'One only does what one can,' he begins. 'If I were the Emperor of Russia, I wouldn't agree to any expansion of the Duchy of Warsaw, just as I would choose death and the loss of all ten of my armies if that was what was needed to defend Belgium. And I would create an eleventh army, of children and women, to attack anything that might be a threat to France. The re-establishment of Poland at this point is not possible for France. I do not want to make war on Russia.'

He shakes his head and feels the burning sensation at the nape of his neck again.

HE HAS ALREADY consulted Doctor Yvan, who dressed his wound at Ratisbon and, as chief surgeon to the Emperor, has accompanied him on all his travels for a number of years.

But Yvan is no genius. So Doctor Frank, the most celebrated practitioner of the moment, came from Vienna to examine his neck. He looked grave, like an expert discovering an incurable illness.

Napoleon rubs his neck. Should he believe this Austrian? He heard him speak of a dartrous condition, courses of blisters, medicine, ointments.

'Doctor Corvisart arrived from Paris last night,' Duroc reports. Justifying himself, the grand marshal of the palace explains that he decided to invite Corvisart to Schönbrunn after Doctor Frank's diagnosis.

Napoleon shrugs. He remembers his night with Marie. He doesn't think it's a bad attack, whatever it is – perhaps just the anxiety and strain of war, the cruelty of everything he's seen, all those dead – Lannes, Lasalle, over fifty thousand others – and the smell of burning flesh hanging over the Wagram plateau.

In Paris, he says, news of the great Corvisart's departure, His Majesty's doctor, is bound to have provoked the wildest speculation.

They're bound to be talking about my succession again.

'I am forty, Duroc. If I die . . .'

He stops, takes a pinch of snuff and then tugs roughly at his coat collar, which is chafing.

He wants a son. He must divorce. It's now, at forty, or never.

HE RETURNS TO the palace, sends for Méneval and starts on the dispatches. Within minutes, he looks up.

Last night, Marie told him she thought she was pregnant. He laid both of his hands on her stomach. A son, in there: further proof of his ability to give life. He must divorce. As soon as peace is concluded in Vienna, he will return to Paris and resolve the matter, brutally, in one fell swoop, the way a limb is amputated on a battlefield.

But when will he be able to leave Schönbrunn? The Austrians are negotiating skillfully, refusing his proposed settlement: the abdication of Emperor Francis, who was responsible for the war, in exchange for the integrity of their national territory.

What do they hope will happen while they delay? That the English will successfully complete their landing on Walcheren Island, and then presumably march on Antwerp and Holland? That I will go to war with Russia over Poland? Or that the Catholics of Europe will rise up against me because the Pope has been arrested?

He sends for Champagny, the minister of foreign affairs. The man hasn't a fraction of Talleyrand's abilities, but he is a trust-worthy subordinate.

'I am angry that the Pope has been arrested,' Napoleon declares. 'It is an act of great folly.'

He takes a pinch of snuff and paces up and down. He had mentioned the possibility of locking up the Pope, it's true. But – he stamps his foot – he never ordered it. He never wanted Pius VII chased out of Rome and established in Savona. He just wanted to annex Rome, that's all!

'It is an act of great folly,' he repeats, 'but there is no undoing it. What's done is done.'

His fury mounts. His neck smarts and the more he raises his voice, the worse the itching and pain.

There are so few people who understand him, who genuinely help him, who don't, sooner or later, disappoint him.

Take his brother Jérôme, whom he has made a king. Jérôme thinks the place to wage war, like a satrap, is a long way from the fighting.

He starts dictating a letter to him,

You must be a soldier, and again a soldier, and always a soldier! You must bivouac with your outposts, be in the saddle night and day, march with the advance guard to get information, or else remain in your seraglio. My brother, you wage war like a satrap.

But the minister of war, Clarke, is no better. He hasn't taken any measures to oppose the British landings on Walcheren Island. Does he want to be caught in his bed by the British?

As for Joseph, he's still trying to impersonate Charles V in Spain while letting Wellesley's English win the Battle of Talavera. Now Wellesley has been made Duke of Wellington.

'I have opened a military college in Spain,' he cries. 'The peninsula is where the English send their army for training!'

Meanwhile Fouché has appointed Bernadotte, whom I dismissed from the army, Commander in Chief of the National Guard! The devious, jealous, inept Bernadotte. Dismiss him immediately!

And these are the men who claim to serve me.

His mouth is full of bile, his skin irritated, his nerves on edge. He has to write yet another reply to Josephine, whose letters are full of a jealous woman's innuendo.

Some good, kind souls must already have informed her of Marie Walewska's presence at Schönbrunn.

She writes as if I've something to be guilty of! It is only for old time's sake that I am gentle with her.

I have received your letter from Malmaison. I am told that you are plump, fresh-faced and in very good health. Vienna is not an amusing city, I can assure you. I dearly wish I were gone.

Farewell, my friend. I watch clowns twice a week; they're pretty mediocre but they liven up the evenings. There are fifty or sixty women in Vienna, but they sit in the stalls, since they haven't been presented at court.

Napoleon

Now for the grand parade in the main courtyard of the palace. He walks out. The sun is dazzling.

He sees Marshal Berthier behind a cordon of gendarmes and grenadiers. He goes up to him and declares, 'You are the Prince of Wagram.' Then he turns to Marshal Masséna, 'You are the Prince of Essling.'

He loves moments like these when he rewards men who have fought well, who have served him with devotion. He tells Macdonald, Marmont and Oudinot: 'You are marshals of the Empire,' and Davout, 'You are the Prince of Eckmühl.'

The drums roll. The parade begins. From the courtyard he cannot see the house where Marie Walewska lives.

He returns to the palace and laughs when he sees the astonished look on Doctor Corvisart's face. He goes up to him. He has a great regard for this amiable-looking man whom he sees almost every day in Paris and whose diagnoses have always proved reliable. Corvisart must have thought he'd be bedridden, at death's door.

'Well then, Corvisart, what news? What are they saying in Paris? Do you know they're saying I'm gravely ill here? I've just got a little rash, a slight headache.'

He turns, undoing his cravat, and shows him his neck.

'Doctor Frank claims that I'm suffering from a dartrous condition which will require a long and intensive course of treatment. What do you think?'

I am forty. Death can take me, now more than ever.

Corvisart laughs.

'Oh sire, making me come all this way for a course of blisters that any doctor could apply as well as I! Frank is talking through his hat. This little complaint is the result of a poorly treated rash and it won't survive four days' blisters. Your health is wonderful!'

Is CORVISART RIGHT? The question occurs to him from time to time during those summer weeks of 1809. Some days he feels overwhelmed with tiredness. Others the opposite; he is brimming with energy.

ON THIS 15 August 1809, he decides to go incognito into Vienna with Marshal Berthier to see the city's illuminations and watch the firework display in honour of his birthday.

He senses Berthier's anxiety, as he shoots worried glances at the crowds of passers-by. If the Emperor were to be recognized . . .

'I abandon myself to my star,' Napoleon says. 'I am too fatalistic to take any precautions against someone trying to murder me.'

They amuse him, all these people who push past him not realizing who he is. He feels joyful, youthful. He is going to spend the night with Marie Walewska.

'I am in good health,' he says to Berthier on their way back to Schönbrunn. 'I don't know what people are talking about. I haven't been this well for years. Corvisart was of no use to me at all.'

He goes to Marie Walewska's house, and is delighted to see her so pink-cheeked and blooming.

She is carrying my child. It is her youth, her fecundity, that are the cause of my good health.

He must divorce in order to marry a woman worthy of an emperor, a woman who will give him what this sweet Marie has given him.

XXVIII

Autumn is on its way. Already! Is that possible? Napoleon has settled into a routine at Schönbrunn. He goes out exploring the countryside on horseback, walking his horse through the villages where the fighting took place and where the peasants have almost finished rebuilding their houses. On the Essling plain and the plateau of Wagram the harvest is in. The September and October rains have started to churn up the ground; nightfall now brings dusk to a brutal close.

The soldiers cantoned in Nokolburg, Krems, Brunn and Goding, not far from the Hungarian border, greet him with cheers. He reviews them and puts them through manoeuvres.

One Saturday, 17 September 1809, he sets off on the Olmutz road on a lively grey that jumps every ditch and hedge and brings him out onto the battlefield of Austerlitz far ahead of his staff and escort. When the troops of III Corps catch sight of him, they yell, 'Long live the Emperor!' He caracoles his horse and remembers.

The Princes of Dietrichstein are waiting for him in their castle. He is served nuts and a glass of Bisamberg white wine. He carries on to Brunn where he decides to spend the night in the town hall. He feels at home wherever he goes; it would be the same way anywhere in Europe. General Clarke has just reported that the English are preparing to re-embark and abandon Walcheren Island. Their attempted invasion has failed. Perhaps he will manage to pacify the Empire from the Tyrol to Spain, after all?

He returns to Schönbrunn. He calls on Marie Walewska, and then goes to the theatre where a ballet or play or recital are put on for him almost every night. He congratulates the Italian actors on their performance of *The Barber of Seville*.

After the play, Champagny reports on the state of peace negotiations with the Austrians. What sort of act is Metternich putting on? Napoleon wonders indignantly. He wants to take the discussions in hand himself, here at Schönbrunn; he wants them to be successful.

Suddenly lost in thought, he paces about his study. It is almost six months since he left Paris on 13 April; it's already the middle of October. Marie Walewska is returning to Walewice to have the child at home, among her family. He will have to go back to Paris soon and face Josephine.

The thought of it makes him uneasy. He imagines what might happen. She has disarmed him so many times in the past, when she's been unfaithful or when he wanted to leave her after coming back from Egypt. She is so clever, and they have so many shared memories. If he's not careful, she'll lay siege to him; she'll burst into his study, wringing her hands and sobbing, and implore him not to abandon her.

He does not want to give in to her any more.

He sends for Méneval in the dead of night, and dictates a letter to the architect in charge of renovations at Fontainebleau where he plans to stay on his return. He wants the corridor connecting his and the Empress's apartments to be sealed off.

That way his intentions will be clear. She will understand; it will be plain to all.

He will not give in. He cannot give in.

ON THURSDAY, 12 October 1809, he crosses Schönbrunn's main courtyard at midday to attend parade. A few dozen metres away, a dense crowd is waiting behind a line of gendarmes. He takes his place between Marshal Berthier and General Rapp, his aide-de-camp who, after a few minutes, walks off towards the spectators and the gendarmes controlling them. Napoleon prizes the intelligence and devotion of this Alsatian from Colmar whose grasp of German is a valuable asset on the battlefield. Rapp can interrogate prisoners and peasants and conduct negotiations, and he's a courageous man as well, who led the charge of the fusiliers of the guard at Essling.

After the parade, Rapp approaches Napoleon and asks to speak to him. Napoleon looks at him. Why this grave expression? In his hand he holds an object wrapped in a newspaper, which he takes off.

I see a knife a foot and a half long, edges like razors, sharp, tapered point.

Napoleon takes a step back. He listens to Rapp telling him how a young man in an olive green frockcoat, boots and a black hat, who wanted to give the Emperor a petition in person, caught his attention. As he was trying to send him on his way, Rapp realized the young man was hiding something under his coat.

'This knife, sire.'

The youth, a certain Friedrich Staps, was planning to kill the Emperor with this knife. He will only explain himself to the Emperor.

One must always face one's destiny. He will see Staps.

Napoleon goes to his study where Champagny is waiting for him.

'Monsieur de Champagny,' he says, 'the Austrian plenipotentiary ministers haven't talked to you about any plans for my assassination, have they?'

Champagny seems unsurprised by the question.

'Yes, sire, they told me it has been proposed to them on a number of occasions and that they have always rejected it with horror.'

'Well, someone has just tried to assassinate me.'

He opens the doors of the drawing room.

So this young man standing near General Rapp is the one who wanted to kill me. He has a round, gentle, naïve face. I want to know why. Rapp will translate my questions.

Friedrich Staps answers calmly, disconcertingly so. Is this pastor's son mad or sick or an illuminato? Can one, at seventeen, wish to kill a man without any personal motive?

'Why did you want to kill me?'

'Because you are ruining my country.'

'Have I harmed you personally?'

'As you have all Germans.'

Can I believe him when he says that he acted on his own initiative, and that he had neither inspiration nor accomplice? I am hated in the courts of Berlin and Weimar, just as I am at Vienna. Queen Louise of Prussia, her vanity wounded, is just the sort of woman to have me assassinated by a fanatic like this young fellow with his angelic face and lunatic mind.

'You are a hothead,' Napoleon says. 'You will ruin your family. I will grant you your life if you ask my pardon for the crime you wanted to commit and for which you should be sorry.'

I'm watching him. His lips quiver only slightly before he starts talking.

'I do not want your pardon. I feel the keenest regret that I was not successful.'

'Damnation! Does a crime mean nothing to you?'

'Killing you is not a crime, it is a duty.'

So much calm, implacable hatred of me!

Napoleon looks at Rapp, Savary, Champagny, Berthier and Duroc, who are standing in a circle around Friedrich Staps. All of them seem fascinated.

'But come now, if I pardon you, would you be grateful?'

'I would try just as hard to kill you again.'

Napoleon leaves the room.

IS THIS HATRED *and determination shared by the entire German people, like the Spaniards and Tyrolese who are still fighting against my armies?*

He sends for General Rapp. Schulmeister must conduct Friedrich Staps's interrogation. Perhaps that shrewd fellow will be able to make him confess the names of his mentors and accomplices.

Rapp persists in thinking Staps was acting alone.

Napoleon shakes his head.

'There is no precedent for a young man of that age, German, Protestant, well educated, wanting to commit such a crime.'

He takes several pinches of snuff as he paces about his study.

If this hatred is the people's, if the rulers of Prussia, Austria, England, Russia, 'my fine ally', and the Pope have deflected the conflagration that should be threatening them onto me, if the people prefer fanaticism to reason, customs and religion to the civil code and the enlightenment, then I have to come to a compromise as quickly as possible and sign a treaty of peace with Vienna at all costs.

Perhaps I should even, as has occurred to me before, ally myself with one of these dynasties, given that the people still support them.

Who shall I marry? A Hapsburg princess or a Russian grand duchess?

But first, no one must hear about this attempt. Assassins are always imitators.

HE WARNS FOUCHÉ,

A young man of seventeen, the son of a Lutheran pastor from Erfurt, tried to get near me at the parade today. Some officers stopped him and as the youth seemed troubled, suspicions were aroused. He was searched and a dagger was found on him. I ordered the little wretch to be brought before me; he seemed fairly well educated and he told me that he wanted to kill me to rid Austria of the French.

Always as important as an event is people's opinion of it.

I wanted to inform you of this so that its importance is not exaggerated. I hope it will not get out. If it should become talked about, make out the fellow is mad. If not, keep it to yourself. There was no scandal at the parade; I didn't even notice that anything had happened.

He must stress this.

I repeat, and you will clearly understand this, that not a word is to be said about this affair.

He remains on his own. He is not afraid of death. He goes up to the desk on which the long, finely sharpened knife Friedrich Staps was hiding lies.

My hour had not come. I have known since my first battle that it is useless trying to protect oneself against the cannonballs. I have given myself up to my destiny. Being emperor means being on a perpetual battlefield. At peace or war, there is change: simply that, in peacetime, it is conspiracies that are the cannonballs.

But he must act. Destiny is a great river that a man must navigate, using its current and steering between its whirlpools.

He sends for the minister of foreign affairs.

'Monsieur de Champagny, we must make peace. You and the Austrian plenipotentiaries are at odds over contributions of fifty million. Split the difference. I authorize you to compromise at seventy-five million, if you cannot get more. In everything else, I rely on you; do the best you can and have the peace signed in twenty-four hours.'

HE DOES NOT SLEEP. He imagines what might have been. He thinks about Friedrich Staps.

If that young fanatic represents German popular feeling, then I must win over Germany, because it is at the heart of the Empire. I must conclude this family union with the Hapsburg dynasty and, in the process, possibly disarm further Staps. Besides, the eldest sister of my fine ally, the Tsar, married the Duke of Oldenburg on 3 August, perhaps so as not to have to marry me. His other sister Anne is said to be too young.

He dozes, reads, dictates. Marie Walewska has left. The nights are long and cool.

At six in the morning, Monsieur de Champagny appears. Is this peace?

'Is the treaty signed?'

'Yes, sire, here it is.'

All the tension in his stomach, which is so often painful, suddenly seems to lift.

He listens to Champagny read out the treaty: Austria loses all access to the Adriatic and three and a half million of its subjects, who become members of the new Illyrian states, incorporated into France. Galicia is divided out between the Grand Duchy of Warsaw and Russia. The Tyrol reverts to Bavaria.

'This is very good; it is an excellent treaty,' he says.

He takes a pinch of snuff and coughs.

BUT WHO REALLY respects treaties? He will have to marry a Hapsburg princess to bind their two dynasties together and make this treaty unalterable. Unless his fine ally in St Petersburg agrees to give him his young sister in marriage. Austria would then be caught in a vice between France and Russia and would have no choice but to respect the treaty.

Champagny, silent for a moment, resumes. He has obtained an indemnity of eighty-five million francs rather than the seventy-five million fixed by the Emperor.

'This is admirable. If Talleyrand had been in your position, he would have given me my seventy-five million and pocketed the other ten!'

He gives orders for the cannon at the end of the Prater to fire a salute when the treaty is ratified, on Sunday, 15 October, to celebrate peace.

ALL THAT SUNDAY, he hears the cheering and singing of the Viennese borne on the wind.

On Monday, 16 October, as he is leaving Schönbrunn, he turns to General Rapp and orders, 'Find out how he dies.'

Staps has been sentenced to death for spying and is to be executed that Monday.

Autumn is beautiful on Germany's roads.

On Saturday, 21 October, he reaches Munich.

HE HUNTS IN the forests nearby. A thick carpet of fallen leaves muffles the horses' hoofs. He doesn't chase down the game but lets it escape, indifferent to the dogs' barking and the shouts of the beaters.

All he can think of is Rapp's report.

Staps refused the meal he was offered, saying he still had enough strength to go to his execution. He shuddered when he was told peace had been signed. He said, 'O my God, I thank you. Peace has been signed and I am not a murderer.'

At four in the morning, on Sunday, 22 October, Napoleon scribbles a few words for Josephine,

My friend, I'm leaving in an hour. I so look forward to seeing you again; I await the moment impatiently. I shall reach Fontainebleau on the 26th or 27th. You can go there with some ladies-in-waiting.
Napoleon

When will he talk to her?

PART EIGHT

Politics has no heart, only a head

27 OCTOBER 1809 TO 20 MARCH 1811

XXIX

WHERE IS SHE? Napoleon's eyes dart around, searching for Josephine. He leaps down from his travelling berline and stops for a moment at the foot of Fontainebleau's great staircase. The grand marshal of the palace, Duroc, who left Schönbrunn a few hours before he did, comes forward to greet him. Aides-de-camp and officers press round. Where is she? He had requested that she be there with her ladies-in-waiting, but she has put her comfort first, as usual.

It is true that the sun has barely risen, on this Thursday, 26 October 1809.

Napoleon spots Arch-chancellor Cambacérès, leads him off and, on the way to his study, congratulates him on his punctuality and starts to question him. What is the state of opinion? Why have they been so slow repelling the English landing on Walcheren Island? What folly led to Bernadotte being put in charge of the National Guard whose responsibility this was? Bernadotte is an incompetent, obsessed with his own petty intrigues and sick with jealousy and ambition. It was Fouché who appointed him, wasn't it?

What do people know in Paris about young Friedrich Staps, the fanatic, the madman who wanted to stab me?

Napoleon stops in front of Cambacérès, who is standing in the middle of his study.

He is not afraid of death, he says. Daggers and cannonballs and poison will be powerless against him, because he has a destiny to fulfill.

HE SITS DOWN and studies Cambacérès closely. This sensible, prudent man tends to keep his counsel, but he has always taken Josephine's part. Every time rumours have spread, he has been against a divorce. Fouché's opponent in this respect, he is afraid of how the public will react if the Emperor marries a descendant of the Hapsburg dynasty, an Austrian or an heir of the Romanovs.

'Where is the Empress?' Napoleon asks.

Sovereigns come to me, armies and fortresses capitulate, my marshals and ministers are up at dawn waiting for me, and this old woman isn't even able to welcome me back after I've been gone for months. What does she think I'm going to do? Is she afraid? Either way, she will have to accept my decision.

He gets up and starts to pace about. He takes a pinch of snuff. He doesn't give a thought to Cambacérès any more; in any case, all he really expects of the arch-chancellor is that he listen to what he has to tell him.

He has decided to get divorced, he says: the sooner the better. But Cambacérès must keep it a secret. He must talk to Josephine first, then have either Eugène de Beauharnais or Hortense explain his reasons to her. He would prefer the Viceroy of Italy to the Queen of Holland. Eugène is like a son to him. He cares about his dynasty's interests. He will give his mother good advice.

'I have really loved Josephine,' says Napoleon.

Lost in thought, he walks away from Cambacérès and then turns back.

'But I do not respect her. She tells too many lies.'

Cambacérès is silent.

'She has something, some quality, that is pleasing,' Napoleon continues. 'She is a real woman.'

He laughs, then murmurs, as if to himself, 'She has the sweetest little backside imaginable.'

Cambacérès's purple face delights him. That man will never know what a woman is. His tastes lie elsewhere.

'Josephine is a good woman, in the sense that she invites everyone to lunch. But would she deprive herself of something so that someone else might benefit? No!'

Suddenly he loses his temper.

Where is she? In St Cloud, while I'm here, where she should be to greet me.

HE DISMISSES Cambacérès, dictates a letter to Eugène, then sets to work on the dispatches.

Still Spain. The war is dragging on. He reads and re-reads the letter General Kellermann has sent to Berthier.'It is in vain that we cut off the hydra's heads to one side,' writes the son of the hero of

Valmy, now an old marshal. 'They simply grow back on the other, and unless there is a revolution of the heart, you will not bring this vast peninsula to heel for a long time: it will swallow up France's entire population and treasure.'

Spain is ruining me. Joseph is incapable of controlling the country. Marshals Soult and Mortier win victories, but they are never decisive. Must I re-take command of the armies of Spain?

'I'll say it again,' writes General Kellerman. 'It needs the head and arm of a Hercules. He alone, with his strength and skill, could end this great affair, if there can ever be an end to it.'

Berthier will have to leave for Spain to prepare for my arrival. Hercules! Napoleon smiles. Hercules will strike presently, when he has finished with Josephine.

THESE SOUNDS OF footsteps and voices in the corridors, then in the antechamber, must mean that Josephine has arrived at Fontainebleau. Finally!

He walks quickly through to the library, shuts the door and starts to write. He is angry with her for making him feel uneasy, for making it impossible for him to talk to her this evening.

She comes in.

He doesn't want to look up. She says nothing. It's more than seven months since they've seen each other. Why didn't she come when he asked her to? What cunning still underlies her behaviour? Does she think he has no patience?

He lifts his head. She is weeping silently.

'Ah, there you are, Madame. You have done well, for I was on the verge of leaving for St Cloud.'

She stammers excuses. That is not what he wants. He wants her to understand the juncture they have reached in their lives. He wants her to make it easy for him. He wants her to accept the facts.

He kisses her. All he feels is discomfiture.

HE HATES THIS situation. He cannot talk to her although that is what he ought to do. He can't stand her appearing ashen-faced, with tear-filled eyes and the look of a hunted animal.

In the days that follow he leaves the château whenever he can.

He hunts with a sort of controlled fury all over the Île de France during that radiant autumn. He hunts at Fontainebleau, the Bois de Boulogne, Versailles and in the forests around Melun and Vincennes.

When he returns to Fontainebleau and sees Josephine hosting her salon, he does not even glance at her. Until he talks to her, until she accepts the situation, he cannot be in her company. Why doesn't she help him? Why doesn't she have the dignity to submit herself to this law of destiny, which dictates that he needs a fecund 'womb', a young womb, a woman from a family on a par with what he has become?

HE SENDS FOR Champagny, the minister of foreign affairs.

He is to instruct France's ambassador in Russia to remind the Tsar of their meeting at Erfurt, where divorce was mentioned and Alexander spoke of the possibility of a marriage to Anne, the youngest of his sisters. Champagny should tell Caulaincourt that 'the Emperor, urged by all France, is preparing for a divorce'. They need to find out where they stand and what their 'fine ally' of the north's intentions are.

But how much is Alexander to be trusted, anyway? The Austrian embassy councillor in Paris, Chevalier Floret, insists that Metternich and Emperor Francis are disposed to 'cede' the Archduchess Marie Louise, a young girl of eighteen, to Napoleon.

A Hapsburg! He tries to picture it. An Austrian, like Marie Antoinette. He remembers those revolutionary days of June and August 1792; the shouts, still fresh in his mind, of 'Death to the Austrian!' ringing around the Tuileries gardens.

He paces up and down his study. An Austrian, like Marie Antoinette. But he is not Louis XVI. If the Tsar proves elusive, as he fears and senses he will, Austria could become an essential ally. This Marie Louise is eighteen. She is the granddaughter of Charles V and Louis XIV.

I have become myself. I am entitled to her if I wish.

IN THE TUILERIES, he entertains the Kings of Bavaria, Saxony and Würtemberg with Murat, the King of Naples, Jérôme, the King of Westphalia, and Louis, the King of Holland.

He presides over the parades of the new Grand Army at the Arc de Triomphe on the Carrousel, and he hears the cheers of the crowd, 'Long live the Emperor! Long live the victor of Wagram! Long live the peace of Vienna!'

He holds Josephine's hand by the fingertips, since he sometimes has to appear at her side. He cannot look at her. She is still trying to appeal to his feelings.

But I am only faithful to my destiny.

Rather than sit next to her, he prefers to ride with his sister Pauline, Princess Borghese, in her barouche. Pauline, his confidant, who has always been in favour of a divorce; his accomplice, who makes herself scarce when one of her ladies-in-waiting appears, an impudent, cheerful, blonde Piedmontese who does not lower her eyes.

Tonight he will see Christina, this Piedmontese. Tomorrow he will talk to Josephine.

I am the Emperor of Kings. No one can oppose my destiny.

It is Thursday, 30 November 1809; he is dining alone with Josephine. He doesn't speak. He can't. When he looks up, all he sees is the large hat she is wearing to hide her red eyes and worn face.

He cannot swallow a mouthful of food. He taps the glasses with his knife, setting them ringing like bells. He gets to his feet, says, 'What's the weather like?' then goes through to the adjoining drawing room.

When a page brings coffee, Josephine moves to pour the Emperor a cup. But he helps himself before she can. Then he signals that they should be left alone and the door shut.

Already she is sobbing, wringing her hands.

'Do not try to sway me,' he says in a brusque tone, turning his back on her. 'I still love you, but politics has no heart, only a head.'

He turns to face her.

'Do you want this to be easy or hard? I am resolved on it.'

She seems stupefied.

'I shall give you five million a year and the sovereignty of Rome.'

She lets out a cry, then murmurs, 'I will not survive it,' and then she falls to the ground, moaning, and seems to faint.

He opens the door, calls in Bausset, the prefect of the palace, a corpulent man, whose movements are hindered by his sword.

'Are you strong enough to lift Josephine and help me carry her by the private stairs to her apartments so that she can be looked after?' he asks, grabbing a torch to light the stairs.

His mind is a whirl: he doesn't know what to think.

On the stairs, Bausset stumbles and Napoleon, who's in front, turns round. He hears Josephine whispering in Bausset's ear, 'You are holding me too tight.'

Did she lose consciousness at all?

HE LEAVES HER room and, within moments, feels weighed down, as if he is suffocating. He goes to his apartments and gives instructions that Hortense, her daughter, and Doctor Corvisart be sent to the Empress.

He sits down. Josephine probably exaggerated her grief and pretended to faint because she is a liar. But even so she must be suffering and he feels overwhelmed at the thought of it. This is a wrench for him too. A whole part of his life is coming to an end. Sorrow grips him.

He hears footsteps. It's Hortense.

He goes to her.

'Have you seen your mother? Did she speak to you?'

They trade harsh words. He tries to check his mounting feeling of helplessness. It would be so simple never to make any decisions, never to choose, never to submit oneself to the law of one's destiny.

'My mind is made up,' he says. 'The decision is irrevocable. All France wants this divorce. It calls for it openly. I cannot resist its wishes.'

He turns his back on Hortense. He cannot look at her any more.

'Nothing will make me change my mind, neither tears nor prayers. Nothing,' he roars.

Motionless, he listens to Hortense reply in her clear, calm voice. He remembers the very young girl, barely thirteen, who he first set eyes on; the tenderness she'd aroused in him then and the affection he still feels for this woman, wife of Louis and sister to the man he thinks of as a son – Eugène, who was himself only fifteen the first time they met. They are his second family, and have been for so many years.

'You are free to do whatever you wish, sire,' Hortense is saying. 'No one will try to thwart you. It is enough that your happiness requires it. We shall be able to perform this sacrifice. Do not be surprised at my mother's tears. It would be more surprising if, after a union of fifteen years, she did not shed any.'

Memories flood back. He feels tears in his eyes.

'But she will submit to your wishes,' adds Hortense, 'I'm sure of it, and we will all take our leave, carrying the memory of your kindness with us.'

He cannot part from them. He wants to add something to his life – a royal wife, a blood heir – but he doesn't want to lose Hortense or Eugène, or their children, or their political loyalty; he does not even want to lose Josephine.

He feels tears brimming over, sobs choking him. Don't they understand the harshness of the choices he is forcing on himself, the struggle he must endure to decide? Why must they make the fulfillment of his destiny so difficult? Why don't they help him?

'What, will you all leave me, will you all abandon me?' he exclaims. 'Don't you love me any more?'

It can't be. He can't accept it. It's not a question of his happiness, but of his destiny, France's destiny.

'Pity me, pity me, don't feel you are constrained to renounce my fondest affection,' he says over and over, sobbing all the while.

He senses how moved Hortense is. Neither she nor Eugène will leave him.

No one abandons the Emperor of Kings. His choices become theirs.

XXX

JOSEPHINE IS HERE. And he wants her to be here – she must be here – at his side, as he walks up the aisle of Notre Dame on Sunday, 3 December 1809. She is still the Empress.

The bells ring out under the vaulted roof. The cannon roar. The Te Deum rises up to celebrate the victory at Wagram and the peace of Vienna.

My kings, my marshals, my generals and my ministers are gathered around me. I can hear the crowds cheering. In a moment I will see the troops massed in front of the cathedral and I will get into the carriage I rode in for my coronation.

Josephine is here. As she was before, on the day of his coronation. She tries to smile and return the gaze of everyone staring at her. They all know. To prepare public opinion, Fouché has spread the news through the salons and taverns: the Emperor is divorcing; the Emperor wants to marry a womb; the Emperor wants a son.

I know how cruel, mean and cowardly they are, these stares. Josephine hides her puffy eyelids and red eyes behind her veil, while everyone revels in her pain.

Her sadness and despair are unbearable. It's as if they were the price I have to pay for my victory. When I see her, grief chokes me; I have tears in my eyes. Must someone always die for me to triumph?

He thinks of Marshal Lannes's trembling body on the battlefield of Essling. He looks at Josephine. She is like a soldier facing the enemy.

SHE SITS NEXT to him in the vast Hall of Victory in the Hôtel de Ville, at a banquet in honour of the kings. She is in the Legislative Body's box when, on Tuesday, 5 December, he steps up to the podium.

He begins to speak. The words sweep him along; after a while, he no longer sees her.

'People of France, you have the strength and vigour of Hercules! Three months have seen the start and end of this Fourth Punic War ... When I show myself on the other side of the Pyrenees, the terrified leopard will seek the ocean to avoid the shame of defeat and death. The triumph of my armies will be the triumph of the genius of good over that of evil, of moderation, order, morality over civil war, anarchy and malicious passions.'

The delegates cheer.

He takes Josephine's hand. After the dazzling brilliance of the triumph, the agony of the wounded. She is going to return to Malmaison. He whispers in her ear, 'I want to hear that you are in good spirits. I will come and see you in the week.'

NOW SHE'S NOT here any more and already he suffers from her absence. She has been a part of his life for so long. He immerses himself in work to get her out of his mind. Now that the divorce is definite, the future must bring a son.

He pauses for a moment. Marie Walewska has written to him from her château in Walewice. Her pregnancy is progressing. The child will be born in spring, in April or May. She can feel the baby already, she says. She is sure it will be a boy.

'A son.'

When finally he has a legitimate son, the Empire he bequeaths to him must have only one ruler.

'I want to absorb Holland,' he says, 'so that it can become French. Paris will be the Empire's spiritual capital, the capital of my son to be. Rome will be the Empire's second city, a French city, and my son will be its king. All the Church's institutions and archives will be in Paris, and the Pope will be stripped of his temporal powers.'

He pictures this great empire stretching from Holland to Catalonia. 'I shall be in Spain shortly,' he tells Berthier. But he won't be fighting for Joseph; he will be fighting for himself and for this son of his who must reign north of the Ebro, just as he will in Rome. And meanwhile, the states of the Confederation of the Rhine, the kingdoms of Naples and Spain, and further to the east, the Grand Duchy of Warsaw will form a solid block around the Empire like an immense glacis.

The hours pass. He paces up and down his study, drafts the decree annexing Rome to France, writes to his generals in Spain.

He needs a son so that, at long last, all the effort he has expended, all the victories he has won, can merge into a single force that will change Europe's destiny. This son will be with him – and thanks to him – the cornerstone of an empire of the West.

After me, everything will depend on what he will become, this child whose mother I don't yet know. He is the one who will crown this novel that is my life. I shall be part of a long chain, the last link before him, my future son.

Such a long line of kings and emperors.

'I feel solidarity with each one of them,' he says, 'from Clovis to the Committee of Public Safety.'

And I don't want this chain to be broken after me. I'm divorcing so as to be able to prolong it.

He's nervous, exalted. Dreams swirl about in his head. He cannot spend the rest of the night alone.

He sends Constant to fetch that blonde, merry, little, plump Piedmontese lady-in-waiting, Madame Christine de Mathis, from Princess Borghese's house.

HE WAKES UP from his dream and from the night. Everything has been said and yet nothing has been settled, neither the divorce nor the marriage. It's like a battle that has begun and yet on all fronts still hangs in the balance.

Perhaps Josephine is still hopeful? Sometimes she gives him insistent looks in which he senses expectancy, as if she were waiting for a gesture, a word that will dispel her nightmare. But he stops himself from saying anything tender, because he can feel her clinging on to him, trying to plunge him back into their past, their well of memories.

He doesn't want that. But every moment he has to struggle with himself, force himself to keep his feelings in check – as when, for instance, he sees Eugène on his return from Italy. He loves Josephine's son. He has watched him grow into a man and a soldier in Egypt, Italy, and Germany. He listens to him say, 'It would be better for us to make a clean break. Otherwise we will be in a false position and my mother may perhaps end up making things awkward for you. Give us somewhere where we can help our mother endure her misfortune, far from the court and its intrigues.'

Napoleon shakes his head. He's already told Hortense he can't accept this. He cannot stand this wound; he doesn't see why it's necessary.

Can't they make this easier for me?

He approaches Eugène. Once a boy of fifteen, now, thanks to him, Viceroy of Italy.

'Eugène,' he says, 'if I've been of any use to you in your life, if I have been a father to you in any way, do not abandon me. I need you. Your sister cannot leave me. She has a duty to her children, my own nephews. Your mother does not wish it.'

He grasps Eugène by the shoulders. He must convince him.

'With all your exaggerated notions, you will bring sorrow on me. But more importantly, think of posterity. Stay, if you do not want it said that the Empress was dismissed, abandoned and that perhaps she deserved it.'

He feels he is swaying Eugène. Although deeply moved himself, he must endeavour to win him over completely.

'Isn't it a fine enough role for her to remain close to me,' he asks, 'to retain her rank and privileges and to prove that this is a purely political separation which she wants, thereby acquiring further claims to the esteem, respect and love of a nation for which she is sacrificing herself?'

He has won. He clasps Eugène to his breast. He wants Eugène to go to his mother, reason with her and make her agree to the separation.

ON FRIDAY, 8 DECEMBER, the three of them meet in the morning. Josephine speaks calmly in front of her son. Napoleon studies her. Even that sharp look in her eyes has come back, part desire and part greed. He is immediately on his guard.

'France's well-being,' she says, 'is too dear to me not to make it my duty to act in accordance with it.' He sees her take Eugène's hand.

Continuing in a voice that is suddenly cold, she says that she wants Napoleon to bestow the crown of Italy on Eugène.

So that's her price. Even suffering, she is still what she has always been: a cunning, voracious woman.

Eugène is on his feet.

'Your son,' he cries, in response to Josephine, 'would not want a crown that was the price of your separation!'

The son is worth more than the mother.

Napoleon embraces him.

'That is Eugène through and through,' he says. 'He is right to rely on my kindness.'

But it is my son to be who will be king of Rome. I have already decided that.

And so she accepts it.

Now, on the other front, he must choose the bride. He sends for Champagny, the foreign minister. They urgently need to find out Alexander's exact position. Does he or does he not want to give his sister Anne to him in marriage? Or is he hedging? They have to have a quick answer. And Ambassador Caulaincourt, when he sees the Tsar, must make it clear that they attach no importance to their conditions, not even on religion. It's children they want – a fertile womb, in other words. And a straight answer. Otherwise they will look elsewhere, Vienna, for instance.

This chain of events getting under way thrills him. At last he has set something in motion.

He attends the lavish fête Marshal Berthier throws at his château in Grosbois. He goes hunting with *his* kings, the Kings of Naples, Würtemberg and Saxony. He is their Emperor. Some are his blood brothers: the King of Holland or Westphalia. He has made all this possible and soon he will be able to do more for his son.

Suddenly, he sees Josephine. She wasn't expected. She takes a seat in the room where there is to be a performance of *Cadet Rousselle*, a play that is all rage at the moment in Paris.

He doesn't know it, and he is only watching distractedly, half-listening, when suddenly some dialogue makes him jump. An actor declares, '*One must divorce to have descendants, or ancestors.*'

Who chose this play? Napoleon gives his full attention to the comedy, which is full of allusions. He feels cold and ashamed.

At the end he goes up to Josephine, takes her arm and walks

slowly with her through the middle of the guests. He stops in front of Hortense and Eugène. He embraces them and forces the dignitaries surrounding them to lower their eyes. Then he escorts the Empress to her carriage.

He doesn't want to endure this false situation any longer. He doesn't want to expose himself to, or be the cause of, any more pointless suffering and humiliation.

Now that Josephine has agreed, he must resolve the situation quickly and publicly. No gangrene, just a clean amputation.

HE SENDS FOR the cautious Cambacérès, a shrewd jurist and loyal servant. Tomorrow, 15 December, a senatus consultum will promulgate the dissolution of their marriage. The Empress will retain the titles and rank of Empress Dowager, and her endowment will be fixed at an annual income of two million francs payable by the state treasury.

Napoleon looks at Cambacérès. With a gesture he asks him not to note down what he is about to say.

Naturally he will let Josephine have Malmaison, he says. He will also give her another château, far from Paris, because she cannot stay at the Elysée. Her presence could be awkward for her, as well as for him. Why not the Château of Navarre, near Évreux?

Cambacérès isn't saying anything. What is he thinking? It doesn't matter.

In addition, all the Emperor's provisions for the Empress Josephine will come out of the civil list, and will be incumbent upon his successors.

'Am I not generous?'

He does not wait for an answer. He wants the imperial family to assemble later today, Thursday, 14 December, at nine in the evening in the Emperor's study, to hear the couple's decision and the contents of the senatus consultum.

He bows his head, suddenly anxious. He is about to cross a boundary between two parts of his life without any possibility of going back. He wants to make this transition, but it makes him nervous.

He remains alone for most of the day. He goes hunting at Vincennes, galloping until his body feels shattered.

When he returns, he sees the kings, queens, marshals and dignitaries assembled in the Throne Room in their ceremonial regalia. The women wear necklaces and diadems, the sovereigns the broad ribbons of their orders.

He sees the black, thin figure of his mother, Madame Mère, who, like her daughters – *my dear sisters* – cannot hide her joy. At last they've got what they've wanted for so long, divorce, because they've never accepted Josephine, always denouncing, criticizing, harassing and mocking her.

In his apartment, he quickly has Constant dress him in his uniform of a colonel of the Guard, and then he passes though to his study, where he sits down at his desk and orders the doors to be opened.

HE SEES JOSEPHINE coming towards him in a white dress. She is not wearing any jewellery. She is as poignant as a sacrificial victim going to the altar.

He does not look at her, but gets to his feet after the members of the imperial family, Cambacérès and Regnaud de Saint-Jean-d'Angély, secretary of the imperial household, have entered the room.

Napoleon starts to read the text he has dictated, rejecting the official speech prepared for him by Maret, his principal private secretary.

'The politics of my monarchy, the interests and the needs of my people, which have constantly guided all my actions, require that I should leave this throne, on which Providence has set me, to children when I die, to heirs of the love I bear for my people.'

He lifts his head, looks at Josephine whose face seems even whiter than her dress.

'However, for several years now, I have lost hope of having children from my marriage with my beloved wife, the Empress Josephine.'

He takes a long breath, then says in a hollow voice, 'It is this that has brought me to sacrifice my dearest affections, to consider only the good of the state, and to desire the dissolution of our marriage.'

He has uttered the decisive words, at last. His voice grows

firmer. He looks hard at his mother, his sisters and each of the dignitaries in turn.

'Having reached the age of forty, I may yet entertain the hope of living long enough to bring up in my own spirit and to my own way of thinking such children as it may please Providence to grant me. God himself knows how much this resolve has cost my heart, but there is no sacrifice beyond my courage when it is shown to be in the interests of France.'

He turns towards Josephine. She must not doubt his feelings, he says.

'I have only praise for the attachment and tenderness of my beloved wife, and I wish her always to consider me her best and her dearest friend.'

Friend: that word like a dagger thrust in his flesh, and in hers too.

Friend: that is what he has become.

He remembers the letters he wrote to Josephine during the Italian campaign. He cannot look at her any more.

She starts to say something, but sobs choke her and it is Regnaud who reads out her consent to the divorce.

Napoleon does not look up until he is given the divorce papers. He presses down hard on the paper, underlining his name with a broad line. He sees Josephine's hand slowly start to write her name underneath in that small, childlike writing of hers. He turns his head away. He hears the scratch of the quill. When the room falls silent again, he goes over to Josephine, embraces her and escorts her back to her apartments with Hortense and Eugène.

So, it's all over. He does not attend the council meeting, which will adopt the text of the senatus consultum, on which the Senate will vote, after which all that's needed is the religious bonds declared null and void by an ecclesiastical commission, which he will have no trouble forming or dominating. From 14 December 1809, he knows he is going to get what he wants, even if some people will challenge the legality of the procedure.

So, he has succeeded. He has broken with the woman who tied him to his past, to the start of his rise to power.

He sits down on his bed. He has severed his links with his

youth. It is what he wanted. But he feels no joy. He wanted this to be true to his destiny. But is he still true to his origins?

He gets into bed. The door opens. He sees Josephine. She walks slowly towards the bed. He takes her in his arms.

'Be brave, be brave,' he murmurs.

He holds her tight while she cries, then he calls Constant, who leads her back to her apartments.

Wretched night.

WHEN HE GETS up the following morning, he feels as if he has no energy left. He lets himself be dressed, slowly raising his arms above his head. His body aches. There's a bitter taste of bile in his mouth. His stomach is knotted with tension.

He sends for Méneval, but he cannot dictate. He's exhausted. He sinks onto a sofa. His body feels heavy. He doesn't move, but just holds his head in his hands, his forehead damp.

He brusquely gets to his feet when an aide-de-camp announces that the Empress's carriages are ready to leave for Malmaison.

This is the last test.

He goes downstairs by the little dark staircase. He sees her, a haggard look on her face. He opens his arms, embraces her, then feels her slide to the floor. She has fainted. He carries her to a sofa.

She opens her eyes, stretches out her arms. But he backs away. What can he say? What can he do? He has made his choice.

He calls his grand chamberlain. He does not want to stay at the Tuileries; he will spend a few days at the Trianon.

He must live.

He gets into his carriage. Princess Borghese is to join him with her lady in waiting, Christine de Mathis.

Living is a choice too.

XXXI

He has only been at the Trianon for a day, yet already the isolation is oppressive. It seems as if this December, this whole year 1809, will never end.

He hears Pauline Borghese and her ladies-in-waiting laughing. He can't stand it. He goes out into the park. It feels as if he'll never recover his energy.

Méneval and his aides-de-camp have been dismissed. He has his horse saddled; he wants to hunt. He rides through Versailles's wood, up onto the Satory plateau, and comes back soaked, after being caught in a rainstorm, but he feels better. He catches sight of Christine de Mathis, who he's going to dine with. But as soon as he is sitting opposite this young woman chattering and twittering away, he sinks into despair. He remembers Josephine, the complicity that bound them together. He stands up and walks out of the room.

Perhaps he's incurred the evil eye by leaving Josephine? Perhaps she was the only woman who allowed him to forge ahead? The only thing that will reassure him is if she is taking this divorce calmly, light-heartedly.

He wants to see her again. He only left her a few hours ago, but he needs to see her. He must convince himself she is still alive. He is so afraid that she suddenly won't be able to cope with the separation and will die.

He goes to Malmaison and sees her walking alone in the park. She turns round and hurries towards him like someone lost. He gives her his arm and leads her round the gardens. He grows calmer. He cannot regret this divorce. She is his past – and the past is behind one: you don't mourn it; you don't try to bring it back to life.

He embraces her, and then returns to the Trianon. But suddenly his anxiety returns: Josephine must be able to survive this ordeal. If she were to succumb, what a wound it would be for him, what a blow politically! The egotistical Emperor, people would say, the

Emperor who rejects his wife when she gets old and then she wastes away and dies. He writes to her,

> My friend, I found you weaker today than you should have been
> ... You must not give way to dangerous melancholy; you must
> be content and, above all, take care of your health, which is so
> precious to me. If you are attached to me and if you love me,
> you must be strong and see that you are happy. You cannot
> doubt my constant and tender friendship and you should know
> me and all I feel for you very little, if you should suppose that
> I can be happy when you are not, or content when you have no
> peace.
>   Farewell my friend, remember that I want this.
>   Napoleon

*I must support her. If she goes under, I shall drown too. My marriage
will be compromised by the scandal and the echo of her death or,
simply, of her despair.*

*She cannot, she must not, let herself go. I need her life; I need her
to be happy.*

He repeats what she whispered to him in a calm voice in Malmaison's park.

'Sometimes it seems I'm dead,' she said, 'and all I have left is a vague faculty for perceiving that I no longer exist.'

He receives letters which all exude the same despair and the same misery. He can't hold it against her. She has done what he wanted. But he can feel himself becoming irritated. He has not inflicted this suffering on her for nothing.

He summons Champagny. Have they had a reply from the Tsar?

*Does he or doesn't he want me to marry his sister Anne? What do
his qualifications really amount to? Anne's mother has reservations?
Just excuses, all of it. I must look to Austria then. Champagny must
talk to Vienna's new ambassador in Paris, Prince Charles Schwarzen-
berg, an estimable prince who saved his men at Ulm and fought at
Wagram. I must know if Francis is disposed to give me his daughter
Marie Louise in marriage – me, the Corsican, Attila, the Antichrist.
Isn't that what all the young duchesses in Vienna call me?*

HE GROWS IMPATIENT. He needs a response immediately; he needs to conclude a marriage quickly. Who can be certain of the future?

He thinks of Josephine. His anxiety about her is suddenly so intense that he goes stag hunting and gallops until he has worn out his horse. He returns at nightfall, but the Trianon, despite the officers of his household and the servants, seems cold and deserted.

He sends for General Savary. He is to go to Malmaison, see Josephine, and report back to him on the Empress's state.

SAVARY COMES BACK with a letter from Josephine. The Empress is crushed, he begins. Napoleon listens to his account impatiently, reads her letter, then begins his reply,

> I have received your letter, my friend. Savary tells me that you cry the whole time: this is not good . . . I shall come and see you when you tell me you are reasonable and your courage has the upper hand. I'm seeing my ministers all tomorrow.
>
> Farewell, my friend, I am sad today: I need to know that you are satisfied and hear that you are recovering your composure. Sleep well.
>
> Napoleon

What can he do to compel her to live, to recover? Go and see her!

> I long to see you, but I have to be sure that you are strong and not weak; I am a little so myself and it afflicts me terribly.

On Monday, 25 December, he invites her to the Trianon for dinner, but as soon as he sees her, he regrets it. She has that victim's air of defeat that he cannot stand. He feels unable to speak, sitting opposite her with Queen Hortense and Caroline, Queen of Naples, on his right.

Sometimes he bows his head because his eyes have filled with tears.

He wanted this; it was his choice.

He leaves the Trianon the following day and returns to the Tuileries. He walks along the corridors, through the drawing room where the Empress used to hold her circle.

Without a wife, this palace is dead.

He feels isolated. He cannot stop himself writing to her again,

I was very bored being back at the Tuileries, Eugène told me
that you were quite sad yesterday: it's not good, my friend, and
contrary to what you promised me.

I'm going to dine alone.

Farewell, my friend, look after your health.

It is the last day of the year, 1809, a Sunday. He goes to the
Arc de Triomphe in the Carrousel to attend a parade of the Old
Guard who are roundly cheered as they march past.

He returns to the Tuileries at three in the afternoon. This
31 December is sunny; the rooms are brightly lit.

He sits at his desk in his study. He is going to write to
Alexander.

*I must know in the next few days which womb, Austrian or
Russian, will carry my son!*

He dictates the letter in a clipped voice.

I leave it to Your Majesty to judge which of us is closer to the
language of an alliance and friendship, You or me. If we begin to
mistrust one another, it means we have already forgotten Erfurt
and Tilsit.

It is a harsh thing to say. But he does not want to change it.
Perhaps a confidence will smooth the effect.

I have been living a retired life, genuinely afflicted by the course
of action I have been obliged to take by the interests of my
empire. Your Majesty is aware of all the attachment I feel for the
Empress.

He signs the letter.

*The year about to begin must be the year of a new life, a new
woman and still greater glory. I shall be forty-one.*

XXXII

NAPOLEON READS THE letter Josephine has just sent him. She's recovering, whatever she says. It's no longer divorce that is driving her to desperation, but the state of her financial affairs!

He takes a pinch of snuff, goes to the window. He has been feeling better for several days now. 1810's winter is cold, but the skies are clear. The days have started to get longer.

He picks up the letter again, reads it through and, bending down, writes a few lines in reply.

> You do not trust me; every rumour going around affects you; you would rather listen to all the gossips in a big city than to what I tell you; you should not allow people to make up stories to upset you.
>
> I am angry with you, and unless I hear you are in good spirits and happy, I will come and scold you very severely.
>
> Farewell, my friend.
>
> Napoleon

Josephine has reverted to what she has always been. A woman who spends and sings like a cicada, whilst at the same time displaying all the prudent greed of an ant; and who, now she has agreed to the divorce, is calculating the contents of her coffers. *Let's do the sums for her.*

> I've spent today working with Estève, the main treasurer of the crown. I have set aside one hundred thousand francs for Malmaison's extraordinary expenses for 1810. You may therefore order as much planting as you wish; you shall distribute this sum as you see fit. I have instructed Estève to transfer two hundred thousand francs to you. I've given orders that your jewellery shall be paid for and valued by the Intendance, because I do not want any more jewellers' swindles. That cost me four hundred thousand francs.
>
> I've ordered that the million the civil list owes you for 1810 be put at your accountant's disposal to pay your debts.

You should find between fifty and sixty thousand francs in the cabinet at Malmaison; you can take it for your silver and linen.

I've commissioned a very beautiful porcelain service for you; they will take your instructions so it should be very fine.

Napoleon

He re-reads this accountant's letter. It's like a clause in a peace treaty. The battle has been fought; now the indemnities are being established. But here it's the conqueror that is paying the contributions of the conquered.

It's the price of my freedom and my peace of mind. I've done what I must. For her and me.

HE SITS DOWN at his desk. The police bulletins Fouché passes on to him all harp on the same theme: 'the party that voted for the King's death' and what it thinks. He knows its members – Fouché, Cambacérès and, at their backs, everyone who's risen from the ranks of the Revolution, including Murat and a good number of the marshals.

They were the regicides. They've seen Louis XVI's head drop into the basket. They don't want me to marry an Austrian, the niece of Marie-Antoinette, which would make me the nephew by marriage of Louis Capet.

Louis XVI, my uncle!

He reads the police bulletin. 'While all the coteries are agitating about political questions and intrigues, the population of Paris pays little attention to anything except accumulating provisions; it does however have strong reservations about an Austrian princess.'

Have I any choice?

The Tsar, according to Caulaincourt, is proving evasive. Whereas Metternich in Vienna and Ambassador Schwarzenberg in Paris are candour itself.

Can I wait on the Tsar's goodwill? Besides, what confidence can one have in a court where a son has his father strangled and where a change of sovereign overthrows an alliance, whereas in Vienna emperors come and go but the government's policies stay the same?

He hesitates. It's like the moment in a battle, when one has to choose whether to launch one's squadrons on the left wing or the right.

ON MONDAY, 29 January, Napoleon decides to convoke a Grand Privy Council in the Tuileries. He takes his place on the dais, facing the glittering assembly. To his left he sees the presidents of the Senate and the Legislative Body, the ministers, his uncle Cardinal Fesch, Archbishop of Paris, and high-ranking officers of the Empire and, to his right, the kings and queens. Murat is in the front row, sitting next to Eugène. Fouché has chosen a seat a long way from the pallid Talleyrand.

Before they even open their mouths, I can guess what they are going to say.

'I can,' Napoleon begins, 'marry a princess from Russia, Austria, Saxony, one of the royal houses of Germany or a Frenchwoman.'

They are all frozen, their faces straining towards me.

'All that remains is for me to single out who will be the first woman to pass under the Arc de Triomphe and enter Paris,' he adds.

He stretches out a hand. Let them each express their thoughts.

Lebrun ventures to speak first. But the arch-treasurer has chosen prudence: he favours a Saxon princess. Murat, in a furious rage, says what the Emperor expects him to say: an Austrian princess will be a reminder of Marie Antoinette, the nation will hate her, and any rapprochement with the ancien régime will alienate those attached to the Empire without winning over any of the nobility of the faubourg St Germain. The Emperor must marry a Russian princess, Murat thunders.

Eugène speaks next, in favour of the Austrian. Now it is the turn of the venal, pallid Talleyrand who, in his calm voice, agrees with Eugène. 'To absolve France in Europe's eyes, and in its own, of a crime which was not its own but merely that of a faction,' he says, the Emperor must marry a Hapsburg. Fontanes, the Grand Master of the University, chimes in, 'The alliance of Your Majesty with a daughter of the House of Austria will be an expiatory act on the part of France.'

Let them all talk. Let them think France is atoning for the past, if that will mean my Empire, my dynasty and my imperial nobility are finally accepted by those who continue to have influence over part of Europe.

'My mission is to lead the West,' I wrote to the Pope who is 'ruled by pride and worldly pomp', and if I have to marry an Austrian and become Louis XVI's nephew to fulfill my destiny, why not?

A Hapsburg, a descendant of Charles the Fifth and Louis XIV — what better womb for my son? What security for the future! As for me, I know that nothing will make me change. I will never be Louis XVI.

Napoleon leans forward and whispers to Cambacérès, who is sitting next to him in his capacity as arch-chancellor, 'So, people are overjoyed about my marriage, are they? I see, they think the lion will go to sleep. Well, they are mistaken.'

He nods his head.

Sleep would be as sweet to him as anyone, he goes on. 'But don't you see that, although I seem constantly to be on the attack, my only real concern is to defend myself?'

Suddenly he catches sight of Fouché slipping away without having said anything. Prudent, cunning Fouché, a supporter, like all the regicides, of a Russian marriage, but preferring to remain silent. He should know that the Austrian bride is the only one still under consideration.

Eugène, Napoleon concludes, must go to Prince Charles von Schwarzwenberg and obtain an immediate response concerning this young, eighteen-year old archduchess, Marie Louise.

For the first time Napoleon wonders: is she beautiful?

People have only talked about her age and her education. He wants to know, now.

The session of the Privy Council draws to a close. He hears Lacuée, the minister of war administration, expostulate, 'Austria isn't a great power any more.'

Napoleon gets to his feet.

'It is clear, sir, that you were not at Wagram,' he says scornfully.

WHAT DO THEY know of the real world? Of the game I have to play? The Tsar keeps me waiting because he does not dare openly refuse me his sister. I choose Marie Louise, but do not want to break with Alexander, and have to be sure of the Austrian response. Does Schwarzenberg have the powers to commit Vienna without consulting his Emperor and Metternich?

Eugène returns from the Austrian embassy on Tuesday, 6 February.

Napoleon stares at him. Eugène gives no indication of Schwarzenberg's response but launches into a long account of his interview with the ambassador. Napoleon interrupts him. Yes or no? he asks.

'Yes,' says Eugène.

So, it's done. Napoleon gesticulates and bursts out laughing. He strides up and down his study, clenching his fists.

I have them. They have given me their archduchess. She is mine.

HE SENDS FOR Berthier and Champagny. The marriage contract must be drawn up immediately. Everything must be done in a matter of days. They will sign a contract here, in Paris, and another in Vienna, where a proxy marriage will be celebrated. Berthier will represent the Emperor.

'I want her here before the end of March so the marriage can be celebrated at the start of April.'

He turns to Champagny.

'You will attend my levée tomorrow. Bring me Louis XVI's marriage contract and all the relevant correspondence.'

His reign has taken its place in a continuum from Clovis to the Committee of Public Safety. He is the nephew of Louis XVI.

'Write this evening to Prince Schwarzenberg to arrange an appointment for midday tomorrow.'

He stops Champagny as he is about to leave. Now they are sure of an Austrian marriage, they have to extricate themselves from any possible arrangement with Alexander.

Napoleon jubilantly takes a pinch of snuff. A beautiful manoeuvre on two fronts, like a trap sprung on a battlefield. They will appear to concede the arguments advanced by the Tsar. His sister Anne is too young, did he say? Then they will agree.

Napoleon dictates the letter that Champagny will give to Caulaincourt for the Emperor of the North. 'Since Princess Anne is not yet formed, and sometimes girls remain for two or three years between the first signs of nubility and maturity, it would mean more than three years without the hope of children.' That would be too long a delay and, as the Tsar has himself emphasized, there is also the question of religion.

This first letter to Alexander should go off forthwith.

'Tomorrow evening,' continues Napoleon, 'when you and Prince Schwarzenberg have signed a contract, you will send a second courier with the news that I have decided to marry the Austrian.'

HE WANTS – he needs – to see everything, check everything personally.

'We will send the trousseau and wedding presents from Paris. It is no use doing anything from Vienna,' he tells the French ambassador to Austria, Otto.

He wants to see the fichus, court gowns, dressing gowns, nightcaps, dresses and jewels – the magnificent diamond *parure* and numerous brilliants.

He sends for the court artists. The Archduchess Marie Louise's shoes will be like this, he explains.

He asks Hortense to give him dance lessons.

'I must make myself amiable. My serious and severe air will not appeal to a young woman. She is bound to like the pleasures of one her age. Let's see now; Hortense, you are our Terpsichore, teach me to waltz.'

He tries his hand. He feels clumsy, ridiculous. He leaves the drawing room.

'Let us leave to each age that which is appropriate to it, he says. 'I'm too old. In any case, I see that dancing is not where I am meant to shine.'

The next morning he looks at himself in the mirror for a long time as Constant and Roustam busy themselves around him. He already has a paunch. His hair is sparse. He sends for Corvisart, and as soon as the doctor comes in, he questions him without looking round.

How long can a man retain the ability to father children? Until he is sixty, seventy?

'Possibly,' Corvisart replies circumspectly.

Definitely. But what is she like, this Austrian princess? He only has several medallions, and a drawing of her. He wants to speak to the officers who've seen her at court in Vienna. How tall is she? Her complexion? The colour of her hair?

'I have trouble getting them to say anything,' he tells Corvisart. 'It's obvious my future wife is ugly, since none of these confounded youngsters has been able to tell me she's pretty. I can see she has Austrian lips,' he adds picking up the drawing. 'But anyway, as long as she's kind and gives me strapping boys . . .'

With a stroke of his quill, he underlines the names of those he has chosen to comprise the future Empress's household. They should be of good aristocratic stock; the household is to be modelled on Marie Antoinette's.

That is reality. Fouché can grumble all he wants. The time of the regicides is over. I want to re-establish all the old ties.

ON 16 FEBRUARY 1810, in Vienna, the provisional marriage contract is ratified. The ceremony of marriage by proxy will take place in Vienna on 11 March. Marie Louise will set off on 13 March. And the marriage will be celebrated in Paris on 1 April.

I have become the nephew of Louis XVI and I have not changed; I am still myself.

My son will be born of the union of all the dynasties; I am the Emperor of the West.

EVERYTHING IS IN place. He thinks of Josephine. He has done what he ought for her, but her presence must not cast a dark, oppressive shadow. She must leave Paris. He wants the Château of Navarre to be restored as a matter of urgency. She must go there. Normandy is not exile. He writes to her,

My friend,
I hope you are happy with what I've done with Navarre. You will have seen there fresh testimony of the desire I have to be agreeable to you.
See that you take possession of Navarre. You can go on 25 March and spend April there.
Farewell, my friend.
Napoleon

April, the month of my marriage. Josephine will understand.

HE SHUTS HIMSELF away in his study in Rambouillet. He is going to write his first letter to Marie Louise. He has Méneval prepare the quills and paper, then he begins, but he tears it up after a few lines. His writing must be more controlled, legible.

He picks up the little portrait of himself that he wants taken to the archduchess. Berthier will give it to her.

He starts writing again:

> My cousin, the brilliant qualities that distinguish your person have inspired us with a longing to serve and honour you by addressing the Emperor, your father, and begging him to entrust us with the happiness of Your Imperial Highness.

He stops. He feels like giving up. He prefers charging the enemy to these politesses. But he carries on regardless,

> May we hope that you will take a favourable view of the feelings which lead us to take this step? Can we flatter ourselves that you will not be solely determined by a duty and obedience to your parents? To whatever extent that the feelings of Your Imperial Highness may be partial to us, we will cultivate them with such care, and endeavour to please you in all things, that we flatter ourselves that we shall one day succeed in making ourselves agreeable; this is the object which we wish to attain and for which we beg Your Highness to be favourable to us.
>
> On which, we pray God, my Cousin, that he keeps you in His holy and worthy keeping.
>
> Your good cousin,
> Napoleon

Rambouillet, 23 February 1810

He wants what he says, not just to win her because she has submitted to her father's wishes.

He has only ever loved what he has taken, what he has conquered.

XXXIII

HE IS HUMMING A tune on this Sunday morning, 25 February 1810. He pulls Constant's ear as his valet tries to dress him, then waves him away and goes and stands in front of the mirror again.

So, this is his forty-first year. Is it really? But he is only just starting to live! He has never felt so free, so sure of himself, so young. He has finally scaled that sheer cliff which has been his life up till now. The last weeks of December were undoubtedly the darkest of his life. He felt that he would never be able to tear himself away from his past; that it was clinging on inside him, trying to keep him from reaching the summit. Now he's there, and he is not going to turn back. He is waiting for this eighteen-year-old Hapsburg princess, this fertile virgin in whose veins the blood of old dynasties flows. She will share his bed.

He goes through to his study and sits down. If he didn't control himself, he would write to her every minute of the day. Steadying his hand in an attempt to form the words elegantly, he begins,

Every letter that comes from Vienna does nothing but speak admiringly of your fine qualities. My impatience is extreme to be close to Your Majesty. If I heeded just myself, I would set off at full gallop and I would be at your feet before anyone even knew that I had left Paris.

He sings a song and daydreams. He could do that, gallop to Vienna and take the Austrian court by surprise.

But it cannot be. Marshal Berthier, Prince of Neuchâtel, will take your orders during your journey . . . I have but one thought, which is to be agreeable to you. Seeking to please you, Madam, will be the most constant and sweetest undertaking of my life.
Napoleon

I have never known this before. Perhaps it's the only thing left to me to discover. A woman, for whom I shall be the first man. A princess, the daughter of an emperor. A virgin who will become the mother of my son.

What a long way from that 'creature' in the Palais Royal, when I knew nothing about a woman's body! All the others were sly and cunning before they met me. Only one was tender, soothing: Marie. But even she had given herself to a man before me.

Now I am waiting for a wife worthy of an emperor. A woman of the same rank as me who will be mine alone, who will bear my son, my dynasty's future.

This is what I am going to discover.

When, though? When? He badgers Constant. Why must he wait another month?

He feels such energy that sometimes he is amazed by the sort of fury that sends him out hunting almost every day, that keeps him shuttling from one palace to the next, from the Tuileries to St Cloud, from Compiègne to Rambouillet and Fontainebleau.

He races through the rooms, then stops: those pictures commemorating an Austrian defeat must be taken down; the apartments must be hung with cashmere from the Indies; the furniture, all the furniture, changed. Nothing must imply that another woman lived here before her. Everything must be new for the new woman.

He tries to imagine life with her. He wants an etiquette as strict as that at the court of Louis XIV. He turns to his grand chamberlain, Count Montesquiou Fezensac. Four women, of noble blood, will keep watch over the Empress. No man, no matter who, may enter into a tête-à-tête with Her Majesty.

He walks away irritably, muttering, 'Adultery is an affair of the sofa.'

He knows what fidelity consists of: remove the men and the sofas, and women will be faithful!

But one only holds onto a fortress if one convinces its inhabitants that one is the better prince. Marie Louise must be attached to him. The love she bears him must be such that the only need she feels is to see him; he must be the only one she truly thinks of.

Her mind must be primed to receive me, docile.

He writes to her to influence her, since it is all he can do. He knows that she has set off after the proxy marriage and the festivities in her honour in Vienna, but the convoy of a hundred carriages will take more than ten days to reach Paris.

Knowing that she is approaching while he is here waiting for her makes everything even more unbearable.

I hope that Your Majesty will receive this letter at Brunau or even past there. I count the minutes; the days seem long to me. It will be like this until the moment I am fortunate enough to receive you . . . Believe me that there is no one on earth who is as attached to you and desires to love you as I do.

Napoleon

10 March 1810

From time to time he notices the astonishment on the faces of his aides-de-camp, his secretary and his sisters. He could simply be satisfied with this as a political marriage, they're bound to be thinking. As a Bourbon, he is now connected to the Hapsburgs. This union completes the network he has long wanted to create between his family and the ruling dynasties – Würtemberg for Jérôme, Bavaria for Eugène, Pauline and Prince Borghese. He has become the 'brother' and 'cousin' of all the ruling heads of Europe.

'I am the nephew of Louis XVI, my poor uncle,' he murmurs in front of his minister of foreign affairs, Champagny.

'The principal tactic the English were using to rekindle war on the continent was to insist that I intended to dethrone the other dynasties.'

He takes a pinch of snuff, and grimaces disdainfully. One would have to be blind to think that. What he has always wanted is to calm the sea that the Revolution whipped into a fury; to soothe it by retaining its creations – the new principles, namely the civil code – and at the same time keep it in check it with the monarchist principles – the Empire, in other words, and these alliances with the other dynasties.

'Nothing seemed more appropriate to calm general anxieties than to ask an Austrian archduchess for her hand in marriage,' resumes Napoleon. 'We have never been so close to peace,' he insists.

With a quick sweep of his hand, he brushes aside the dispatches piled up on his desk. Spain is unchanged, but he plans to go there once the marriage is concluded. Italy is calm and the Pope back in line, reduced to what he should always have been, a bishop deprived of all temporal powers. 'His kingdom is not of this world.' And as for the Church of France, it will be Gallican, as it was under Louis XIV.

He takes a few steps, his expression suddenly sombre. That leaves his fine ally of the north, Alexander.

The Tsar has fallen into the trap he wanted to set me.

Napoleon picks up the latest dispatch from Caulaincourt. The ambassador morosely requests to be recalled in the face of what he says is Russian discontent.

'I find Russia's complaints ridiculous!' Napoleon exclaims. 'The Tsar misjudges me if he thinks there has been any double negotiation: I am in too great a position of strength for that. It was only when it became clear that the Emperor of Russia is not master of his own family and that he was not keeping the promises he made at Erfurt that we negotiated with Austria, negotiations that began and ended within twenty-four hours because Austria had allocated her minister full powers to act on its behalf.'

They gave him Marie Louise without a moment's hesitation.

But he is not satisfied with just a young woman's body. He wants her mind, her heart. He needs passion.

How could one live if one didn't give oneself wholly and impulsively to everything one undertakes? How do other people manage to exist other than in the absolute truth of a dream?

He ponders this as he exhausts himself hunting or going to fêtes.

HE ENTERS THE magnificent residence of Count Marescalchi, ambassador to the King of Italy (*me, Napoleon*) to the Emperor (*me, Napoleon*). Marescalchi's mansion, on the corner of avenue Montaigne and avenue des Champs-Élysées, is teeming with guests in masks and fancy dress. Everybody is scrutinizing everybody else, trying to work out who is who.

Napoleon leans on Duroc's arm. He feels suffocated suddenly and retires to a small drawing room in which there's an officer he recognizes, Major Marbot. 'Iced water, quickly,' he says. He feels faint. He splashes water on his forehead and the nape of his neck. A woman comes in, speaks to Marbot.

'But I must speak to the Emperor,' she says. 'It is imperative that he double my pension. I know that people have been trying to run me down, that in my youth I had lovers. Lord above! You just have to listen to the conversations in every alcove downstairs to know that everyone is here with a paramour! Besides, don't his sisters have lovers? Doesn't he have mistresses himself? What is he here for, if not to talk more freely with pretty women?'

Napoleon gets to his feet. He walks past the woman dressed as a shepherd with a long plait down to her heels. The insolent gossip – he will make sure she leaves Paris. There are a dozen cantankerous shrews like her spreading their poison about the capital.

It's true that one of the reasons he came to the Marescalchi house was because he knew Christine de Mathis would be there. But that life must be erased now; Marie Louise must be kept in the dark about all of it. It must not even cross her mind that he was another woman's husband before her.

HE SENDS FOR Fouché.

Monsieur Regicide looks very happy. His police reports continue to say that the people are grumbling about my Austrian bride. His agents are impounding works exalting the memory of Marie Antoinette and the royal family. I have had to make him responsible for building six state prisons – the Bastille, he muttered, arbitrary detention. What, shouldn't I defend myself against murderers; against my adversaries who are so determined they would actually assassinate me?

And now, after he supported the divorce, here he is allowing the newspapers to talk about Josephine constantly.

'I told you to see that the newspapers didn't speak about Empress Josephine, but that is all they do,' says Napoleon, snatching up a newspaper lying on the table. 'the *Publicist* is full of her again today.'

He turns his back on Fouché, which is his way of dismissing him.

'Make sure that tomorrow's newspapers don't repeat the *Publicist's* story!' he calls out.

He waits impatiently for Fouché to leave the study. He re-reads the dispatches sent by the Strasbourg telegraph announcing that the one hundred carriages and four hundred and fifty horses, which comprise Louise's suite, have arrived at Sankt Pölten. Eight grey horses draw Marie Louise's carriage, and Caroline is sitting next to her sister-in-law. There was a small disturbance in Vienna shortly after Marie Louise's departure when the execution of Andreas Hofer, the leader of the Tyrolese insurrection, became public.

Napoleon crumples up the dispatch. He wants peace, but nothing will make him give way – not even the fact that nothing must spoil this marriage or compromise the relations that he hopes to have with his wife.

He writes to her,

At this hour you will have left Vienna. I sense the regrets you feel. All your pain is mine. I think of you very often. I would like to know what may be agreeable to you and may earn me your heart. Allow me, Madam, to hope that you may help me to win it, to win it entirely. This hope is crucial to me and makes me happy.

Napoleon
15 March 1810

He cannot wait any longer. What is he doing at the Tuileries when he should be with Marie Louise, since their marriage by proxy has been concluded? She should already be in his bed.

On Tuesday the 20th, he decides to leave Paris for the Château of Compiègne. That is where Louis XVI received Marie Antoinette.

And I shall receive Marie Louise there as Emperor.

He wants his whole court at Compiègne, with Hortense and Pauline Borghese at his side.

Pauline should come with her lady-in-waiting, Christine de Mathis. Why not? I am alone, for the moment.

But being at Compiègne does not calm him.

When Murat joins him, he takes him off on long hunts. He spurs his horse so hard he draws blood. He wants to win every race. His energy is inexhaustible. He dismounts, aims, fires. Then suddenly he wearies of it all, returns to the château, writes to Marie Louise,

I've been on a very fine hunt, yet it seemed insipid to me. Anything that is not you no longer interests me. I feel I shall lack nothing when I have you here with me.

He wants to take absolute possession of her. Nothing, not her body, nor her mind, nor her dreams, must elude him.

He has barely finished one letter, on Friday, 23 March, before he starts another. 'The Emperor can only be contented and happy if Louise herself is happy,' he writes.

He has barely finished that one, before another dispatch arrives.

The telegraph tells me that you have a cold. I beg you, look after yourself. I went hunting this morning; I send you the four first pheasants I shot as a duty most owing to my sovereign for all my most secret thoughts. Why am I not in a page's place, swearing an oath on bended knee as your liegeman, with my hands in yours? Even so, accept this oath in thought; and, in thought also, I cover your beautiful hands in kisses . . .

MARIE LOUISE IS drawing closer. On Tuesday, 27 March, she is expected at Soissons. It would be madness to wait. Patience is impossible. He calls in Constant. Over his uniform of a colonel of the chasseurs of the Guard, he wants to wear the overcoat he wore at Wagram. That was the day, the victory, that won him Marie Louise.

He sends for Murat, whose wife Caroline is travelling with Marie Louise. Let's be on our way. A barouche is ready. They set off at a gallop.

He badgers the coachmen. At relays, he gets out in the driving rain to hurry along the postilions. At the entrance to the village of Courcelles, one of the barouche's wheels breaks. He runs through the downpour to the church porch.

He loves these unexpected events, the rain and wind that have to be braved, this meeting he has planned that will flout all protocol and take Murat and the soldiers of the escort by surprise.

He paces up and down by the side of the road, looking out for the cortege. Who did they think he was? Louis XVI waiting quietly on his throne at Compiègne? He is Napoleon.

HE SEES THE team of greys pulling Marie Louise's carriage. He stands in the middle of the road and when the barouche stops, hurries towards it. An equerry unfolds the steps. He darts forward. He recognizes Caroline Murat, who murmurs, 'Madame, it is the Emperor.'

So this is her, Marie Louise. He smells her perfume. She is pink-cheeked, so young. He takes her hands, kisses them. So fresh. He smiles, studies her. He senses her heavy breasts pushing into him, her full hips, her supple body there to be taken. Her skin glows; her hair is ash blond. He didn't imagine she would be so full, so strong. And he wants to clasp her to him, like a fleshy spoil of war. He recognizes the features that had struck him in her portrait, the thick Austrian lips. She is fertile ground, lush, fecund. He's sure of it. He wants to fondle her, to burst out laughing.

He gives the order not to stop at Soissons. Too bad for the banquet, for the notables they can see under the awnings waiting to present their compliments to the Emperor. He laughs. What he wants is a bed, as quickly as possible.

The night draws on. He holds her in his arms, fusses over her. She is scared, and then he feels her relax. She starts to laugh too.

A bed, quick.

It is ten in the evening when they arrive at Compiègne. He sees the whole court waiting at the foot of the main staircase, ready to surround them and suffocate them with their compliments and deference. He parts the crowd with a gesture, and goes to a little dining room where he dines with Caroline and Marie Louise alone.

SHE IS MORE beautiful than he could have imagined. Fantastically beautiful! But healthy too, and plump and rosy and as fresh as a spring that has just gushed up out of the ground.

An eighteen-year-old Hapsburg, to be sure!

He wants her tonight.

'What instructions did your parents give you?' he asks.

He notes her candid gaze, her naiveté, approvingly.

'To be wholly yours and to obey you in every way,' she murmurs in her heavily accented French.

This profession of obedience excites him.

She must be mine, mine immediately!

Bowing her head, she protests that the religious ceremony has not yet taken place. He sends for Cardinal Fesch, who reassures her and convinces her that everything is in order.

Napoleon leads her to the Chancellery near the château, which is where he is meant to sleep, alone. With Marie Louise a few hundred metres away? He is not the sort of man who can accept that.

He leaves her for a few minutes with Caroline. She is a virgin. She doesn't know anything. He has been told she has never even been allowed male pets.

I AM THE first male.

He enters her room.

She is mine, as I wish her to be.

He lets her sleep as dawn approaches.

He would like to claim his victory, his triumph now but he leaves her room.

He goes up to Savary, his aide-de-camp, who is waiting in the drawing room near her bedroom.

He pulls his ear, laughs and says, 'My dear sir, marry a German. They are the best women in the world, gentle, kind, innocent and as fresh as roses.'

HE SPENDS WEDNESDAY, 28 and Thursday, 29 March 1810 with her in the Château of Compiègne. He has breakfast served in her room.

He senses people's curious looks when he appears with her at a concert in the great hall of the château. He has to present her to his court, of course. But he is impatient to be alone with her again, to surprise her and make her scream and laugh and introduce her to the jousts of love. He has already sensed her delight, after a few minutes of surprise and pain, at what she is feeling.

This is completely unknown to him. He is the teacher giving the lessons. He no longer feels in a hurry. He sees a slightly sarcastic look of surprise on Pauline Borghese's face. Two days without leaving Marie Louise's side!

'I have a young, beautiful, agreeable wife.' He shrugs. 'Aren't I allowed to express some joy at that fact? Can't I devote a few moments to her without being criticized?'

He leans towards Pauline, whose turbulent life is a succession of pleasures.

'Aren't I, like anyone else, allowed to abandon myself to a few moments of happiness?'

Before returning to Marie Louise's bedroom, he quickly dictates a few lines to Francis, Emperor of Austria.

My brother and father-in-law,

Your Majesty's daughter has been here for two days. She fulfills all my expectations and for two days I have not ceased to give or receive proofs of the tender sentiments that unite us. We suit one another perfectly.

I shall ensure her happiness, and mine I shall owe to Your Majesty.

We leave tomorrow for St Cloud and on 2 April, we shall celebrate the ceremony of our marriage at the Tuileries.

XXXIV

HE HAS GIVEN INSTRUCTIONS for these volleys of cannon fire and these fanfares to mark the moment of their arrival at St Cloud on Friday, 30 March 1810, a little after five in the afternoon.

He watches her. Ever since the entire cavalry of the Guard surrounded their carriage at Porte Maillot, there has been a look of astonishment on her face, a combination of fear and delight. He loves surprising her.

At Stains, when they entered the *département* of the Seine, there was a crowd of courtiers, ladies-in-waiting and curious onlookers to greet them. Prefect Frochot started to give a speech of welcome, but Napoleon interrupted him and gave the order to set off immediately. She stared wide-eyed at him like a child who has been shown a magic trick. He wants to be all-powerful in her eyes; the magician who gives her every pleasure, who introduces her to an unknown world, of which he holds all the keys.

He takes her hand and helps her out of the carriage. The cannon roar. The drums roll. Together they walk slowly along in front of his old grenadiers. This is his finest victory. He has conquered the young daughter of the enemy emperor, the leader they defeated; Marie Louise is the spoils of Wagram. They must see her.

But he is equally impatient to be alone with her again. This is the fourth night about to begin, but still he feels the same passion. She undergoes a complete transformation under his touch. He has made her a woman. And now he's the one surprised by her curiosity and her innocent audacity. He no longer thinks of anything. Sometimes, in a flash, he remembers how he never stopped thinking before, even with a woman he desired, even with the experienced Josephine who showed him what a woman could do when her whole body becomes a pair of lips.

'I am always working,' he used to tell Josephine. 'Nothing can stop me thinking. I work at dinner, in the theatre, at night I wake up to work.' I work while I am making love.

But now his mind is empty when Marie Louise is next to him, her submissive, generous body, ample and supple, like a young mare he wants to school. And he thinks of nothing except what this mare's stable master would do.

He's impatient for these days of ceremonies to be over, but at the same time he wants all this pomp so that she'll know he is the Emperor of Kings and see that the splendour of Paris, his capital, is more dazzling than anything she's known before, anything she could have possibly imagined. And she must be seen too – the Emperor's wife. So young!

ON SUNDAY, 1 April, at two in the afternoon, he leads her to their seats on a dais, sheltered by a canopy, at the end of the long gallery in St Cloud.

The whole court presses round. He squeezes Marie Louise's hand when she says after him, yes, she wants to be the wife of Napoleon.

'In the name of the Emperor and of the law, I declare joined in marriage . . .' begins Cambacérès.

Then the cannon drawn up on the terrace of the château start firing and the shouts of the crowd mingle with the explosions.

That night he leads her to the window, which she likes to keep open. The park is brightly lit; a large crowd is still out there.

He hides her behind the curtains. He does not want her to be seen. At night she is no one else's but his.

BUT ON MONDAY, 2 April, he wants her adorned with the Empress's crown and robes. He strides forward as his sisters carry the train of the gown that Josephine once wore.

But today is my real coronation. With this marriage I am joining the family of kings. As its senior member.

He looks at Marie Louise, her eyes wide. A phalanx of troops lines the road from Port Maillot to the Tuileries. The cavalry of the Guard caracole their horses. Crowds are everywhere. On the Chaillot esplanade, they are massed in two vast amphitheatres. Salvos of cannon fire punctuate the cortege's procession. He leans closer to Marie Louise to catch her surprise at the Arc de Triomphe, as they're about to pass under it. Barely started, he has had the monument completed with scaffolding and veils; the illusion is perfect. He is filled with pride. This is the capital of which he is the master.

She has never seen the Tuileries, the Louvre. The sun flashes in the windows, floods the galleries, which are thronged with almost ten thousand people. He recognizes Prince Kourakine, Russia's ambassador, who cuts a fine figure. *Here's Metternich, triumphant. And look at all these women pressing forward to see her, the woman whose hand I am holding, the Empress, the Archduchess of Austria, who's barely eighteen years old.*

He enters the rectangular salon that has been transformed into a chapel. Suddenly he feels hot in his black velvet cap, his overcoat and his white satin breeches. He feels restricted in these diamond-encrusted clothes. He sees Marie Louise, her face red under her crown, on the verge of fainting. Cardinal Fesch must start immediately and keep this religious marriage ceremony as brief as possible. He's impatient to get it over with. Suddenly he sees empty chairs, where the cardinals would have sat if they had not refused to attend the ceremony, out of loyalty to the Pope and in protest against the measures taken against him. A wave of anger sweeps over him.

He wants Bigot de Préameneu, minister of public worship, to convene these cardinals, charge them with grievous insult and forbid them to wear any external sign of episcopal rank; from now on they'll be 'black cardinals', like crows.

'I alone choose cardinals in my Empire ... The Pope is not Caesar, I am! The popes have done too many foolish things to consider themselves infallible. I will not suffer these demands; the century we live in will not suffer them! The Pope is no Grand Lama. The administration of the Church is not an arbitrary matter. If the Pope wishes to be the Grand Lama, then we are not of the same religion.'

Sombre-faced, he passes through the gallery and senses the surprise his expression arouses on all sides.

The doors giving on to the gardens are opened. Fresh air, at last! The Guard marches past. The grenadiers wave their caps on the tips of their sabres. 'Long live the Empress!' they shout. 'Long live the Emperor!

He clenches his fists.

'I will send a hundred thousand men to Rome if I must,' he murmurs.

He leads Marie Louise, now relieved of her robes and crown, towards the auditorium where there is to be a banquet.

A few more hours and I'll be alone with her.

But he must sit on the dais again, at a table under the canopy, then show himself on the balcony, watch the fireworks, acknowledge the crowd's cheers. He must content himself with looking at her while the senior chaplains of France and Italy bless their bed.

Napoleon cannot help dismissing them with a brusque gesture.

The doors are closed, finally!

She is exhausted. He feels vigorous, young, conquering.

He is her Emperor, her master.

He forgets everything except this room, this young woman.

HE WANTS TO enjoy spending a whole day with her. He has never known such a feeling before. It is as if time has changed rhythm. He decides to leave the Tuileries for Compiègne. He will be able to enjoy her better there. He dismisses any aides-de-camp that try to bring him dispatches. He keeps Murat waiting for several days, vainly soliciting an audience. He skims through the latest reports from Spain. Joseph is in despair. General Suchet has not been able to take Valencia. Berthier asks when the Emperor will take command of his armies to put an end to 'the canker of this Spanish war'.

He does not want to leave Marie Louise. He summons Masséna and appoints him head of the army. Isn't he 'the Favourite Child of Victory'? Masséna should be able to bowl over Wellington's thirty thousand English and fifty thousand English-trained Portuguese.

He watches Masséna ride away. He sees Marie Louise, surrounded by ladies-in-waiting, trying to mount a horse in the château's park and laughs at her clumsiness. He rushes over, feeling light, carefree. Has he ever had this feeling of having no duty except to amuse himself, to give and take pleasure? Is this what life is?

He must devour this life, just as he wolfed down his other life, before Marie Louise. He lifts her up and puts her in the saddle. He holds the horse by the bridle and jogs along at its side. He laughs when she screams with fright. He has a horse brought up and mounts it without riding boots. He is free. He is happy. He doesn't remember ever feeling so carefree, except perhaps on the quays of Ajaccio's port when he was a child.

She is a child who doesn't know anything and he wants to be lead off by her into one those games of blind man's buff she loves so much. He lingers over meals because it gives him pleasure seeing her eat. He no longer wants to rush off to his study after bolting a couple of mouthfuls of each dish. He wants to stretch out his legs, slip his left hand in his waistcoat. He starts to put on weight and has his clothes let out to hide it. He takes less snuff. He uses eau de cologne. He waits for night to fall.

IN THE MORNING he sees Corvisart who examines him carefully. A few boils, occasional irregular heartbeat, stubborn cough. He shrugs the doctor off. He feels fine. Fatigue? Nonsense! Forty-one years old? One is as old as one's desires! Young man's nights? Why not, since he can?

Doesn't Corvisart know that I am not of the ordinary run of men?

Even those close to me forget this. Everyone judges me by their own standards. Josephine, for instance. The letters she sends from Navarre are a litany of complaints and reproaches. Who does she think I am?

Napoleon goes through to his study. These letters from Josephine are getting on his nerves; they remind him of the past.

My friend, I received your letter of 19 April. Its style is bad. I am the same as I have always been; men like me never change.

Can't they understand that, even in bed with an eighteen-year-old Hapsburg, I'm not putting on an act, pretending to be someone else, but simply revealing a suppressed part of myself? But they're so simple, all these people around me, they can't conceive how various I am.

I don't know what Eugène can have told you. I didn't write because you didn't and because I only want what will be agreeable to you.

I see with pleasure that you plan to go to Malmaison and that you are happy. It would make me so to hear your news and give you mine. I won't say more until you have compared this letter to yours and then I will let you be the judge of who is the better and more friendly, you or I.

Farewell, my friend, keep well and be fair to yourself and me.

Napoleon.

But who is fair to me?

My brother Louis, since I made him King of Holland, has been playing his own game, refusing to abdicate to let Holland become French and trying to turn the Dutch against me. He is negotiating with the English: the police reports are categorical about that. He has joined forces with Fouché and Ouvrard, the army contractor, and they're all working towards peace with England without consulting me.

The Tsar, fair? He can't fool me. He is rebuilding his army, stealthily moving it westwards, threatening the Grand Duchy of Warsaw, leaning on Denmark, sending emissaries to Vienna and renewing ties with London as if he is contemplating going to war against me!

But all I want is peace! I want Russia to remain my ally. Haven't I become the cousin or brother or nephew of each of these sovereigns?

Aren't I the husband of one of their daughters?

Everyone must realize this; my subjects must know that there is no reason to oppose me any more.

If they are loyal to their old rulers, let them think of the woman who I have married. And if they believe in the new values, let them remember that I am the Emperor who drew up the civil code!

They'll know the truth if they can see us.

ON SUNDAY, 27 APRIL 1810 at seven in the morning, he leaves Compiègne with Marie Louise. Laughing, he comforts her. She is sleepy, tired by another change. He likes the way she looks at him with those startled eyes that say, who is this inexhaustible man? He wants to show her off to the countries in the north of his Empire previously under Austrian rule; the people will see a Hapsburg duchess at their Emperor's side.

He gives the signal to set off to the six hundred horsemen of the Guard who are escorting the long train of carriages which, on his wishes, includes Eugène, his ministers and the King and Queen of Westphalia.

It rains. The roads are muddy and the receptions interminable in Antwerp, Breda, Bergen op Zoom, Middelburg, Grand, Bruges, Ostend, Dunkirk, Lille, Le Havre and Rouen.

He observes Marie Louise. She doesn't know how to smile at the officials welcoming them to a town, or flatter the dignitaries who are waiting for a sign of recognition that will remain with them all their lives. He remembers the talent Josephine had for charming everyone who came into contact with her. The memory irritates him. He flies into a rage with Louis who he meets in Antwerp and who reveals, with a mixture of naivety and self-importance, the negotiations he, Fouché and Ouvrard have entered into with England.

Who gave them the right? Napoleon bellows.

Luckily there are nights, walks on the beach, Marie Louise's squeals of joy when the long waves break at high tide. And there is the feeling of joy that floods Napoleon for several days when Marie Louise thinks she is pregnant.

But on their return to Paris, Friday, 1 June, he sees her walking towards him, pale, sulky, shaking her head. She won't be having a child this time.

HE GOES OFF alone, disappointed. It feels as if he's woken up to find everything he's been doing was just a dream.

On a table he recognizes a letter from Josephine; it is plaintive, humble, the letter of a sick old woman. He has to reply.

My friend, I have received your letter. Eugène will give you news of my trip and of the Empress. I very much approve of you going to take the waters. I hope they will do you good.

I want to see you. If you're at Malmaison at the end of the month, I will come and see you. I plan on being at St Cloud.

My health is excellent; I just need to know you are happy and well.

Never doubt the truth of all my feelings for you; they will last as long as I live; it would be most unjust of you to doubt them.
Napoleon

He has the other dispatches brought in and sends for Cambacérès. He reads, listens and grows furious. He has only loosened his grip on the reins for two months, but is two months too long? It seems that all the springs of the Empire have gone slack.

Caulaincourt is snivelling in St Petersburg as if he's ceased to be the ambassador of the French Empire and become a loving subject of Alexander's instead! Joseph — who I gave the Spanish throne to — writes to his wife in one of the letters the police have intercepted, 'The trial of two kingdoms is enough for me. I want to live peacefully, acquire an estate in France . . . I desire you therefore to prepare the means for us to live independently in retirement and justly recompense those who have served me well.'

Is this how a king speaks? Is this the character of the Emperor's older brother?

Meanwhile Louis is degrading himself with Fouché to negotiate without my consent!

He wants a council of ministers convened tomorrow at St Cloud.

On Saturday, 2 April, he watches them taking their seats like naughty schoolboys, apart from Fouché, who is merely paler than usual. He has character, that one, but who can trust him?

'Well, Monsieur the Duke d'Otranto,' Napoleon calls out. 'Are you making war and peace now?'

Napoleon gets to his feet and paces up and down in front of the ministers without looking at Fouché who, in a steady voice, justifies his actions, blaming Ouvrard for making all the overtures to London.

'It is the most unprecedented breach of duty to take the liberty of negotiating with an enemy country without the knowledge of one's sovereign, on conditions that the sovereign knows nothing of and in all probability would not accept,' Napoleon replies. 'It is a breach of duty which even the weakest of governments should not tolerate.'

Fouché begins to say something.
'You should put your head on the block!' Napoleon cries.

I DON'T WANT this man anywhere near me any more. People will say I've removed him because he voted for Louis XVI's death and I'm now the King's nephew. But really I don't want a minister of police who has his own agenda. I want someone to carry out my policies; someone dedicated to me, body and soul, who can inspire terror without even needing to take action.

He thinks of General Savary, Duke of Rovigo, formerly aide-de-camp to Dessaix, the colonel in command of his elite gendarmes, his personal Guard. The man who arrested the Duke d'Enghien and saw he was executed.

'The Duke of Rovigo is shrewd and resolute and he is no troublemaker,' Napoleon tells Cambacérès. 'People will be afraid of him and that alone will make it easier for him to be lenient than it would be for someone else.'

He summons Savary to St Cloud and scrutinizes this rugged-looking fellow who acquitted himself well at Marengo, Austerlitz and Eylau.

He takes his arm, leads him out into the park.

'Good policing requires a complete absence of passion,' he starts. 'Be wary of hatreds, listen to everything and never give your verdict without allowing reason and time to prevail. Don't let yourself be swayed by your officers; hear them out, but it is you who they must listen to and your directives they must carry out.'

He walks on a little.

'Treat men of letters well; they have been turned against me by people claiming I don't like them. It was malicious; if I didn't have so much to take care of, I would see them more often. They are useful men who must always be singled out for distinctions, because they do France honour . . .'

Will Savary understand? Fouché has already tricked him by burning all his ministry's files and hiding my correspondence with him. Fouché must leave Paris as soon as possible, either abroad or to his senator's province in Aix.

'I replaced Fouché because, deep down, I couldn't count on

him any more. He defended himself against me when I wasn't troubling him and considered his interests at my expense.'

In addition to which Fouché embodied a faction, that of the party that voted for the King's death.

'I espouse no party other than that of the mass,' Napoleon thunders. 'Do not try to do anything other than reunite. My policy is to complete the work of fusion. I must govern with everybody at my side without watching what every individual is doing. People rallied to me to enjoy security. They'd leave me tomorrow if everything regressed and became difficult.'

He catches sight of Marie Louise who seems to be waiting for him on the stairs, surrounded by her ladies-in-waiting. He leaves Savary and quickly goes to her.

She wants to play billiards.

XXXV

HE WAVES THE LETTER in the air. He wants to shout. He goes over to Méneval, gives him several friendly slaps on the shoulder, then pulls his ear. He wants to see the grand marshal of the palace, Duroc, immediately. Left alone, he goes to the window, opens it and the soft air of a June morning and the smells of St Cloud suddenly touch him deeply. He hears Méneval return with Duroc, but he cannot move. He stays leaning on the windowsill, the letter crumpled in his fist.

He has only read it once but he knows every word. In his mind, each of them has the gentle lilt of Marie Walewska's voice. She whispers that her son was born on 4 May in Walewice Castle.

He is called Alexander Florian Joseph Colonna. He has the same shaped face as his father, his forehead, his mouth and jet-black hair. She asks for nothing. She is happy simply waiting and hoping for her son Alexander.

He would like to clasp them both in his arms, broadcast his joy, show them off to everybody, even Marie Louise. What would be the harm in that? His life contains several lives and he can live them all while still protecting those he loves and has loved. He turns to Duroc and laughs. It was Duroc who introduced Marie Walewska to him; he will be the repository of this secret.

He goes up to the grand marshal of the palace.

'A son,' he says in a loud voice.

He wants Duroc to make preparations for Marie Walewska and Alexander to move to Paris. He will endow this son more handsomely than he did Count Léon, his firstborn. But how could he be entirely certain of Louise Éléonore Denuelle de La Plaigne? It was the same with his daughter Emilie, who has Madame Pellapra for a mother.

'Two sons,' he murmurs and laughs again.

As soon as Marie is set up in Paris, in the town house in rue de la Victoire, she will be presented at court as the daughter of one of the Polish families that are France's oldest allies. Doctor Corvisart will attend to her and the child.

He paces about his study. How many lives there are contained in his life! He feels mutilated having to conceal some of them like this. Why should he? He is like a great river that flows through different countries, its banks at times gently sloping, at others sheer. But he is always the same river, from its source to its mouth.

He goes outside. If Marie Walewska were in Paris, he would visit her regularly as a friend, as the mother of his son. And how would that change Marie Louise's life?

He wants unity among all his lives. He cannot live as if his destiny has exploded into countless different pieces. He is one.

HE RIDES WITH a single aide-de-camp to Malmaison. It moves him to be back, to recognize everything, even the scent of the flowers. Everything is deathly quiet; he is concerned. He hails a footman who is panic-stricken when he sees who it is. Napoleon takes his arm, shakes him.

'Where is Josephine? Hasn't she risen?'

He is impatient to see her, anxious.

'There she is, sire, walking in the gardens.'

He sees the white silhouette in a light dress, her hair pinned up at her neck. He wants to take her in his arms.

He runs towards her, embraces her.

He has several lives.

HE NURTURES THEM all, constantly vigilant. He gives his orders, presides over the Council of Ministers every day.

Where would these men take him if he let them lead?

Savary, the minister of police, hasn't Fouché's shrewdness or adaptability. He sees Jacobin plots everywhere. He breaks them up, but people should know that, even if I'm the husband of a Hapsburg, I'm not favouring the aristocrats. I am the founder of a nobility and dynasty, not a branch grafted onto the old trunk of the ancien régime. I am simply drawing the sap from centuries-old trees to make my branch grow.

He sends for Cambacérès.

'I do not want there to be any dukes other than the ones I have created or may still create. If I make any exceptions with the old nobility, they will be very restricted and only concern old family names that it will useful to keep.'

Cambacérès is listening, but has he understood?

'My goal is to support the present dynasty and cause the old aristocracy to be forgotten.'

HE GOES OUT into the Trianon's gardens. This is the most pleasant of his residences in the intense summer heat.

He joins in the parlour games Marie Louise is so fond of. She gets out of breath quickly, drops into one of the armchairs set out in the shade of the trees. She is a young, healthy woman, yet she doesn't seem to have much energy. During a splendid reception at the Hôtel de Ville with fireworks, she tired immediately. At Pauline Borghese's château at Neuilly, she appeared bored during a dazzling party organized by Pauline that had a trompe-l'oeil recreation of Schönbrunn specially to please her. She is the same at the opera or at parades of the Guard.

Perhaps she is scarred by that tragic party given by Prince Schwarzenberg on 1 July at the Austrian embassy? A fire started and the specially built wooden ballroom, with its canvas walls hung with netting, taffeta and garlands of paper flowers, suddenly went up in flames, the blaze fuelled by thousands of candles, and the guests trampled one another as they tried to get to the only exit not blocked by flames.

Napoleon left with Marie Louise, took her as far as the Champs Élysées and then went back to the embassy. It was like a battlefield with the same smell of burnt flesh as at Wagram and bodies piled on top of one another, among them Prince Schwarzenberg's sister-in-law.

Napoleon saw the naked bodies, already robbed by looters who'd torn off their rings, necklaces and earrings, mutilating them if they had to.

Horrible party.

Every time he thinks of it, he remembers the curses, the evil omens spoken about so often when he was a child.

He dismisses the thought. He goes and finds Marie Louise, red faced and perspiring as she joins in the roundelays making fun of Prince Borghese or runs among the trees at the Trianon.

It is the start of August. Tonight, as almost every night, there will be a play. This Thursday, 9 August, it is *Les Femmes Savantes*. He leans over towards Marie Louise. She prefers circuses. He stretches out his arm, showing her the amphitheatre that is being constructed in the Petit Trianon's gardens. The Franconi brothers, Italian maestros, are putting on a show tomorrow.

She is radiant. He kisses her. She whispers in his ear, several times.

'Perhaps,' she adds.

He takes her hand, squeezes it. He is sure, and it will be a son.

He has several lives.

He gets to his feet, walks through the gardens. He has several lives. This one is beginning with this young woman pregnant by him.

He goes back in to her. No more riding for her, no more dancing, no more lavish, draining fêtes, no more exhausting trips, but a calm, peaceful life at court here at the Trianon, and at Rambouillet, Fontainebleau and St Cloud. He strokes her like a child. Shows, concerts, the games she loves – that's what he wants for her.

She grasps his hands. She wants him always to stay with her.

He reassures her. He will not leave her.

BUT HE STILL needs to feel the wind as he gallops, to smell damp grass.

He hunts stag at Meudon, Rambouillet and Fontainebleau. Several times a week, he rides to hounds at the head of a cavalcade that charges through the undergrowth like a cavalry squadron. He sets off at midday and comes back at six, having changed horse six times.

He takes a bath, then goes downstairs to join Marie Louise who is growing fuller. He touches her. This is another life for him, this woman carrying his child, filling out. He is light-hearted.

He writes to Francis, Emperor of Austria:

I don't know if the Empress has let you know, but the hopes we have of her being with child increase daily and we are as sure as one can be at two and a half months. Your Majesty will readily understand all that this adds to the feelings your daughter inspires in me and how much these new ties accentuate my desire to prove agreeable to her.

He showers her with presents, attention and consideration. She is carrying the future. He wants to be certain he is making her happy, and so he asks to see Metternich, who is staying in Paris. He likes this intelligent fellow who decides Vienna's policies and strongly supported Marie Louise's marriage. He wants Metternich to have a tête-à-tête with the Empress. Laughing, he acknowledges what an exception this is, since she wouldn't otherwise be allowed to meet a man without a third party being present.

He waits for their conversation to end and when Metternich emerges, goes up to him.

'Well then, did you have a good chat? Did the Empress say anything bad about me? Did she laugh or cry?' he asks.

Then, with an indifferent wave, he says, 'But I'm not asking for a report, these are secrets between the two of you which don't concern a third party, even if that third party is the husband.'

He leads Metternich to his study.

'I will never quarrel with my wife,' he says, 'even if she were infinitely less distinguished than she is in every respect. An alliance of two families is a considerable thing.'

He picks up a portfolio on the table and shows it to Metternich.

'I no longer set any store by the secret articles of the treaty of Vienna concerning the Austrian army,' he says. 'I want to please the Emperor Francis and give him new proofs of my esteem and high consideration.'

The Emperor of Austria will be the grandfather of my son. This rapprochement with Austria could be the key to my policies. But what of the alliance with Russia?

'All I get from Russia is continual complaints and insulting suspicions.'

Alexander is afraid I will re-establish Poland. If I'd wanted to, I would have told him and I wouldn't have withdrawn my troops from

Germany. Is Russia trying to prepare me for her defection? I shall be at war with her the day she makes peace with England.

His voice grows harsh.

'I do not want to re-establish Poland. I do not want to conclude my destiny in the sands of its desert wastes, but I will not dishonour myself by stating categorically that Poland will never be established.'

He thinks of Marie Walewska and his son Alexander, scion of an aristocratic Polish patriot and himself, the Emperor.

I have several lives.

'No,' he goes on. 'I cannot commit myself to take up arms against a people who have shown me constant goodwill and great devotion. For their own good and Russia's, I will exhort them to be peaceful and submissive, but I shall not declare myself their enemy and I shall not tell the French, "Your blood must be spilled in order to bring Poland under Russia's yoke."'

He bangs his fist on the desk.

'Nothing in the world could make me subscribe to a dishonourable course of action or compel me to put my signature to the statement "Poland will not be re-established". That is worse than any stain on my character.'

He walks away from the desk.

'I would have to be God to decree that there will never be a Poland. I cannot make promises I cannot keep.'

He turns back towards Metternich and seems to hesitate. It's been months since he has used the words 'war', or 'army'.

'St Petersburg should not be under any illusions that I am in no position to wage war again on the Continent. I may have three hundred thousand men in Spain, but I have four hundred thousand in France and elsewhere. The army of Italy is still intact. The moment war broke out, I could appear on the banks of the Niemen with a larger army than I had at Friedland.'

He smiles at Metternich. He doesn't want war. But can he count on Vienna? He doesn't wait for Metternich to reply. He takes him by the arm and sees him out.

'The Empress will have told you she is happy with me, that she has no complaints to make.'

He stops Metternich at the door.

'I hope you will tell your Emperor. He will believe you more than anybody.'

HE REMAINS ON his own, lost in thought.

War a possibility again, at the height of summer 1810, when I am expecting a son. What will he inherit from me, this descendant of Charles the Fifth and Napoleon?

I must make my Empire unassailable for him. And anyone who does not plan ahead is defeated.

England and Russia could come to an agreement tomorrow. Who can I rely on? The kings I've made are nothing: Louis has finally abdicated the Dutch throne, but without coming to an agreement with me, and fled abroad, like a coward, deserting Hortense and the children.

I shall write to Hortense.

My daughter,
We have no news of the King. We do not know where he has retired to and cannot understand his hare-brained behaviour at all.

That man, my brother, has gravely offended me.

A man who I have been a father to. I raised him on the meagre funds of an artillery lieutenant's wages; I shared my bread with him and the mattress of my bed . . . Where is he going? Among foreigners in Bohemia under an assumed name to make it seem he's not safe in France.

I shall write to my mother.

Louis' behaviour can only be explained by the state of his illness.

I intend to govern the country myself.

What has Holland become? An entrepôt for smuggled English goods.

Do the Dutch take me for a grand pensionary? I shall do what suits the interests of my Empire and the clamour of those lunatics who think they know my interests better than I fills me with nothing but contempt.

Contempt for Lucien, my brother, who has fled Rome because I declared it French, the second city of the Empire, just as I decreed that Amsterdam will be the third. Now he wants to go to America and fall into the hands of the British!

Joseph is incapable of waging a war except to make things difficult for the marshals, who are stamping their feet with impatience and then getting beaten by Wellington's men.

Hand-me-down kings, like Murat, who's trying to land in Sicily without telling me, because the Queen of Sicily is Marie Louise's grandfather, and so he's afraid I'll stop him, the King of Naples, conquering the island! Which, in any case, he is incapable of doing, although I've urged him to do it a hundred times!

All mediocrities and the ones with any talent are hostile to me. Talleyrand, the police spies are convinced, has just asked Alexander for a loan of one and a half million francs — the cost of the information he gave him at the Russian embassy. As for Bernadotte, he's got himself elected hereditary prince of Sweden. Am I entitled to hope that he won't go to war with me because I haven't prevented him becoming Swedish? Beneath all his declarations of loyalty, though, I can feel how proud he is to be king and how ready he is to do anything to stay king, this husband of Désirée Clary.

So many lives contained in mine!

He receives Metternich again who is concerned at a marshal being elevated to the rank of king like this, the suspicions it will provoke in St Petersburg.

Napoleon spreads out his correspondence with Charles XII, King of Sweden, and Bernadotte in front of Metternich.

He had nothing to do with Bernadotte's rise. He merely tolerated it.

'I was only too pleased to see him leave France. He is one of those old Jacobins with their minds in a whirl. But you're right, I should not have given a throne to Murat, or even to my brothers. But one is only wise with hindsight.'

He crosses his arms.

'I ascended a throne I had created; I did not assume another's legacy. I took something that belonged to no one. I should have stopped at that and only appointed governor-generals and viceroys.

Besides, you only have to consider the behaviour of the King of Holland to be convinced that relatives are often far from being friends. As for the marshals . . .'

He shakes his head, shrugs his shoulders.

'You are absolutely right, all the more so because some of them have already begun dreaming of their own greatness and independence.'

IT IS HIS responsibility, his alone, to plan for the future, to watch over the Empire.

In the Trianon gardens, he sees Marie Louise, surrounded by her ladies, applauding a juggler.

He suddenly thinks of Marie Antoinette, the Empress's aunt, who lived here. He has before him police reports of talk, often hostile, about the 'new Austrian'. Some people are saying the fire at the Austrian ambassador's party is a sign of the curse Viennese women and alliances with the Hapsburgs always put on France. They find Marie Louise stiff, cold, haughty.

They don't share her bed!

There's so much heat inside her that she can only sleep with the windows open, whereas I loathe the chill night air.

He re-reads the reports.

He must be wary of the people's prejudices. He does not want the newspapers to start reporting ridiculous details. He sends for Savary, minister of police, and Count Montalivet, Home Secretary. They must stop 'the publication of anything that might come from foreign correspondence. The Germans are so notoriously silly that they'll say that I pressed Princess Louisa's slipper to my lips when I don't even know her!'

He turns to Count Montalivet. He knew this former member of the Grenoble Parliament when he was at Valence.

One of my lives, when I was an artillery lieutenant.

'I will only sleep easy when I am assured that you are performing your special task of checking Paris's supply of corn. There is no measure more apt to contribute to the people's well-being and the administration's peace of mind than a guarantee that this means of supply exists.'

Montalivet, like me, lived through 1789. The people must have bread if one doesn't want them marching to the Trianon calling for the baker and his wife.

And there must be money in the coffers too, and work for the factories.

At St Cloud, Trianon and Fontainebleau he dictates decrees calling for vigilance against the smuggling of English merchandise. Importing such merchandise will incur taxes representing half the total value of the imported goods: those who do not respect the continental blockade will have to pay a high price.

When Eugène tries to defend Italian interests, as Louis had tried to protect Dutch merchants, he says, 'My principle is France first. You should never lose sight of the fact that if English commerce dominates the seas, it is because the English are strongest in that realm. It is therefore conceivable that, since France is strongest on land, she could secure her commerce's domination of that realm . . . England is really in dire straits and I have a glut of merchandise which I need to export and I'm procuring colonial goods to its cost.'

But for this he needs to exercise greater control over the European coastline. Smuggled merchandise must be seized and burned at Frankfurt, Hamburg, Amsterdam and Lübeck.

'You have plenty of staff officers, get them cracking,' he tells Davout who's in command of the troops in Germany. 'I am making you responsible for stamping out, once and for all, English smuggling and traffic between Holland and Swedish Pomerania. Make this your affair.'

But he knows Davout can't achieve the impossible. Since the start of October 1810, twelve hundred English merchantmen laden with merchandise have been plying the Baltic.

Bernadotte has closed the Swedish ports to them. But there are still the Russian ports. What will Alexander do? And if he allows them access, what should I do?

HE GOES DOWN to the large drawing room, which he has chosen as the best place to work for the Venetian sculptor whom he has brought to the Tuileries. He has known him since his first time in

Italy. He didn't much care for the way Canova represented him, naked, holding a small victory in his hand. But Canova is the greatest sculptor alive. He has been commissioned to make a bust of Marie Louise, and Napoleon is going to attend the sittings.

He takes a seat. Marie Louise is fidgeting impatiently.

'This is the capital of the world,' Napoleon tells Canova. 'You should stay.'

He admires the movements of Canova's fingers, the lack of servility in his conversation.

'Why isn't Your Majesty reconciled with the Pope?' Canova asks.

'The Popes have always prevented the Italian nation rising up. The sword is what you need!'

Marie Louise coughs. Canova speaks of imprudence, since the Empress is pregnant.

'You see how she is. But women always want everything to be as they wish ... I am always telling her to take care of herself. What about you, are you married?'

He barely listens to Canova talking about his freedom.

'Oh women, women ...' Napoleon murmurs.

MARIE LOUISE astonishes him, just as Josephine and Marie Walewska had, each in their own way.

He receives Hortense, who has come to talk about her mother. Josephine is afraid she will be sent into exile, not just outside Paris but actually away from France.

He does not want that. He has several lives that should coincide and co-exist side by side. But Marie Louise can't understand this desire.

'I have to think of my wife's well-being,' he tells Hortense. 'Things have not yet settled down the way I hoped they would. She is frightened of your mother's charms and the influence she is known to have over my mind. That is it, I'm sure.'

He stops walking. It is autumn. In St Cloud's park, the gardeners are heaping leaves into piles. Wisps of smoke are rising at the edges of the russet-coloured forest. They've started to burn the fallen leaves over there.

'Recently I wanted to go for a walk with her at Malmaison. I don't know if she thought your mother was there, but she started crying and I had to change route.'

It seems so natural and simple to me that my different lives should meet. When will the day dawn when men and women are no longer prisoners of their prejudices?

'However that may be, I shall never constrain the Empress Josephine in any matter. I shall always remember the sacrifices she performed for my sake. If she wants to settle in Rome, I shall make her governor. In Brussels, she can still have a superb court and do that country good. Close to her son and her grandchildren, things would be better and more suitable for her. However . . .'

He spreads his hands. He knows perfectly well she doesn't want any of this!

'Write to her that if she would rather live at Malmaison, I shall not raise any objections.'

Going back inside, he scribbles a few lines to Josephine himself.

My opinion was that the only fit places for you to pass the winter were Milan or Navarre. Anything you want to do thereafter I approve of, because I do not want to inconvenience you in any way.

Farewell, my friend. The Empress is four months pregnant and she has appointed Madame de Montesquieu governess of the children of France. Be happy and do not trouble yourself. You must never doubt my feelings for you.

Napoleon

He feels the same affection for Josephine he has always felt, and he is very attached to Marie Louise, who touches him deeply.

He follows her along the long gallery at St Cloud. Her gait is heavy. He exclaims, 'Look how her waist has grown!'

They walk side by side through the congregation of dignitaries gathered in the chapel at St Cloud. He watches Marie Louise distributing diamond-rimmed lockets among the mothers whose children are going to be baptized on this Sunday, 4 November. There are twenty-six children, including Charles Louis Napoleon, the son of Louis and Hortense, and Berthier's son – all children of princes and kings – who are going to be baptized in the presence of the Empress and Emperor.

Hortense's son, Charles-Louis Napoleon, the future Napoleon III and Josephine's grandson, is becoming the godson of my second wife, for whom I repudiated Josephine.

And I'm going to be the father of a son born to a Hapsburg mother.

He announces Marie Louise's pregnancy to the crowd of guests. They burst out cheering.

He dictates a letter to the Emperor of Austria officially informing him of the news.

I am sending one of my equerries to convey to Your Majesty the news of the Empress, his daughter's, pregnancy. She is almost five months pregnant now. The Empress's health is very good and she is experiencing none of the discomforts common to her state. Knowing all the interest Your Majesty shows us, we are sure this event will be agreeable to him. Greater perfection than that possessed by the wife whom I owe to him is impossible. I beg Your Majesty to be convinced that she and I are equally attached to your person.

He stops and listens to his secretary's quill flying over the paper.

Méneval presents him with the text to sign.

He dashes off his signature with a flourish.

What a novel my life would make!

XXXVI

NAPOLEON WALKS THROUGH the empty, high-ceilinged rooms alongside the grand marshal of the palace. Duroc opens the gilt double doors; Napoleon briskly follows and pulls his ear.

The grand marshal used to live here, in this wing of the Tuileries overlooking the Carrousel. *But this is where my son, the King of Rome, is going to live.*

He sends for the architects. Everything must be repainted. The walls will be padded to a height of three feet so that the child doesn't hurt itself when it falls over.

Napoleon goes over to a window. The cold November sun glints on the gilded statues of the Arc de Triomphe in the Carrousel.

I had that built, to the glory of my army.

He imagines the child looking out, discovering this symbol of greatness and victory. The King of Rome will know he is the son and grandson of emperors the moment he opens his eyes.

Napoleon dictates instructions as he walks back to his study. He lists the contents of the child's trousseau, the dignitaries to be sent for when the Empress's pains begin, the ceremonies that will follow the birth, the hundred-and-one gun salute, the parade of the grenadiers of the Guard. He turns towards Duroc who has murmured a question, which he has sensed rather than actually heard. A twenty-one-gun salute if it is a girl, he declares regretfully. But it will be a boy. Witnesses to the birth will be Eugène, Viceroy of Italy, and the Duke of Würzburg.

He goes into his study. He wants everything to be submitted to him for approval, from Prudhon's sketches for the vermeil cradle to the list of doctors who will attend to the Empress. Everything.

THREE MONTHS IS barely enough to foresee and plan everything and make sure everyone has their instructions.

'There's never enough time,' he says. The forthcoming year, 1811, is the forty-second of his life. Everything he has done until now feels as if it has only been a preparation for this phase of his destiny.

His real life as an emperor is just beginning. He has military power, an obedient people, experience and the vigour of youth still.

He can hunt for hours on end – on the Rozoy plain yesterday, today at the Croix de Saint-Hérem, and it was he who started the stag. He is the fleetest of all the riders.

And in Marie Louise's bed, or with that vivacious brunette, the stepdaughter of Commandant Lebel, Deputy Governor of St Cloud, who has offered herself and he has accepted on several nights (because one does not refuse what life offers), he is sprightlier than the second lieutenant he used to be who, he remembers, was awkward, shy even, too brusque and in too much of a hurry.

He is at his peak.

All the kings have been forced to recognize his dynasty, to admit it into their number. He has won his throne and a nineteen-year-old Empress is going to give him a son.

No one will cast a shadow over this noontide of his destiny.

He will not allow it.

HE SITS DOWN and looks at the police bulletins, dispatches and reports filed in their different trays on his desk. He would rather not have to immerse himself in this sea of paper. His life has become so full without it!

Marie Louise asks for him constantly. He loves their tête-à-têtes, her naivety, her skin, especially her skin and her body that's changing with motherhood. All that is so new for him, whereas here it's the same grey routine, the same brutality and insidious manoeuvrings, the same reality he has been wading through since childhood without any illusions.

He reads the first police report, 'The most hard-headed businessmen are panicking about the future. The crisis is so dire that, every day, any banker who has got to four o'clock without misfortune exclaims, "That's another one got through!" '

Farewell, insouciance! Farewell, reverie! Let us plunge back into the mire!

BUSINESS IS BAD because English smuggling is rampant and it is impossible to export French merchandise. Europe is overrun with produce from England and its colonies. The blockade's flaw is the north.

He sends for Champagny. What do the Russians want? What does our ambassador have to say? Napoleon scowls disdainfully. Caulaincourt has become a courtier of Alexander's. He is more Russian than French.

'I know . . .'

He indicates the reports Davout, the commander in chief in Germany, has sent him.

'. . . that the twelve hundred merchantmen the English escorted with twenty men-of-war, having masked them with Swedish, Portuguese, Spanish and American flags, have unloaded part of their cargoes in Russia.'

He bangs his fist on the table.

'Peace and war are in the Russians' hands.'

Perhaps they don't know that.

'It is possible that they are exposing themselves to war without wanting to. It is a habit of nations to do foolish things.'

But I must take it into account anyway. I must consider war.

Alexander is creating new regiments. He has massed three hundred thousand men on the border of the Grand Duchy of Warsaw. He is even thinking, it is claimed, of putting General Moreau in command of one of his armies.

Moreau, who I merely exiled! Moreau, already eaten up with jealousy ten years ago when he fled to the United States. What about Bernadotte? How can I trust him when he receives Russian envoys and prepares for his future as hereditary prince of Sweden?

He gives an audience to one of Bernadotte's French aides-de-camp, Major Genty de Saint-Alphonse, an officer devoted to his marshal who it's useless to try to intimidate.

'Do you think I don't know,' Napoleon begins, 'that Bernadotte is saying, "Thank God, I am no longer in his clutches" to anyone who will listen and similar wild nonsense that I do not care to repeat?'

As the price of his loyalty, Bernadotte is asking for Norway, which belongs to Denmark. But if I give it to him, what will that guarantee me?

Greedy, jealous men betray one. Bourrienne, my former schoolmate at Brienne, my secretary for seven years, the venal Bourrienne, who I expelled from Hamburg, has been amassing millions – six, seven, eight? – selling licences to import English goods. What does he care about the welfare of the Empire?

Once more, I can only trust myself.

HE PONDERS THE situation. He cannot ask anyone for advice. Who knows better than he what the Empire needs, what is necessary for his dynasty's future? Is that peace?

Count Czernichev, Alexander's envoy in Paris, a self-important, unctuous character, who is also a womanizer and habitué of the salons, has been found to be running spies. Savary's police have discovered half-burnt papers in the ashes of his fireplace that come from Marshal Berthier's staff, where Czernichev is paying a spy to report on the state of French troops in Germany. And what about the way Alexander is imposing prohibitive taxes on French goods coming into Russia – is that a step towards peace?

Aren't I going to defend myself? Can I let English merchandise overrun Europe?

Napoleon dictates a senatus consultum by which the French Empire annexes the hanseatic cities of northern Germany and the Baltic, and the Duchy of Oldenburg, which belongs to Alexander's brother-in-law.

Is my fine ally of the north jibing? Who contravened the spirit of Tilsit first? I must speak plainly to the Emperor of Russia.

Napoleon writes to Alexander,

My feelings for Your Majesty will never change, although I cannot disguise from myself that Your Majesty no longer has any friendship for me. Already our alliance has ceased to exist in the eyes of England and Europe. Were it as complete in Your Majesty's heart as it is in mine, this widespread state of opinion would be no less of a great evil.

Will Alexander understand? Will he be able to keep the dogs of war in check?

I feel the same towards you, but I am struck by the evidence of facts and the implication that Your Majesty is disposed, the moment the circumstances present themselves, to come to an understanding with England, which would be the same as igniting war between our two countries.

He signs the letter, then, with the back of his hand, sweeps the dispatches from Caulaincourt off his desk.

'That man has no brains, he can't write, he's just an excellent stablemaster, that's all.'

He must be recalled to France, since he neither can nor wishes to do his job, and General Lauriston, his aide-de-camp at Marengo, must be appointed in his place.

BUT WHAT ARE these men around me here worth? Even a councillor of state like Joseph-Marie Portalis, the son of the former minister of public worship, has become an accomplice of the Pope in his attempt to challenge the authority of the Archbishop of Paris, Maury, who I appointed.

The Pope is plotting with various ecclesiastics, such as the Abbé d'Astros who has been caught carrying, hidden in his hat, Pius VII's denouncements of Maury. Let Astros be thrown into Vincennes and the Pope 'who combines the most terrible behaviour with the most blatant hypocrisy' be kept under close surveillance; the troops guarding him in Savona must be reinforced.

Why such criticisms of me? Haven't I restored religion? Have I provoked a schism, like the English or the Russians?

Napoleon is standing at the window of his study. He turns his back on Cambacérès and Savary. The latter has brought him a copy of the speech Chateaubriand intends to deliver at the Académie Française, to which he has just been elected in place of the regicide Chénier. This speech will reopen old wounds.

'I am surrounded by adherents of all parties,' Napoleon begins. 'I have even admitted émigrés and soldiers of the army of Condé to my inner circle.'

He walks towards Cambacérès, shows him the text of Chateaubriand's speech.

'I should say to the author if he were in front of me, 'You are not from this country, sir. Your admirations, your wishes are elsewhere. You understand neither my intentions nor my actions.'

He raises his arms, goes back to the window.

'Well then, if you are so ill at ease in France, leave, sir, leave, because we do not understand one another and I am in charge here. You do not like my work and you would spoil it if I let you have your way. Leave, sir, cross the border and leave France in peace and unity, under a power it has such need of.'

HE HOLDS THIS power in his hands. He stops in front of the map he has had drawn up which shows the new borders of the Empire: it contains one hundred and thirty *départements*, from Hamburg to the Adriatic and from Amsterdam to Rome. He rules over forty-four million inhabitants.

This is what my son will inherit; perhaps there'll be even more, since he will be the King of Rome and one day, when the Kingdom of Italy reverts to him, he will be able to govern the peninsula and perhaps annex the Kingdom of Naples.

And who knows, why he may not extend his Empire further, to the Confederation of the Rhine, and he will have the Grand Duchy of Warsaw as his ally, which one day perhaps another of my sons will rule.

He often thinks of Alexander Walewski.

He steals into the house on rue de la Victoire with Duroc. He has had Marie Walewska presented at court, to Marie Louise herself. And even if only he and a few others allowed into the secret could appreciate it, it has given him pleasure to see his lives brought together like this.

But Marie Louise mustn't know. How could I expose her to any shocks, when she is carrying my child?

She wants him to be present at every moment. And he agrees.

The weather at the start of 1811 is cold and wet. He barely leaves the Tuileries. He loves humouring her whims, surprising her with presents, parures and earrings. He senses she is anxious about the birth. He reassures her, often taking her in his arms despite court etiquette.

In the evenings, during the plays performed in their private apartments, he watches her drowse off, her body heavy.

He feels moved. It is the first time he has seen a woman pregnant with his child.

ON TUESDAY, 19 MARCH, at eight in the evening, he waits with the Court in the Tuileries' theatre. He goes up to the Grand Duke of Würzburg and Eugène, who have just come from Paris to be witnesses at the birth.

He is starting to grow impatient when, all of a sudden, the Duchess of Montebello, Marshal Lannes's widow and Marie Louise's lady-in-waiting, appears. He does not like her. He appointed her in Lannes's memory and yet every day provides further evidence of her attempts to sow a web of discord around the Empress. She is a greedy, jealous, antagonistic woman but Marie Louise has become besotted with her.

He hears Madame de Montebello announce with great gravity that Marie Louise's pains have begun.

He orders the men to put on their uniforms. This birth must observe the court ceremonial he has decreed. The drawing rooms soon fill with over two hundred people.

He enters her room, into which are crowded six doctors. He has never experienced this before, this feeling of tenderness for a woman who is being made to suffer by the life she carries within her. He takes her by the arm, supports her as she walks about, the two of them taking matching small steps. He feels her growing calm. He helps her back into bed and she falls asleep.

He crosses the drawing rooms where the dignitaries are dozing. He asks for his supper to be served. He feels hot and takes a bath. He would like to do something and this impotence to which he is reduced to irritates him. He dictates through the night.

At eight o'clock, when it is already light, Doctor Dubois rushes in, pale and distraught.

Suddenly Napoleon is chilled to the bone.

'Well? Is she dead?' he calls out. 'If she is dead, we shall bury her.'

He feels nothing. He is a block of stone. He is used to the unexpected, to death.

Dubois stammers. The child is presenting badly. Corvisart has been sent for. Can the Emperor go down to see the Empress?

'Why do you want me to go down? Is there any danger?'

He looks hard at Dubois, who seems to have lost all self-control. Dubois is muttering that he will have to use forceps; he has delivered women before whose children were presenting like this.

'Well, how did you do it? I wasn't there, was I? Proceed in this case just like in the others; take your courage in your hands.'

He claps Dubois on the shoulder and escorts him out of his study.

'Don't think you're delivering the Empress but a bourgeoise of rue St Denis.'

Before they enter the Empress's room, Dubois stops.

'Since Your Majesty gives his permission, I will do so,' he says.

The doctor hesitates, then murmurs that a choice may have to be made between mother and child.

'The mother, it is her right,' Napoleon answers.

So perhaps he won't have the son he has hoped for so dearly. He grasps Marie Louise's hand. She cries out, doubled up in pain. He sees Doctors Corvisart, Yvan and Bourdier approach. She screams as Dubois prepares the forceps.

He doesn't want to stay there, a helpless spectator. He feels the sweat running down his forehead, down his neck. He clenches his fists. There's a bitter taste in his mouth. He'd like to howl with rage. He shuts himself in the dressing room. He hears Marie Louise's screams. The door opens.

He tries to read the expression on Doctor Yvan's face. The doctor murmurs that the Empress has delivered.

He sees the body of the child lying on the carpet of her room, inert. Dead.

He grasps Marie Louise's hand, kisses her. He doesn't look at the child. That is the way of things.

He won't have a son.

He strokes Marie Louise's face, his eyes staring fixedly into hers.

Suddenly, a wail.

He straightens up.

The child is wrapped in swaddling clothes on Madame de

Montesquiou's knees; she is rubbing it and putting a few drops of brandy in its mouth.

The child screams again.

Napoleon takes the bundle, lifts it up. It is like the sun rising on the morning of a victory.

He has a son.

It is nine o'clock in the morning, on Wednesday, 20 March 1811.

HE HEARS THE reports of the cannon, then the shouts rising up from the Place du Carrousel.

He cannot speak. He signs the birth certificate of Napoleon François Charles Joseph, then goes to the window. He sees the crowds converging on the palace from all directions; he sees the hands waving.

He hides his face behind the curtain and starts to cry.

HE WANTS TO show the child to the people and the army. This King of Rome, this child Madame de Montesquiou is holding or putting on a white satin cushion covered in lace, will be their sovereign.

While waiting for the provisional baptism that will take place in the evening, he dictates a letter to the Emperor of Austria.

> The Empress, much weakened by the pain she suffered, showed throughout the courage she has given so many proofs of . . . The child is in perfect health. The Empress is as well as her state allows; she has already slept a little and taken some food. This evening at eight the child will be provisionally baptized. Since it is my intention to have him fully baptized in six weeks, I am charging my chamberlain, Count Nikolay, who will convey this letter to Your Majesty, with another which will ask him to be godfather to his grandson.
>
> Your Majesty can have no doubt that all the satisfaction I feel at this event is increased immeasurably by the prospect of it perpetuating the bonds that unite us.

He takes another sheet of paper himself and writes a few lines to Josephine.

My son is big and healthy; I hope he will come on well. He has my chest, my mouth and my eyes.

I trust that he will fulfill his destiny.

PART NINE

And so the war will take place,
despite me, despite him

21 MARCH 1811 TO 21 JUNE 1812

XXXVII

HE LEANS OVER THE cradle. He could look at this child forever. He touches him, talks to him, caresses him and takes him in his arms for a few moments before Madame de Montesquiou takes him back and walks away with him.

He has a son.

He proudly presents him to the senators and state councillors who process in turn through the child's room.

'I have ardently desired what Providence has now granted me,' he says. 'My son will live for the welfare and glory of France. My son's great destiny will be fulfilled. With the love of the French, everything will be easy for him.'

My son: these words fill his mouth; he repeats them over and over. When he says them, his chest seems to puff out. And yet, after a few weeks he is amazed to find that each day his joy grows more fleeting. He feels weighed down by fatigue. His legs become swollen. He cannot sleep. He does not share his bed, and he bolts his food, as he used to do.

He sees Marie Louise every day, but she does not get up. Still exhausted from the birth, she dozes most of the time and only sees her son for a few seconds each day; not overly concerned about him, she entrusts him to Madame de Montesquiou, behaving like the archduchess she is, who was separated from her mother at birth.

When he leaves her to return to his apartments, he walks slowly through the galleries of St Cloud, then spends a long time in his bath. He feels morose. Everything about his destiny has changed: he has the heir he has set his heart on, and yet nothing is different.

Getting out of the bath, after Roustam has dried him, he lies down on a sofa. He stays there for a long time, deep in thought.

All around him, despite the King of Rome's birth, he senses anxiety and weariness. He is obeyed, but only slowly.

He has flown into a rage with Clarke, the minister of war, about the time being wasted by the units from France, Italy and

Westphalia who should be converging on northern Germany to confront the Russian threat. Alexander, it is clear, is pushing his armies towards the Grand Duchy of Warsaw.

'An order must always be executed,' he tells Clarke. 'When it isn't, a crime is committed and the culprit must be punished.'

HE GROWS INDIGNANT about these shortcomings. He cannot sleep. He dictates orders for entire nights at the start of April 1811, because he wants to pull the reins tight again. He cannot accept that the Empire might slip away from him, just when the birth of a son has assured his future.

Will he have to fight again? He will, if he has to. Against the marshals who are unable to get the better of the Spaniards in Spain. Ney refuses to obey Masséna and Junot has been forced to evacuate Portugal. Masséna is falling back and Wellington advancing. Can this be possible? He removes Masséna from his post.

In the north, on the border of the Grand Duchy of Warsaw, all his information confirms the concentration of Russian troops.

On Monday, 15 April 1811, during the Easter celebrations, he harries his ministers. He emerges from his study from time to time to receive the delegations that come to congratulate him on the birth of the King of Rome. He listens to the compliments, the speeches. He accompanies the Empress onto the terrace of the Tuileries for her first walk; the crowds cheer her.

But what is the good of these homages, of this son, if the Empire founders?

So, fight.

He returns to his study. He spends several nights there. He is convinced that the Russians may attack any day. He sees Champagny. The minister seems at a loss, unable to face up to the situation. A loyal servant but he hasn't been able to anticipate these threats of war.

'The Emperor Alexander is already a long way from the spirit of Tilsit,' Napoleon starts. 'All the ideas of war are coming from Russia. If Alexander does not reverse this tide immediately, it will carry him away next year despite himself. And so the war will take place despite me, despite him, despite the interests of France and those of Russia.'

He takes a few steps, stares at Champagny.

'I have seen this so often that it is my experience of the past that's revealing such a future to me,' he continues.

He raises the tone of his voice; his whole body tenses to show his anger.

'All this is an opera set and the English are working the scenery.'

Champagny hasn't understood this. He must replace him.

'Monsieur the Duke of Cadore,' he says, going up to Champagny, 'I have nothing but praise for the services you have rendered me in the different ministries to which I have entrusted to you, but foreign affairs are of such a complexion that I feel it necessary for the good of my service to employ you elsewhere.'

Champagny bows his head.

I do not want to humiliate anyone, but my duty is to choose capable men and dismiss those who are incompetent.

Maret, Duke of Bassano, who works with me every day, will replace Champagny.

HE IS TENSE and goes to find Marie Louise in the Trianon gardens or in Rambouillet or Compiègne's parks. The feelings she inspires are just as strong, but since the birth of the King of Rome it is as if a carefree interlude of happiness has come to an end.

He submits himself once more to the rigorous discipline of work. Sometimes, in the middle of the night, he breaks off and thinks he has never spent so much time administering the Empire, dictating. And gradually he sees that the machine, which had wound down for a moment, is righting itself. He feels a sort of exhilaration. The stakes are higher than ever now. He has a son. He holds all the cards of Europe in his hand except three: Spain, which is an open wound; England, which is suffocating under its economic crisis, and Russia, which he must bring to heel.

Will he have to wage war against it?

'I don't want war,' he says to Maret, 'but I at least have the right to demand that Russia stay true to our alliance.'

He studies the troop returns. He needs new regiments. New recruits must be levied, the cavalry and artillery remounted. Troops must be sent through Germany without attracting attention.

'I'd rather have enemies than doubtful friends,' he says. 'They would be more useful to me, in fact.'

OFTEN, AFTER a night's work, he feels as if his whole body is going to explode. He needs to move about. He goes hunting at St Cloud or St Germain. He pushes his horse into a wild gallop, streaking out in front of the little troop of generals and aides-de-camp that ride with him.

The exertion allows him to forget all the problems that assail him.

Joseph is complaining, claiming to be ill; he wants to leave Madrid. Murat is doing what he pleases in Naples, like a sovereign who doesn't owe me his throne and needn't carry out my orders.

'If he thinks that he is ruling in Naples for anything other than the general good of the Empire,' he tells Maret, 'Murat is mistaken. If he does not change, I will take charge of his kingdom and put a viceroy of Italy on the throne.'

He rides back and sees Marie Louise sitting in the park. She seems drained. Corvisart has told him that he strongly advises against a second pregnancy. Is it possible that such a young, vigorous woman can be so affected by childbirth? He sits down next to her, teases her. Madame de Montesquiou comes up with the 'little king'.

My son.

He takes him in his arms, plays with him for a while, makes him drink Chambertin and laughs at his grimaces. Then suddenly he thinks of the years ahead until this son will be able to reign.

He hands the child back to Madame de Montesquiou.

I must protect this Empire my son will inherit. That is my obligation.

He speaks to Marie Louise in a low voice. The Empress must understand that she has duties too. She must – and she can, because she must – accompany him on the journey he is about to take to the west of France to inspect the port of Cherbourg and check that the fleet which he has ordered rebuilt will one day soon be able to face England's.

He pays no heed to Marie Louise's sighs. He does not want to think of her tiredness. They will leave Rambouillet on Wednesday, 22 May at five in the morning, he says. This is a sovereign's work.

He does it. She is the Empress, so she must submit to her duties. When he sees her bored expression, he remembers Josephine who was so good at listening to dignitaries' compliments, smiling and then getting back into the berline to spend another few hours on the road.

THE FIRST DAY they drive for almost nineteen hours at a stretch. The next stages are each twelve hours long. They pass through Hudan, Falaise and Caen, and stay at Cherbourg. He wants to visit the ships. On the *Courageous*, he orders all the frigate's cannon to open fire while she is having a rest. Laughing, he carries her over to a scuttle.

'Do you want me to throw you in the sea?' he asks, as the officers look on in astonishment.

She is only a young woman, his wife, who should follow her husband and adopt the rhythm he sets her.

He stands looking out to sea, surveying the port he has had made where his squadron will be able to shelter when it has taken on the English. Cherbourg will be the most advanced of the Continent's dispositions against the eternal enemy, England.

He goes to Querqueville Château and inspects it with Marie Louise following slowly behind, exhausted. He will establish one of his headquarters here. Then he sets off for St Cloud again, which he reaches on Tuesday, 4 June at one in the afternoon.

He watches Marie Louise go off to her apartments. He has to chair a council of ministers now, then tomorrow he will see Caulaincourt, when he returns from St Petersburg.

He stands motionless in the gallery for a moment, observing Marie Louise's silhouette. He feels full of energy.

In Caen, while Marie Louise was resting from the journey, he had time to see Madame Pellapra, an old mistress who offered herself to him again and talked about Emilie, the child he is the father of.

One never refuses anything life gives one.

He is a husband and father. A lover. A conqueror, always. An emperor.

HE CALLS CAULAINCOURT, the Duke of Vicenza, into his study at St Cloud, at eleven o'clock in the morning on Wednesday, 3 June. He is suspicious of the man. Alexander has pampered him, and, what's more, Caulaincourt is close to Talleyrand. He is a dedicated equerry, an expert on horses, but a malleable ambassador.

He studies him severely. The man does, however, have the courage of his convictions.

'The Russians want me to make war; they want to force me to evacuate Danzig. They think they can control me like their King of Poland!'

Napoleon stamps his heel.

'I am not Louis XV; the French people will not endure this humiliation.'

He listens to Caulaincourt speak in Alexander's defence.

'You are enamoured of Alexander then!'

'No, sire, but I am of peace.'

'As I am too. But Russia has broken off our alliance because it is incommoded by the Continental system. You are fooled by Alexander's arguments because he showers you with flattery.'

He smiles.

'I am an old fox, I know the Greeks.'

He goes up to Caulaincourt.

'What side would you take?'

'Maintain the alliance, Sire. It is the path of prudence and peace.'

How can Caulaincourt not see that the Tsar has abandoned the spirit of Tilsit?

'You're always talking of peace,' Napoleon exclaims. 'Peace only amounts to something when it is lasting and honourable. I don't want a peace that ruins my commerce, like that of Amiens. For peace to be possible and lasting, England must be convinced that it will find no support on the Continent. The Russian colossus and its hordes must therefore no longer be able to threaten the countries of the south.'

Now Caulaincourt is talking to me about Poland again, about me wanting to re-establish it!

'I don't want war! I don't want Poland, but I want this alliance to be useful to me, which it isn't when one of us receives neutral vessels.'

Napoleon walks away. Caulaincourt repeats Alexander's words: 'Our climate and our winter will wage war for us. You only achieve remarkable feats when the Emperor is present, but he can't be everywhere, nor away from Paris for years.'

He thinks of the quagmires in Poland, of the Battle of Eylau, of the mud and snow.

I don't want war.

'Alexander is false and feeble,' Napoleon says. 'He has the Greek character. He is ambitious. He wants war, since he refuses all the accommodations I suggest.'

He breaks off.

'It is this marriage with Austria that has caused us to fall out.'

Caulaincourt shakes his head.

'War and peace are in your hands, sire,' he says. 'I beg Your Majesty to reflect, for your own good and that of France, that You are going to choose between the risks of the one and the certain advantages of the other.'

'You speak like a Russian, Monsieur the Duke of Vicenza.'

Napoleon turns his back on Caulaincourt.

WHO CAN HALT the tide of events?

Napoleon wonders this a few days later when he hears the volleys of cannon fire saluting the imperial cortège's departure for Notre Dame.

He thinks of the cannon bumping along Germany's roads on their way to reinforce the troops. He takes his seat next to Marie Louise in the coach used at his coronation. As the horses swing into motion, he sees the carriage in which Madame de Montesquiou is sitting, holding the King of Rome on her knees.

He looks at the huge, silent crowds massed behind the lines of soldiers. He feels anxious. No one is applauding, as if the crowd were overwhelmed by the splendour of the procession accompanying the King of Rome to his baptism.

Are the people imagining a time after war, like me?

Napoleon walks slowly down the nave, which is crowded with dignitaries. When his son is brought past, he stops Madame de

Montesquiou, takes the child, kisses him three times and holds him up at arm's length above his head.

Then the cheering erupts. 'Long live the Emperor! Long live the King of Rome!'

He feels elated for a few moments.

In the coach that takes him from Notre Dame to the Hôtel de Ville after the baptism, his anxiety returns. The horses stamp and whinny and are difficult to control. Suddenly there's a crash. The traces have snapped. Equerries rush forward to repair them. He gets out of the coach. He'll have to wait.

He doesn't like this incident, this omen.

XXXVIII

THE STIFLING HEAT ON this Sunday, 23 June 1811, puts him on edge.

He is sitting under a shade in the gardens at St Cloud. He turns towards Marie Louise. Beads of sweat are rolling down the Empress's face. Her hair is stuck to her forehead and temples. She is breathing heavily, like someone about to fall asleep. He studies her. She hasn't recovered from the exertions of childbirth yet. She has lost some hair; her body has sagged. The trip to Cherbourg seems to have exhausted her. And since their return to St Cloud, one fête has followed another. They are vital.

He hears the shouts of the throngs gathered in the park, in which lights are beginning to appear as it grows dark, but no cooler. He has had buffets laid out for the massive crowds. Wine gushes from fountains. Further off, in the Bois de Boulogne, the grenadiers of the Imperial Guard are banqueting. And now the fireworks are about to start for everyone's entertainment.

He takes Marie Louise's hand. It is damp. The first explosions ring out in the overcast sky; sheaves of colour light up the clouds. Then suddenly a storm breaks, driven by a cold wind.

He doesn't move. He watches the dignitaries get drenched, yet still not dare to leave the gardens. Dresses cling to women's bodies; the most lavish and colourful uniforms are soaked.

'There's some new orders for the Empire's factories,' he remarks to the Mayor of Lyons who happens to be sitting at the back, under the awning.

But the fireworks have been interrupted. The rain carries on coming down in sheets, emptying the park.

Will the biggest celebrations always end like this from now on, washed out by storms?

HE RETURNS TO his study and squats down on his heels. That morning, he had set out on the carpet the little mahogany bricks of differing lengths and colours that represent divisions, regiments and battalions. He rearranges them, creates a new order of battle.

Yesterday afternoon, the governess had come in with the 'little king'. The child started playing with the bricks and he let him. Now he is alone and it is silent, without the child's laughter and screams, he replays the scene in his mind's eye. At one point, he tried to take one of the pieces away from the child. The boy sulked, then refused the other piece he was given. Wilful child, 'proud and sensitive, just the way I like,' he told Madame de Montesquiou.

My son. What sort of a man will he be? What are we?

Recently he has had a long conversation with the members of the institute, Monge, Berthollet and Laplace.

They are thoroughgoing atheists. Are they right? Sometimes, like them, 'I think man sprang from the earth's silt heated by the sun and combined with electric fluids.' *But I believe in destiny. What will be my son's destiny?*

'Poor child, what tangled affairs I'll leave you.'

But I believe in the utility of religion.

He gets to his feet.

Like my prefects and gendarmes, the clergy must assure peace in the Empire and obey me.

He cannot sleep. The weather is still stormy. It is going to break again, like during the fête.

He must control all the cogs of the Empire. He wants to see the minister of public worship, Bigot de Préameneu, tomorrow. This councillor of state, a member of the Académie française, is a skilled lawyer and devoted servant who he has made Count of the Empire.

He has given him the task of convening a national council of the bishops of the Empire to remind them of their duty of obedience, bring them to heel and remove them from the Pope's temporal authority.

Pius VII who is continuing his rebellion against me. The Pope has done everything to make my people and my armies forsake me.

Now the bishops are putting up resistance.

He will tell Bigot de Préameneu to remind the Pope that, if he does not stop opposing the Emperor, he can forget the concordat with the Church.

Napoleon gets up, paces about his study for part of the night.

If an example must be made, I shall order the arrest of a handful of bishops so that the others will submit. I know men. Fear is what guides them. The bishops will come to heel just like anyone else. I will ask the minister of police to open their correspondence, find out who they see. I will tell them, 'You should know whether you want to be princes of the Church or just vergers.' They will give in.

HE IS RESTLESS. The days and nights of that summer, 1811, are swelteringly hot. Sometimes he gallops for hours through the forests of St Germain and Marly. When he returns and catches sight of the King of Rome, he rushes forward, picks him up, plays with him for a few moments, takes Marie Louise's hand and forces her to walk with him in the park. She has no energy, whereas he is impatient within minutes, wanting to move, to do something. He should be everywhere: in Spain, where his marshals are failing to put an end to the insurrection and the activities of Wellington's men, and in northern Europe, especially, where the English merchantmen are continuing to ply the Baltic with the complicity of Bernadotte, who is dictating Sweden's policies as its ruler more and more frequently now.

Are they still French, these men who've become what they are thanks to me?

All they dream about is outlasting me. They don't care about my son. They only think of their kingdoms. Hasn't Murat just replaced the imperial standard with the flag of Naples?

In a furious voice, he dictates a letter to Murat,

All French citizens are citizens of the Kingdom of the Two Sicilies . . . You have surrounded yourself with men who feel hatred for France and want to destroy you . . . I shall see from your actions whether your heart is still French.

These men don't realize the energy that courses through me. I shall be forty-two this year, on 15 August 1811, but I feel able to crush all my enemies.

He wants to see Caulaincourt, now grand equerry again, to instruct him to prepare a tour of inspection of the ports of Belgium and Holland so that he can assess, after the trip to Cherbourg, the state of the coast's defences and the resources for a fleet to attack England.

As for Russia, it had better be on its guard.

ON FRIDAY, 15 AUGUST, he crosses the Tuileries' Throne Room. The cannon roar. He passes slowly through the middle of his court, then with a gesture, indicates to the grand chamberlain that he may show in the members of the diplomatic corps. He waits for the ambassadors to form a circle. Then he immediately walks towards Prince Kourakine, the Russian ambassador, who is flanked by the Austrian and Spanish ambassadors.

One must be able to corner one's enemy, force him to reveal himself. He is calm, composed, but anger is a weapon he wants to use.

'Do you have any news, Prince?' he asks.

The heat is stifling. Kourakine is already sweating in his parade uniform studded with gold and diamonds.

'You have been defeated by the Turks,' Napoleon continues. 'The reason being that you were short of troops, and you were short of troops because you have sent five divisions of the army of the Danube to the army of Poland in order to threaten me.'

Kourakine seems to be suffocating; his face is bright red.

I am speaking bluntly. My power comes from refusing to use the dead language of diplomacy. I know that five hundred English merchantmen have been allowed into Russian ports and have landed merchandise that will now infest the Empire.

'I am like primitive man. Whatever I don't understand arouses my suspicion.'

He raises his voice.

The court and all the ambassadors must hear this warning. My anger is an act.

'I am not stupid enough to believe that it is the Duchy of Oldenburg that concerns you. I am beginning to think that you want to take Poland.'

Kourakine stammers something incomprehensible, his face turning redder and redder.

'Even if the Russian army appeared on the hills of Montmartre,' Napoleon continues, 'I would not cede an inch of Warsaw's territory. If you force me to war, I will use Poland as an instrument against you.'

He walks away a little.

'I declare that I do not want war,' he thunders. 'And I will not wage it this year, unless you attack me. I have no interest in waging war in the north, but if this crisis has not passed by November, I shall raise one hundred and twenty thousand more men. I will carry on like that for two or three years and, if I see this system is more draining than war, then I will wage war on you and you will lose your Polish provinces.'

He goes up to Kourakine and suddenly adopts a milder tone, his voice calm.

'Whether it's luck, or the bravery of my troops, or because I understand a little about this profession, but I have always had success, and I hope to have more if you force me to make war. You know that I have money and men. You know that I have 800,000 men, that each year puts 250,000 conscripts at my disposal and that consequently I can increase my army by 700,000 men in three years, which will be enough to continue the war in Spain and to wage it against you. I don't know if I will beat you, but we will fight . . .'

He listens to Kourakine's protestations of friendship and alliance. The Prince has fallen into his trap. Napoleon interrupts him.

'Well, as for coming to an agreement, I am prepared to do that. Do you have the necessary powers to treat with me? If you do, I authorize negotiations immediately.'

'It is very hot in Your Majesty's palace,' Kourakine says, mopping his forehead.

He cannot answer Napoleon. He has no powers to negotiate.

'You are like a hare when it has been shot. It stands up on its hind legs and waves its paws about in a panic, exposing itself to another barrelful right in the belly,' Napoleon says, walking away. 'When two gentlemen quarrel, when one, for instance, has slapped the other, they fight and then they make up. Governments should do the same: wholeheartedly either make war or peace.'

He catches sight of Caulaincourt through the crowd of dignitaries. The grand equerry is standing off to one side, near a window. Napoleon stretches out an arm in his direction.

'Whatever Monsieur de Caulaincourt may say, the Emperor Alexander wants to attack me. Monsieur de Caulaincourt has become Russian. The Emperor Alexander's flattery has monopolized him.'

Caulaincourt protests that he is a good Frenchman, a loyal servant. Napoleon smiles.

'I know you are a brave man, but the Emperor Alexander's flattery has turned your head and you have become Russian.'

He leaves the Throne Room. It is 15 August 1811, the day of his forty-second birthday. Now he must go to Mass.

HE RETURNS TO St Cloud at ten that evening. He takes a bath and tries to sleep, but his thoughts go endlessly round and round, facts falling into patterns, plans taking shape. He wants to see Maret tomorrow – Saturday – morning. The minister of foreign affairs must bring all the pieces of correspondence with Russia since the meeting with Alexander at Tilsit. He wants to study them. It is already too late for hostilities with Russia to begin this year. But they could start in June 1812.

He also wants to consult all the books in French on the Swedish King Charles XII's campaign in Poland and Russia. War is not a matter of improvisation.

LITTLE BY LITTLE the future is taking shape, and little by little Napoleon feels himself freed of the bonds shackling him.

He receives Lacuée de Cessac, the minister of war administration. He trusts this clear-headed sixty-year-old who has been a deputy in the Legislative Assembly, a councillor of state and governor of the École Polytechnique.

'Let us go for a walk,' he says.

He goes out ahead of him onto the terrace that overlooks St Cloud's park, and then stops. Here no one can hear them, and they can see when they are about to be interrupted.

'I need to talk to you about something which I haven't talked about to anyone, not to any of my ministers, nor is it something they need to know about,' Napoleon begins.

He leans on the balustrade.

'I have decided on a large expedition. I will need a considerable number of equipages and transports. I shall have no difficulty getting the men, but the hard thing will be preparing the transports.'

He looks at Lacuée de Cessac for a long time.

'I will need an immense number,' he continues, 'since my point of departure will be the Niemen and I will be operating over large distances and in different directions. That is why I need you, and why this must be secret.'

He listens to Lacuée, who speaks of the cost first, and then, after hesitating, mumbles that he is not in favour of a war with Russia.

Napoleon stops him. He knows what the Empire needs, and, as for expenses, he adds emphatically, 'Come to the Tuileries the next time I'm there. I will show you four hundred million in gold. So don't dwell on the cost; we will meet whatever is necessary.'

Then he turns to go back inside.

'The world needs peace and, for that, we must strike this final blow,' he says. He lowers his head, his lips pursed, then adds in a loud voice, 'Afterwards we shall have years of rest and prosperity for ourselves and our children, after experiencing so many years of exhaustion and hardship but also of glory.'

In the doorway of his study, he declares, 'When we are finished with war, and God willing it will be soon, we will have to get down to work, because everything we have done so far is only provisional.'

Now HE CAN leave, race over the dusty northern roads, revisit Boulogne and Dunkirk, go aboard the *Charlemagne* off Flushing and spend several days at sea when a heavy storm springs up on Tuesday, 24 September, harrying all the ships at anchor.

He is alone. It is the first time since they met that he has left Marie Louise. She cried at their parting and hung on his neck like a little girl. She told the Duchess of Montebello within his earshot,

'He is abandoning me.' She is to join him at Antwerp and they will continue on together to Amsterdam. He wants the Dutch who are now citizens of the Empire to see their rulers.

He writes to her every day. From Boulogne,

> My dear Louise, it has been terribly hot and dusty . . . I hope you have been sensible and are now enjoying a good sleep. It is midnight. I am going to bed. Farewell, my friend, a very tender kiss. Nap

From Boulogne again,

> Please take good care of yourself. You know that the dust and the heat don't suit you. I have given chase to an English cruiser for four leagues out to sea . . . Farewell, Louise, you are right to think of the man whose only hope is you. Nap

He writes these lines quickly. She has learnt to read his messy writing. She must think about him. He must be with her every day. He is doing his job as soldier and Emperor. 'You know how much I love you,' he tells her again. 'You are wrong in thinking that professional matters could in any way diminish the feelings I have for you.'

He visits the forts, the ships of his squadrons, 'vessel by vessel'. He wants to see everything. If he is committed in the north against the Russians; the English must not be able to land here, as they have tried before.

He does his Emperor's duty and writes to his wife every day, because that is his duty as a 'faithful husband'.

This is what he is.

He remembers the letters he wrote to Josephine.

He neither can, nor wants, to write declarations of passion to Marie Louise like those that left him dry-mouthed when he wrote them to Josephine from Italy.

He says, 'Take care of yourself and be well. You cannot doubt all the feelings your faithful husband has for you.'

And because he has demanded daily reports about the King of Rome, he is the one who writes, 'The little king is in very good health.'

Then he adds, 'I have never been angry with you, because you are good and perfect and I love you. The stars are bright; the day I am going to spend on board my squadron tomorrow will be fine.'

MARIE LOUISE JOINS him in Antwerp, exhausted by her trip. But that night he is enchanted by her yielding languor.

In the morning, he watches her sleep for a few minutes, then goes off to the naval shipyards or to manoeuvre troops in Amsterdam or Utrecht.

She dozes in the theatre or at the daily receptions. She's only light-hearted and happy when they go for a walk alone and the escort keeps its distance.

But the time for leisure is over. He must do his work; the festivities are duties, and she must fulfill them with him, like him. She must acknowledge the cheers of the crowds that are waiting for them in Amsterdam.

Then they set off again, because the dispatches have arrived from Paris and they have to return directly. When she asks to have lunch or stop, Napoleon reacts with a flash of bad temper, then agrees, giving her a kiss.

But they are on the road again by dawn and they reach St Cloud on Monday, 11 November 1811, at six in the evening.

Napoleon ignores the dignitaries and ministers and officers waiting at the foot of the main staircase. He rushes forward when he sees his son in the door of the great hall in his governess's arms. It's been almost two months since he kissed him.

He takes him and presses him to his breast.

Marie Louise, meanwhile, slowly gets out of the carriage.

XXXIX

HE GETS UP. It is the middle of the night. The fire in the fireplace lights up the room. Napoleon wakes Roustam, goes through to his study, sits down at his desk and begins to read the table Marshal Berthier sends him every day of the distances covered by the troops marching towards the Niemen.

He runs his finger down the columns of figures indicating the different corps, the cavalry, artillery and wagons. He cannot leave his desk, despite his growing tiredness. His legs are heavy. His lower abdomen aches. He has shooting pains in his stomach. But how can he dwell on these minor details, these ailments?

He has to check everything, plan everything: a million bushels of oats for the horses, four million rations of biscuits for four hundred thousand men. He needs bridge trains for the Niemen and the other rivers.

He goes to the library. He needs to read the accounts of the campaigns waged in Russia by other invading armies, then analyse them all. How can he sleep after that? He has to talk to somebody.

EARLY NEXT MORNING he receives Count Narbonne. He has made this former minister of Louis XVI's, who was in office when war was declared in 1792, an aide-de-camp.

Narbonne is a subtle negotiator and a man of experience. He should understand me. I need to think out loud in front of him; that way my mind will be more at ease.

'Aren't you convinced,' Napoleon begins, 'having the knowledge of history that you do, that the extermination of the Cimbri can claim to be the founding moment of the Roman Empire? And it was in theirs or similar blood that the Empire steeped itself time after time, under Trajan, under Aurelian, under Theodosius.'

The Cimbri of today are the Russians.

'I am therefore impelled to embark on this hazardous war for political reasons. It is the forces of circumstance that decree it. Remember Souvarov and his Tartars in Italy? The answer is to drive them back past Moscow. And when will Europe be able to do that, if not now?'

He sits down. Sometimes the tension in his body is so great he has dizzy spells. He is short of breath and he feels the heaviness of his body. He has to make an effort of the will, like a rider digging his spurs into his mount, to keep going. What has become of that sinewy, supple body he once had, as sharp as a blade that slashes through the air?

He speaks in a slow voice, 'I shall make war on Alexander on courtly terms, with two thousand pieces of ordnance and five hundred thousand soldiers, but without insurrections. War has been an antidote to anarchy in my hands. Now that I want to use it again to preserve the West's independence, it mustn't revive what it has suppressed, namely the spirit of revolutionary liberty.'

He shrinks into a corner of the sofa.

Recently there have been riots in the markets of Caen, Eure-et-Loir and the Bouches-du-Rhône. He has had to use harsh measures. The Guard was sent in to Caen: men and women were arrested, some sentenced to death and shot. He cannot risk an uprising. He fixes the price of bread.

'I want the people to have bread – that's to say, I want there to be plenty available, and I want it to be good quality and cheap.'

I need the people to be calm. I can feel them stirring again. Sparks from the Spanish fire are spreading to Germany. Marshal Davout, General Rapp and my brother Jérôme are worried. Everyone would take up arms against us if we suffered a defeat, according to Rapp, Governor of Danzig. Why should I listen to rubbish like that? As if I didn't know that those who have been conquered and wounded are never finished, and that weakness causes people to rise up against one. But I won't be defeated. Why should I read such reports?

'My time is too precious to waste on such rubbish . . . All it does is begrime my imagination with absurd pictures and suppositions . . .'

He looks at Narbonne.

'You will accuse me of imprudence no doubt. But you fail to see that even my temerity is calculated, as the head of an Empire's should be. I strike at a distance to keep the home front in check and, of an extraordinary enterprise, I only want to undertake that which is useful and inescapable.'

He goes up to Narbonne.

'After all, my dear sir, the road to Moscow is also the road to India,' he murmurs. 'One just has to touch the Ganges with a French sword to bring down all of India, that great edifice of mercantile splendour. So you see, the certain and the uncertain, politics and the unbounded future – everything launches us on the great Moscow road and won't allow us simply to bivouac in Poland.'

He starts pacing up and down.

'This is our first move: the greater part of Europe and the West confederated, one way or another, under our eagles; a spike of four hundred thousand men driving into Russia and marching straight on Moscow, which we shall take.'

He grabs the tables charting the progress of the various armies. They are approaching the Oder; the advanced guards have been thrown on the Vistula.

'So you see, my dear Narbonne, all this has been planned with some care, apart, of course, for the hand of God, which must always be allowed for and will not, I think, fail to play a part in our affairs.'

He adds in a grave tone, 'I have pacified the people by arming them and I have restored the *majorats*, the aristocracy and the hereditary nobility in the shadow of the Imperial Guard, which is composed of peasants' sons, small-scale purchasers of national property and simple working folk.'

Then, in a louder voice, after asking Narbonne to go to the Tsar to make a final attempt at negotiation, he adds, 'Make no mistake, I belong to the race of Caesars, the founders of dynasties.'

LEFT ALONE, HIS tiredness and anxiety return. He must divert the court, the people and the ambassadors with balls and fêtes, and dispel the anguish he feels inside and all around him.

He holds a costumed ball at the Tuileries on Thursday, 6 February 1812. He draws up the guest list himself and walks among the crowd of nine hundred, the Empress on his arm. But despite the beauty of the dresses, women and costumes, despite the grace of Pauline and Caroline, his sisters, he feels no joy. He barely eats anything at dinner, which is served in the Diana gallery at one-thirty in the morning. And he returns to his apartments without visiting Marie Louise.

These fêtes are a duty, like the strict etiquette he imposes on the court; they are a way of showing one's authority, and he likes order and hierarchy. But everything seems frozen to him. He decides to move to the Élysée Palace, which Josephine has made over to him.

But he gets a cold there and on 11 February, Shrove Tuesday, it is at the Tuileries that he gives another fancy-dress ball, masked this time. He half-heartedly puts on a blue domino and grey mask. When he enters the ballroom, he immediately recognizes the Empress dressed as a woman from Caux.

The guests are joyfully dancing the quadrille as if my absence was liberating.

He does not stay long. He goes up to his study. Only work, constant work, can calm him now.

BUT SOME DAYS, suddenly, he feels as if he can't breathe. He wants a horse saddled in minutes. Then he gallops through the forests of St German and Raincy or the Bois de Boulogne. He barely notices whether there's game to hunt and catch; the physical effort is what he needs. He loves gripping the horses with his thighs and riding them to exhaustion, whether they're from Persia, Spain, Arabia or even South America. He wants to have more stamina than them. He breaks them. He feels reassured that he can still master tiredness like this, as he used to, and recover all the vigour of his body.

At dawn, he sometimes has the Empress woken so she can ride with him or follow in a barouche. He knows he is the only one who has this inexhaustible energy; he's proud of it, but he does wish those close to him had it too.

He watches his son playing on a big woolly sheep on wheels, tinkling the bells hanging round the animal's neck. Delightedly he makes him repeat his first words, 'papa', 'mama'. He counts his teeth, scrutinizes his features. He looks at himself in a mirror with the child next to him. The likeness seems striking. But at the same time, this child is too sensitive, too delicate. At his age, wasn't he more enterprising, livelier?

He turns away. He has had so many disappointments with his brothers and sisters, he so wants this son to live up to his hopes, that he is shaken to the core when he sees him. He has to leave not to suffocate with emotion.

He ventures out of the Élysée Palace.

It is a beautiful March afternoon in 1812, Tuesday 24th. He goes for a walk through the streets of Paris. He looks at the crowds on the boulevards, then crosses the Pont d'Austerlitz and strolls along the embankments on the left bank.

The air is mild; the trees are in bud. But he doesn't feel spring burgeoning in him; rather as if the greyness of winter is lingering on.

He has learnt that Josephine has commissioned a portrait of the King of Rome and put the picture in his room. Naturally she has been robbed blind. And he has had to pay her debts. He writes to her:

> Put your affairs in order. Only spend a million and a half francs and set aside the same amount every year. In ten years that will be a fund of fifteen million for your grandchildren: it is a pleasure to be able to give them something and be useful to them. Instead of which, you have debts. Look after your affairs and don't be profligate. If you wish to please me, let me hear that you are extremely wealthy. Think how poor an opinion I will have of you if I find out you are three million in debt.
>
> Farewell, my friend, be in good health.
> Napoleon

'She can't count on me paying her debts any longer,' he tells the treasury minister Mollien. 'The fate of her family cannot rest solely on my head . . . I am mortal, more so than anyone.'

But he cannot be angry with Josephine. He knows she has received Marie Walewska and Alexander Walewski at Malmaison.

My son.

My lives are intertwining independently of me.

What will become of them after I'm gone?

HE PONDERS THIS as he sits next to Marie Louise in the front row of the Tuileries' court theatre. He doesn't listen to the exchanges between the Comédie-Française actors performing *Andromache*. He feels as if his face is drooping, as if his whole body is pulling his eyelids down.

He wakes with a start, glancing to left and right. Has anyone seen him fall asleep?

He stands up as soon as the curtain falls. He is not going to watch the following acts. Work will dispel sleep.

The following day, Monday, 27 April 1812, he receives Prince Kourakine, the bearer of a message from Emperor Alexander.

HE READS A copy of it that night. Alexander is demanding the withdrawal of all French troops from Prussia to behind the Elbe. Furthermore, he wishes to be free to trade as he desires with whom he desires.

It is an ultimatum.

Napoleon receives Kourakine in the main reception room at St Cloud. Does the ambassador remember what he said on 15 August 1811?

Napoleon goes up to him. 'Is this the way you wish to come to an agreement with me?'

He speaks loudly, in clipped sentences.

'This demand is an outrage. It is a knife to my throat. My honour will not permit me to have anything to do with it. You are a gentleman – how can you dare present such a proposal to me? What are people thinking of in St Petersburg?'

Kourakine trembles.

NAPOLEON SUDDENLY CHANGES his tone.

The split mustn't be my doing. I must have time to take command of my troops.

He smiles at Prince Kourakine. 'Why not declare neutral all the territory between the Niemen and the Passarge?'

Kourakine is enthusiastic.

This gives me a few days.

He must leave Paris discreetly to be able to take the Russians by surprise and yet leave the door to negotiation open. Be ready simultaneously to make war and welcome peace.

But how is that going to be possible? England hasn't even replied to my peace offers and Alexander wants to impose his law on me.

It will be war then.

He decides to leave St Cloud on Saturday, 9 May 1812 for Dresden, with the Empress.

Her presence will guarantee the loyalty of the German princes and the Emperor of Austria.

On Tuesday, 5 May 1812, he goes to the opera with Marie Louise. The spectators cheer them.

When will he see the people of Paris again?

He whispers to Prefect Pasquier, who is sitting near him, 'This is the biggest, most difficult enterprise I have ever attempted, but I have to finish what has been started.'

XL

HE IS SILENT. Marie Louise is drowsing next to him in the carriage. They have already passed Meaux, Château-Thierry. They should reach Châlons by evening, from where they will set off again at four in the morning. He hears his escort's galloping horses. When they stop to change teams, he gets out of the berline. The road is full, as far as the eye can see, with the vehicles of his convoy. He is going off to war, but this has never seemed so like a sovereign going off to visit his allies' states.

He looks at Marie Louise. She has the unperturbed face of a tired but happy woman who, for the first time since her marriage, is going to see her family in Dresden. Does it occur to her that war awaits him? He thinks of Josephine who, when he visited her secretly a week before, clung to him in tears, anxious and haunted, she said, by black thoughts and nightmares. He held her in his arms, reassured her. But he was very moved when he left.

HE GETS BACK into the carriage. He opens one of the portfolios and begins to read that day's *Monitor*, Saturday, 9 May 1812. It reports, as he had requested, that the Emperor has left Paris to inspect the Grand Army gathered on the banks of the Vistula. Suddenly he trembles with surprise and rage. The newspaper has printed the first of a series of articles entitled *A Study of the Places Where Varus and His Legions Perished.* Varus, the Roman general under Augustus who was defeated by the German Arminius, which compelled Augustus to abandon Germany, with the Elbe as his border, and make the Rhine the *limes* of his Empire. A bad omen or someone intentionally trying to do him harm?

Who can he truly rely on?

He sees the peasants gathered at the side of the road to watch him go past. They are silent, as are the populations of Mainz, Frankfurt and Bayreuth who watch his cortege without any display of emotion.

Do they think I want war?

When they stop at Mainz, he goes up to Caulaincourt and asks what he thinks.

'Your Majesty probably doesn't want to go to war with Russia just for the sake of Poland,' his grand equerry tells him. 'But also to have no more rivals in Europe, only vassals, and to indulge a dearly held passion.'

'What passion is that?'

'War, sire.'

Caulaincourt is impudent and stupid. Napoleon pulls his ear, gives him a little slap on the neck.

'I have only ever waged political wars in France's interest,' Napoleon replies. 'She cannot remain a great state if England maintains its claims and usurps all maritime rights.'

He wants to convince the princes, kings and the Emperor of Austria, whom he's going to meet in Dresden, of this.

Caulaincourt repeats that Europe's sovereigns are anxious. They don't want to be deprived of their rights. It will be difficult to persuade them to act alongside the Emperor.

Napoleon shrugs his shoulders.

'When I need someone, I don't look too closely, I just kiss his backside.'

What was Caulaincourt thinking?

At Tilsit and Erfurt, didn't I try my utmost to win over Alexander? I shall do the same at Dresden with the kings and the Austrian Emperor.

I need allies to fight the Russians.

The Austrians are due to supply me thirty thousand men under Prince Schwarzenberg's command. Could they refuse me this contribution when I am the husband of the daughter of Emperor Francis? I need peace in Germany and Prussia. And I need troops from twenty nations, from Croatians to Dutch, Italians to Bavarians, and Spaniards to Würtembergers.

HE DRIVES THROUGH the night. The fires that have been lit on the slopes pick out Marie Louise's face in the shadows. He wakes her as the carriage slows at the entrance to Dresden.

The volleys of cannon fire reverberate, drowning out the sound of the bells. The cuirassiers in great helmets and white uniforms lining the approach to the royal palace hold torches. The King and Queen of Saxony are waiting in front of the château.

He gets out, gratified by the splendour of his reception. During the 'Te Deum' that is sung on Sunday, 17 May 1812 in the presence of all the German princes and ambassadors, he is reminded of Tilsit and Erfurt, when the kings and princes were his courtiers.

But he must win them over again. On Monday, 18 May, he respectfully greets the Emperor of Austria, Francis, and Queen Maria Louisa. He pays a visit to the King of Prussia Frederick William III.

They know, despite his benevolence, that he is the Emperor of Kings.

It is he who leads the assembled company into dinner each evening, going in first on his own, wearing his hat. A few paces behind comes the Emperor of Austria, offering his arm to his daughter Marie Louise; he is bareheaded. Then the other kings and the princes follow, their hats doffed.

Napoleon presides over the table. He tells stories, smiles, exerts his charm. He recalls episodes from the Revolution and gauges the intense silence that falls on the table. He revels in this extraordinary situation. Him, a lieutenant in the Revolution's army, sitting here between kings and married to a Hapsburg. He says that the events he witnessed then would have had a different outcome if 'my poor uncle had shown more firmness'.

He is the nephew of Louis XVI.

What is he proud of? Of this alliance that has made him a relative of these rulers, or of the destiny he has fulfilled which makes him a man of a different calibre to these heirs. He is a founder, a Caesar.

He walks through the drawing rooms, addressing remarks to left and right, and then takes Francis aside and strikes up a conversation that turns into a soliloquy. This 'sickly Francis' has nothing to say.

At the theatre, before the performance begins, a curtain falls with a dazzling sun on it and an inscription that reads, 'Neither as great nor as splendid as him'. The audience applaud.

Do they think he's fooled?

He shrugs his shoulders.

'These people must think I'm very stupid,' he murmurs.

He hunts boar in the countryside near Dresden. On a white horse with a scarlet, gold encrusted bard, he rides over the hills behind the city at the head of a crowd of princes and dignitaries and an escort of cuirassiers.

In the evening he rejoins Marie Louise, who is happy in a way he has never seen her. She is in the bosom of her family and she is his.

He reads her the dispatches he gets from Paris every day with news of their 'little king'.

ON TUESDAY, 26 MAY 1812, an aide-de-camp announces that Count Narbonne has just returned from Russia. He has seen Alexander, who has left St Petersburg to be with his troops at his headquarters in Vilna.

Napoleon receives Narbonne and paces up and down as he listens to his report. He is silent for a long time, until suddenly he bursts out furiously, 'So, every means of understanding one another is becoming impossible. The mood of the Russian cabinet is hastening it to war. All you have reported is the re-statement, and confirmation, of what Kourakine proposed me. This is Russia's sine qua non! The princes here were right. There isn't a single one who hasn't received correspondence to that effect. People know that we have been summoned to take the Rhine road. The Russians vaunt themselves on it, and now this publicity is the final insult.'

He breaks off for a few seconds.

'We have no more time to waste on fruitless negotiations,' he cries.

HE SHUTS HIMSELF away and writes. It is imperative that calm reigns in the troops' rear, throughout the Empire. He gives orders for Pope Pius VII to be moved from Savona to Fontainebleau. The concordat has been broken.

Then he consults his maps, writes to Davout,

Everything is subordinate to the arrival of the bridging train, for my whole plan of campaign is founded on the existence of a well-horsed bridging train that is as mobile as cannon.

In the hours that follow, he learns that the Russians have signed a peace treaty at Bucharest with the Turks whom they have been at war with for some months. Another signal. He won't be able to count on Turkish attacks weakening Alexander's troops. So be it. He writes a letter immediately appointing the Abbé de Pradt, Archbishop of Malines, French Ambassador to the government of Warsaw. The Poles must enter the war against the Russians.

Everything is in order.

Now he must join the Grand Army.

ON THURSDAY, 28 MAY, he spends the whole day with Marie Louise. He is moved by her sadness, her whispers. She is unhappy, she says.

'I try to master myself but I will be like this until the moment I see you again,' she whispers.

He must tear himself away from this tenderness, this gentleness, the luxury of palaces.

Suddenly he feels weary.

He must bring this war to an end so he can get back to Marie Louise and see the 'little king' again.

What is driving him on like this into the maelstrom?

At four o'clock in the morning of Friday, 29 May 1812, he frees himself from Marie Louise's embrace. He hesitates in the guard-room, kisses her again, and then suddenly turns his back on her.

THE BERLINE DRIVES off into the night. It is not yet five.

At eleven, in Reitenbach, he writes his first letter,

My good Louise,

I am stopping for a moment to have lunch. I am taking this opportunity to write to you and to commend you to be cheerful and not let yourself be affected. All the promises I made you will be kept. So our separation will only be a short one. You know how much I love you; I need to know that your health is good and that you have peace of mind.

Farewell, my sweet friend, a thousand kisses.

Nap

Then he sets off again.

HE DRIVES ALL day and the following night without getting out of his carriage. At seven in the morning, he writes again,

> I have been travelling very fast, only a little dust. I'm setting off and should arrive at Posen this evening, where I will spend the day tomorrow, the 31st. I hope you will have written me that you are in good health and cheerful and reasonable.

I am the one who supports them all, whose duty it is to lead other people.
I, who can never lay down my arms, who can never slacken.
He takes up his quill again.

> It would be good if, when I send you officers, Montesquiou, the grand chamberlain, gives them presents of diamond rings, with the quality depending on the news they bring.
> Your father will have left by now, which will have increased your loneliness.
> *Addio, mio dolce amore,* a thousand tender kisses.
> Nap

He hears the shouts of the crowds in Posen who are greeting him as if he is the liberator of Poland.
I have no consolations other than glory.

XLI

IT IS SEVEN IN THE evening on Sunday, 31 May 1812. Napoleon goes up to the window in the room of the house in Posen where he has been studying troop numbers and situation reports. The sun has not set. Shouts ring out. The crowd that surrounded the house when he entered it is still there, enthusiastically milling about the paved streets, every station of life intermingled – soldiers, local peasants, notables, women. On his way to mass at lunchtime, he noticed faces and silhouettes like Marie Walewska's, and he was moved and happy to be here, in Poland, among this people. Since then he has shut himself away in this room with Méneval, dictating his dispatches and going through the regimental reports.

He feels a sense of pride and power. Never has an army like this been assembled: 678,080 men from twenty nations. 11,042 French officers and 344,871 French NCOs and soldiers; 7,998 foreign officers and 284,169 foreign NCOs and soldiers. *Foreign!* He doesn't want to hear that word, he tells Marshal Berthier. These contingents come from *départements* of the Empire or its allies.

He needs to be informed of every detail about every unit; he'd like to know every soldier in the army. That morning, on the outskirts of Posen, he reviewed the 23rd corps of *chasseurs à cheval*. He went up to the major, who he recognized as Marbot, a brave officer. He bombarded him with questions without taking his eyes off him.

'How many carabineers have you from Tulle and Charleville? How many Norman horses? How many Breton? How many German? What is the average age of your men? Of your officers? Of your horses? Have you provisions for everyone, for how long? Have your men got five kilos of their flour in their packs, four days' bread and six days' biscuits as I demanded?'

Marbot answered well. Wars are only won by a combination of high strategy and meticulous concern for detail.

He turns towards Méneval and begins to dictate an order of the day.

'The officers will carry out inspections to check that each soldier has only eaten his day's entitlement and that he still has the correct number of days supplies.'

Eugène must delay his army's movement until further orders, 'because more than anything you must have supplies. Let me know how much bread you have. Then I shall decide whether to order you to advance. In this country, bread is the main thing.'

Now Marshal Davout needs to be questioned.

'I assume you have twenty-five days' provisions for your army corps?'

He stops. Maret has just arrived. The Duke of Bassano, minister of foreign affairs, left Dresden a few hours before. Has he any letters from the Empress? He holds them out. Napoleon puts them on the table, then indicates that he wishes to be left alone. He reads them, and starts a reply.

My friend, I have received your three letters. I am beginning to find two days a very long time to be without news of you. I am sorry to hear that you are sad and I am grateful to Princess Thérèse for taking you on a walk. I am tired from having worked all day. I am going to go riding for an hour. I shall set off tonight so as to reach Thorn tomorrow morning. Give all my best to your aunt and the King and the family.

You should think of me. You know I love you and feel very vexed at not being able to see you two or three times a day any more. But I think it will be finished in three months.

Addio, mio dolce amore.

Ever yours,
Napoleon

He calls Maret back in. He listens to what he has to pass on from Bernadotte, who is prevaricating, hesitating over how to commit Sweden on France's side while keeping Russia happy, and essentially letting time pass until he can choose the winner's side.

Napoleon kicks a chair over.

'The wretch! This is a unique chance to bring down Russia and, if missed, he won't get another, because you don't see a warrior such as me marching with six hundred thousand soldiers against the formidable Empire of the North twice ... The wretch, he fails his glory, he fails Sweden, he fails his country: he is not worthy of our attention.'

He kicks the chair again.

'I do not want anyone to mention him to me again and I forbid him to be given any response, official or unofficial.'

HE GOES OUT, rides for an hour, accompanied by a light escort and then tries to sleep when he gets back. But at three in the morning he gives the signal to leave. As dawn is breaking, he observes the troops on the march. Plenty of stragglers. The gendarme's units will have to round them up and escort them back to their regiments.

At the entrance to Thorn, his carriage comes to a standstill. He gets out. The streets are choked with Jérôme and Eugène's troops. He passes through the soldiers. Most speak German or Italian and pay him no mind. He goes into the monastery where Caulaincourt has prepared his headquarters. The vaulted rooms are full of allied officers, Germans.

'Tell these gentlemen to leave and not follow me so closely from now on; they're to keep several days' march behind.'

He gets down to work. Have plans been made to establish hospitals? Has the bridging train arrived? He dictates, gives orders, reviews the Guard and the artillery, and then goes out in the middle of the night to inspect the cantonments.

He needs to breathe the cooler night air, to hear the voices of soldiers and immerse himself again in the feeling of the night before a battle. He returns to his headquarters. He cannot sleep. But he feels well. He hums, then his voice rings out, thunderous,

> From North to South
> The martial trump
> Peals its blare, its warlike dance
> Tremble then, you enemies of France ...

He stops. Singing like this has finally calmed him. He loves 'The Song of Departure'. He murmurs the last words pensively.

Kings drunk on blood and pride
Lo, the sovereign people draw nigh
Down, you tyrants, in your coffins hide

'I am the people's King,' he thinks.

HE GOES TO sleep for a few minutes. When he wakes up, he immediately sits at his desk.

> My dear friend,
> It is very hot, like Italy. Everything about this climate is extreme. This morning I was in the saddle at two o'clock. It agreed with me very well. I am leaving in an hour for Danzig; everything is very quiet on the frontier. The Guard I saw yesterday was very handsome.
> I have been told that you have been vomiting. Is that true? Give all my best to all your family and your father and the Empress.
> I want to see you as much as you do me and I hope it can be soon: three months apart and with you at every moment.
> A thousand kisses.
> Your Nap

Night, the road.
Perhaps Marie Louise is pregnant?
Dust, then the paved streets of Danzig and General Rapp, governor of the town, coming forward and launching into a string of complaints.

Napoleon listens to his former aide-de-camp, this valorous general, once a comrade of Desaix and Kléber, scarred with wounds, who feels like a 'lost child' in Danzig.

'What are the merchants doing with all their money?' Napoleon interrupts him. 'The sums they are earning, and that I am spending on their behalf?'

'They are in desperate straits, sire.'

'That will change. It is well known. In the meantime, I will keep their money myself.'

He reviews the troops, sees Murat and Berthier.

'What is wrong with you, Murat? You look sallow, not your

usual handsome self. Are you sad? Aren't you glad to be a king any more?'

'Oh, sire, I barely am one.'

'That's what the matter is. You so want to fly with your own wings that you confuse your situation. Believe me, forget the petty politics that reek of Naples, and be French first and foremost. Your profession of king will be much simpler and easier than you imagine.'

He leaves Murat, and walks a little way off with Caulaincourt.

'Murat is an Italian *pantaleone*,' he murmurs. 'He is good hearted and, at bottom, he still loves me more than his *lazzaroni*. When he sees me, he is mine, but far away, like all people without character, he belongs to whoever flatters him and is close to him. If he has come to Dresden, his vanity and interest must have made him commit a thousand foolishnesses to keep the Austrians happy.'

He looks at Caulaincourt for a long time. Aren't all men like that?

HE IS SITTING opposite Rapp in the main room of Danzig's fortress. He picks at some food and observes Murat and Berthier, to his right and left respectively.

'I can see, gentlemen, that you have lost the desire to make war: the King of Naples does not want to leave his beautiful kingdom, Berthier would like to be hunting at Grosbois, and Rapp living in his splendid residence in Paris.'

Murat and Berthier lower their eyes.

'I agree, Sire,' Rapp replies. 'Your Majesty has never indulged me; I know the pleasures of the capital very little.'

He has to convince them, lead them, and forget that he too would like to feel Marie Louise's body next to his and take his son in his arms.

Is she pregnant again? There's been no other mention of her feeling sick.

'We are approaching the dénouement,' he resumes, looking at Rapp, Murat and Berthier in turn. 'Europe will not breathe freely until the affairs of Russia and Spain are settled. Only then will it be able to count on a deeply rooted peace. A renascent Poland will grow stronger. Austria will concern itself more with the Danube and less with Italy. Lastly, England will resign itself to sharing the world's trade with the Continent's fleets.'

He gets up.

'My son is young,' he says. 'The way must be paved for him to have a peaceful reign.'

Then he stops. He needs his generals, his marshals, he says.

'My brothers don't support me. The only thing princely about them is their stupid vanity; they have no talent and a complete lack of energy. I have to govern for them. My brothers only think of themselves.'

He raises his voice.

'I am the people's King, because I only spend money to encourage the arts and bequeath glorious memorials to the nation that will be of use to it. It shall not be said that I endow favourites and mistresses. I reward service to the nation, nothing else.'

He walks quickly out of the room. He wants to see the troops and fortifications and inspect the roads in a small boat. Then he shuts himself in his study to consult the dispatches, maps and situation reports.

He looks up and asks for a quill.

My good Louise, I have no letter from you. I am in the saddle at two in the morning; I return at midday, sleep a couple of hours and then see the troops the rest of the day. My health is excellent. The little king is very well; he is going to be weaned. I hope you have been kept informed.

Everything is very quiet. The weather has become slightly rainy, which is welcome. I will be in Königsberg tomorrow.

I am very impatient to see you. Despite my occupations and fatigue, I feel something is missing: the sweet routine of seeing you several times a day. *Addio, mio bene.* Take care of your health, be cheerful and happy, that is the way to give me pleasure.

Your faithful husband,
Nap

He is so impatient to set off again that without waiting for the carriages to be ready, he mounts a horse and tears off at full tilt. He passes through Marienburg, Königsberg. He receives Prévot, the secretary to the French embassy in St Petersburg, who explains that Alexander has refused to grant their ambassador, General Lauriston, an audience.

'There, it's done,' says Napoleon. 'The Russians, whom we have always conquered, are using the tone of conquerors; they're provoking us, and no doubt we will be expected to thank them for it. Halting on such a road would mean missing the most propitious opportunity that has ever presented itself.'

He remains silent for a few minutes.

'Let us accept this turn of events that forces us to act as a favour and let us cross the Niemen.'

He is cold all of a sudden. He goes outside. The countryside is covered with snow. A June night has been enough to turn a spring landscape into a vista of winter.

But the sun is rising. The snow will melt.

A courier arrives with letters from Marie Louise. He reads through them, replies immediately.

You know how much I love you. I want to know that you are well and in very good spirits. Tell me you're haven't got your nasty cold any more. Never suffer anyone to say anything equivocal about France and its politics in your presence.

I am often in the saddle; it does me good. I hear good news of the King; he is growing, walking and in good health.

I am sad to see that what I hoped for has not happened. Well, we'll have to put that off until autumn. I hope to hear from you tomorrow . . .

She is not pregnant.

Where will he be in the autumn?

ON SUNDAY, 21 JUNE 1812, he reaches Wilkowiscki. The small town is overrun by Marshal Davout's troops. Beyond the trees, he sees the woods and sandy hills behind which the Niemen runs.

The heat first thing in the morning is stifling. That one night's snow has come to seem like a mirage.

In the parlour of thatched house, he starts to dictate.

A spring wells up in him as powerfully as ever, after years of war. It forces out the words as he paces up and down the beaten earth floor, his hands behind his back.

Soldiers, the second Polish war has begun; the first ended at Friedland and Tilsit. At Tilsit, Russia swore eternal alliance with France and war with England. Today she has broken her undertakings!

Russia is carried away by fate; her destiny must be fulfilled. Does she think that we have degenerated? Are we no longer the soldiers of Austerlitz? She places us between dishonour and war: the choice we will take cannot be open to doubt.

The second Polish war will reflect as much glory on French arms as the first. Forward then; let us carry the war into her territory. Let us cross the Niemen!

He sleeps for a few hours. When he wakes up, on Monday, 22 June 1812, he starts to write,

My good Louise,

I am here, but I am setting off in an hour. The heat is extreme, the dog days of summer. My health is good . . . Let me know when you plan to set off. Take care to travel at night, because the dust and heat are very tiring and could affect your health, but if you travel at night and in the early morning, you will manage the journey fine.

Farewell, my sweet friend, with my sincerest love.

Nap

He leaves the house. The air is motionless. He cannot breathe. He looks at the pine forest ahead covered with a grey haze.

'To horse,' he says. 'To the Niemen.'

Coming in January 2005, Volume 4 of the *Napoleon* series,

THE IMMORTAL OF ST HELENA